Sir Ian Rankin is the multimillion-c
bestseller of over thirty novels and creator of John
Rebus. His books have been translated into thirty-six
languages and have been adapted for radio, the stage and
the screen.

Sir Ian is the recipient of four Crime Writers' Association
Dagger Awards, including the Diamond Dagger, the UK's
most prestigious award for crime fiction. In the United
States, he has won the celebrated Edgar Award and been
shortlisted for the Anthony Award. In Europe, he has
won Denmark's Palle Rosenkrantz Prize, the French
Grand Prix du Roman Noir and the German Deutscher
Krimipreis.

He is the recipient of honorary degrees from universities
across the UK, is a Fellow of the Royal Society of
Edinburgh and a Fellow of the Royal Society of
Literature, and has received an OBE for his services to
literature. In 2022 he received a knighthood as part of
the Queen's Platinum Jubilee celebrations.

Website: IanRankin.net
X: @Beathhigh
Facebook: IanRankinBooks

Ian Rankin
The Iconic Number One Bestseller

'Whatever he writes, it will be worth reading . . . Rankin
has redefined the genre'
Guardian

'Rankin is a phenomenon'
Spectator

'Britain's No. 1 crime writer'
Mirror

'One of Britain's leading novelists in any genre'
New Statesman

'Worthy of Agatha Christie at her best'
Scotsman

'Quite simply, crime writing of the highest order'
Express

'Unmatched in the field of British crime fiction'
The Times

'Delightful, impossible-to-fault crime writing from a
virtuoso of the craft'
Daily Mail

Also by Ian Rankin

IAN RANKIN

MIDNIGHT AND BLUE

ORION

First published in Great Britain in 2024 by Orion Fiction,
an imprint of The Orion Publishing Group Ltd.,
Carmelite House, 50 Victoria Embankment
London EC4Y 0DZ

An Hachette UK Company

1 3 5 7 9 10 8 6 4 2

A CIP catalogue record for this book
is available from the British Library.

ISBN (Hardback) 978 1 3987 0942 3
ISBN (Trade Paperback) 978 1 3987 0943 0
ISBN (eBook) 978 1 3987 0948 5

Typeset by Deltatype Ltd, Birkenhead, Merseyside

Printed in Great Britain by Clays Ltd, Elcograf S.p.A.

MIX
Paper | Supporting
responsible forestry
FSC
www.fsc.org
FSC® C104740

www.orionbooks.co.uk

Before

A quick in and out, just as a favour. A big favour, a favour meriting repayment at some point down the line. A quick in and out – not even that actually. Breaking without entering. The alarm would kick in, though it always took time for anyone to respond. There might be cameras, but he was in his balaclava, the one that covered everything except the eyes. Gloved too, of course.

'You don't have to go in,' he'd been told. 'Leave that to us.'

The main door was almost too easy, though, and once it was unlocked, what was to stop him? Might even be a bit of petty cash lying around, a phone or an iPad, nothing anyone would bother about. He knew he had a couple of minutes. Maybe even five or ten.

But looking around the inside, it was just a nail bar. Not much to pocket other than manicure files and varnish. No cash register, just a card reader. If there'd been a computer, it had been unplugged and carried home for the night. Two more doors at the back of the room – toilet to the left and office to the right. The office was locked, too. Yale lock. He pulled off his gloves with his teeth so he could get a better grip on the smaller of his picks. Ten seconds was all it took. He crossed the threshold and switched his phone's torch on. When he recognised what was

3

sitting on the desk, he clenched his free hand, the one holding the pick. Clenched his teeth, too, and let out a hiss of breath between them.

Then he turned and ran, not noticing that the sharp little lock pick had pierced the flesh of his palm, a few tiny droplets of blood left behind on the fake wooden floor as he made good his escape ...

Day One

1

Rebus sensed that something was wrong even before the alarm sounded. He was in the queue for breakfast, listening to the Wizard coughing up half a lung as usual. Nobody ever mentioned the hierarchy; it just happened naturally. Those liable to throw their weight around or go off on one ended up closest to the food while everyone else gathered behind in a ragged line. The Wizard was two places ahead of Rebus, which was fine. He probably wasn't any older, but he looked it, and he'd been in prison longer than just about anyone else on the hall. His real name was Gareth Wallace, the nickname stemming from his long grey locks and longer beard. He arched forward as he coughed, not bothering to cover his mouth. New arrivals would make COVID jokes until they realised none were being heard for the first time. When Rebus turned to look behind him, he found Ratty there, seemingly more shrunken with each passing day. Ratty's eyes, narrower even than usual, were for once not focused on the progress of the queue. He gave a slight nod when he realised he had Rebus's attention.

There was a blur of movement as one of the white-shirted officers hit the alarm. The ringing was sudden and piercing, accompanied by other officers arriving, milling, conferring. Then the order – back to cells – followed by complaints and questions.

'Room service today,' an officer called Eddie Graves announced, beginning the process of shepherding the reluctant flock. 'Wish I was as lucky.' Graves had a complaint for every occasion, as if fortune was forever favouring the inmates.

'How long but?' someone asked.

'Soon as we get you indoors,' Graves answered.

Though Ratty was a good eight inches shorter than Rebus, he had the knack of seeing and knowing everything. 'It's Jackie,' he told Rebus. Sure enough, two officers – Novak and Watts – filled Jackie Simpson's doorway, faces close together, conversing in an undertone. Though other officers were forming a makeshift cordon, Rebus and several others had to pass this cell to get to their own.

'Keep moving,' came the order, hands flapping, arms outstretched. But as with a motorway crash, traffic inevitably slowed for a gawp. There were two more officers inside the cell. On the lower bunk Rebus could make out a prone and bloodied figure. Another man lay on the upper bunk and seemed in slightly better shape, in that the officers were trying to rouse him while ignoring his cellmate. Rebus remembered the name of the upper bunk – Mark Jamieson. He'd known him briefly on the outside. Not that he'd ever mentioned as much in here; Jamieson wouldn't have thanked him.

'Come on, John,' Graves said, pressing a hand to his shoulder. 'Don't make things difficult.' They locked eyes for a moment. Graves's jaw was tensed and some of the colour had drained from his face.

'It's not in my nature to make things difficult,' Rebus assured him. 'Unlike some.' He gestured over Graves's shoulder to where Darryl Christie sat at one of the circular tables near the food station. Two officers were flanking him while he finished his breakfast, taking his time, savouring each drop. Neither officer seemed minded to interrupt.

'Darryl!' Graves called out. 'Back to your cell, please!'

Turning his head slowly, Christie took in both Graves and Rebus. 'Right you are, Michelle,' he called out. Michelle for

8

Michelle Mone. Graves, the serial moaner, tried as ever not to show that the name irritated him. Rebus sensed that the grin Christie threw in Graves's direction was meant not for the officer but for him.

John Rebus had a cell all to himself. It consisted of a narrow bed, toilet and sink. The toilet had no door but was in an alcove, allowing a modicum of privacy. There was a small desk and some storage space, plus a shelf for personal effects. He had piled here all the books he had promised himself he would read. Inside one of them he kept photos of his daughter and granddaughter. He wasn't sure why he wanted them to remain private, but he did. A wall-mounted flat-screen TV had a slot at the side for DVDs, and there was also a landline telephone, again fixed to the wall. Calls had to be prearranged and paid for, and of course were monitored if there were any staff available. Beneath the bed was a small safe for valuables, which Rebus never bothered to lock.

This was his home now, and had been for the past six months. When he'd first arrived at HMP Edinburgh, they'd assessed him and put him in an overnight cell. Because he was ex-police, it was then decided that he should transfer not to one of the general halls but to the Separation and Reintegration Unit. This was where they kept the prisoners who were either in danger or were a danger to themselves. Some of them Rebus never saw. They remained in their cells, occasionally yelling a complaint but mostly staying silent. There was an enclosed yard where exercise was taken, its walls heavily graffitied with names, sometimes with the word 'paedo' or 'nonce' added.

Rebus felt hemmed in, not only by walls but by the same daily faces too. He had visited the prison many times during his detective years – he recalled being shown the Hanging Shed, now long demolished – but this was different. The various smells were never going to be showered away. Testosterone and wariness filled what air there was. Drug use was hard to miss. He had always known the place simply as Saughton, though the branding on the officers' shirts these days declared it HMP Edinburgh. Prison, nick, jail, chokey, inside – many names but only one game: incarceration.

There were four general halls – Gyle, Swanston, Trinity and Whitecraig. Gyle was for women prisoners while Whitecraig housed the sex offenders. Trinity and Swanston were a mix of those awaiting trial on remand and those already convicted. One day, three months into his life sentence, the governor, Howard Tennent, had summoned Rebus to his office. It was large and modern and had a table and chairs for meetings. Tea was offered and there was even some shortbread.

'How would you feel about joining the general population in Trinity?' Tennent had asked while Rebus bit into a biscuit.

'What's happened?' Rebus had asked back.

'Two things. For one, we're short of accommodation in the SRU, so we could do with your bed.'

'And?'

The governor had shifted slightly in his chair. 'Darryl Christie is ready to vouch for you, meaning you'll be protected. He seems to think you did him some sort of favour a while back.'

'He means getting rid of the competition – not that I did. My lawyers are busy with the appeal.'

'You were there when Cafferty died, though.'

'Again, not true. The coronary came after.' Rebus had paused. 'Is Trinity Christie's patch?'

Tennent swept a few crumbs from the table in front of him. 'He's guaranteeing your safety, John, and we have a single cell that's just been vacated. You've been off the force a good few years – I doubt you'll come across too many guys you put in here. In fact, I've had a look. Just a few minor habituals, none of them minded to get on the wrong side of Darryl and his lads.' He had fixed Rebus with a look. 'So what do you say?'

'I say that if someone does me in, I want you grieving at the graveside.'

Tennent had given a thin smile before rising to his feet, Rebus snatching a final biscuit as he was ushered from the room.

Well, it'll make a change, he had thought to himself, while all too aware that ex-cops were unlikely to be welcomed with open arms. Aware, too, that Darryl Christie might at any time change his mind, leaving him wide open to attack.

It was an hour before his cell door was unlocked long enough for cold toast and a mug of stewed tea to be handed over. The officer's name was Kyle Jacobs – nicknamed Kylie by the men on the hall. Rebus had made friends with him over the past weeks, Jacobs eager to hear tales from Rebus's CID days. He was in his late twenties with short, well-groomed hair and heavily tattooed arms. He had two uncles who'd been Lothian and Borders Police and Rebus had pretended to know the names.

'This looks appetising,' Rebus said as he took the plate.

'Best we could do. The eggs would have walked in here by themselves.'

'So what's happening out there?'

'Someone stabbed Jackie in the neck. He's done for.'

'How about Jamieson?'

'Doped to the eyeballs. A nasty gash on his forehead.'

'Taken out of the game, basically. Found the weapon?'

Jacobs looked around. 'I've already said more than I should.'

Rebus had edged forward, hoping for a glimpse down the hall, but the young officer crowded in on him. A raised voice came from behind the door of the next cell along.

'Will you hurry the fuck up, Kylie! My belly thinks my throat's been cut!'

Jacobs started closing Rebus's door.

'Don't be a stranger,' Rebus told him.

He settled on the edge of his bed, listening to the door locking. The normal routine would have had him helping at the library. He'd been offered floor polishing or the kitchens, but being around books had appealed more. The library wasn't far from the NHS unit and its nursing staff. Rebus got his regular supply of COPD inhalers there, always with the warning that he shouldn't pass them on – 'Some users tweak them to make bongs,' he'd been told. Not that cannabis was the biggest problem inside. Spice and its chums had been causing havoc for several years. Ketamine, nitazene, etizolam, bromazolam – Rebus couldn't keep up, which didn't matter as most of the prisoners just called them 'benzos' and didn't seem to mind exactly which doses and combinations they were being offered. The drugs were easy to hide and there was no giveaway aroma. From noon onwards you could see the benzos taking their toll, slack faces atop immobile frames. There were ketamine users whose addiction had led to bladder problems and colostomies. They were known as Pissbag One, Two and Three. Nursing staff carried oranges with them because they diluted the effects of spice. Rebus had also seen plenty evidence of self-harm, prisoners whose arms bore scarring, some of it fresh and raw from the razor blade's work. No one ever discussed it; it was just another fact of life behind bars.

Tennent had been right about one thing: Rebus hadn't become aware of any real grudges against him. There was one guy, JoJo Peters, three murders to his name, who'd been put away after a cold-case trawl that Rebus had been involved in. But he was suffering from dementia these days and barely left his cell. The other prisoners made regular checks on him and took him treats. Rebus had stopped by one day and Peters had stared straight through him while chewing a toffee with the few teeth he'd managed to keep.

'Shouldn't be here,' a younger prisoner had commented, arriving with another handful of sweets. 'Home or a hospice if they had any heart.'

Word had obviously filtered down to Darryl Christie, who had stopped Rebus in the hall later.

'Reckon JoJo could pose a problem?' he'd asked.

'Definitely not.'

Christie had nodded slowly and turned away, watched by a couple of officers. Rebus doubted they'd have been quick to respond even if Christie had launched himself at him. The place was short-staffed – all prisons were – and it was at near-capacity. Other jails were even more crowded, but life here was made easier for all concerned if someone like Christie exerted a level of control.

The day Rebus had moved into his permanent cell, Christie had come calling. He'd gained some weight and wore his hair long, swept back from his forehead. He'd wanted to thank Rebus for getting rid of Morris Gerald Cafferty. But Rebus had been convicted of attempted murder rather than murder proper. Even so, the judge had handed down the mandatory life sentence, despite Rebus's protestations that he'd only meant to scare Big Ger by putting a cushion over his face. The prosecution hadn't liked that, presenting Cafferty as a wheelchair-bound Mother Teresa rather than a thuggish career criminal. Rebus's past run-ins with the man had been dusted off and held up to the jury for their consideration and condemnation. Still, Cafferty had died, leaving a vacuum of sorts – once his cocky lieutenant, Andrew Downs, had been scared off and run out of town. Christie's town, controlled at a distance, while inside HMP Edinburgh he sat on his throne – or at least the chair at Rebus's desk.

'Settling in? Anything I can get you? I know you had a bit of a thirst on the outside – harder to source in here. Pills, on the other hand – uppers and downers – you'll soon forget you've got four walls around you. You'll forget everything bad.'

'No chance of any Sanatogen then?' Christie looked blank. 'Forget it,' Rebus said. Then: 'Am I supposed to thank you for this?'

Rebus had known him since Christie was in his late teens, keening for retribution after his sister's murder. Paths were open to him back then and he'd chosen the one leading here. Rebus had been in the room the night Christie had shot and killed an enemy. He'd seen a madness behind the young man's eyes and had assumed he'd end up in the secure unit at Carstairs. But the law dictated otherwise.

'One thing you can do for me, lifer to lifer,' Christie had said that day in the cell, rising to his feet so he was eye to eye with the standing Rebus.

'What?'

'Run me through it. Help me picture the scene.' His voice had dropped, but his eyes glittered. 'Was he scared? Did he show it? Did he beg?' He ran his tongue across his lips. His breath was bad and his skin sallow. 'Come to think of it, how did *you* feel? It was a long time coming. Too long for many ...'

'I actually had a bit of respect for the guy,' Rebus had eventually replied. 'He had a code of sorts, things that were beyond the pale. Not every toerag can say the same.'

Then he'd sat down on his bed, picked up a book and pretended to start losing himself in it, leaving Christie to stand his ground, dragging a hand through his hair before walking out.

A few of the prisoners referred to Christie as 'the Don'. The first few times it had happened, Rebus had felt it necessary to respond that he was no Vito Corleone. But it kept happening anyway. Rebus knew all too well that Christie's protection was a mixed blessing; it didn't do to rile the guy unnecessarily. So he kept himself to himself, worked all the hours he could in the small but well-stocked library, and got to know a few of his companions, finding out who could be trusted to any extent and who should be avoided. He thought of Cafferty sometimes, not quite with remorse. The life sentence felt like Cafferty having one last laugh at Rebus's expense.

The level of noise rose as the morning progressed, complaints from behind the locked doors. Rebus's neighbours on both sides – Billy Groam and Everett Harrison – gave occasional kicks and thumps. Harrison had music playing as usual. Rebus had given up asking him to turn it down. Harrison was of Caribbean descent and had a Liverpudlian accent. He worked for a Merseyside-based trafficker of drugs and people, and had been caught in Edinburgh with a consignment of the former.

Rebus had asked him once if encroaching on Christie's turf meant he had to watch his back.

'Anyone comes at me, they better have nuclear capability,' Harrison had retorted. And it was true that he seemed to get on well with Christie, the two men playing pool together and sometimes even sharing a console game. Smiles and laughs, pats on the back and handshakes. Rebus was almost convinced.

His door was unlocked at one o'clock. An officer he didn't recognise told him that food was being served in Swanston Hall, so he'd need to get changed. On your own hall, you could wear what you liked, but when visiting elsewhere, prison-issue polo shirts and sweatshirts were required, their colours indicating what level of inmate you were. Blue for short-term, brown for those not yet tried in court, maroon for sex offenders. The long-termers like Rebus wore dark green. He'd been told it was so the officers watching on CCTV could keep tabs. Last thing they wanted was lifers meeting kiddie-fiddlers during free flow.

Having swapped his faded red polo for green, Rebus stepped out of his cell and saw that a cordon had been set up around the crime scene, courtesy of blue-and-white-striped POLICE tape draped between some parking cones. A scene-of-crime team was still busy, those inside the cell covered head to toe to prevent trace contamination. The governor meantime was in conversation with a cop Rebus recognised – Detective Sergeant Christine Esson. Spotting Rebus, she raised an eyebrow before turning her attention back to Howard Tennent.

'We all know what happened,' Billy Groam muttered, walking a few paces ahead of Rebus. 'Bad blood between Jackie and that bawbag Chris Novak. You saw him this morning same as I did, standing outside the cell making sure all his mates had their stories straight.'

Yes, Rebus remembered the two officers, faces almost touching as they talked. Novak and Valerie Watts. Rumour was they were more than just colleagues. But then rumours were like oxygen in a place like this, keeping the heart pumping and the mind active.

15

The line had slowed to a shuffle, giving Rebus time to check out who else he might know from the old days. He couldn't see Haj Atwal, who usually ran scene-of-crimes, but then he could be outside, busy at his well-equipped van. Rebus wondered if any of the crew had their phones on them, or had they been locked away as they would be for normal visitors? Whatever had been brought in would be taken out again, the prison staff would make sure of that.

Speculation and information ran up and down the line as it moved. Mark Jamieson had been taken to hospital to be checked over. Chris Novak had been on the overnight shift, which meant he was pulling a double, since he'd still been on duty at breakfast. Same went for Valerie Watts – and wasn't *that* a happy coincidence? The lads in the cells either side of the crime scene hadn't heard raised voices or anything, though Billy Groam across the way swore he'd heard a cell being un-locked at some point before dawn.

'Jackie's cell?' Rebus checked.

'Who else's?' Groam muttered.

Rebus had known Jackie Simpson. He would visit the library for DVDs while boasting that he'd never read a book in his life.

'The streets were my school,' he'd told Rebus once. 'And now I'm the teacher!'

By which he meant that he taught other prisoners how to get through a locked door, *any* door. He'd even offered to show Rebus.

'What makes you think I don't already know?' Rebus had replied.

He'd also told Rebus about his feud with Officer Novak. 'Bastard grabbed me by the throat one time. Inside my cell so it wasn't on camera. Told me my boy was a deadbeat like his dad. It'll be a different story when I get out of here.'

'In which case you'll be paying this place a return visit pronto,' Rebus had warned him.

As the line moved closer to lunch, Rebus asked Groam how he reckoned Novak had killed Simpson.

'Smuggled in a shank, didn't he? Or maybe he confiscated it, kept it tucked away for future use. Cell door was locked, John – you reckon one of us magicked our way in there?'

'Simpson got on okay with his cellmate?'

'Mark's a pussycat, barely out of his teens. Plus the size of him, you could fit him in Jackie's back pocket. Jackie would have ripped his head off if he'd tried anything.'

'Benzos can make a man act out of character.'

'Tends not to turn them into the Hulk, though. Plus, aye, Mark was zonked as usual. Zonked *and* whacked across the head with something. You've seen the batons Novak and his gang carry. Way he sees it, cops aren't going to break sweat. Jackie's just another con to them. One less to worry about.'

There were some wolf-whistles and whoops as they trooped into Swanston, the prisoners there letting them know what they thought of the incursion. But they were curious, too, wanting to know what had happened and why, so there was a charm offensive of sorts. Rebus studied each and every face, recognising none, for which he was grateful. On his home turf, Darryl Christie reigned, but Rebus didn't know how far his kingdom stretched. Christie himself settled with his food, seemingly unconcerned, but his eyes remained wary and he made sure he was flanked by two of the bigger bastards from Trinity, one of them Everett Harrison. Rebus watched as a prisoner approached and tapped Harrison on the shoulder. Harrison got up, all grins, and the two men hugged, then patted each other's upper arms, checking the musculature. Rebus realised they must have known one another on the outside, and he felt his gut clench.

'His name's Bobby Briggs,' Groam confided. 'From the west coast.'

'I know him,' Rebus admitted in an undertone.

Groam fixed him with a look. 'From your days in the filth?'

'Where else?'

'Half Trinity thinks you were moved in because Tennent wants someone on the inside.'

'Wasn't like that.' Rebus scooped up more potato. The food was lukewarm at best, but anything tasted better than confinement. It reminded him of fare from a primary school or some second-rate holiday camp. One day a week they got burgers. After that, a lot of prisoners started counting down the days till next time. Everybody liked burgers. But today it was chicken in a white sauce, plus mushy potatoes. Rebus didn't finish his, and Groam angled his head towards the plate.

'Fill your boots,' Rebus said.

He was thinking of Christine Esson. In days past, he might have known her phone number. He assumed she was still based at Gayfield Square. Time was, she worked under DI Siobhan Clarke, but Clarke had moved on. Esson hadn't looked at all fazed by her surroundings, every inch the professional. Whatever mentoring Clarke had done, it had paid off.

He realised that someone was staring at him from the far side of the hall, that someone being Bobby Briggs. Then Briggs was on his feet and lumbering in Rebus's direction. Rebus got up and backed towards the nearest officer.

'Trouble's coming,' he informed him.

'Easy, Bobby,' the officer cautioned, holding up a hand in warning. Briggs stopped a couple of feet short of Rebus, jabbing a finger as he spoke.

'Bastard stitched me up,' he snarled, eyes glowing, teeth showing. Spittle flew from his mouth, flecks of it hitting Rebus's face.

'That was in another century, Bobby,' Rebus argued. 'And it's not why you're in here now.'

Everett Harrison had approached, pressing a palm to Briggs's shoulder. 'Everything all right, Bobby?'

Briggs didn't take his eyes off Rebus. 'Lied through their teeth in the witness box, him and his lot. I got five years.'

'That's right, Bobby,' Rebus offered. 'The victim kicked his own ribs till they broke – I keep forgetting.'

'Maybe you forget, but I never will. Your card's marked, Rebus.'

'Whatever you say, Bobby.'

Briggs looked ready to pounce, but Harrison's grip on him had strengthened and the officer's hand was half an inch from the alarm. With effort, Harrison turned the man around and began leading him back into the body of the hall, his arm draped around his shoulders.

'Might take the rest of my meals in my cell,' Rebus told the officer, on whose forehead a sheen of sweat had appeared.

'I'll make a note of it,' he said. 'Bobby's not someone you want to get on the wrong side of.'

'Maybe I'll send him a box of Quality Street as a peace offering ...'

Twenty minutes later, they were on their way again, being waved off and blown kisses by some of their hosts. Outside the deceased's cell, Esson and her colleagues had been replaced by the governor and another man, the latter smart-suited, hair immaculate, tie crisply knotted. It took Rebus the briefest moment to place him – Malcolm Fox, formerly Professional Standards and now Organised Crime. Fox was happiest behind a neat desk, inbox empty and a boss's arse waiting to be peppered with kisses. Rebus almost blurted aloud what he was thinking:

Fuck are you doing here?

Fox clocked him, almost as if he'd been expecting him. While the governor kept talking, Fox's attention was all on Rebus. Rebus in turn narrowed his eyes, letting Fox know he had questions. Fatalities were the preserve of a major incident team, and Fox was not and never would be MIT. Rebus turned his head by degrees as he walked, maintaining eye contact. An officer was gesturing for him to enter his cell.

'We're being cooped up again?' Rebus complained.

'Afraid so.'

'Whatever happened to human rights?' Groam piped up. 'We've hardly been out today.'

'A mate of ours is dead, Billy,' Everett Harrison shot back. 'A few extra hours banged up is fuck all.'

19

'I've nothing to do, though.'

'Haven't you got a toy you can play with?' Harrison cupped his own groin, grinning.

Rebus waited until he had the man's attention. 'I want to thank you for saving my neck back there.'

'Bobby holds his grudges. He wants to see you turning on a spit.'

'I thought I was under Darryl Christie's protection.'

'In here you are, but this is just one hall.'

'Everybody in!' the governor called out.

Everyone went in.

Rebus sat on his bed, rubbing a hand across his jaw and occasionally glancing towards the wall-mounted landline. He was aware of a dull cacophony – more complaints about the lockdown, shouted responses from the officers on duty. Eventually, around four, his door rattled open.

'Stretch your legs,' Graves said. 'There's already a queue for the showers if you feel the need.'

'I'll manage,' Rebus said. The temporary cordon had gone from in front of the murder scene, but there was tape stretched across the closed door. Prisoners mingled, chatted, set up games of cards, trying to avoid looking at that tape. Two of them headed for the pool table and picked up cues. No one was being allowed out of the hall for activities, but freedom was relative and they were determined to savour it, while trying for the solemnity they felt the day required. No jokes for a change, no teasing or gentle bullying.

'You're not due to see the nurse or anything?' Graves checked. 'Enough meds?'

'Plenty meds,' Rebus confirmed.

'Lucky you. I could do with some myself. Back's been giving me gyp.'

'I'm sure Darryl can sort you out. You only have to ask.'

Rebus walked past Graves's scowl, shaking his legs as if loosening them. He tried to look as if he was just circling the hall, no real destination in mind. He'd done four circuits before

20

the queue at Darryl Christie's table was cleared. Rebus took the seat opposite him.

'What's with you and Bobby Briggs?' Christie asked.

'He thinks I lied in court.'

'And did you?'

'Pious perjury, we called it.'

'In other words, you *did* fit him up?'

Rebus shook his head. 'He'd done the crime. We just couldn't quite prove it.'

'So you gave the jury a version they'd fall for?' Christie nodded his understanding.

'He was about to rip my head from my shoulders back there.'

'Everett had you covered,' Christie said with a shrug. 'So if you've come looking for an apology ...'

Rebus shook his head again. 'I need a phone for an hour.'

Christie took his time folding his arms. 'What makes you think I have a phone?'

'You've probably got a dozen of them. Either smuggled in up someone's arse or brought in by one of the staff for a bung. If there's a choice, I'd prefer something from the latter batch.' Rebus watched a thin smile spread across Christie's face. 'I can pay the going rate, if that's what you're wondering.'

'You don't know what the current rate is.'

'So enlighten me.'

Christie unfolded his arms and pressed his palms flat against the table. 'What's wrong with the landline in your cell? Let me guess – you need to make sure no one's listening in. But that still begs the question. My guess is it's to do with what happened to Jackie Simpson.'

'So what *did* happen to Jackie?'

'How would I know?'

'By pressing a few pills into the right hands.'

'I'd be wasting good product. Even the uniforms know it was one of them, maybe more than one. They're going to have trouble keeping a lid on it, too. Jackie was well liked. Lot of the guys want to do the right thing by him.'

'Start a riot, you mean?'

'Do I?' Christie leaned across the table, eyes level with Rebus's. 'My office in five minutes,' he stated, getting to his feet and turning away.

Rebus stayed where he was and counted the seconds. There were plenty of looks from those who wondered what was going on.

'Just getting my Special K order in,' he told the nearest of them, raising his voice for the benefit of everyone else.

Eventually he took the short stroll to Christie's cell. The door was ajar a few inches. Rebus nudged it further open with his foot and stepped inside. It was comfortable enough – TV and music player and a pile of recent car and bike mags. There were photos on one wall, including several of Christie's murdered sister and one of him astride a Harley-Davidson.

'They won't let me carpet the place,' Christie pretended to complain. He was standing under the high window, legs parted, hands behind his back. 'Do you mind shutting it?' He nodded towards the door. Rebus did as he was told.

'So how much?' he asked into the silence.

'A grand,' Christie informed him. Then, having watched Rebus take this in, he gave a snort. 'Just this one time then.' He held out his right hand. There was a small, basic-looking mobile phone sitting in it. 'Passcode is four zeroes. Reception can be dodgy, so try clambering onto your toilet seat. Bonus is, they can't see you from the peephole. They can hear you, though, so keep your voice down, and best phone while things are lively. At dead of night sound carries even further, and your neighbours will have their ears pressed to the wall.'

Rebus reached out for the device, but Christie had wrapped his hand around it again.

'Something to consider: you take this, you're not on their side any more, you're on ours. If you're found with it, you'll be locked down solid for a while. You get that, right?'

Rebus gave a slow nod. 'I get it.'

'And if the boss finds out you've been naughty, there'll be

no more tea and biscuits in his office. So you need to be really sure.'

'I'm sure.'

'And it *is* to do with Jackie Simpson?'

'Maybe,' Rebus confessed. As Christie's fist relaxed, he plucked the phone from it and slipped it into his pocket. 'How do I get it back to you?'

'It's yours till breakfast. Hand it over then. Fair warning – it's got about twenty minutes' battery left on it. Call it a free taste. If you decide you need to up the dosage, we can talk numbers.' Christie held out his hand and Rebus took it, returning the grip as best he could while they shook.

'One last thing,' Rebus said. 'How come you're so pally with a guy who plays for another team?'

'Harrison, you mean?' Christie considered for a moment. 'His manager's a Scouse wanker called Hanlon. But maybe there's a transfer window opening. Could be he'll change strips ...' He gave a slow wink before turning his back on Rebus, angling his head to gaze at the high window. It was open as far as it would go – a scant few inches – but air was air. Christie seemed to be appreciating it as he clasped his hands behind his back again.

Meeting over.

As soon as he was back in his cell, Rebus headed to the toilet pan and stepped onto it. But nobody was being locked up yet, meaning anyone could yank his door open and catch him in the act. So he bided his time, and after twenty minutes a couple of prison officers arrived accompanying two detectives, presumably from the MIT. One male and one female, late twenties or early thirties, the male looking the more senior. Rebus couldn't put names to either of them. This was the signal for the prisoners to be herded back into their cells, amidst the usual volley of complaints, bluster and cursing, plus queries as to whether they'd be allowed out in time for their next meal. As soon as

Rebus's door was locked, he climbed onto the lavatory again and made the call. A female voice answered.

'Yes?'

He remained silent, wondering how long it would take her. The answer: eight seconds. Then a sigh.

'John?'

'Hello, Siobhan.' He cupped one hand around his mouth and the phone.

'There was no voice telling me the call's being monitored.' Again Rebus waited. Again Siobhan Clarke sighed. 'Oh Jesus, John, what if you're caught?'

'You thought I'd be phoning, though, didn't you?'

'It's Christine Esson you need to speak to, not me.'

'Yes, I saw her earlier. She looked the part.'

'That's because she *is* the part.'

'Do I detect a note of jealousy?'

'Sod off.'

'It's good to hear your voice, Siobhan. How've things been?'

'Sammy and I went to check your flat a few days back. Starting to smell a bit damp, so we're putting the heating on an hour a day. Is that all right?'

'Did Sammy have Brillo with her?'

'He was looking all over for you. We gave him a run on the Meadows and he was looking there, too.'

'Give him a scratch behind the ears for me.'

'Will do.' Clarke paused. 'Carrie wants to see you. She's gotten good at drawing. There's one of Brillo she wants you to have.'

'I can't have her seeing me in here, Shiv. You know that.'

'She'd be fine, John.'

'She might, but I wouldn't.' He paused. 'How about you – you doing okay, all things considered?'

'How long have you got?'

'Maybe ten more minutes.' Rebus held the phone away from him. The battery indicator was already flashing. 'Can you get me Christine's number?'

24

'Not a good idea.'

'How about Malcolm Fox? Is he speaking to you?'

'What's Fox got to do with anything?'

'He was at the crime scene, getting the lowdown from the governor by the look of it.'

'Bit odd.'

'That's what I thought. Reckon you can shed any light?'

'I'll do what I can. No promises. But you'll owe me, and you know what I want.'

It was Rebus's turn to exhale. 'I'll think about it.'

'She's missing you rotten.'

'I said I'll think about it. Nice talking to you, Shiv. Don't be a stranger.' He ended the call but stayed where he was. The battery light was still flashing red. How many minutes did he have? He tried to think who else to call. His solicitor? They'd have clocked off for the day, or be out of the office – the receptionist would have her excuses ready as per. There was always Deborah Quant, but then she'd done the autopsy on Cafferty and given evidence at Rebus's trial, and somehow that had cooled whatever ardour there had still been. He could talk to Sammy, but he'd be seeing her at the next visit. The Oxford Bar? He smiled at the thought – the sounds of the regulars in the background as Kirsty picked up. But then what? No, there really wasn't anyone. Besides, the light was no longer flashing. The burner phone was dead.

2

Cammy Colson opened the car door and started climbing into the passenger seat.

'Sorry to keep you waiting,' he said.

Siobhan Clarke obliged with the briefest of smiles. Detective Sergeant Cameron Colson moved through life at the pace of a snail. Even now, having seated himself, his hand was creeping with painful slowness towards the handle. Watching him pull the door shut was like watching tectonic plates shifting. Clarke couldn't bear the thought of his seat-belt manoeuvres, so she pressed the ignition button and got going.

'Who were you on the phone to?' he asked, pulling the belt across his chest.

Slow-moving, yes, but little escaped his attention.

'Personal,' was all she said, pulling out of the car park at St Leonard's police station.

She hadn't been in position long, didn't really know her colleagues well enough as yet to think of them as a team. She knew anything she let slip to Cammy Colson was bound to get back to the others. They were all curious, of course – and wary. Curious because Clarke had been promoted to Professional Standards (the feared and infamous 'Complaints') but had then jumped ship and returned to CID. Too late, however, to return to her old station at Gayfield Square, where she'd already been replaced. St Leonard's was not new to her – she'd worked there with John Rebus before his retirement – but she was new to it. The faces had changed, and those faces were wary precisely because she was linked, however tenuously, to Professional Standards. As a result, colleagues were careful how much they divulged. When she walked into a room, the small talk ceased. She could have told them the simple truth – that she hadn't lasted at Professional Standards because she didn't like it and felt it a waste of whatever talent she possessed. But would they believe her? Never apologise, never explain. She wasn't sure who it was who first said that, but she was content to abide by it.

Maybe one night over drinks it would all come out. Except that none of them drank. Or if they did, they did it quietly at home. At the end of each shift, as jackets and coats went on, there was never mention of stopping for a quick one across the road. Then again, maybe everything was arranged by text message, keeping her in the dark. She didn't think so, though; had even wandered into two or three pubs in the vicinity, finding no one she knew lurking there. It was a different generation, that was all. Younger than her; taking better care of themselves. Pete Swinton ran half-marathons for fun. Colson, despite his heft, was 'vegetarian verging on vegan'. Trisha Singh did yoga and Pilates. And all of them worked under Detective Chief Inspector Bryan Carmichael, who, as well as looking young enough still to be at college, swam every morning in the nearby Commonwealth Pool, having been on the national team as a schoolboy. Though she tried not to feel nostalgic, she missed the old days with John Rebus, crossing the occasional line to get results. 'The bad old days', Carmichael would no doubt call them, but they'd been good days too.

She thought about Rebus often, between the weekly visits and the occasional monitored catch-up by phone. His weight had been dropping, the skin loose around his jaw and neck, and he'd lost what little colour his face had once had. He managed

27

to joke about his incarceration, but they both knew Saughton would always be a dangerous place for an ex-cop, even one with the guile and instincts of John Rebus. His imprisonment had brought Clarke closer to his daughter, Sammy, and granddaughter, Carrie. They often walked Rebus's mutt Brillo together, finding things to talk about that didn't always involve the man himself.

By the time Clarke stopped at the first set of red lights, Colson had got his seat belt fastened.

'So what do you reckon?' he asked.

She took a moment to gather herself. 'Met someone at a party or in town, head over heels for forty-eight hours, rest of the world just disappears.'

'So she'll be back any time?'

'Here's hoping.'

They were talking about a fourteen-year-old schoolgirl, Jasmine Andrews, who had left school for home the previous afternoon but not arrived. By 6.30 p.m., wondering where she was, her mother had phoned Jasmine's best friend, Carla, who'd told her Jasmine wasn't there and wasn't picking up texts or answering her phone. Nor had she been active on social media.

Jasmine's mother had ended the call and made another to her husband, a business developer who was on a job down south. He hadn't answered and she'd left no message. Instead, she'd headed out in her car to trawl the streets around the neighbourhood and beyond. She'd paused at some point and texted Carla, asking her to keep trying to track Jasmine down. When her husband phoned her an hour or two later, she'd burst into tears and then, on his advice, called the police.

That had been last night. Jasmine still hadn't come home, and her disappearance was out of character. If she was with someone, it wasn't any of her gang of friends. Either that or someone was covering for her. She'd left no note, taken no obvious clothes. It would take time for them to check whether she was using her bank card for purchases or withdrawals.

28

Time, too, for them to scour CCTV footage from street cameras, public transport and shops. Jasmine's mother, Helena, had been asked if they'd fallen out, or whether Jasmine had seemed herself recently. Did she have a boyfriend? (No.) Any ex-boyfriends? (Just the one, never very serious.) Her bedroom had been visited, a few photographs borrowed, her contact details noted. Service providers would be asked for their help. Jasmine's friends had already alerted the online world, and their concern had been picked up by the media. The *Evening News* had run the story on their website, and Jasmine's picture would be in the next physical edition of the newspaper. She was a fresh-faced teenager with a winning smile and long blonde hair. Everyone was interested.

Clarke and Colson were on their way to Jasmine's school in Marchmont, where the head teacher was rounding up all the pupils who knew her. Though Clarke had told Colson she reckoned Jasmine had just met someone and was hanging out with them, she wasn't sure she believed it. It was a best-case scenario, something to say to the worried parents so they wouldn't lose their minds. She had visited the Andrews home, a Victorian semi-detached on a leafy street in the Grange. She had watched Helena Andrews just about fail to raise a mug of tea to her mouth without spilling it, due to the tremble in both hands. She owned and ran a designer shop in nearby Bruntsfield. Her sister was due to arrive soon from Glasgow to be with her. Her husband probably couldn't get home until late evening or even the next day.

'Jas is only fourteen,' she kept saying between sniffles. 'You've got to bring her back.'

'Of course we'll do that,' Cammy Colson had said, beginning the onerous process of reaching across the table for his own mug.

A member of staff was waiting for them at the gates to the car park, indicating the bay for visitors. She guided them into the modern building and up a flight of stairs to the only other floor, where she opened a classroom door and signalled for them

29

to enter. The head was waiting and shook hands, introducing herself as Tara Lindsay.

'Do you want me to stay, or ...'

Clarke looked at the thirty or so pupils, seated behind desks, dressed in a uniform of white shirt, yellow-and-red-striped tie, dark blazer with the school's crest on the left breast. Charcoal-coloured trousers for the boys, clingy black skirts and dark tights for the girls. Knowing they were in the presence of authority figures, they all wore looks Clarke had seen before, frightened that their minds could be read and their secrets revealed, desperate that their body language or a slip of the tongue didn't give them away.

'Sit yourself down,' she told the head. Colson was resting his backside against the edge of what would be the teacher's desk and had started folding his arms. Clarke placed herself in front of the group of teenagers and took a deep breath.

'My name's Detective Inspector Clarke and this is Detective Sergeant Colson. I want to thank you for coming along. As you know, your friend Jasmine hasn't been seen since yesterday afternoon and we all want to see her back here safe and sound. You probably knew her better than anyone, and that's why we need your help. Anything you can tell us, no matter how trivial you might think it, could be of help.' She broke off as a hand went up.

'Is Jas in trouble? When she's found, I mean.'

Clarke focused on the girl. 'That's a good point. She needs to know she's not in any kind of trouble. I can't stress that enough. Her mum and dad just want to give her a hug. Whatever the reason might be for her leaving, there's going to be no punishment. Can any of you think why she might've wanted to disappear, even for a short time?'

The pupils looked at each other, some of them offering shrugs.

'Anybody she might've gone to visit, out of town maybe? Someone she knew online?' Above the sea of shaking heads, Clarke saw two girls at the back share a look.

'You're all keeping a lookout for her on TikTok, Snapchat and whatever, aye?' Colson piped up.

'She uses WhatsApp too,' one girl replied.

'Everybody online knows she's gone,' another added, 'but nobody knows where.'

'Can any of you think of places she might have headed? Maybe somewhere you all congregate that none of your parents know about?'

The room shared a variety of glances, twitches and shrugs. The silence stretched until Clarke broke it.

'Is there a Craig Fielding in the room?' she asked.

'He's the year above, but he's not in today,' a boy answered, his voice much deeper than his skinny frame would suggest. There were wisps of a nascent moustache either side of his upper lip.

'Is he off sick or what?' Clarke addressed this to Tara Lindsay, who said she would check, taking out her phone and starting to text.

'Craig and Jasmine split ages back,' one of the girls at the back announced.

'Were they both okay about that?' Clarke enquired, receiving a shrug in response.

'You think someone's taken her?' another girl interrupted, voice shaking slightly. 'Do we need to be extra careful?'

'There's nothing to suggest that,' Colson drawled. 'But it always pays to keep your wits about you – cars or strangers following you, maybe tailing you home ...'

Seeing the fearful looks on a few faces, Clarke butted in. 'I'm sure there's nothing to worry about, but we all want to know that she's safe and not in any sort of bother.'

Lindsay was reading an incoming text. 'Feeling a bit off-colour. His mother phoned the office this morning.'

'We'll need his contact details,' Clarke stated. She turned to the whiteboard, picked up the marker pen next to it and wrote down a phone number and email address. 'Keep a note of these,' she said to the pupils. 'You can talk to us confidentially, any time day or night.' They all got out their phones and started entering the details, mostly by dint of photographing the board. Clarke turned to Tara Lindsay. 'Maybe you can make sure the staff get the same message?'

'Absolutely.'

She turned again and addressed the classroom. 'Thank you for coming. I think that's enough for now.' She watched them start to gather up their bags. 'Oh, one thing – is there someone here called Carla?'

The two girls at the back shared another look. One of them raised her hand with some reluctance.

'If you could maybe stay behind a couple of minutes,' Clarke told her.

Tara Lindsay was entering the information from the whiteboard into her own phone. She came and stood next to Clarke as the teenagers filed from the room. When she spoke, she kept her voice low.

'I wouldn't say Jasmine's super-bright or super-confident. She's one of the quiet ones. A camp follower, you might say. Never gives us any trouble or cause for concern, unlike some others I could name.' Clarke got the feeling those 'others' might include Carla and her confidante, who were having a whispered conversation as they dawdled. The eyes of those making their exit were on them both, and some colour had risen to Carla's cheeks.

'We'll talk to Carla in private,' Clarke told the head, 'if that's okay with you. We can find our own way out when we're done.'

Lindsay seemed reluctant, but eventually nodded her agreement. She left the room just ahead of Carla's pal, Carla herself sitting back down in the same spot on the back row of desks. Clarke didn't mind letting the girl win that one. She walked from the front of the classroom, Colson a few steps behind. When the pair of them came to a stop, they loomed over the seated figure.

'What's your last name, Carla?' Clarke asked.

'Morris.'

32

'Where's that accent from?'

'Bradford. We moved here four years ago.'

'Is that how long you've known Jasmine?'

'Pretty much.'

'We hear from her mum that you're her best friend – is she yours?'

'Jas is all right. A good laugh. We like the same music.'

'If she wanted to confide in anyone, it would be you, though, yes?'

'Maybe.'

Clarke studied the girl. She was clear-skinned, still carrying some puppy fat but readying for adulthood. Her eyes were filled with a degree of knowledge but maybe even more bravado. Shoulder-length dark hair and a bit of eyeliner. Her school tie boasted an oversized knot, the top button of her white shirt undone. Clarke tried to think back to her own schooldays and to girls like Carla, but too much time had passed.

'Who was that next to you?' Colson asked, pointing towards the vacated chair.

'Stephanie.'

'Would she be *your* best friend, Carla?'

The girl looked at him for a brief second. 'I wish I could help you, but I can't.'

'No clue as to what Jasmine might be doing? Where she could be hiding?'

'She was fine last time I saw her. We shared YouTube clips two nights back. She didn't say anything about ...' She twirled a finger in the air, indicating anything and everything.

'What sort of clips?'

'Music videos ... funny animals ... just things she thought I'd like.'

'Did she do that a lot?'

'Most nights.'

'Things she thought *you'd* like – so it was mostly one-way traffic? Would you say she's a needy sort of friend?'

When Carla met Colson's eyes, it was as if she were pulling

up a drawbridge. 'I've told you everything I can.' Her voice was low but determined.

Clarke held up her phone and waved it. 'Can we have your contact details, Carla? I'm not saying there'll be more questions, but just to be on the safe side.'

The girl considered for a moment, then reeled off her number.

'Thanks for that,' Clarke said.

'So I can go?'

'You can go,' Colson agreed.

Carla lost no time grabbing her bag and making for the door.

'No current boyfriend?' Clarke called out to her.

'Me or Jas?'

'Jasmine.'

'Not that I know of.'

'And how about you – you're not seeing Craig Fielding, are you?'

The girl answered with a roll of her eyes as she left.

'Craig Fielding?' Colson asked when the door had closed.

'Just something about Carla and her mate Stephanie. Something they didn't want us to know.' Clarke gave a twitch of the mouth and approached the whiteboard. 'I think I'll leave that up,' she said.

'When you started writing, I could sense you enjoying it. Ever plan to go into teaching when you were younger?'

'I don't think so.' She turned towards him. 'We need to speak with Craig Fielding at some point.'

'I suppose.'

Clarke glared at him. 'You *suppose*?'

'Case is neither one thing nor the other just now. If she waltzes back home later today, we've been wasting our time.'

'You're saying you can't really get motivated until she's lying on a slab in the autopsy suite?'

'Christ, Shiv, nobody wants that.'

'It's Siobhan, DS Colson.'

He started to hold up his hands in a show of surrender. 'Just

34

answer me this, then – do you think she's been abducted, or do you think she's a hormonal teen who's gone off in some kind of strop?'

Clarke thought for a moment. 'You've got a point – we need someone to start going through the register of sex offenders. Anyone local we should know about, maybe only recently back on the streets.' She saw the look he was giving her. 'We need to cover every contingency. That way we're better prepared if bad news comes.' Her tone became more conciliatory. 'Maybe you're right and she's gone walkabout. Maybe she really is about to waltz back home. But if she hasn't, our boss is going to want to know that we were on top of it from the get-go.' She paused. 'Yes or no?'

The fight seemed to drain out of Colson. 'Fine, yes, of course you're right. So the ex-boyfriend and then the paedophiles?'

'Not forgetting Strawberry Switchblade.' Colson looked blank. 'I mean Carla and Stephanie.'

'Strawberry Switchblade?'

'Before your time, Cammy,' Clarke said, trying not to show how painful it was to admit that.

Malcolm Fox's office in the Scottish Crime Campus's modern building at Gartcosh was a glass box, identical to the others either side of it. He'd just had a rare visit from his boss, Detective Chief Superintendent Phil Pratchett. Pratchett's whole demeanour had changed in the past year. Retirement was coming for him and he had yielded to its inevitability. Fox had the notion that Pratchett had at one time reckoned him a potential successor, but Fox's judgement had been called into question by the farce with Siobhan Clarke. She'd been his enthusiastic pick for Professional Standards and she hadn't lasted two minutes. Fox was all too aware that he needed a result that would plaster over the resulting cracks.

Which was why Jackie Simpson's death was such a blow.

Simpson had been Fox's eyes and ears inside Trinity Hall,

as he had been on the outside. Darryl Christie continued to be a malign presence in Scotland's capital. New drugs were being parachuted onto the city's streets. Nobody in Police Scotland wanted the country to appear too welcoming to suppliers. Fox's department had been charged with stopping the flow and identifying the main players. Those players, however, were not all home-grown, which was why Fox had been introduced to a DI in London called Thomas Glaze. (Always Thomas, never Tom – Fox had made that mistake only once.) The two had not yet met, only ever speaking by phone, but Fox liked to think a rapport had been established.

Glaze worked for SO15 and had a special interest in drugs and people-trafficking. A year back he had given Fox the name Shay Hanlon. Hanlon was suspected of smuggling refugees through Europe and then selling them into a sort of slavery where they worked menial jobs in order to pay off a debt that kept rising exponentially. One of these operations was a nail bar in Edinburgh. Could Fox's team glean anything that might prove helpful? Fox didn't bother telling Glaze that he had no team as such. There were few enough officers working within the Organised Crime and Counter-Terrorism Unit, and the budget had just been slashed yet again. So he had undertaken the work himself, often on his own time. Then one night, sitting in a quietly anonymous bar with Jackie Simpson, a plan had been conjured up. Say the nail bar was broken into. Police would then have reason to enter the premises and have a good look around. Something might well turn up.

And something had. Street drugs. Lots of them. Delivered by one Everett Harrison, and with his prints and DNA smeared across the packages. Charged, found guilty and sent to HMP Edinburgh.

But then Jackie Simpson had slipped up and found himself there too.

'Bit of a bonus,' Glaze had commented. 'Harrison's a good catch, but it's his boss we really want. If the two are in touch, maybe your man can learn something. How long is he in for?'

'Just a few months.'

'Better get busy then, eh, Malcolm? Don't think we're not grateful, by the way. Your name's getting mentioned down here in ways that would make you blush.'

Which was the point at which Fox had decided he'd better talk to his boss and apprise him of *most* of what he'd been doing and what had been achieved.

But time had passed and all Fox really had to show was a deceased snitch – which was what had led the chief super to his door.

'This better not be about to get messy, Malcolm,' had been the message.

'It won't,' Fox had assured him, maintaining eye contact.

But that meant depending on Edinburgh CID to solve the case satisfactorily. And Fox had no confidence at all in that scenario – hence his visit to HMP Edinburgh with the governor as his tour guide. He had left with the promise that he would be kept up to date with developments.

'Good man,' he had said, his smile genuine for once.

Clarke stayed in the office at St Leonard's after everyone else had gone home. She liked the place when it was quiet like this. She had space to think. Mostly she was thinking about Colson and Swinton and Singh. Colson never offered up much about his private life. She knew Swinton and Singh were both married, Swinton to someone who worked in finance and Singh to a doctor. The boss, Bryan Carmichael, was gay and in a relationship, though again he never brought it up.

If asked about her own circumstances, she would have told the truth – that she was on a sabbatical from all that. There had been a brief thing a while back with Fox, but it had been awkward and unsustainable. Before that there had been names, faces and dates she barely recalled. She picked up one of the photos of Jasmine Andrews and studied it. They hadn't bothered pinning anything to a corkboard yet. No one was discussing search parties or river dredging. Officers had sourced the available footage from bus and train stations, ignoring the airport for now. Cab drivers had been alerted. A family liaison officer was visiting Jasmine's parents this evening, the father having travelled north.

The father's name was James. He'd met Helena at work when he'd been lower in the pecking order and she'd been a secretary. She'd quit the job when she became pregnant. With James's career going well, they'd decided she needn't go back to her old position. What she'd always fancied was running her own retail business. Clarke had taken a detour from the school in order to drive past the shop. It looked cheerful, even under lock and key, its window filled with knick-knacks, tweed and cashmere.

'Quality tat,' Colson had commented, leaving it at that.

The liaison visit was a formality; Clarke doubted much would be gleaned. Though as they'd not yet had the chance to size up the father, she'd asked for an evaluation.

'If the hair on your neck starts to prickle,' she'd told the officer, 'I want to know.'

St Leonard's was one of the city's more modern cop shops, but it still felt jaded, its surfaces chipped and scuffed, windows ill-fitting and heating reduced to a game of chance. In purely aesthetic terms it could be considered a step up from Gayfield Square, but it managed to feel like a demotion. She missed her old crew. She missed being able to walk to work from her tenement flat just off Broughton Street. Placing the photograph to one side, she lifted her phone and called Christine Esson.

'You've heard, then,' Esson said.

'First decent murder case in a while,' Clarke responded. 'Everyone's green with envy.'

'I doubt they'd be jealous if they had to spend all day in the place. I only got out half an hour ago and the smell is clinging to me.'

Clarke listened to a car horn sound. 'You're stuck in traffic,' she speculated.

'The joys of rush hour. Where are you?'

38

'St Leonard's. You live just down the road, don't you?'

'You know damned well I do. Want me to pick you up?'

'You've read my mind, girl.'

'I'm only staying for one, though. Can't risk a breathalyser.'

'One will do the job,' Clarke assured her.

'We used to tell ourselves that, but it never quite turned out that way.'

'Thank God we're older and so much wiser.'

'I'll be there in ten, fifteen at most.'

'I'll be waiting out front,' Clarke said.

The bar they ended up in was a neighbourhood place on the edge of Newington, no tourists to speak of, and quiet, as most post-COVID pubs tended to be outside of weekends and the city centre. They ordered G and Ts with a spare bottle of tonic apiece and settled at a corner table with a view of the door. When their eyes met, they smiled – it was a cop thing; you always wanted to know who might be coming in, just in case you didn't want to meet them.

Having clinked glasses, they sipped in silence for a moment. Esson stretched her neck to left and right, loosening it.

'So what's keeping you busy just now?' she asked.

'Teenage girl gone AWOL.'

'I heard about that.'

Clarke held up her phone, showing Esson a picture of Jasmine.

'How old?' Esson asked.

'Fourteen.'

'Looks older, but then they always do, or so predatory men keep telling me.'

'It'll either be something or nothing.' Clarke spoke over the rim of her glass. 'So how's it going with my replacement?'

'I thought you said you never wanted to talk about him?'

'I don't. I just need to hear that he's a bitter disappointment with the charisma of a tin of paint.'

Esson pretended to consider this. 'What colour paint?'

'Battleship grey.'

'He's okay really. I think you might even like him.'

'Personable? Hard-working? Collegiate?'

'All that and more.'

'You've taken a shine to him?'

'"Taken a shine"? Remind me what century we're in.'

'But you're working well together?'

'So far.'

'Including in the nick.'

'He's actually on less sure ground there. I think maybe he's claustrophobic.'

'Remind me of his name.'

'Jason Mulgrew.'

Clarke rolled the words around in her mouth.

'We did some interviews on site today, but a slew more are due tomorrow.'

'It's not like anyone's going anywhere.'

'The guards go home occasionally.' Esson dribbled some more tonic into her glass. 'We've been checking the CCTV. This is a prison, right? Surveillance an absolute must. Yet one of the cameras has been on the blink for over a week.'

'The one pointed at the cell where the murder happened?'

'How did you guess?'

'You'd have had it solved by now otherwise. Quite the coincidence, though ...'

'That's what we're thinking.'

'How many suspects?'

'There were only a dozen staff on that particular night shift for north of eight hundred prisoners – can you credit that? Cell door locked, nobody saw or heard anything – nothing they're willing to divulge to us, at any rate. Well, apart from a single solitary inmate who says he heard a key rattling at some point in the night.'

'Pity about that camera.'

'We've got the lab looking at all the other footage. Plenty of

40

comings and goings, but nothing showing anyone heading for the locus until the morning shift.'

'The victim had enemies?'

'There are stories of a bit of needle between him and one of the officers.'

'And this officer was on duty that night?'

'Alibied by his co-workers, never alone for more than five minutes at a stretch.'

'How convenient. What about the cellmate?'

'Outside the high walls we might term him a habitual user. They ran tests at the hospital and the story that he was out of it rings true. He was cracked over the skull, too. They've had to staple his forehead back together.'

'So the killing happened while he was crashed out?'

'Like everyone else, he didn't hear or see anything.'

'Nothing he's going to divulge at any rate.' Clarke followed Esson in adding more tonic to her drink.

'No blood on him anywhere. He was top bunk, victim bottom. Plenty of blood on the bedding, wall and floor.'

'Footprints heading back to the door?'

Esson shook her head. 'No footprints, no fingerprints, no weapon.'

'A knife, though, yes?'

'Bladed weapon, serrated edge. We might know more after the autopsy – it's due in the morning.'

They were silent for a moment. 'Has to be someone with a key,' Clarke commented.

'Bringing us back to the night shift,' Esson agreed. 'And here's another thing – a couple of staff cars have been torched in their parking bays over the past month and a half. It's not the only jail it's happened at and no one's been caught as yet.'

'The officer who didn't get along with the deceased ...?'

'His car was targeted.' Esson was nodding slowly.

'What was our victim inside for?'

'Entering lockfast premises. This wasn't his first time at the rodeo. Only had another month or so to serve. Governor reckoned he wouldn't be out for long before he reoffended.' Esson half turned her head towards Clarke. 'Fancy some crisps?'

'I'd prefer nuts.'

'They do salt-and-pepper ones. Back in a tick.' Having got to her feet, Esson paused. The first round had been bought by Clarke. 'I assume we might manage just one more?'

'Entirely at your discretion, Officer.'

While Esson waited to be served, Clarke felt herself relax. This was what she missed: the unwinding that came with each day's post-match discussion. Rebus had taught her the trick in the Oxford Bar's back room. They would talk tactics and angles, find things they'd potentially missed. It was as if everything got filed away in the right place, so that you were better organised for the next day. Esson returned to the table with two little plastic pots of peanuts, the lids already removed. She sat back down and waited for Clarke to say something, but Clarke had already seen the barman making his approach, carrying their fresh gins.

'Thanks, Gerry,' Esson said. She tipped the measure into her original glass, a second slice of lime joining the first. 'That's how you keep tabs on how many you've had,' she told Clarke.

'What about your car?'

'I'll leave it out front. Ten-minute walk and I'm home. Pick it up again in the morning before the wardens get busy. Cheers.'

Their glasses met again.

'So,' Clarke said eventually, 'you've started interviewing the inmates? Have you got as far as our friend yet?'

Esson smiled into her glass. 'I wondered when you'd get round to him. I saw him this morning, actually, though not to talk to. Couldn't quite believe he's in with the general population.'

'Darryl Christie vouched for him.'

'Really?' Esson puffed out her cheeks and blew.

'So what do you think's got Malcolm Fox so interested?' Clarke tried to make the question sound casual, but Esson was having none of it.

42

'Who mentioned Malcolm Fox?' She exhaled loudly. 'You've been talking to JR.' Her voice had risen slightly.

'Guilty as charged. He clocked Fox and it got him wondering. And now it's got me wondering too.'

'Welcome to the club. He breezed in without anyone clearing it with us.'

'So he's attached to the team?'

'Not as such – just wanted briefing, plus the promise of regular updates.' Esson broke off and leaned back as far as her seat would allow. 'That's what this is all about? Pumping me for gen on Fox that you can feed back to John Rebus? You can't ask him yourself because he's still angry at you for ducking out of the Complaints – you were his pick and you left him in the lurch.'

'It just wasn't for me, Christine.'

'I told you that before you went – didn't stop you, though.'

'Look on the bright side. Now you've got hunky Jason Mulgrew.'

'I never said he was hunky.'

'Is he, though?'

Esson considered the question. 'Maybe a bit,' she conceded. Then: 'Why *do* you think Fox is sniffing around?'

'He's got a bit of history with Darryl Christie,' Clarke speculated. 'This gives him a chance to see what Christie's up to on the inside.'

'Not exactly a reformed character, the way I hear it.'

'He runs more of the city than ever before.'

'That might be it then.' Esson scooped up a few more nuts. 'We do miss you, you know,' she said as she chewed.

'Thanks, Christine. I appreciate that.'

'How's John doing, anyway? I thought his lawyers would have had him out by now.'

'That's pretty much what they've been telling him since day one – but now they've gone quiet and it's driving him crazy. On the other hand, there are aspects of prison life I think he quite likes – suddenly there's a shape to his days.'

'A shape that doesn't include visits to the pub.' Esson moved her chair an inch closer to Clarke. 'He didn't drop any hints, did he?'

'Hints?'

'As to who did it and why?' Esson watched Clarke shake her head. 'Well, we'll be questioning him sooner or later. I'll ask him myself when I see him.' She pushed the last few nuts towards Clarke and drained her glass. 'You sticking around?'

'On my own? What do you take me for?'

'We both know,' Esson said with a wink. 'Plenty cabs go past if you want to pick one up. Or Gerry can call one for you. Busy day for some of us tomorrow.' She lifted her scarf and wrapped it around her neck, then leaned across to give Clarke a hug. 'Good to see you, Siobhan – even if you *did* need an ulterior motive.'

And with that she was gone, phone in hand, checking the screen for messages. Clarke picked up the empties and carried them to the bar. The background music wasn't bad. Burt Bacharach or similar. Gerry nodded his thanks as she placed the glasses in front of him.

'Apparently you can arrange a taxi,' Clarke said.

'I certainly can. And one for the road, too, if you like?'

'Go on then,' Clarke said, resting her elbows on the bar.

'Fresh tumbler?' her new best friend enquired.

Clarke studied the two slices of lime resting atop melting ice cubes in front of her. 'Fresh tumbler,' she confirmed.

Day Two

3

Esson and Mulgrew went to the prison straight after the autopsy. Both were sombre during the twenty-minute drive. It always took time to adjust, time for those sights, sounds and smells to dissipate. Esson was grateful that Mulgrew seemed to feel the same, steering his sleek silver Audi as though it were a hearse. He had switched on some music, which they listened to in silence for the first five or so minutes.

'So who is this?' Esson eventually enquired.

'Pentangle.'

'Is it recent?'

He took his eyes off the road briefly. 'Late sixties. Seriously, you've never heard of them?' She shook her head. 'How about the Fairports then – Sandy Denny and Richard Thompson?'

'Sorry.'

'Incredible String Band? They were from Edinburgh.'

'But then so were the Bay City Rollers.' She watched a sliver of a smile appear on Mulgrew's face. A handsome face – Siobhan Clarke had used the term 'hunky', and that wasn't far off the mark. He was fair-haired, broad-chested, with just a bit of excess weight around the middle. And he was single. 'You'd get on great guns with John Rebus,' she told him. 'He has a lot of stuff from back then.'

'I hope someone's looking after it for him while he's inside.'

'You can probably ask him.' Esson stared out of the passenger-side window. 'So what did you get up to last night? Anything exciting?'

'Not much. What about you?'

'Much the same.'

They had stopped at a red light and he was fussing with his phone. The music broke off, a new tune replacing it.

'This is Bert Jansch,' he said.

'Not easy to dance to,' she commented. Mulgrew started drumming his fingers against the steering wheel.

'We could do with finding the weapon,' he said after a couple of minutes, and suddenly they were back in the autopsy suite, being shown the ragged two-inch gash. Would the wound have gushed? It was the pathologist's opinion that it would. So blood on the attacker's clothing? Almost certainly, though the towel pressed into the victim's mouth had caught a lot of it. Staff lockers would be checked again – forensically this time. And every bin on the prison grounds, the prison whose main car park they were already approaching.

They parked next to the other visitors, the music ceasing.

'I liked it,' Esson offered.

'I can lend you some CDs.'

'And something to play them on?'

Mulgrew shook his head, almost pityingly, as he locked the car. The pair of them stood for a moment studying the prison's high walls. They shared a look and pulled back their shoulders. It was time.

Being part of a major incident team didn't make for short-cuts here, though they did have a special dispensation to hang on to their phones – everyone else's got locked in a box in the reception area. They signed in and took their temporary passes, then went through the airport-style screener. An of-ficer had been assigned to them. She wore more make-up than Esson and moved casually, sure of herself in these surround-ings. Door after door unlocked then locked again behind them, corridors and stairs, cameras watching from the ceilings. A couple of prisoners were running a cleaning machine over one of the floors. They greeted the officer by her first name.

'Bit casual,' Mulgrew commented.

'I get ma'am sometimes,' she replied. 'Beats being called slag or rug-muncher.'

'I suppose it does,' he agreed.

They were being led to the pastoral care office, which had been set aside for them for the duration. There were positivity posters on the walls and stacks of pamphlets and feel-good books with titles like *Living Your Best Life*. The desk drawers and filing cabinet were locked, but there was a tea and coffee station, supplemented by a variety box of biscuits with a note attached inviting them to 'Help yourselves!'

Instead of bringing in cumbersome recording equipment, they were relying on their phones for audio and video. Mulgrew had brought his charger and a small tripod. The tripod had been checked over by the officer manning the X-ray machine.

'I want to see it again when you come out,' he had warned, adding it to his list. His tone hadn't been friendly. Esson reckoned she knew why. They were here to ask questions of his colleagues – because those colleagues had become their chief suspects.

Pastoral Care was in a large modern extension to the original jail. The adjacent offices housed the further education unit, which, the signage made clear, was run by staff from Fife College. They'd passed the medical unit too, which was NHS. A large meeting room, meantime, was where charities could run workshops and open houses, dealing with topics such as drug addiction, alcoholism and self-harm.

A third chair had been added to the furnishings in Pastoral Care, which made for cramped conditions. Esson got busy brewing up while Mulgrew set up his phone. Hers would be used for audio backup. They'd had a meeting with the fiscal depute, who had advised on protocols. Normally witnesses would be interviewed in a room at St Leonard's. The fiscal

49

had warned them to keep things as similar to that format as possible. Nobody wanted to aid and abet a mistrial, or – worse – make a mistake that led to no trial at all.

'We're not bloody kids,' had been Mulgrew's remark afterwards. And yes, the talk had seemed at times more like a lecture given by a sceptical teacher. All the same, they were doing as they were told. By the time Chris Novak arrived, giving three solid raps on the door and waiting to be invited in, they were settled behind the desk, arms and thighs almost touching.

'Officer Novak,' Esson said, 'please take a seat.' She introduced herself and Mulgrew. The offer of a drink was turned down.

Novak had heavy-set features and cropped hair stiffened with product. Tattoos covered both arms, and he seemed almost ready to burst from his tight white shirt.

'No rest for the wicked,' Esson commented, studying a sheet of paper in front of her. 'You worked the night shift when the incident happened, and then the day shift straight after – and here you are on duty again.'

'I got plenty of kip last night.'

'Do you do a lot of double shifts?' Mulgrew asked, adjusting the tripod slightly.

'We're short of staff. Plus the extra cash is useful.'

'What do you spend your money on?'

Novak glared at Mulgrew. 'How is that any of your business?'

'Just making conversation. Maybe you like cars, or holidays, or nights out ...'

'You know about my car,' Novak stated. He sat with his legs apart, meaty hands clamped to his knees.

'Any idea why someone wanted to turn it into a bonfire?'

'Wasn't just me.'

'Yes, it's been happening at other jails. Targeted, do you think?'

'More likely random.'

'So no specific grudges against you in here?' Esson asked,

watching Novak give a slow shake of the head. 'Sure about that?'

'I know where this is going. Okay, some prisoners I get on with better than others. Every officer in here will tell you the same. Clashes of personality, bams who want to prove themselves, guys who should be in a psych ward rather than the nick.'

'Which was it with Jackie Simpson?'

'He kept trying to get my goat up. Said he knew where I lived, and he'd be paying a visit when he got out.'

'You've probably heard similar before?'

'Plenty of times.'

'And did Mr Simpson manage to get your goat up?'

Novak locked eyes with Esson. 'Not even close. There was plenty of verbal between us, but it never went further than that.' He leaned in towards the desk, chair creaking under the strain. 'I know how it must look from the outside, but no way any of the officers in here did what was done. Must've happened just before the cells were locked for the night. A quick in-and-out.'

'You lock up without checking?' Mulgrew asked. Novak turned his attention to him.

'Not usually, but sometimes maybe someone gets sloppy, or they're distracted by something.'

'Who locked Mr Simpson's cell.'

Novak shook his head. 'Can't remember.'

Esson checked her notes. 'Witnesses say it was an officer called Valerie Watts.'

Novak's eyes remained blank. 'If you say so.'

'It would be hard to miss a bloodied figure on the lower bunk.'

'Not if they were covered with a blanket or something.' Novak shifted slightly in his seat.

'Pity about that one wonky camera,' Mulgrew said.

'We reported it over a week ago.'

'Who would know it wasn't functioning?'

'Everyone.'

51

'Prisoners as well as staff?'

'They had a guy up a ladder trying to fix it. That sort of thing doesn't go unnoticed.'

'I suppose not.'

'Funny, though, isn't it,' Esson added, 'that a single row of cells was left without surveillance, and someone turns up dead in one of them?'

'Depends on your sense of humour.'

'But there was nothing else unusual about that night, no feeling that anything was about to happen?'

'Same old same old – after bang-up and lights-out, you do a bit of patrolling, and when you're not doing that, you tend to bounce between the control room and the break room.'

'We noticed checks on a few of the cells during the night.'

Novak nodded. 'Sometimes a prisoner can't sleep. They get restless and noisy, and out of boredom they might call for us.'

'Nothing like that from the deceased's cell, though?'

Novak shook his head, sat back and folded his arms, biceps bulging.

'Someone will talk,' Esson went on with calm certainty. 'Someone always does.'

Novak turned his attention to Mulgrew's phone, speaking directly towards it. 'This is a waste of time, and whenever you march one of us in here, you're leaving us short elsewhere. Anything kicks off, it's your fault.' He shifted his gaze to Mulgrew and Esson. 'We're done here, aye?' He pressed his hands against the chair arms, readying to rise.

Esson studied another sheet of paper. 'Is Valerie Watts on duty today, do you know?'

'Day off.'

'That's unusual.'

Halfway to his feet, Novak stopped.

'It's just,' Esson went on, 'the days she's on duty seem to match yours, even the same double shifts.'

'So what?'

She just shrugged, waiting for him to say something else. But

52

instead he straightened up and marched out, while Mulgrew ended the recording.

'Is Novak married?' he asked Esson.

'Two kids.'

'And Watts?'

'Not so much.'

There was a gentle knocking at the door. It opened far enough for Howard Tennent's head to appear around it.

'Everything all right?' he enquired.

'Fine, sir, thank you,' Mulgrew said.

'I just passed Chris Novak; he didn't look exactly full of the joys. A prison only works when the staff are engaged and focused. Otherwise you're inviting trouble.'

'Mr Novak told us much the same. But we still have a job to do.'

'Of course, of course.'

'And normally we'd be dragging your staff to our own station for interview ...'

The governor held up his hands. 'I appreciate you're trying to minimise the disruption, but everyone knows you're questioning my POs, and they're starting to put two and two together.'

'Sooner we find out what happened, sooner things will start to calm down.'

'Only if it turns out a fellow resident is to blame,' Tennent cautioned.

'I can see how you'd like that to be the case,' Esson said, 'despite the odds being against it.'

The governor's face fell a little further. He made a noise at the back of his throat and retreated into the hallway.

'Reckon we should be questioning him?' Mulgrew asked.

'He's going to take his officers' side, whatever happens.'

'So what now?'

'Biscuits,' Christine Esson replied.

*

53

Rebus was visiting the Wizard in his cell. Or rather, he was standing in the doorway while they talked. Proximity to the Wizard meant you took him back to your own cell with you. It wasn't body odour or decay, but every prisoner commented on it. A particular aroma that lingered. The Wizard liked to do puzzles – crosswords and Sudoku especially. There were books of them piled high on his desk, along with a pencil and eraser.

'You were in the police,' he was saying between coughing fits. 'You know nobody's going to be punished for what happened. People out there don't give a shit who topped him or why. He just stops being a drain on the public purse.' He looked up from his puzzle, meeting Rebus's eyes. 'When you were on the outside, you always saw it as Us and Them – you being the good guys and us the bad. But you've been here a while now, John, so tell me – wouldn't you say we're all pretty much the same at the end of the day?'

'You mean apart from the small fact that I didn't ram a screwdriver into a pal's eye socket?'

The Wizard's face darkened a little. 'He was asking for it, John. And when the red mist descends, all bets are off. Don't tell me it was any different with you and Cafferty.'

Rebus thought for a moment. 'I didn't kill him, though,' he said.

'Ah, pure as the driven – plenty more like you in here.' The Wizard gave a chuckle, breaking off to listen as someone in the hall shouted something about a cover-up.

'Despite what you say,' Rebus began, 'the guys in here seem to give a shit who killed Jackie. Any ideas of your own, Wizard?'

'Who put you in charge of the case?'

'I'm just naturally nosy.'

'Not always a good thing in a place like this.'

Rebus glanced in both directions along the hall. He'd been keeping an eye open for Christine Esson or Malcolm Fox but so far had caught sight of neither. He knew an incident room had been set up elsewhere. The scene-of-crime team had done all they could. The tape was still stretched across the door of the locked cell. At one end of the hall, Darryl Christie was seated at one of the round tables, the calm centre of a swirl of activity, prisoners circling him, their complaints rising and falling and rising again. There were two officers keeping watch, neither of them too far from a panic button. Their jaws were tense, arms folded, all too aware of the waves of enmity directed at them. Loud music was coming from one of the cells, a soundtrack ranging from The Killers to 'Killer Queen' via NWA. Rebus felt sure the officers would glean the theme behind the selections.

When the governor appeared, flanked by two more POs, things calmed slightly, though the music remained loud. He made straight for the Wizard's cell, nodding a greeting in Rebus's direction before starting to speak. Rebus noted that he too stayed just the right side of the threshold.

'Sorry about this, Gareth,' he told the Wizard, 'but we need to switch your single bed for a bunk. Probably only for a week or so.'

'I'm getting the kid?' the Wizard guessed.

'He has to go somewhere.'

'How is he doing?' Rebus asked.

'Doctors are finished with him. He'll be back here later today.'

'Nobody else can take him?' the Wizard was asking.

'Thing is, you'll look after him, Gareth. And if he wants peace and quiet, you won't keep jabbing away at him.' The Wizard nodded his understanding. 'The officers here will help you shift your bedding and stuff. Someone'll be along shortly to unbolt the bed and move it out.' Rebus noticed that the governor was looking not at the Wizard but at him. 'A quiet word, John?' Then he was walking in the direction of Rebus's cell.

Rebus knew everyone was watching, especially Darryl Christie. As he followed Howard Tennent into his cell, the governor told him to pull the door to. Once inside, some of the man's public show of bravado fell away, his cheeks sagging.

'Can't have this place erupting, John. Can't have it.'

'Absolutely,' Rebus agreed, fairly sure he knew what was coming.

'Police are only doing their job, of course, and that's fine as far as it goes. But they're not in *here*.' He jabbed at the air with a finger. 'They can't see or hear the things you do.'

'There's plenty I don't get to know about.'

'You had a name in your day, though. You got things done.'

'If I start acting like a detective, the whole hall will know, and pretty soon after that I'd be as useful in solitary.'

'I'm not asking for much, John. But anything you hear, any inkling ...'

'I bring it to you? And if the only inklings I get are that a PO did it?'

The governor looked more doleful still. 'Will you do it, though? As a favour to me?'

'I suppose it might help pass the time.'

Tennent held out his hand for Rebus to shake. 'One other thing. You and Bobby Briggs?'

'Best kept separated by a locked gate or six.'

'Understood.'

When the two men emerged from the cell, Darryl Christie was standing directly opposite, back to the wall, hands in pockets. His eyes said he knew exactly what had just finished being discussed. When the governor moved off, he took a couple of steps in Rebus's direction until his attention was diverted by cheers and clapping. Mark Jamieson, stapled forehead swathed in a bandage, had returned to Trinity. He was immediately mobbed, hand after hand patting him on the back. His injuries were examined and someone offered to make him a hot drink.

'And if you've any medication surplus to requirements ...'

Jamieson laughed along with them, right up until the moment he saw the cell door and the crime-scene tape. Then he dry-gulped, his Adam's apple bobbing, and had to be helped to a seat.

'Just tell us it was Novak,' someone demanded. 'That's all we need to hear.'

But Jamieson started to shake his head. 'I don't know,' he said in a voice not much above a whisper. 'I was out for the count.'

'Bastards, the lot of them,' someone spat. Stares were once more directed towards the white-shirted officers, one of whom whispered something in Howard Tennent's ear, receiving a nodded reply. The governor was then ushered briskly towards the nearest exit.

'Run all you like!' a prisoner yelled after him. 'The truth's coming for you!'

There were roars of agreement. Darryl Christie, having decided that Rebus could wait, approached the gathering around Mark Jamieson. He stretched his arms out in front of him, palms down, gesturing for calm. More officers were arriving. Eddie Graves paused alongside Rebus.

'Be just my luck to end up taken hostage,' he muttered before moving away.

Billy Groam was standing in the doorway of the neighbouring cell. 'No way that guy's becoming a hostage,' he commented for Rebus's benefit. 'Way he moans, we'd end the siege in ten minutes tops.'

'How close are things to kicking off, Billy?' Rebus enquired.

'That depends on Darryl,' Groam answered with a shrug. 'What Darryl wants, Darryl usually gets ...'

The men around Jamieson had formed a huddle, shoulder to shoulder, Christie leaning in to talk tactics like a football coach. Rebus took a couple of steps forward.

'I wouldn't,' Groam warned him. And it was true that a couple of the prisoners were giving Rebus a good hard look. 'Cell might be the best place for you right now, John.'

'I'm not so sure about that, Billy,' Rebus said quietly, his eyes on the crime-scene tape opposite ...

4

Clarke and Colson sat in the car outside the Andrews house. DCI Carmichael had gathered the team together first thing. Time had passed and Jasmine still hadn't shown herself. The case was therefore being upgraded. A media briefing had taken place and enough uniforms had been mobilised to enable a sweep of the local area. Jasmine's phone provider and bank were being pressured to hurry up with details of recent usage. A press photographer had stopped his car just long enough to take a few shots of the family home from the pavement. Spotting the two detectives, he'd had the good grace to look slightly sheepish as he dived back into his car and drove off.

Clarke and Colson were sitting there digesting what they'd just been told during a phone call from family liaison.

'I sensed a bit of friction,' the liaison officer had said. 'Not the most obviously loving and close of couples. She sat on a chair, him the other side of the room on the arm of the sofa, as if there was somewhere else he needed to be. Bit of sniping and snark back and forth. I'd say he blames her for whatever Jasmine's done. She had a go at him for the amount of time he spends away ...'

Colson shifted in the passenger seat. 'So we don't put them in front of any journalists just yet,' he suggested.

Clarke was still staring at her blank phone screen when she heard the sound of raised voices coming from the direction of the house. No one was visible behind the living-room window, but Colson had already made his decision and was out of the car. It was the fastest she had ever seen him move. Helena Andrews' Nissan Leaf was plugged into a charger on the driveway. Behind it was her husband's Mercedes, its interior a riot of sandwich wrappers, paperwork and crushed coffee cups. Clarke passed both vehicles and caught up with Colson as he was trying the front door, which rattled but stayed locked. He was raising his fist to give it a thump when the door flew open.

James Andrews was tall and looked in decent shape for his age, despite the exhausted eyes and stubble. His shirt was untucked, and he wore socks but no shoes.

'What?' he growled.

In answer, Colson held up his ID. The air went out of Andrews, and he scraped a hand through unruly salt-and-pepper hair.

'It's the police,' he called over his shoulder to his wife.

'Everything all right here, sir?' Colson enquired.

'Apart from our missing daughter, you mean?'

'We thought we heard voices.'

Helena Andrews had appeared by her husband's side, curling a hand around his arm in a show of apparent solidarity.

'We were in different rooms,' she tried by way of explanation. 'I think maybe the pair of us should get our hearing checked – we're always needing to shout.' Her smile would have convinced some, though her heart didn't really seem to be in the deception.

'Mind if we come in?' Clarke asked.

'I forget your names,' Helena said, cocking her head.

'DI Clarke and DS Colson,' Clarke reminded her.

'Is there any news?'

'We'd like to take another look at Jasmine's bedroom, if that's all right.'

'Don't you need a search warrant or something?' James Andrews asked.

'Would you like us to fetch one? It'll take time, and in cases like this, time is the one thing that's often against us.'

'What does that mean?'

'Just that if she wants to disappear, the longer she's given for that to happen, the less chance we have of finding her.' Clarke paused. They still weren't inside the house and she directed her gaze to the doorstep, hoping they'd take the hint. Helena tugged on her husband's arm.

'Whatever we can do to help,' she said.

'That all right with you, Mr Andrews?' Colson demanded.

'Of course,' Andrews mumbled, taking a step back.

Clarke and Colson brushed past him and entered the living room. An open bottle of wine, mostly gone, sat on the coffee table.

'Last night,' Helena Andrews explained. 'Shouldn't have, but, well, you know ...'

'You think there might be some clue in her bedroom?' her husband interrupted. 'You've already got her computer and iPad.'

'But no passwords as yet. I don't suppose you can help with that, Mr Andrews?'

Andrews shrugged and shook his head, then began to tuck his shirt in.

'Maybe we could just sit down for a minute,' Clarke added. She watched as Helena settled into her regular chair and James perched on the edge of the sofa across the room, maximum distance attained.

'How often do you talk to Jasmine when you're away from home, Mr Andrews?' Colson asked.

'Call me James, please. We FaceTime once a week.'

'*Most* weeks,' his wife corrected him. 'Sometimes you're too busy.'

'I work long days,' James explained to the two detectives. 'Whatever it takes to put food on the table and clothes on my family's backs.'

'You're a business developer?'

'That's right.'

'Meaning?'

'Meaning I help companies grow, develop, modernise.'

'And how long do these trips last?' Clarke asked.

'Four to six weeks, sometimes longer. I get weekends off, mostly, but the thought of the drive north ...'

'You poor thing.' Helena had folded her arms and crossed her legs, one foot wagging furiously.

'I've learned my lesson, though.' Her husband's voice had hardened. 'Seems I can't depend on things not to fall apart here when I'm elsewhere.'

Clarke watched as husband and wife continued to refuse to make eye contact with one another. 'You told us your sister was coming to stay?' she said to Helena.

'Yes, well ... once James came back ...' Helena glanced in his direction. Clarke got the feeling husband and sister-in-law did not get on.

'Why do you think Jasmine might have wanted to go off somewhere?' Clarke asked him.

'Her mum would know better than me.'

'Because you don't know much of anything at all, do you?' Helena shot back.

'None of this is really helping,' Clarke stated quietly but firmly, causing the pair to try for a look of contrition.

'Jas has become a bit of a closed book to me,' James eventually admitted with a sigh. 'Maybe all girls are like that in their teens. I'll ask what she's up to and she won't have an answer. What she does with her friends, how work's going at school – replies of one syllable and the feeling she'd rather be left alone. I thought she'd open up to her mum, maybe, female solidarity and all that ...'

'She knows I'm there if she needs me,' Helena said quietly. Whatever rage had existed in the room had been earthed, at least temporarily.

'I've always been told that parenting is teamwork,' Clarke

said into the silence. 'Sometimes one takes the strain, sometimes the other. There's got to be give and take.'

Helena expelled air. Her eyes were on the wine bottle, hopeful of a glass in her near future. 'Tea!' she said suddenly. 'I should have made you some.' She started to get up, but Clarke waved away the offer.

'Maybe if we could just go look at Jasmine's room again?'

'Of course.' She ran a hand across her forehead, trying to wipe away the fatigue.

'We know the way,' Siobhan Clarke said.

There were three bedrooms upstairs, one turned into an office with a sofa that looked as if it would unfold into a bed. Jasmine's room was tidy, with pictures on its walls of K-pop groups and anime characters. The only books looked like school texts, and a Bluetooth speaker meant there was no need for a music collection. There was a gap on the desk where her computer had sat until bagged and removed by CID. The view from the window was of a biggish back garden, wooden fencing separating it from near-identical neighbours. The barbecue looked to be gathering rust, as did a Swingball set-up that stood in the middle of what lawn there was, most of it having been sacrificed for a patio. Jasmine's bed was a double, its base including drawers, which Colson pulled open. There was nothing inside other than a spare duvet and pillow plus a rolled-up yoga mat.

'For sleepovers?' he suggested.

Clarke couldn't disagree. Wardrobe and chest of drawers contained nothing out of the ordinary, and certainly nothing hinting at any interesting or quirky facet of Jasmine's personality. An ordinary girl growing up in an ordinary street among ordinary friends but with two warring parents she needed to sidestep as much as possible.

After a few more minutes, Colson shook his head. Clarke was staring at the pop-star posters. The performers were young, the girls dressed in short skirts, the boys immaculately coiffured. She had read stories in the press about the stresses imposed by the lifestyle – crack-ups and suicides. The glamour was only ever two-dimensional, but it served its purpose, decorating the dreams of teenagers like Jasmine Andrews.

Downstairs, thoughts of wine had been replaced by the brewing of coffee. The aroma filled the hallway.

'Can't tempt you?' James Andrews said, hoisting an over-sized mug. It had writing on it – *World's Best Dad* – and was showing its age. Clarke wondered if he'd chosen it in the hope of making some kind of statement.

'We'd best be off,' she told him.

'You'll let us know when there's news?' He tried not to let the desperation in his voice show too much. Helena stood in the doorway between kitchen and living area. No mug for her but a china cup and saucer, decorated with roses. Another statement of sorts?

'Promise,' Siobhan Clarke said, while Colson opened the door behind her.

But instead of heading directly to the car, she took the path around the side of the house to the back garden. Three bins sat in a line just around the corner. She raised the lid of the recycling bin and looked in. Half a dozen wine bottles, some of them green glass and some clear.

'You were expecting to find it filled to the brim?' Colson guessed.

As she turned towards him, she caught a glimpse of some-thing – a figure darting away from an upstairs window in the house the other side of the fence. Young and male, she thought. She stood her ground until Colson looked quizzical. He followed her back to the car. Rather than start the engine, however, she sat with her hands on the steering wheel, peering into space.

'Do me a favour, Cammy,' she eventually said. 'Find me the address we were given for Craig Fielding.'

Having switched on the power in the car, Clarke waited for Colson to recite the address from his phone, tapping it into her satnav. They then both watched as the map appeared, Clarke magnifying it until there could be no doubt.

'One street over,' Colson remarked.

'With a view right into her bedroom,' Clarke added, starting the engine.

They turned left and left again, into Craig Fielding's street. A figure was walking along the pavement towards them, hood up, hands tucked into the front of his jacket.

'What do you reckon?' Colson said, sliding down his window.

They had their answer when the figure dashed in front of the car and then ran.

'You've got to be kidding,' Colson said.

'Not so stupid,' Clarke retorted. 'Plenty of footpaths we can't take the car down.'

'Then we just come back to the house later. What's he going to do – hide in the woods?'

Clarke was studying the satnav as she drove. They caught sight of him a couple of minutes later. He disappeared down the side of a house, but then came back.

'Fence must've been too high,' Colson commented. 'He doesn't run like an athlete.'

'Fancy our chances against him on foot, do you?'

'I'd rather not have to try.'

They were drawing alongside him when he darted left across a patch of grass and flower beds, almost tripping. He was limping as he rejoined the pavement, and after another thirty seconds he gave up altogether, stopping with his hands on his thighs, head lowered, breathing hard. Colson rested his forearm against the sill of the passenger window as Clarke pulled to a stop.

'Get in the back, Craig,' he ordered.

'That's not my name. You've got the wrong person.'

'Show us some ID then and we'll be on our merry way.' Colson's hand stretched out towards the boy, who looked at it, sweat trickling down either temple. Then he took a couple of steps towards the car and got in.

'Not too bad for someone who's off sick from school,' Clarke commented, twisting in her seat to face him, while Colson adjusted the rear-view mirror, content to make eye contact that way.

'That was yesterday. A bit better today.'

'Odd coincidence, though, eh?' Colson added. 'Your old girl-friend goes missing and suddenly you need to stay in the house?'

'Maybe you've seen her,' Clarke chimed in, 'or you know what she's up to?'

'I'm in the dark, same as everybody else,' he said, still trying to get his breathing under control. Clarke studied him. A boyish face, ready to grow handsome, was hidden beneath the acne. He looked gawky enough, but there was intelligence there too. He might have just stepped out of *Gregory's Girl* and be about to lecture her on Caracas or choux pastry.

'How long since the two of you split up?'

'Couple of months.'

'Who dumped who?'

'She dumped me, I suppose.' He was looking at the floor as he spoke. 'Not for anybody else, she said. She just ...' His voice trailed off.

'You're the year above her, aye?' Colson checked. 'So you're fifteen? Leaving school next year or sticking around for uni?'

'Uni if I get the grades.'

'What plans did Jasmine have?' Clarke asked.

'She never really said.'

'Any idea what's happened to her, Craig?'

A vigorous head-shake.

'And you've definitely not heard from her?'

'I've tried phoning and texting. We've all been trying.'

'And this came out of the blue? She'd not seemed different recently?'

The boy thought for a moment. 'She'd sort of stopped hanging around with any of us. Soon as school was done for the day, she was off.'

'Off home, you mean?'

'Not necessarily. She'd take the bus into town or head off in the opposite direction from her house.'

65

'Going where?'

'She never said. I wondered if she did have somebody else.'

'From a different school, you mean?'

'Maybe.' He shifted in his seat.

'Would that have made you jealous?' Colson asked.

'No.'

'You sure about that?'

'You can see into her bedroom from yours,' Clarke added. 'Ever see anyone in there with her?'

'Just her mum sometimes.' He met Clarke's eyes. 'How's Helena doing? She must be worried sick.'

'She wants Jasmine home, same as the rest of us.'

'I saw her dad's car. He won't stick around.'

'Why would you say that?'

'Because he never does.'

'And Jasmine didn't like that?'

Craig shrugged.

'You're not hiding her in your bedroom, are you, Craig?' Colson asked.

Another shake of the head.

'So you wouldn't mind if we took a peek?'

'You won't find her – I don't know where she is!'

Colson and Clarke shared a look.

'Off you go then,' Clarke told the boy. 'Unless you want us to give you a lift?'

But Craig Fielding was already out of the car. He'd taken a couple of steps when he paused, returning to the open window.

'She had money,' he said. 'Notes, I mean. Suddenly everything was cash. And she wanted us to notice, wanted us asking about it.'

'I'm assuming you did just that?' Colson enquired.

'But then all she did was ...' Craig made show of zipping his lips shut. 'She seemed to get a kick out of that.'

'Bank of Mum and Dad, maybe?'

'Maybe,' he said, but he didn't sound convinced.

5

Rebus tried to make his next visit to the Wizard's cell seem casual, though he doubted anyone paying attention would be fooled, not least when he sauntered in rather than stopping on the threshold. The bunk had been installed and Mark Jamieson was lying on the top one while the Wizard sat at his desk with a Sudoku, trying to look like he was fine with this new arrangement. Jamieson had one arm flung across his eyes, but he was awake.

'You okay, son?' Rebus asked.

'Everyone keeps asking him that,' the Wizard answered. 'Answer's always the same – he's fine, so far as it goes.'

Rebus took a couple more steps towards the bunk. 'I knew him on the outside, you know,' he said, making show of addressing the Wizard. 'This was years back, mind, when he was a teenage tearaway. Running with the wrong crowd and doing too much blaw. I tried to warn him ... even thought some of it might have seeped in.'

Jamieson had removed his arm, turning his head and levering himself upright, his face only inches from Rebus's.

'I often wonder what happened,' Rebus finished, voice dropping a fraction.

'I never moved on from that wrong crowd,' the young man

said by way of explanation. 'I know your face now. Never knew your name back then.'

'You had a lot going on. My name probably didn't seem important.'

'Money was what I was interested in.'

'Money and drugs,' Rebus corrected him. He studied Jamieson's pupils. 'And at least one of those is still the case.'

'They gave me painkillers at the hospital.'

'But who was it dosed you the night your cellmate died? Do I have to guess?'

'It's hard to sleep without a bit of something.'

'You were comatose, Mark. You either did that to yourself or someone did it to you.'

'Tea tasted funny.'

'Tea?'

'That night. When we were eating. Actually, maybe the food, too ...'

'Who was it served you?'

'Christ knows.'

'Maybe so, but he's a hard guy to reach.'

'Usual evening crew,' the Wizard stated. 'Ratty, Devo and Malachi.'

'Which one, though?' Rebus persisted.

'What's it to do with you?' Jamieson demanded, eyes suddenly lucid, voice sharp-edged.

'Officers are always there too, mind,' the Wizard mused, stroking his beard. 'Valerie Watts and Blair Samms.' He nodded slowly to himself.

'You were asleep when you got hit,' Rebus continued, eyes on Jamieson. 'So you were in bed when the cell was unlocked. And you didn't hear it happening?'

The arm had gone back over the eyes. 'Can you just leave me the fuck alone? Can every fucking one of you just give me peace?'

'Everything all right here?'

Rebus turned towards the voice, expecting to see an officer.

Instead, he found himself face to face with Darryl Christie.

'Just passing the time,' he told him.

'Plenty of it to go around,' Christie countered. 'Maybe you'd like to pass some with me instead?'

'And maybe not.'

'But you've got something for me, John. Something you borrowed and forgot to give back.'

'Aye, right enough. It's in my cell – go help yourself.'

'Where in your cell, though?'

'Lying on the bed.'

Christie's eyes smouldered. 'On the bed?' he echoed. Then he spun around and was gone.

The Wizard had risen from his chair and was patting Jamieson's shoulder. 'The lad's been through a lot, John. Bit of rest would do him no harm.'

'Neither would speaking to me.'

Voices were rising again in the hall. 'Slain in your bed and nobody to blame!' someone cried out. 'Which one of us is next?'

There were roars of agreement. The Wizard held up a finger.

'Hear that?'

'I hear them all right.'

But the Wizard was shaking his head, eyes turned upwards towards the cell's small window. 'I mean the church bells. You can't always make them out for all the noise in here. It drowns them. Eight hundred angry men will do that. But they're there.' He broke off and began one of his hacking coughs.

Jamieson looked towards Rebus from beneath his arm. Rebus gave a slight shake of the head, indicating that the Wizard was harmless. He turned towards the sudden movement in the doorway. Christie was back, glaring at him.

'Under your pillow, like that isn't the first place they'd look!' he seethed, the shape of the phone obvious in his tracksuit pocket. Then he was gone again.

'You might just have lost a fan,' the Wizard informed Rebus, catching a breath between coughs.

'I reckon I can live with that.'

'The decision might be out of your hands, though.'

Rebus pressed a finger to Mark Jamieson's chest. 'I'm just along the hall. And I'm a good listener.'

'A listener who can't even hear the church bells,' the Wizard countered.

'Maybe I'll only hear them when they want me to,' Rebus said, making his exit.

Out in the hall, he realised why the complaints had grown vociferous. The door to the murder cell stood open. There were a couple of figures inside, and plenty of POs making sure no prisoners got in the way. The cell had been stripped of its movable contents. Rebus realised that there was nothing belonging to Mark Jamieson in the cell he now shared with the Wizard. Probably bagged as potential evidence. The two suited men in the cell turned to look at him. The governor and Malcolm Fox. Fox then turned back to the governor and said something, receiving a nodded reply.

Rebus returned to his cell and lay on the bed. His feeling was, Fox would want to come and gloat. Years back he'd tried hard to put Rebus inside, regarding him as a cop too bent ever to be straightened. An uneasy truce had eventually come to pass, yet here Rebus was. As he lay staring at the ceiling, the walls seemed to close in. It happened a few times a week, the realisation that he was stuck here. Some nights he'd open his eyes in the darkness, heart pounding, wondering if he might be about to breathe his last. No final words, no bedside gathering. He turned his head now to look towards the doorway, but it was Kyle 'Kylie' Jacobs who stood there.

'Governor's office,' he said. Rebus heaved himself off the thin mattress, pulled a green sweatshirt over his tee and followed.

Fox was seated at the table with the plate of shortbread biscuits, the governor handing him a mug of tea as Rebus arrived. Fox was chewing while sucking crumbs of sugar from his fingers. He then pulled out a crisp white handkerchief and proceeded to wipe them clean. A nod told the governor that he could make himself scarce.

'I'm fine, honestly,' Rebus said, unnecessarily – there was to be no offer of a drink. No biscuits either, as Fox lifted the depleted plate and shifted it to a shelf behind him. Having seated himself, Rebus waited for the door to close. Fox stared at it, as if trying to ascertain whether the governor might be listening from the other side.

'Hello, John,' he eventually said, cupping his hands around the mug.

'Long way from your desk, Malcolm. How are things at Gartcosh?'

Fox blew across the surface of the mug. 'Settling in all right?'

'It's not like I'm at a new job.'

'I was surprised to see you, you know. Didn't think they'd let an ex-cop out among the general scumbag population.'

'Those are my friends you're talking about.'

'Friends like Darryl Christie?' Fox gave a thin smile. Always big, he seemed to have put on more weight of late, as if physical heft could make up for other shortcomings. Rebus, who had lost almost a stone inside, sat up a little straighter in his chair. 'Anything you want to tell me?' Fox asked.

Rebus made show of considering the question. 'I could tell you the system's broken, that there are men in here who should be elsewhere – but I doubt any of that would register with your tiny brain, so why bother?'

Fox's face hadn't changed; he hadn't really been listening. 'Mr Tennent told me you're under Christie's protection. That's interesting.'

'Is it?'

'You see much of him?'

'We're in the same hall – what do you think?'

'Plenty to talk about, I suppose.'

'You were always shit at doing interviews, Malcolm. Why don't you just tell me why the Specialist Crime Division is interested in the death of a small-time criminal?'

'It's called OCCTU these days – Organised Crime and Counter-Terrorism.'

'I'm guessing some graduate gets paid a decent wedge for coming up with all these names. Still doesn't explain your interest.'

'Murder is always interesting, John, and especially when it takes place in the vicinity of someone like Darryl Christie. I can't imagine much happens here without a nod from your new best buddy. You'll be shocked to learn that he continues to ply his trade even from inside these four walls, so of course I'm interested.'

'Nobody in here thinks Darryl Christie sanctioned what happened.'

'Of course not – they reckon it was one of the staff. Seems obvious, doesn't it? Those same staff who've been receiving anonymous threats and had their cars attacked with petrol bombs and acid.' Fox rested his elbows against the table. 'Why do you reckon that's been happening, John?'

'Not doing what's been asked of them,' Rebus surmised.

'And who do you think might have been doing that asking?'

'Darryl Christie.'

'Noticed a drop in the amount of drugs getting in here? The phones and other illicit goods?'

'I know it's hard to find a decent malt.' The two men stared at one another. 'I've not heard about these threats, though.'

'Not the sort of thing you want to publicise – makes inmates think their guards might be fallible.'

'Just here, or other jails too?'

'Not just here.'

'Any names?'

'That's not something I can divulge.'

'Chris Novak?'

'Not something I can divulge,' Fox echoed, his body language betraying him. 'But here's one name I *can* give you – Shay Hanlon.'

'Liverpool gangster.'

'You've got one of his team in a neighbouring cell. Does he ever talk about his boss?'

'No, but Harrison's chummy with a Neanderthal on another wing, name of Bobby Briggs.'

'I don't know him.'

'He's Glasgow.'

'Connected to anyone?'

Rebus offered a shrug. 'You're the detective here, Malcolm. I'm just a con. But even I can see that nothing you've said explains why Christie or anyone else would want Jackie Simpson dead.'

Fox grew a little less animated. 'True enough,' he admitted. 'But then we've barely started digging.'

'We? You're not asking me to ...?'

'Christ, no. I meant the MIT. With additional assistance from OCCTU as required.'

Which told Rebus that Howard Tennent hadn't revealed anything to Fox about the mission he'd handed him.

'Your days in the sun are long gone, John,' Fox went on, relishing the sound of the words.

Rebus turned his head momentarily towards the window and the overcast sky beyond. 'So dragging me in here was just by way of rubbing it in?'

'I felt a bit bad that I've never had the chance to visit. I know Siobhan sees you regularly ...'

'How did that go down at Gartcosh, by the way?' Rebus asked casually.

'What?'

'You'd groomed her for Professional Standards ... vouched for her. And after a few weeks she tells you to stuff it. Bet your bosses were thrilled.'

'Siobhan's loss, not ours.' Fox's cheek muscles were moving, and Rebus knew he'd got to him.

'Tell you what,' Rebus added. 'Give me a number I can reach you on. If I do hear or see anything, I'll give you a bell.'

'Really?'

He nodded slowly, watching Fox start to dig into his inside

73

pocket for a card. 'I'll do it on one of Darryl's burners if you like.'

Fox froze, realising he'd been had. Rebus got to his feet, reached past Fox to grab a biscuit from the plate and left the room, almost bumping into the governor, who was loitering in the outer office. With a wink and a smile, Rebus was gone.

Kyle Jacobs was waiting for him in the outer hall. 'What was that all about?' he asked.

'Nothing much.'

'It wasn't one of us, you know.' Jacobs was speaking out of the side of his mouth as they walked. He clammed up as they passed a couple of prisoners who were cleaning the floor. Then, once he and Rebus were through yet another of the locked doors: 'Morale's bad enough. Staff calling in sick, new recruits thin on the ground, you lot ready to kick off ... And now Gartcosh arrive and start sniffing around. I'm not saying we're all angels, but the bad ones don't last long. And I know for a fact none of us did for Jackie Simpson.' As he unlocked the barred gate leading to Rebus's hall, he made eye contact for the first time, looking suddenly all too human. 'We're sick and tired, John, and that's not a good state of mind for a job like this.'

'It's not just the residents who might kick off, is that what you're saying?'

'I'm saying we need calm heads and I'm seeing precious few. Maybe a quiet word with Darryl Christie would—'

'Everybody seems to think we're bosom buddies,' Rebus interrupted. 'We definitely aren't.'

'He listens to you, though. Just have a word, that's all I'm saying.'

'Can I ask you something in return?'

'What?'

'The night of the murder, Mark Jamieson reckons his dinner tasted funny. Your colleagues Watts and Samms were on duty while it was served up. How easy would it have been to slip him something?'

Jacobs gave Rebus a hard stare.

'I'm not saying one of them did it necessarily, but could—'

'Get through that gate!' Jacobs snarled.

Rebus did as he was told, Jacobs staying the other side, locking it again. Rebus tried meeting his eye, but Jacobs had already turned away.

He hadn't been in his cell more than two minutes when he sensed Darryl Christie in the doorway, waiting to be told. Rebus gave a heavy sigh. 'Malcolm Fox wants your head delivered to him,' he confessed.

'And he thinks you're the man for the job?'

'He knows better than that. But it's why he's scratching around. Meantime, the staff reckon we're on the verge of anarchy and only you can calm things down.'

'Hard to do when I've had my head cut off. Looks like you're stuck in the middle, eh, John? Good luck in no man's land. You won't know a thing until you step on a mine.'

Christie turned and left Rebus to his thoughts. Something Jacobs had said stayed with him. *I'm not saying we're all angels* ... Maybe Jacobs thought that was what had brought Fox to the prison – not gangsters, but bent prison officers. Bent POs, however, only came into Fox's orbit if they connected to organised crime. Fox had mentioned threats and attacks. Chris Novak's car had been targeted – Rebus wondered if Jacobs had been on the receiving end, too. And what did it mean if he had? Yes, such an attack could imply that the victim was refusing to go along with whatever was being asked of them. But it could just as easily be an attempt to make someone look like a victim if they were in danger of being investigated.

Rebus closed his eyes and played the conversation through again. But it was Malcolm Fox he kept seeing.

Your days in the sun are long gone, John ...

Well, they'd have to see about that.

*

75

Clarke and Colson sat side by side at Clarke's desk. They were calling it a 'brainstorming session', but progress had so far been limited, which hadn't stopped them eating half a multi-pack of KitKats washed down with several double-strength coffees from a local café.

Clarke had typed up a list on her screen, which they'd been staring at for several minutes without any bright ideas emerging from the exercise.

'Okay,' Colson said, 'so her bank tells us Jasmine hasn't withdrawn any cash or used her debit card since her disappearance. On the other hand, she might not need to if her ex is to be believed about the cash she was suddenly parading.'

'And her parents say they'd not been dishing out any more than usual.'

'Nicking it from her mum's purse?'

Clarke offered a shrug.

'Dad handing it over because he feels guilty at not being around?'

She tapped the screen with her ballpoint pen, next to the name James Andrews. A background check had revealed that Jasmine's father had been in a bit of trouble back in his twenties – drunken brawls, fights with nightclub security. Seventeen years ago now, but even so ...

'A good woman can soothe the savage beast,' had been Colson's response. Clarke hadn't bothered to correct him. She had tried playing out the scenario – father grabs daughter from wife he sees as unfit – but dismissed it. Nothing on the screen added very much to the sum of their current knowledge. But then, just as she was about to give in to the lure of yet another KitKat, her phone vibrated against the desk.

She picked it up and answered. She listened for a moment, a crease forming above her nose as she concentrated.

'Hang on,' she eventually said to the handset, 'I'm putting you on speakerphone.' She did so, laying the device flat on the desk halfway between her and Colson.

'Okay, PC Galvin,' she said, raising her voice slightly to compensate. 'Repeat what you just told me.'

'We're outside the home of Kevin and Martha Fielding. They're the parents of Craig Fielding. They've made a complaint about a neighbour called James Andrews. Apparently he attacked their son.' The constable paused. 'Well, between the address and the name Andrews, I realised the connection and thought I better call it in.'

'You did the right thing,' Clarke told him. 'Is Craig injured?'

'Mr Andrews shook him about a bit and gave him a slap, but nothing that needs medical attention.'

Clarke saw that Colson was already starting the process of putting his arms into the sleeves of his jacket. She'd been about to tell the constable that they'd be there in fifteen minutes.

'Stay there,' she said instead. 'We'll be with you in the next half hour.'

Colson had grabbed another biscuit, which he gnawed at while Clarke drove.

'What do you reckon?' he asked between bites.

'I reckon you better not get chocolate on my seats.'

The traffic was in a good mood and they made it to the Fielding house quicker than expected. The patrol car was parked kerbside, and Clarke pulled to a stop next to it. A dog-walker had paused across the street, keen for some drama and ignorant of the fact that his dog had done its business on the pavement behind him. Colson pointed a warning finger and advised him to clean it up.

The door to the house was being opened by PC Galvin, who didn't yet look out of his teens. His partner was the same age and only half an inch taller. They told their story a final time in the hallway, the door to the living room closed, keeping their voices low. Then Clarke dismissed both officers while adding her thanks. They replaced their caps on their heads as they

77

walked down the path. Colson closed the front door behind them. Clarke was already in the living room.

Craig Fielding sat on the sofa, hands squeezed between his knees, while his agitated parents stayed on their feet. Clarke started introducing herself and Colson, but Kevin Fielding interrupted.

'We want him charged,' he said, voice quavering. His hair was thinning and he wore round, thick-framed glasses, his movements reminding Clarke of nothing so much as a marionette.

She crouched in front of Craig, seeking eye contact. 'You okay?' she asked.

'Of course he's not okay, he's been attacked!'

'This isn't doing any good, Kevin,' Martha Fielding said, her voice strained. Clarke had the feeling she was one of those people who would always try to do the right thing and see the best in people. The room was cluttered with little glass ornaments. A pipe lay forgotten in a large ashtray by the fireplace, a pouch of tobacco alongside.

Clarke got back to her feet. 'Maybe if you just tell me what happened.'

'Jasmine's father beat up my son, that's what happened!'

'Would you like to sit down, Mr Fielding?' She looked from husband to wife and back again. 'Both of you.' As if to help them come to a decision, she settled on the sofa next to their son. His left cheek was still red from the slap and he looked like he'd shed a few tears.

'He was in such a state when he came back,' Martha Fielding said, sitting down on one of the two chairs. 'And all he'd wanted to do was offer sympathy.' Colson was resting on the arm of the sofa, next to Clarke. When he took all of this in, Kevin Fielding decided to give up the fight, throwing himself onto the one empty armchair.

Clarke turned towards Craig. 'You went to Jasmine's house?' she coaxed. 'To show sympathy?'

'I just wanted them to know that we all care about Jas.'

78

'So thoughtful,' his mother added quietly.

'And what happened?' Clarke asked.

Craig stared at his hands, still pressed between his knees. 'Helena was pleased to see me,' he began. 'She went to the kitchen to pour me a glass of water.' He paused to take a breath. 'But then *he* came home. Pulled me to my feet, shouting at me, asking me where she was.' Fresh tears were forming at the corners of his eyes. 'He kept shaking me ...'

'Just a boy,' Martha stated.

'Helena told him to stop, and that's when he slapped me. Then he let me go. I ran for it, ran all the way back here.'

'He was in such a state,' his mother added.

'The man's clearly out of control,' Kevin Fielding muttered, though much of the fight seemed to have gone out of him.

'I doubt you'd be in your right mind, sir,' Colson advised, 'if your child had gone missing.'

'Doesn't excuse it.'

'Maybe it does *a bit*,' Martha piped up.

'How about if we go speak to Mr Andrews?' Clarke suggested. 'We'll give him a warning and get him to apologise.'

'I don't want to see him,' Craig blurted out.

'A written apology, then – and a promise not to fly off the handle again. If he can't stick to that, he'll find himself in custody.' Clarke broke off and made eye contact with both parents. 'Do we all think that would suffice?'

Eventually there were nods from husband and wife. Clarke turned her attention to their son. 'That okay with you, Craig?'

'Suppose,' he said.

'Right then,' she said, rising to her feet, followed by Colson.

'Thank you,' Martha Fielding said, as though they'd just made a donation to a cause close to her heart.

'I bloody knew they'd call the cops. That wanker was never going to show his face himself.'

James Andrews turned and strode back into his living room,

Clarke and Colson following. There was a bottle of red on the coffee table, three-quarters drained, flanked by two emptied wine glasses. There was also a crystal tumbler with some whisky still in it. Andrews wasn't quite drunk, but his eyes were glassy.

'Do you mean Craig or his father?' Colson asked.

'The dad, obviously. Smug streak of piss that he is.'

Helena Andrews had appeared silently in the doorway from elsewhere in the house. She nodded a greeting towards the detectives and sat down, looking almost ghostly.

'How is Craig?' she asked.

Her husband flung out an arm to indicate the two detectives. 'Called the cops on us, sweetheart – *that's* how he is!'

Clarke and Colson had already decided to remain on their feet, their faces stern. Andrews waited for them to say something, then started to shake his head when they stayed silent.

'I'm not about to say sorry, if that's what you're asking.'

'He's a child, Mr Andrews,' Colson stated.

'He's fifteen,' Andrews countered. 'A year from now he could be in the army. We're not talking about a toddler here. At fifteen I was smoking and sneaking a drink—'

'And fighting?' Colson enquired. 'A lifestyle choice that ended up getting you in a bit of bother.'

'Half a lifetime back.'

'Still quick to anger, though, sir, wouldn't you say?'

Andrews took a step towards Colson, so they were face to face. 'I walk in and he's sitting there like he owns the place.' He gestured towards the chair his wife was now occupying. 'Calls me "James" like we're old pals. Cocky little git at the best of times – there was only ever one thing he wanted from our Jas.' He broke off, eyes flitting towards his wife.

'Sex, you mean?' Clarke asked.

'What else?'

'Even if that were true,' Helena broke in, 'he didn't get it. She'd have said.'

Her husband looked unconvinced. 'The kid was a leech,

80

coming here at all hours uninvited. When I walked in and he was sitting there ... where *she* should have been ...' He exhaled loudly, anger spent for now.

'Is James in trouble?' Helena asked, eyes on Clarke.

'A written apology would help.'

'He'll do that.'

Andrews stared at her but didn't say no.

'We're on tenterhooks,' she went on. 'Neither of us sleeping, worried sick. We just want her to walk through that door ...' She bowed her head so the tears would remain hers and hers alone.

'You'll write something down?' Colson nudged James Andrews. Andrews nodded, but his attention was on his wife. For a moment, Clarke thought he was ready to go to her and wrap her in his arms. But instead he started heading towards the front door.

'I'll let you out,' he said.

6

DCI Mae McGovern had gathered the major incident team at Gayfield Square police station. It had been decided to move the base from HMP Edinburgh because there were too many restrictions inside the prison and it took too long for the team to get in and out. Besides, they had all they needed in terms of the crime scene. There were some interviews still to be carried out, but those did not require everyone's presence. Two team members – DCs Allbright and Tilley – were absent, one at an emergency dental appointment and the other with COVID, leaving what could best be described as a skeleton crew.

They had listened to selected recordings from the interviewees, focusing on the night-shift POs and the deceased's cellmate. The autopsy report had been discussed and photos of the locus projected onto a screen so they could discuss theories. The lack of the murder weapon was proving a major frustration. Forensics had picked up no blood traces on the floor outside the cell. CCTV footage showed no POs looking agitated or attempting to hide stained clothing. Nothing had come of a search of staff lockers and rubbish bins. And yet the pathologist, Deborah Quant, had been clear – there would have been blood.

'So we're going to have to come at this from an angle,' DCI

McGovern was telling her team. She stood at the front of the room with arms folded. She had removed the jacket of her trouser suit and rolled up the sleeves of her olive-green blouse. Her hair was auburn and Christine Esson reckoned it had to be dyed. McGovern was in her late forties, not far off qualifying for a full police pension. Two grown-up kids, each with a child of their own. The windowsill behind her desk was festooned with framed photos of her family. Her husband was a senior civil servant. Like him, she had grown up in Glasgow and attended university there before joining the police. She was never going to lose the accent and often made fun of herself when playing to an east-coast audience. But she had a sharp mind that belied her apparently easy-going nature, and when she rolled her sleeves up you knew she meant business.

'We need to focus on motive,' she went on, eyes scanning the room, making sure she had every officer's full attention. 'Who wanted Jackie Simpson dead? We know he had a lengthy criminal record, but never for anything violent. He'd been breaking into premises since he was at school – jail had become an occupational hazard. He was due to be released shortly and had behaved impeccably while serving his sentence.'

'Not exactly impeccably,' Jason Mulgrew interrupted, 'if you speak to Chris Novak.'

'Agreed, a fair bit of niggle there, but enough to merit murder?'

'There was a threat to pay the officer's house a visit,' DC Zara Shah piped up. McGovern nodded slowly, allowing this.

'Once Simpson was out, Novak couldn't get to him so easily,' Mulgrew added, meriting a smile from Shah for backing her up.

'I'd say just the opposite,' Esson couldn't help arguing. 'If Novak really wanted to harm Simpson, why not wait until he was released? Much more chance of getting away with it. Attacking him in his cell brings the list of suspects down to a handful.'

'Heat of the moment, who's to say?' Shah argued back. McGovern held up a hand, silencing them.

'We need to know all there is to know about the victim, the officers on duty and the prisoners on that wing. If Chris Novak continues to be the main suspect, then we can zero in on him, but I want to be confident that we're not missing something. Did the deceased have a beef with anyone else – prisoner or staff? Could one of Novak's colleagues have decided to do him a favour by taking matters into their own hands?'

'Let's not forget his good friend Valerie Watts,' Mulgrew added. 'The night-shift team all say the same thing – they pretty much knew where everyone was from minute to minute. But CCTV shows Novak leaving the control room, and two minutes later, so does Watts. It's a good ten minutes before they pop up again. Loo break apparently, but there's no sign of either of them on the tapes.'

'What do we make of the broken camera?' Shah asked.

'It had been reported and there had already been one attempt to repair it,' McGovern stated.

'On the other hand,' Shah continued, 'someone could have decided that with it out of action, the timing was right for the assault.'

Mulgrew lifted his laptop from his desk and turned its screen to face the room at large. 'Couple of other cameras *were* still working. They show sections of the hall, officers patrolling, but nobody particularly lingering.' He had speeded up the footage. They'd all watched it more than once, knew every single frame. 'Patrols aren't frequent – they don't have the staffing level. Unless an alarm's hit or a con requests a visit.'

'The governor would rather we used the term "resident",' Esson reminded him.

'How about the prisoner who heard a key in a lock?' Shah asked.

'His name's Billy Groam,' Mulgrew answered. 'Seemed pretty confident when we talked to him, but maybe he was high on something that night.' He turned his screen back towards him and worked away at the touchpad. 'There are blind spots throughout the prison – and the POs would know them.

Mostly officers stick to two rooms away from Trinity Hall. One houses the CCTV screens and comms with the cells, the other is for downtime. Usual kettle, microwave, fridge and sink, plus a corkboard where they pin up photos of recent weapon finds and the like.'

'I also want us to think a bit more about the cellmate,' McGovern added. 'He was high as a kite, but was that voluntary? Had someone slipped him a much bigger dose than he was used to? Had he been more or less ordered to take enough spice or whatever to put himself out of the game? Was he really unconscious when he got hit on the head or did he maybe hear or see something or somebody? Could be he's blocking it out and it'll come back with a bit of nudging. Plenty for us to be considering and a lot of work ahead. Anything you need from me, you only have to ask.'

'Does that include a few more pairs of hands?' Esson asked.

'You know what budgets are like these days, Christine.' McGovern's tone was cold, but her eyes were sympathetic. Nobody blamed her for the fact they lacked bodies, funds and sometimes the equipment to do the job.

Once McGovern had left for her own office down the hallway, Esson settled at her computer, trying to get it to do something, anything. Not for the first time, it wasn't minded to oblige. An arm suddenly reached down past her shoulder, Mulgrew's fingers busying themselves on her keyboard. The screen sprang to life.

'I could have done it,' Esson commented.

'A simple "thanks" will suffice, Christine.'

Over by the tea bags, Shah was shaking an empty half-litre milk carton.

'Whose job was it to bring fresh?'

'Allbright's,' Mulgrew said, walking towards her. 'Probably curdling in the dental surgery as we speak.'

'You mean the milk or Allbright?'

Mulgrew snorted at the joke, Esson refusing to join in even though Allbright's name really did sometimes seem to be in

85

itself a joke on nominative determinism. She got up and joined them as the kettle came to a boil.

'If you followed my example, it wouldn't bother you,' she said, pouring the boiled water into her empty mug.

'Don't know how you can do that,' Shah said, wrinkling her nose.

'I like it,' Esson replied. She watched Mulgrew offer Shah the last peppermint tea bag, which Shah accepted with a look not unadjacent to a simper. Esson tried to remember if the DC was attached right now. She thought not. She was about four inches shorter than Mulgrew and eight years younger. Her family had moved to Scotland from the Middle East a generation back. Esson envied her flawless skin and those huge hazel eyes, currently fixed on Jason Mulgrew. When Mulgrew passed Esson's desk on his way to his own and half raised an eyebrow, she wondered if something had been showing in her face.

'Do we have the victim's file?' Shah asked the room.

Esson hoisted it and let it fall with a thump back onto her desk. 'Like the boss says, he's been on our radar most of his adult life.'

'We've not really talked to the family yet, have we?'

Esson made show of opening the file. They'd been through this more than once. 'Divorced, one son, Marcus. His ex moved south, the son stayed here. He's been in a bit of bother too, the past few years. Driving under the influence with no insurance, couple of scuffles outside pubs and clubs, possession of hash and speed ...'

'Does he have a job?' Mulgrew asked.

Esson dug a little deeper into the file. 'Don't know if you'd call it a job or not, but he hangs out with Zak Campbell.'

'The footballer?'

'Ex-footballer,' she corrected him. 'Injury did for him.'

'Hell of a player he was turning into, too,' Mulgrew mused.

'He was at the same school as Marcus. Few years above him, but they became pally.'

'Didn't Campbell go into acting or something?'

Shah had been busy on her phone. 'Bit parts in a couple of TV dramas and films I've never heard of. Tried his hand at modelling and singing. Info dries up after that.'

'Who was it that spoke to the son?' Mulgrew asked.

'Me and Allbright,' Shah said, dumping her tea bag into a bin. 'He's still living at the family home – out Edinburgh Park way. Didn't seem that shocked by his dad's killing, but that could've been bravado. Shared precisely no useful information regarding the deceased. It was Allbright who noticed a few photos in the house showing Marcus with Zak Campbell – I had no idea who he was. From the way Marcus then spoke, we got the idea he maybe worked for Campbell in some capacity, or at least was taking money from him.' Shah broke off, watching as Esson held up the report of the interview.

'Allbright's spelling is all over the place,' Esson said.

'Poor guy was mainlining ibuprofen for his toothache,' Shah reminded her.

'How about the deceased's ex-wife?' Mulgrew enquired.

'Using her black-widow charms to persuade one of the other prisoners into doing her dirty work?' Esson sifted the paperwork again. 'Split was amicable. No cheating on either side. She got the cash for her half of the marital home and has hitched her wagon to a car mechanic in Nottingham.'

She closed the file and they sat in silence, drinking their drinks while the seconds passed.

'Stands to reason it was Novak,' Shah eventually offered.

'It does,' Mulgrew agreed.

'We should bring him in here,' Shah went on. 'Proper grill-ing in an interview room. Then do the same for every colleague who's covering for him. My guess is, they either knew he was going to do it, or they helped him carry it out – getting rid of the evidence, cleaning up, handing him a fresh uniform.'

'That being the case, why would they help us?' Esson asked. 'They'd be putting themselves in the frame. Only way this works is if they all stick together.'

Shah held up a finger. 'One link in the chain is always weaker than the rest. Some hard questioning will show us who that is.'

'These people work in a prison, Zara. I doubt we've got anything that won't just bounce off them.' Esson broke off as her phone buzzed with an incoming text.

It's Malcolm F. Can we meet?

She started tapping her response. *Busy.*

Seconds later, Fox replied. *At Gayfield? I'm in my car outside. Need 5 mins max.*

'Anything interesting?' Mulgrew enquired.

'A huge break in the case.' She watched him crack a smile. 'I just need to pop out for five. Is that okay?'

'I suppose so,' he said, 'but only if you make it ten rather than five.' He saw the quizzical look on her face. 'Nip into a shop and fetch us some milk,' he explained.

Fox's car was big and black. The interior smelled and looked brand new. Esson climbed in and closed the door, checking she couldn't be seen from the CID windows across the street.

'Interesting,' she said.

'How so?'

'Well, for one thing, I'd no idea you had my mobile number. And for another, if it's an official visit, why are we down here and not upstairs?'

The smile took a long time spreading across Fox's face, and lacked a certain amount of sincerity. Esson noted that he kept his hands on the steering wheel, as though he might abduct her at any moment. It didn't help that those hands were sheathed in black leather gloves.

'I just thought maybe I could offer you something – trust me, it's something you definitely want.'

'Okay, I'm listening.'

'There's an inmate who's in the same hall as the victim – in fact, their cells are pretty much across from one another. His name's Everett Harrison. I don't think you've got round to questioning him yet. When you do, it might help to have some background. Harrison's an enforcer for a Liverpool crime boss called Shay Hanlon. Our colleagues south of the border got a bit too close to prosecuting Hanlon, and off he went to Brazil – no easy extradition. Hanlon's specialisms are dope and people-trafficking. That was how we got lucky. There was a break-in at a nail bar. The culprit ran off when the alarm sounded, but that same alarm sent a patrol car looking. In the back office they found a chunky consignment of drugs with Harrison's dabs all over it.'

'I'm with you so far, for what it's worth.'

'The intruder cut himself during the break-in,' Fox went on, keeping his voice level as he surveyed the roadway and pavement. 'Took a while – you know what the labs are like with low-level stuff – but we finally got a match.' He turned towards her. 'Jackie Simpson.'

Esson was silent for a moment as she digested this. 'So in a way, Simpson's responsible for this guy Harrison being put inside?'

Fox nodded slowly, his eyes turning towards her as she gnawed her bottom lip, deep in thought.

'Do we have any reason to believe Harrison knows who Jackie Simpson is?' she eventually asked. Fox just shrugged. 'And your interest isn't so much in the victim as this guy Harrison – but Harrison's already doing time, so what's in it for you?'

It was Fox's turn to think for a moment. He drew in a breath, a sign that he had made his mind up. 'We think Hanlon might be on his way back to the UK.'

'"Think"?'

'He uses EncroChat – makes it impossible for us to intercept his phone calls – so as of now it's just a strong suspicion. Doubtful he'd get in touch with Harrison, but not impossible. His gang is almost clannish, and money's been making its way to Harrison's family to tide them over. SO15 asked me to keep an ear to the ground ...'

89

'And of course, you'd want to suck up to London.' Esson managed a wry smile. 'Same old Malcom Fox.' She gestured towards his hands. 'Do those gloves help you climb the greasy pole?'

'I didn't need to come to you, Christine. I could have taken this to Mae McGovern.'

'But you didn't.' She narrowed her eyes slightly. 'And why is that, Malcolm? Siobhan escaped your clutches, so you're on the hunt for a new pet project? Maybe you see yourself as Sir Galahad.' She made show of checking her surroundings. 'No damsels needing saving here, mister.'

Fox's face had grown stony. 'I've told you what I thought you should know. What you do with it is up to you. All I'm asking is to be kept in the loop.' He pressed the ignition button and sat there, hands ready on the steering wheel, staring through the windscreen as Esson wrenched open the door.

She was about to walk back into the station, but changed her mind and headed off in the direction of Leith Walk. There was no point taking the information straight back to MIT when she could add something else of value to the basket.

Milk ...

Fox watched her in his rear-view mirror. She was right, of course, but only partially. Becoming her ally, her confidant, would have annoyed Siobhan Clarke, and perhaps driven a wedge between the two women. Maybe he had miscalculated, but maybe not. She would take the information to her boss, of course she would, and would be praised for it. Which might cause her to reflect and come round to thinking of him as useful, maybe even eventually thanking him. There was more he could have told her, but some secrets had to remain locked away. No need for her to know about his relationship with the deceased or his role in the break-in that had led to Everett Harrison's prosecution. And after all, a result had been secured – drugs taken off the street, a criminal put behind bars. Plus Jackie

Simpson had kept quiet throughout, never mentioning Fox or the plan the two of them had conjured up. That in itself should have kept him safe during his incarceration. Well, relatively safe. Yes, it should have.

Oh well.

As he drove west out of the city, headed for his office at Gartcosh, he thought again of John Rebus, locked up and guilty, yet neither as troubled nor as changed as Fox had expected. He knew Rebus couldn't ignore Jackie Simpson's murder – it wasn't in the man's nature. Then there was Darryl Christie to consider. The consignment found in the nail bar pointed to one thing – Hanlon was barging into Christie's territory. His first foray into Scotland, Glaze had said on the phone. Perhaps a taster of things to come.

'See, Malcolm,' Glaze had purred, 'one strong reason for Hanlon to come back from Brazil would be to improve his chances of taking a grip on the Scottish market. With Christie inside, what's to stop him?'

'Christie might be inside, but his men aren't,' Fox had countered.

'Maybe so, but I'll bet they've never encountered someone like Shay Hanlon before. I'll send you a few stories.'

And so he had, stories of violence meted out and territories gained. Photographs, too, including a couple of shots of Hanlon himself, ruddy-cheeked and curly-haired, freckles covering an almost boyish face – Fox would have taken him for a farmer, or maybe a builder. Six murders at the very least, SO15 reckoned he'd got away with. Old ties with Republican hitmen in Belfast, arms bought and sold, killers given safe passage and new identities. Fox had put feelers out, but had yet to find solid evidence that, Harrison apart, Hanlon had shifted any of his troops to Scotland. He'd also, after speaking to Rebus, done a search on Bobby Briggs, headcase for hire. Briggs had been in trouble all his days, but without straying too far from his Glaswegian orbit. He'd been transferred to Edinburgh because he was judged to have too many enemies with scores to settle in the local prison, Barlinnie. Had he known Everett Harrison on the outside? If so, how? And what was in it for either man?

Fox knew he had many more questions than answers, nor could he rely, it seemed, on Christine Esson to do his bidding, and that meant only one thing: he had to attach himself to the investigation. Using hands-free, he called his boss's office. Then he sat up a little bit straighter at the steering wheel and took a deep breath.

Time to turn on the charm, Malcolm, he told himself, waiting for the call to be answered.

7

Siobhan Clarke opened a bottle of wine, promising herself she only needed the one glass to accompany the dinner she'd cooked. Gnocchi with fried onion, garlic and mushrooms added, then a heaped spoonful of pesto stirred in. She'd even grated some pecorino. Surely that merited a smallish helping of cold white wine. She had the central heating on, the lighting turned low and Chet Baker singing from her Bluetooth speaker. With the curtains closed, the rest of the world could perhaps be persuaded to melt away. Her flat had two bedrooms (one used for storage, since no one ever stayed) and was a couple of storeys above ground level in a traditional tenement. If she wanted nightlife, Broughton Street was around the corner. Plenty of bars where a single woman could sit for a while without being hassled; a decent spread of restaurants; and during the day there were cafés and local shops. There was even an auction house where she sometimes browsed on viewing days. She hadn't bought anything yet, but she was on their mailing list.

Yes, the furnishings in her flat were tired, but she couldn't quite muster the energy to spend her free time changing things. She liked her sofa and she liked her armchair. The mattress on her bed got turned every few months. The in-bath shower was haphazard, but she could do without the bother of plumbers who never turned up. At weekends she caught up with Samantha and Carrie, plus Brillo, of course. They might go check on John's flat and pick up his mail. If Christine Esson didn't have a new guy on the go, they sometimes walked the seafront at Portobello before hitting a wine bar. Fox ... well, Fox had been around for a short time, but that was long past. It often struck her that she was nearer to retirement than to the day she'd joined the force. Much nearer, truth be told. Had CID robbed her of a personal life? No, that had been her choice. But she was beginning to feel that the job no longer wanted her around. Wasn't it more fun a decade or two back, when a few rules could be bent or broken? Rebus and his contemporaries hadn't had to worry about internet warriors, the brandishing of mobile phone cameras or being 'cancelled'. Livelier times; or, as Rebus himself sometimes termed it, 'the wild east'.

Mood dipping, Clarke stared at the speaker. 'It's you, isn't it?' she chided the crooning Chet Baker. Then she scrolled on her phone until she found some Talking Heads, a more upbeat soundtrack to her last few mouthfuls of food. She was just starting to consider a second glass of wine – a smaller helping than the first, naturally – when her phone rang. She saw that it was Laura Smith. Smith was a journalist, ex-crime correspondent of the *Scotsman* newspaper. She now ran a website, podcast and blog and was happier outside the mainstream – and better off financially, too. She had stopped inviting Siobhan to join her as co-presenter, or at least appear on an episode or two (anonymity preserved), but was a good companion, who phoned when she was at a loose end and thirsty.

'Not tonight, Josephine,' Clarke said, answering the call.

'This is business rather than social. I'm parked downstairs – any chance I can come up?'

Five minutes later, Clarke was placing a clean glass in front of her guest. Smith was dressed casually – jeans and an oversized jumper, her hair unbrushed. Something had brought her here in a hurry, so Clarke poured, sat down and waited. After a couple of sips of wine, Smith put the glass down and pressed her fingers against the base of the stem.

'I got a call tonight. Some bloke who wouldn't give his name. He said it was about the missing girl.'

'Meaning Jasmine Andrews?'

She gave a brisk nod and reached into her shoulder bag for her MacBook. She slid the wine glass to one side and opened the screen.

'He said he saw her photo – the one you released to the media – and she looked familiar.' Smith stopped tapping at the keys long enough to make eye contact with Clarke. 'From a porn site.'

'What?' Clarke lifted her chair and carried it around the table, settling alongside Smith.

'That was my first thought, too. Some weirdo trying to wind me up. The site is called Young Fresh East Coast. Sounds innocent enough, but after a couple of clicks you find yourself here ...' Smith sat back and angled the screen slightly towards Clarke. There were a couple of dozen posed photos there. Young people, male and female, semi-clad, their faces digitally distorted. They all seemed to be positioned on the same bed in the same room. Smith slid the cursor to the top right photo and enlarged it.

'What do you think?' she asked. 'Jasmine Andrews?'

'Hard to tell without seeing the face. Can we do anything about that?'

'I can't, but I'm guessing your lab techs might. I've tried getting further into the site, but it's impossible. You have to apply online to join "the community".'

Clarke enlarged the photo a little more. The girl was wearing thong and bra, plus white ankle socks. Her arms were stretched out behind her to support her as she sat, legs bent at the knees and open more than a few inches. The other girls were similarly positioned or else were up on all fours, sometimes photographed from behind, heads angled back towards the camera. The boys wore bulging underpants and sometimes flexed a bicep or knelt with a finger hooked into a waistband.

'There's no video,' Smith said, 'but there is sound.' She clicked on one of the icons and listened alongside Clarke.

'*I'm horny as hell. Please choose me. I'll do anything your heart desires.*' It was a girl speaking, breathy, trying to act older. There was almost a trace of a giggle at the end.

'They all parrot the same line,' Smith explained. 'And they mostly sound Scottish.'

'Different voices for each photo?' Clarke watched as Smith nodded. She tried navigating further into the site without success. 'The guy who phoned?' she prompted.

'Also Scottish. When he hung up, I checked, but he'd blocked his number. He wants money, though.'

Clarke looked at her. 'Money?'

'A hundred to start with. And if I cough up, he promises another phone call.'

'So you've some way of contacting him?'

'It's a pub called the Mallaig Inn.'

'In Mallaig?'

Smith shook her head. 'The badlands of Restalrig. Five twenties in an envelope and the name Pedro on the front. Hand it to the barman and walk away.' She paused. 'Instead of which, here I am, because I *know* you'll give me the exclusive – and you've done me plenty of favours in the past.'

'Did he say when you were to hand the money over?'

'Sooner the better or he might go elsewhere. You do think it's her then? I mean, if it is, and somebody was getting ready to out her – maybe a boy in her year who put two and two together – that's a pretty good reason for getting out of Dodge, wouldn't you say?'

Clarke didn't answer, too focused on the screen and her own thoughts. Smith, knowing that look of old, reached for her wine and waited. Clarke eventually got up without saying anything and left the room, returning with a multipack of envelopes. She placed it on the table and slid one out, fetching a pen from her bag.

'Pedro, wasn't it?' she asked.

'Pedro it was,' Laura Smith confirmed.

The Mallaig Inn sat on a prominent corner site in the middle of a housing scheme. The area looked tired and so did the pub. Its pebble-dashed walls hadn't seen paint in a while (other than graffiti tags) and the M had disappeared from its signage. But it was well lit, and a sandwich board by the door promised real ales and bar food.

When Clarke walked in, the place was moderately busy. A man sat at a corner table, strumming a guitar and singing a Paul Simon song. She wasn't sure if he was hired or just a punter, but the half-dozen whiskies in front of him spoke of an appreciative audience. She ordered a gin and tonic from the barmaid. The girl was young, just out of her teens, and had dyed her hair purple. Nose, ear and eyebrow piercings, round-rimmed spectacles, violet lipstick. There was no sign of anyone more senior, so Clarke placed the envelope on the bar top. It stayed there, ignored by the barmaid, as Clarke handed over a ten-pound note. Taking her change, she tapped the envelope with a fingernail.

'For Pedro,' she said. The girl met her eyes for the merest second before lifting the envelope and placing it beneath the bar.

'I'll see he gets it.'

'Is he due in?'

The barmaid ignored the question and moved off to serve the next customer. Clarke took her drink to a far corner, but there was no real hiding place here. The barmaid turned her back while she made a call on her mobile, but angled her head briefly in Clarke's direction while talking. So Clarke returned to the bar with her untouched drink, thanking the girl as she left. She crossed the road and got into her car, starting the ignition and driving off. In the rear-view, she could see the barmaid in the doorway, checking the visitor had gone. Her phone was in her hand, illuminating her face as she started to make another call.

Clarke drove around the block, found a kerbside parking space and walked back in the direction of the Mallaig Inn. She kept her distance and made sure she wasn't near any street lighting. One or two cars passed her, but she had her phone up to her face as though texting a friend. Then a man sauntered around the corner, exchanging greetings with a smoker in the pub's doorway before stepping inside. He was out again less than a minute later, hadn't even bothered to unzip his thin, pale-coloured jerkin. Clarke caught up with him just as he came to a stop. He had been in the act of opening the envelope, surprised by its contents – a few torn-up pieces of newspaper.

'Sorry to disappoint you, Pedro,' she said.

'You've got the wrong guy, sweetheart.'

He was in his forties, overweight and with thinning hair. There was a wedding ring on his left hand. The shirt below the jerkin was open at the neck but looked as though it might normally sport a tie. An ordinary married man with a job, the quiet type. Clarke had met his ilk a hundred times and knew her line of attack.

'Does your wife know about Young Fresh East Coast? Should we maybe go chat with her?' She had her ID open, held up in front of his nose.

His Adam's apple bobbed as he studied it. 'You're not the reporter.' He looked disappointed rather than angry, used to the world being an unjust place.

'My car's not far. We can talk there or down the station.'

'I haven't done anything.'

'You recognised Jasmine Andrews from her media photo. But on the site's home page her face is obscured. That tells me you've paid for certain privileges. So do we talk here or at the station?' His silence told her all she needed to know, and he followed her meekly to her car, climbing into the passenger seat as though ascending a scaffold. She left him to stew in his juices for a moment while she opened her laptop, accessing the website.

'Won't do you any good,' he said.

'How so?'

'You only get the access code once payment's gone through. And nothing's been going through for a few days.'

'You're a regular customer then?'

'Not really.'

She allowed him this. 'So talk me through it,' she said. 'Payment's accepted, and then what?'

'Then you click on your choice.' He gestured towards the display of photos. 'If they're active, that is.'

'Active?'

'Usually only one or two at a time are. It's live-streamed.'

'From this location?' Clarke tapped a finger against the bedroom and watched Pedro nod.

'Then you type in what you want them to do.' He was beginning to perspire and ran a hand across his forehead and cheeks. 'I didn't know she was underage, not until the news broke.'

'Got any kids yourself?' Clarke asked.

'They're twelve and eight.' His eyes were glistening. 'I'm not ... I just sometimes like to watch ...'

'What does she call herself?' Clarke interrupted, her finger resting against the photo of Jasmine.

'She's Jazz, like the music. All she does is strip off and maybe feel herself up.'

'And you're talking to her while she does this?'

He shook his head. 'You type it in. But there's a microphone somewhere close to her – you can hear what she's saying.'

'I'm assuming there's someone behind the camera?'

'Never see or hear anyone.' He thought for a moment. 'But yes, sometimes the models look to one side of the lens, as if there's someone there.'

'Do they ever seem scared to you, like they don't want to be doing this?'

He gave a vehement shake of the head. 'They're relaxed, happy.' Something else came to him. 'They want whoever's behind the camera to be pleased with them.'

'Does it ever go further? One-to-one phone calls or meets?'

'No. Nothing like that. You pay and you watch and when your time's up the screen goes black.'

'You said "one or two" ...'

'Sometimes there's a double act, but those cost too much, so I never—'

Clarke slapped shut the laptop. 'What's your real name?' she demanded.

'Just Pedro will do.'

'It won't really, though, will it? See, here's the thing – you held back vital information from an ongoing police inquiry. On top of which, you tried to cash in on that information rather than bring it to us the way a respectable, upstanding citizen would. So I need to know your name, address and a contact number before I send you back to play happy families.'

'I'm Peter. Peter Cowan.' He managed to mumble his address, which Clarke duly tapped into her phone, along with his mobile number. She then asked to see proof. He dug out a driving licence, and she scrutinised it.

'You can't get in trouble for looking,' he stated as she handed it back.

'Oh, but you can. Because those weren't "models", Mr Cowan, they were and are children, kids being exploited for money by you and men like you.' She paused, her eyes drilling into his. 'I'll be in touch.'

He placed his hand against the door handle but then paused. Clarke sensed what was coming – further excuses, denials and justifications.

'Get out of my car,' she commanded. Cowan did so, but stood unmoving on the pavement, hands rising slowly and shakily to clutch at his head. Clarke drove off into the night and never looked back.

Day Three

8

After breakfast, there was a chance for fresh air in the exercise yard. Some prisoners took the word 'exercise' literally, jogging a circuit or doing push-ups and squats. These were the ones who spent as much time as possible in the gym, pumping themselves up. Others kicked a ball around. But mostly people just ambled. SRU had an adjoining space, a high wall separating the two. A few of the prisoners on Rebus's side sent up yelled threats, just in case any rapists or kiddie-fiddlers were listening. Rebus had encountered one or two paedophiles during his short time in the unit. They'd tended to be docile and eager to follow orders, but keen also to keep to their cells, the door locked. There was one rapist, too, nicknamed Hair Trigger for his sudden violent outbursts. He'd been locked in solitary throughout Rebus's stay, his shouts echoing down the hall.

The Wizard leaned against a wall, head angled towards the slate-grey sky. Maybe he was listening for those church bells. There was a well-thumbed Bible in his cell and he attended the chapel on a Sunday. Rebus knew that a few prisoners – white, working-class Scots – had converted to Islam during their time inside. They had their prayer times and their assemblies, with Jumah on a Friday. They borrowed religious texts from the library. If Rebus was helping out, he always studied their faces for signs that this was all a front of some kind, but as yet he'd caught no one out.

As Rebus walked, he overheard snatches of growled conversations. Cells and shared spaces were still in the process of being given a methodical search by police officers. The guards were not immune from this, but the prisoners didn't care about that. They had to open the safes beneath their beds and allow cops to rifle through their stuff. Classes were cancelled while meeting rooms were searched. Rebus's own cell had been gone over a second time by two young officers, one male and one female, neither looking thrilled about the task they'd been assigned.

'Didn't teach you this in training, did they?' Rebus had teased, receiving no reply, the officers doubtless having been told to avoid interaction with the cons.

One of the nursing staff had complained to him while refilling his inhaler that even the NHS office had been searched.

'As if we wouldn't notice a bloodstained knife lying about the place.'

'No way it's still on site,' Rebus had replied. She'd looked at him.

'Smuggled out?' she'd guessed. 'Not easy for a resident to arrange that, I'd have thought.'

'I see you got the governor's memo. But to answer your question with another – who says it has to be a "resident" doing the smuggling?'

The library was Rebus's next port of call after exercise. It wasn't a large room, but it was well stocked with books, magazines and DVDs. The librarian was provided by Edinburgh Council. She was a meticulous young woman called Megan Keighley, who hailed from Northumbria and had told Rebus that her name derived from a word for a woodland clearing. She wore a small crucifix around her neck, which she quickly tucked away if it escaped from below her neckline. Rebus had impressed her by knowing so many authors' names. He didn't admit that though in the past he'd amassed a solid collection of books, he'd got to the end of precious few of them.

Keighley was sorting through the latest batch of requests when Rebus arrived. The prisoners were free to order just about anything, but with certain restrictions – no terrorism handbooks or true crime, and nothing involving children. Additionally, none of the DVDs carried an 18 certificate. The most popular book loans tended to be legal texts, whose readership was on the lookout for loopholes and get-out clauses. One of the older lags had become so knowledgeable that other prisoners consulted him. He took his fee in cigarettes, which as he said himself made him quite the bargain compared to his 'colleagues' on the outside.

Rebus was reminded that his own legal team seemed to have forgotten about him. In the weeks following his imprisonment, there had been a flurry of meetings, either in person or via the video-call facility, a row of cubicles where prisoners could also connect with their families if those families lived too far away for physical visits to be practicable. His defence had stayed the same throughout: he hadn't intended to kill the man, just put the fear of God into him. If he'd wanted him dead, he would have made sure. His actions might or might not have had some bearing on the heart attack Cafferty then suffered. That was the whole point: no one could say for certain, so how could he be guilty of attempted murder? When he'd entered HMP Edinburgh the first day, straight after sentencing, the officers in the first-night centre had given him a round of applause, all agreed that the world was better off without Big Ger Cafferty.

Rebus, however, wasn't so sure, because he knew damned well that someone else would replace Cafferty, that someone being Darryl Christie. Siobhan Clarke, on her first visit to him, had sat across the table and cocked her head.

'I actually thought you quite liked him, you know.'

Rebus had replied with a twitch of the mouth, without voicing any denial.

'Managed to get a couple of novels in Polish and Romanian,' Keighley was saying as Rebus stood next to her. 'Thomas

Harris and Michael Connelly. Should keep the troops happy.'
She glanced at him. 'Do you read any languages, John?'

'At a pinch I can manage English.'

'Not even Gaelic?'

'I know how to say "kiss my arse", but in Irish rather than Scots.'

Keighley tucked a stray hair behind one ear. He knew she was good-looking enough that some men would pretend to browse the stacks just so they could drink her in. There was a nurse in the healthcare unit who had a similar effect. No one had ever tried anything, though, not as far as he knew. An officer was always close by when prisoners who weren't trusted were in the room.

'*Pogue mahone*, right?' she said. Then: 'Such a shame about Mr Simpson. You know he offered to show me how to pick a lock?'

'Jackie was generous that way.'

'He always had a twinkle in his eye.'

'Probably on the lookout for anything worth nicking.'

Rebus got to work sorting out the books. He'd hardly started when Chris Novak arrived, accompanied by a prisoner whose face Rebus knew but not his name.

'You're wanted elsewhere,' Novak informed Rebus. 'Jimbo here will swap with you.'

Rebus pretended to check with Keighley, but of course she had no say in the matter. Jimbo was looking around the library like a kid on his first visit to a zoo – so many exotic creatures, all of them new to him.

'Colouring books are over there,' Rebus told him with a nod, following Novak out of the room.

'What's going on?' he asked as they walked along the corridor, unlocking and locking doors after them.

'Who the fuck knows?' Novak shot back. He looked as if sixteen hours' sleep would go at least some way towards easing his many troubles. 'I just do what I'm told, as per.'

'How many times have you been interviewed by CID?' Rebus enquired.

Novak shot him a look, but then relented. 'Twice so far. Same questions over and over.'

'As long as you're stating the truth, just stick to that. And never give more detail than you've been asked.'

'Someone told me I should just keep saying "no comment". But that'd make me look guilty, right?'

'It also annoys the people questioning you, which makes them inclined to dig deeper and wider.'

Novak nodded at the sense of this. 'I've a cousin who's CID. He's the one who suggested "no comment".'

'Would I know him?'

'I doubt it – Cammy would have been joining the force around the time you retired. Big lump of a guy, gives the lie to the idea CID is the preserve of the brightest and best.'

'You know I'm standing right here?'

Novak managed a thin smile. They had come to a stop in front of the door to the pastoral care office. He met Rebus's eyes.

'I appreciate the advice, John.' He knocked and pushed the door open, ushering Rebus in. 'I'll be out here when you're done ...'

Christine Esson sat behind the desk. The other two chairs were empty. Rebus took the one opposite her.

'Thanks for coming, John,' Esson said. The desk in front of her was bare, no paperwork of any kind. The room hadn't quite warmed up, and she was keeping her jacket on. Even so, she looked cold. When she exhaled, it was as if she were checking whether her breath was visible.

'And that's with the heating working,' Rebus commented. 'Cells can get a mite chillier.'

'Do you want a hot drink or anything?'

'What is it I can do for you, Christine?'

'Jackie Simpson was murdered inside a cell on your hall.'

'So I've heard.'

'And what else have you heard?'

'That the man posted outside this room, possibly with his ear pressed to the door, is the likeliest suspect.'

107

Esson turned her attention from the door back to Rebus, lowering her voice so that at first he strained to hear her. 'Something else has come to our attention,' she said. 'The deceased broke into a nail bar that was a front for drug- and people-trafficking. As a consequence, a man called Everett Harrison was charged and sent here.'

'I know Harrison.'

'I expect you do – he's in the cell next to yours. He works for a Liverpool gangster called Shay Hanlon, currently thought to be sunning himself in Brazil.' She gave Rebus another look. 'This doesn't seem to be coming as a surprise to you either.'

'I know a bit of what goes on around here.'

Esson had noticed that she was rubbing her hands together to warm them and tried to stop herself. 'How does Harrison get on with Darryl Christie?' she asked.

'I'd say a truce had been agreed at some point – on the surface everything's hunky and dory.'

'Doesn't that strike you as odd? Harrison works for the competition, no?'

'Maybe "ceasefire" would be a better word than "truce" – doesn't mean the situation can't change.' Rebus clasped his hands around the back of his head as he leaned back in the chair. 'Malcolm Fox gave you this,' he stated matter-of-factly.

'What makes you think that?'

'He's here, he's Organised Crime, and there are organised criminals in the vicinity.'

'His theory is that maybe Harrison found out who Jackie Simpson was and decided to take revenge before Simpson was released.'

'And what does MIT think?'

'We're exploring it.'

'Harrison would need to have an officer in his pocket, someone to spring him after lights-out and take him over to Simpson's cell.'

'Or carry out the killing on his behalf.'

'In either case there'll be a big deposit in that same officer's bank account.'

'I'm not sure these are the sort of people who depend on the banking system, John.'

'What, then? A new house or car? A cryptocurrency wallet?'

'We'll be checking.'

'I assume you'll be asking Harrison himself about all of this?'

'Think that would get us anywhere?'

'Not a chance.'

'Which is why we'd like a bit of evidence first.'

'Like footage showing him tiptoeing out of his cell at dead of night, shank in hand?'

'Listen to you with your prison lingo.' She gave a tired smile. 'CCTV isn't proving particularly helpful.'

'The broken camera,' Rebus stated.

'Coincidence, you think?'

'It's been bust a while. If you're thinking it was tampered with, why didn't the killer take out Jackie a week ago?'

'Then there's the unlocking of a cell door ...'

'Which only Billy Groam seems to have heard.'

'Is he just having some fun at our expense?'

'I don't think he's the type. But one door or gate sounds much like any other, and POs were coming and going ...' He stared at her. 'The fact that you've got teams searching places that have already been searched tells me you're not exactly making progress.'

'Fiscal was adamant it had to be done.'

'Forensics?' She shook her head. He studied her as she rubbed at her eyes. 'Fox came to you specifically, didn't he?'

'Yes.'

'Have you told Siobhan? Because a pound to a penny that's why he did it – to let her know she's no longer his blue-eyed girl.'

'I realise that.'

'Tell me you went straight to your team with it?'

'I did.'

'Because otherwise you're giving him a hold over you. He tells your boss you held it back even for one day ...'

'I took it to my team,' she assured him. Then: 'We're not all like you, John.'

He gave a short laugh, Esson joining in. Then he lowered his arms again and placed his hands on the desk, inches from hers.

'I think I know why you've brought me this, Christine, but I'd like to hear you say it.'

'It's just ... you're in here and we're out there, and we could use all the help we can get.'

'I doubt Harrison's going to open up to me. I mean, I see him all the time, but if I start asking obvious questions ...'

'Then forget I said anything. Last thing I want is you on my conscience.' She tried for a half-joking tone but didn't pull it off.

Rebus kept his eyes on her. 'Give me a number I can reach you on,' he said.

'You've got phones in here?'

'Didn't you see the landline in the victim's cell?'

'I think I was preoccupied.'

Rebus waited while she tore a sheet from a notebook and jotted down a mobile number.

When he tried to take it from her, she held on to it for a moment. 'Nothing more you can tell me just now? Nothing that would help me get a fix on this?'

'Sorry, Christine.' Her grip on the sheet of paper loosened and he folded it into his pocket.

'And you *will* share anything you find?'

'Why wouldn't I?'

'Because you're you, and that means you might well want to present us with a fait accompli.'

'I'm not even sure I could spell it, never mind present it.'

'Just play nice, John. Do the right thing.'

He patted his pocket. 'You'll have heard the rumour, I take it?'

'Which one?'

He gestured towards the door. 'That Chris Novak and Valerie Watts are an item?'

'I'd heard a whisper – you're saying it's true?'

'I'm not one for tittle-tattle. But if I were you, I'd want to know one way or the other ...'

The door opened and a man stood there, staring at them. 'Started the interviews without me?' he said, sounding un-happy.

'I'm ex-CID,' Rebus explained, rising to his feet. 'DS Esson and me go back a ways. We were just catching up.'

The man's eyes drilled into Rebus's. 'You're on our list, though.'

'And all I'll tell you is, I know as little as anyone else.'

'This is DI Mulgrew,' Esson said by way of introduction. Rebus held out a hand, which Mulgrew ignored.

'This isn't exactly following procedures, Christine,' Mulgrew stated.

'I was just passing,' Rebus improvised. 'Happened to see DS Esson, so we sat down for a chat. There was no discussion of the case, if that's what's squeezing your nuts.'

Mulgrew looked unconvinced. Rebus glanced in Esson's direction: *I've done what I can.* Mulgrew was still holding the door open, so Rebus had to negotiate his way around him and out into the corridor, where Novak was waiting.

'Reckon she's in trouble?' Novak asked as they started to walk.

Rebus turned his head long enough to watch Mulgrew close the door. 'She's a big girl, she'll deal with it,' he said.

Though they walked in silence for the next few yards, Rebus knew Novak was on the verge of saying something. Eventually, as they stopped at one of the barred gates, he cleared his throat. He kept his eyes on his chain of keys, took his time finding the right one. A camera was watching, but there was no way of listening in. Nevertheless, he spoke in an undertone.

'When you were a cop, you stuck up for your mates, right? Never grassed them up even when they'd been a bit naughty?

Same rules apply here. But you need to know that some of us might be more honest than others. It's easy to get recruited – short spell of training and you're in. But the past few months and years, some have been resigning almost before the ink's dry on their contract. A matter of weeks and they're done.'

'And why's that?' Rebus asked.

'Because ultimately they've been placed in the system by the scumbags they work for. They smuggle stuff in until they're rumbled or they start to lose their nerve. If you've got a head on your shoulders, you soon start to spot them. Not much you can do about it, though, unless you catch them in the act. Even then, another one steps into their shoes and it all starts again.' Novak broke off, raising his head so that his eyes met Rebus's. 'If told to, it's likely one of them would have done Jackie Simpson ...'

He unlocked the gate and both men passed through. While he was locking it again, Rebus spoke.

'They'd have to have been on the night shift, though. So who on your team don't you trust?'

Novak seemed to be wrestling with whether to answer. He had started walking before he made up his mind. 'Samms,' he eventually intoned. 'Blair Samms.'

Rebus pulled up an image of Samms: early twenties, tall and skinny, cropped black hair, never seeming fully present, as though ticking down the minutes till each shift's end.

And he'd worked the supper service alongside Valerie Watts.

'Have you given him to MIT?' Rebus watched Novak shake his head. 'Why not?'

'Things are bad enough without it coming out that officers are on the take.'

'Was your car firebombed to warn you off?'

'They don't like me because I want security and surveillance ramped up – no more smuggled phones and drugs. More cameras – ones that *work* – inside the jail and on the exterior walls.'

'So why tell me?' Rebus continued. 'What makes you think I won't take it straight back to DS Esson?'

'That's up to you – but it can't have come from me, under-stood?' Novak was ushering him through the last door before the library.

'And this isn't just you covering your own arse?' Rebus risked asking. But Novak wasn't about to answer that. He called out to Jimbo, and the prisoner scurried gratefully from the strange new world into which he'd been hurled. Rebus watched the two men walk away, Novak upright as ever, not a man to be messed with, Jimbo chattering away to him without ever seeming to expect it to turn into a dialogue.

A group of three prisoners plus one guard were inside the library. Books were being borrowed, Megan Keighley noting each one down while the borrowers admired her surreptitious-ly. Rebus's glower in their general direction seemed to have no effect, so he went back to his task and got on with it. When one group left and another arrived, he paid them no heed, until he realised someone was hovering by his shoulder. Turning, he found himself face to face with the scarred and nicked face of Bobby Briggs. Briggs made show of reaching past him to pluck a book from a shelf, his mouth a couple of inches from Rebus's ear, his breath a mix of nicotine and onion.

'Everett tells me it's too soon to do you in – one murder's enough to be going on with. But I can bide my time, and you're not going anywhere. Christie might say he's got your back, but that means nothing to me. Got that?'

'It's not just Darryl you'd be pissing off, though, Bobby,' Rebus improvised. 'It's Shay Hanlon, too.'

'Bullshit.'

'Ask your good pal Everett next time you see him. Better still, borrow a burner and call Shay yourself.'

'Come on then, you lot,' the officer was saying. Briggs looked ready to ignore the request, his eyes bolted on to Rebus. But with a final low growl, he turned away. He was the last to leave, throwing a baleful look at Rebus as he went.

Megan Keighley was clutching an oversized tome to her

chest. 'Not too many people in here give me the heebie-jeebies,' she told Rebus. 'but he's right at the top of my list.'

'Mine too,' Rebus said, realising his heart was pounding and nerves jangling.

After a calmer hour, his time was up and an officer arrived to escort him back to Trinity Hall. It was Blair Samms, Mr Nonchalance himself.

'Having a good day so far?' Rebus asked conversationally as they walked.

'Same old same old.'

'You're far too young to sound so jaded.'

'Is that right?'

'You're in a paying job – you've a lot to be grateful for.'

'You sound like my grandad.'

'What did he do for a living?'

'Lived off benefits.'

'Well, it's a career, I suppose. I hope you treat him right – a few quid now and then for a bet on the horses or a couple of pints.'

'What's it to you?'

'I'm just saying, I hope you appreciate the life you're living. Good career to be had in the prison service.'

'You're joking, aren't you? Soon as I can, I'm out of here.'

'To do what?'

'Anything.'

'All that training wasted.' Rebus made show of shaking his head. 'How many times have you been questioned?'

'That's none of your business.'

'It's just that you were on shift that night.'

'So?'

'So chances are—'

'Chances are, you know fuck all about it.'

'Hence my interest,' Rebus persisted. 'The kid reckons his dinner might have been spiked – I don't suppose you saw any-thing?'

114

'He's spinning you a yarn. Whoever it was killed Simpson, it wasn't a PO.'

'Spontaneous bleeding then, maybe – should we be phoning for an exorcist?' Rebus waited for Samms to say something, but he stayed silent. 'If it wasn't one of yours, stands to reason it was one of mine. Who would your money be on? Darryl Christie? Everett Harrison?'

Samms glanced towards him. 'Why those names specifically?'

Rebus just shrugged.

They had reached the gate leading to Rebus's hall. As Samms unlocked it, Rebus studied him, trying to imagine him slashing another man's throat. He couldn't see it. But on the other hand ... unlocking a door and sending the likes of Everett Harrison through it, knife gripped in his paw? Rebus reckoned Samms might have been just fine with that.

And Harrison, Rebus's next-door neighbour, was the first person he saw as he approached his cell. Harrison gave him a little wave as he headed towards the shower cubicles, a towel draped over one shoulder. A wave and a smile, actually. It wasn't often that Everett Harrison smiled.

Walking into his cell, Rebus had the immediate feeling that someone had paid a visit in his absence – nothing was quite where it had been when he'd left. But nothing obvious was missing either. A third CID search? He didn't think so. He sat on the edge of his bed, facing the doorway. Bobby Briggs's ape-like face morphed into Chris Novak's then Blair Samms's and eventually the smiling Everett Harrison – Shay Hanlon's man. His surroundings began to lose their density, becoming a milky swirl. He placed his hands either side of him on the bed to steady himself, waiting for the feeling to pass. His mouth felt dry, but he lacked the energy to go to the sink for some water. After a while, everything began to stabilise, everything but his heart rate. When Samms passed his doorway, Rebus called to him and said he wanted to book a phone call.

'It'll be tomorrow now,' Samms warned him, but Rebus shook his head.

115

'Tell the governor it has to be today.'

'The governor's a busy man.'

'Just tell him, will you?' Rebus tried to sound less irritated than he felt. He could sense a headache starting behind both temples.

Samms headed off, giving no indication of whether he'd do as Rebus asked. Rebus knew he could always beg Christie for another burner, but he was damned if he'd do that, especially with Christie pissed off about the last one. Could Esson wait to hear what Novak had told him? She was probably still in the building. He could always demand to be taken to her, but then that would get everybody interested. Interested and curious. There was a killer somewhere in this place, almost certainly someone Rebus knew. The governor had come to his cell to talk to him, Malcolm Fox of OCCTU had summoned him to the governor's office for a cosy chat, and Christine Esson had welcomed him to Pastoral Care. Rebus's head was already well above the parapet. He would be patient, wait for word that he could make the phone call, play it safe.

Aye, John. Safe as any sitting duck. He forced himself to his feet, feeling the sudden need to be anywhere but this cell. He walked down the hall towards the body of the kirk. Darryl Christie was there, as were Mark Jamieson – still not looking a hundred per cent – and the Wizard and Ratty and Billy Groam. They all seemed interested in Rebus as he approached. So too did Valerie Watts, who was chewing gum as she patrolled, one hand on the two-way clipped to her shoulder. Someone was whistling the Amy Winehouse song, as they always did when Watts was on duty.

Any one of you, Rebus said silently to himself. Any one of you ...

An hour later, he had his phone call. He unfolded the slip of paper and tapped in Esson's mobile number. The usual recorded voice warned that calls would be monitored.

116

'I'm driving,' Esson said when she answered.

'But not with your DI in the passenger seat?'

'How can you tell?'

'You've got me on speakerphone. Are you on your way back to the station?'

'Yes.'

'Tell me, have you interviewed Blair Samms yet?'

'Twice.'

'Get any sort of a feeling from him?'

'What sort of feeling?'

'You've got antennae, Christine, same as Siobhan, same as me. They didn't twitch at all?'

'Tell me why they should.'

He listened to the clicking as she signalled to turn at a junction. He wondered how his old Saab was doing, garaged at a specialist place in Wardie. 'It's just, I heard he might be on the take.'

'Who told you that?'

'I'm not at liberty to say.'

'You're not at *liberty* full stop, John.' She was beginning to sound annoyed. 'What did I tell you about keeping stuff back from the investigation?'

'You said it was a fine and noble tradition? Besides, here I am doing exactly as asked, sharing information.'

She was silent for a moment, then gave an audible sigh. 'Blair Samms?' she checked.

'That's the one,' Rebus confirmed.

'I'll add him to the mix.'

'Oh, I meant to say – I like your new partner. Total ray of sunshine, he is.'

'He's a good detective.'

'He'll be wondering if he can say the same about you after he walked in on us.'

'Already forgotten. Listen, I have to go.'

'Best of luck, Christine. I mean that.'

'Thanks, John,' she said, ending the call.

*

117

Ten minutes later, when Esson walked into MIT, she saw Malcolm Fox standing in the middle of the floor, Mae McGovern facing him with arms folded. Esson walked over to them.

'Hello, Christine,' Fox said.

'DI Fox has just been telling me that the two of you have worked together in the past,' McGovern said stonily.

'Only at arm's length,' Esson felt it necessary to qualify.

'Well,' McGovern went on, 'he's here today to give us the benefit of his expertise.'

'And what expertise is that?' Esson enquired, eliciting a forced laugh from Fox.

'Same old Christine,' he said, while the two women exchanged a look.

Esson could tell McGovern wasn't entirely thrilled by Fox's presence. Easy to perceive it as a hint that Police Scotland's upper echelons felt MIT needed their hands holding. Shah and Allbright were all but hiding behind their computer screens.

'I've just been explaining to DI Fox,' McGovern said, 'that progress is being made in the case at a rate we're satisfied with.'

'Absolutely,' Esson said.

'Please, call me Malcolm,' Fox told McGovern.

'But he's keen to be taken through the various stages so far – maybe you could facilitate that, Christine?'

'I could, but I do think my time would be better spent on the case itself.' Esson glanced in the direction of the two DCs in the room, but McGovern wasn't minded to take the hint.

'That's settled then,' she said, turning away.

Left alone with Fox, Esson was relieved when Jason Mulgrew walked through the door.

'This is my DI,' she told Fox. 'Jason, Malcolm here's from Gartcosh.'

'We met briefly at the locus,' Fox said, holding out a hand for Mulgrew to shake.

'Good to see you again,' Mulgrew said. 'What is it we can do for you?'

'Just walk me through the investigation,' Fox replied.

'That won't take long – we've not made much headway.'

'Actually,' Esson said, 'that's not strictly true. Less than an hour ago, I got word that one of the night shift, an officer called Samms, might be worth an additional check.'

'Oh?' Fox nudged.

'He could be on the take.'

'Interesting,' he drawled. 'Money from Darryl Christie, you mean?'

Esson gave a shrug.

'Christie manages to run the city from a jail cell,' Fox went on. 'Much easier to do that if he can rely on messenger boys – either a prison officer or civilian staff.'

'This is the first I'm hearing of Officer Samms,' Mulgrew said. 'Did it come from your chum Rebus?'

'It might have.'

'And when were you going to tell me?'

'I just did,' Esson said, hackles rising.

'So you've been talking to our old friend John?' Fox's eyes were on her.

'Bumped into one another, apparently,' Mulgrew stated. 'Supposedly had a chat about things in general but specifically *not* the murder.'

Fox was still staring at Esson. 'So this man Samms was mentioned, but not Darryl Christie or Everett Harrison?'

'You're interested in Harrison, aren't you?' Mulgrew asked Fox. 'Christine mentioned the connection between him and the victim.'

'She told you the information came from me?'

'I don't keep secrets, Malcolm,' Esson said darkly. 'Always better when things are out in the open, don't you agree?'

'Absolutely.' He paused. 'Most of the time, at least.' When he smiled, Mulgrew did the same.

'Jason,' Esson said, 'maybe you'd like to show Malcolm the CCTV footage?'

'You might find it interesting,' Mulgrew told Fox. 'Two of the POs go walkabout – allegedly to the loo.'

'Is Samms one of them?'

Mulgrew shook his head. 'Timeline is proving interesting, though – they're AWOL for a good long while.'

'I have another possible name for you,' Fox added. 'Bobby Briggs. He's in another hall, but he's friends with Harrison and has a notably short fuse.'

'I doubt anyone from outside Trinity Hall could have done this,' Esson felt it necessary to say. 'But then the murder's not really what interests you, is it?'

Fox decided not to rise to her bait. Instead, he pressed his hand lightly to Mulgrew's forearm. 'Lead the way to this camera footage,' he said. 'And please, do call me Malcolm ...'

9

In the days before Police Scotland, the country had been served by eight regional forces, Lothian and Borders being one. Its headquarters was a tall concrete and glass box located on Fettes Avenue. Back then, this building had housed CEOP, the Child Exploitation and Online Protection division, but now Fettes was little more than a warehouse, and one with crumbling walls. There was talk of razing it to the ground and replacing it with housing, but nothing had happened as yet. CEOP no longer lived there; in fact, as far as Siobhan Clarke could ascertain, it was no longer a Scottish concern, falling instead under the jurisdiction of the National Crime Agency in London. Eventually she'd been connected to a single officer in the Scottish Crime Campus at Gartcosh, Lanarkshire. Detective Sergeant Louise Hird had given her a twenty-minute window, starting at 11.30 a.m.

Traffic west out of Edinburgh was the usual crawl, spray from other vehicles meaning she spent every other minute clearing the windscreen. She didn't relish the prospect of a visit to Malcolm Fox's domain and the HQ of Professional Standards. No happy memories there, but at least she was used to the protocols at the well-guarded gatehouse – not at all dissimilar to those at Rebus's prison. She waited in the airy

121

atrium, refusing eye contact and hoping not to be recognised by colleagues she had effectively snubbed.

DS Hird looked to be no older than her mid twenties. Only the set of her jaw and the slight glaze to her eyes hinted at the things she probably saw each and every day. She was dressed fashionably – a red skirt that ended above her knees, sheer black tights, olive-green blouse. Around her neck dangled all the electronic passes she needed to gain access to the inner core of the building. Her hair was cropped and reddish-gold. Her freckled face didn't quite manage a smile as she held out a hand for Clarke to shake.

'The prodigal returns,' she said.

'I was hoping I might have been airbrushed out of the picture.'

'Gartcosh never forgets.' Hird gestured towards the stairs and led Clarke up a level. 'I know you're probably thinking we could have done this on the phone, but I prefer face-to-face.'

'What I'm actually thinking is that we used to have a whole office at Fettes dedicated to kids at risk.'

'And now all the poor mites have is me.' Hird turned her head to meet Clarke's eyes. 'Efficiency savings.'

'So you work for the NCA?'

'I work for the victims.' Hird was taking brisk strides towards a door, Clarke just about keeping up. She risked a glance across the expansive stairwell to where Internal Affairs had its suite of offices.

'You're quite safe with me,' Hird commented. 'Besides, I've not seen Malcolm today.'

Clarke followed her into a small room, its glass walls covered by blinds that were probably kept closed at all times. There was nothing on display – no photos of predators or victims; no notes or lists of names. A single locked cabinet stood in one corner and a solitary desk in the middle of the room. There was a printer, a cable straggling from it, but nothing else, other than a biro and a blank pad of paper. Hird sat down and gestured for Clarke to take the only other chair.

'I'm sorry,' she said, 'we should have stopped at the coffee counter.'

'I had something on the way here,' Clarke said.

Hird nodded, seeming satisfied, and unlocked her desk drawer, sliding out a slim notebook computer and opening it up. Clarke noticed that she locked the drawer again afterwards. She tried not to think about what might be lurking within, just out of sight.

'The bad news is,' Hird was saying as she typed, 'it's a new one to me so there's not much I can tell you.' She paused for a moment before turning the screen towards Clarke. It was displaying the homepage of Young Fresh East Coast. 'They come and they go. The set-up is usually very similar. Sometimes it's even a boyfriend behind the camera.'

'Jasmine's friends think she might have been seeing someone after school. Nobody knows who.'

But Hird was shaking her head. 'Too many on the roster, and both sexes. A bit more organisation required. Therefore not just a persuasive boyfriend with a money-making idea.' She gnawed at her lip as she played with the homepage.

'I've been able to track down one punter,' Clarke explained. 'He couldn't tell me much either. Seems to think the site's gone dead.'

Hird peered over the screen towards Clarke. 'Easier if you bring your chair here.' While Clarke moved it, Hird shifted along a little. She circled the cursor on Jazz's thumbnail. 'This is your misper?'

'That's her,' Clarke stated.

'Wild child, is she?'

'I don't get a sense of that.'

'A quiet one then, easily led?'

'Maybe. Family life is ... Well, the father spends a good deal of time elsewhere, and his relationship with Jasmine's mother could be described as feisty.' Clarke leaned forward, pointing towards the photos. 'I really need to know where this is. What are the chances of making that happen?'

Hird puffed out her cheeks. 'Slim,' she eventually conceded. 'I'll give it to London, but it might take a while. They can definitely decrypt the facial features. But as for following the trail back from the IP address ... You don't know any teenage hackers, do you? They'd probably have about as much luck. The thing about the online world is, the scrotes are cleverer than us and at least three steps ahead. As soon as the internet was born, porn was right there astride it, every taste catered for and no questions asked.'

'But to get ordinary teenagers to do this sort of thing ...'

'I assume you don't know many teenagers? They've grown up exhibiting themselves for the benefit of a screen, craving all those heart emojis. Most of them will have seen worse than this after a couple of clicks.' Hird looked at Clarke. 'I'm assuming all they're doing is stripping and touching themselves?'

'The punter mentioned twosomes.'

'So far, so low-level.'

'He also said the performers never meet the clients – but I'm guessing that sometimes occurs?'

'You think that's what's happened to Jasmine? Found herself a sugar daddy?'

'Is it likely?' Clarke's throat felt dry.

'Probably not without the agreement of whoever's behind the camera. If we can access the clips, we can maybe hear him speak. Doubtful, though – it shatters the illusion that it's just the paying customer and the performer.'

Hird clicked on the speaker icon and turned up the volume.

'I'm horny as hell. Please choose me. I'll do anything your heart desires.'

'They all say the same thing,' Clarke commented.

'It's definitely her voice?'

'I've yet to check.'

Hird nodded. 'Not the easiest conversation to have with the parents.'

'I know.' Clarke leaned forward a little. 'You've come across

124

this set-up before – can you think of people with previous who might be who I'm looking for?'

Hird shrugged. 'Jasmine is in Edinburgh, but what about the others? I mean, could she have travelled to Fife or Glasgow, maybe even Newcastle?'

'It says it's East Coast.'

'Doesn't really mean anything. I once saw a porn film with the word Swedish in the title. First thing I noticed was a car with a German number plate. Ruined the whole thing.'

Clarke managed a weak smile. 'The voices all sound fairly local.'

Hird listened to a couple of them, then lifted the pen and tapped it against her cheek. 'We do have a roll-call of past and present offenders. I can pull it up and see if anyone looks likely. But I know for a fact none of them are Edinburgh-based. Sure you don't want a coffee? I could do with one.'

'Okay then.'

She slapped shut her computer and locked it back in its drawer. 'I'm glad you brought me this. It's actually refreshing.'

'Refreshing?'

'They're usually a lot younger – sorry to be so blunt.'

'I don't know how you can do it.'

'The usual answer is: someone has to.' Hird gestured for Clarke to exit the room in front of her, turning to lock the door after them. 'I get sessions with a counsellor – and the posting only lasts a year or so, with a promotion soon after.' She sucked in some air as she walked towards the coffee counter, where a male barista was busy at the gleaming machine. 'But the first answer I gave you,' she said, 'that gets to the nub of it really, even though it sometimes seems we're trying to push back a tsunami with a handful of sweeping brushes. Will cappuccino do you?'

'Cappuccino is fine,' Clarke said quietly.

They took their drinks to one of the breakout booths, where they wouldn't be overheard. A few passing officers nodded or waved a greeting in Hird's direction. Both women concentrated on their drinks for the best part of a minute, then Hird sniffed and cleared her throat.

'The internet has normalised stuff that would have been off limits two generations back. Girls like Jasmine are bombarded with it. Boys at her school won't have any problem with choking, anal, spitting. And if a girl complains ...' She gave a shrug. 'You've accessed her phone and computer, checked her socials?'

'It's under way.'

'Guy operating the camera could have met her that way – cajoled her and flattered her.'

'Paid her, too – friends say she's been flush of late.'

'No radical mood changes? Absences noticed by her parents?' It was Clarke's turn to shrug. 'It's just that drugs are often part of the equation, keep the performers docile.' Hird took another sip of coffee. 'What have you done about this punter you identified?'

'He basically identified himself – went to a reporter and wanted money for his story.'

'Nice.'

'But to answer your question, I've left him dangling.'

'And sweating, too, I hope?'

'What's the best I should be hoping for here, Louise?'

'Best case, she comes waltzing home unharmed. Like you say, a client could have whisked her off to the south of France for a good pampering.'

'Ever known that to happen?'

'No.'

'I really need to get to whoever's running the operation.'

'I promise I'll talk to London. I wish I could say it'll be a high priority, but ...'

Another passing detective nodded towards Hird, but then seemed to place Clarke and did a double-take before heading in the direction of Professional Standards.

'That's you been clocked,' Hird said.

Clarke drained her cardboard cup. 'I need to be going anyway. Thanks again for seeing me.'

'But you hope we never have reason to meet again – right?'

'Professionally anyway.' The two women shook hands. As Clarke was descending the staircase, she glanced back and saw Louise Hird making her way to her locked office and its drawers filled with nightmares.

Silently she wished the young woman well.

Music kept her mind off things as she left Gartcosh and headed towards the motorway. But her mood remained solemn, not helped by a phone call from the station, Cammy Colson filling her in on the lack of discernible progress in her absence, his funereal pace of delivery adding to the gloom.

'We've cracked her computer password,' he said, 'but there's not a lot for us in there. All her social media must be on her phone. Mobile provider tells us she still hasn't used it. I'd say that's ominous. There's no tracker on the phone either – another dead end. Hope you had better luck at Gartcosh.'

'Not really, Cammy, not really ...'

The sky above was a bruised layer of low, heavy cloud. It seemed to press down on the car, meaning that even with her foot down, she seemed to have the most sluggish possible acceleration. She'd considered phoning ahead to alert Jasmine's parents to her visit but had decided against it. It was always more interesting to catch people unprepared. When her phone rang again, she saw Christine Esson's name on the screen.

'I hope you're going to cheer me up,' Clarke said, answering.

'Depends whether you think Malcolm Fox is a laughing matter or not.'

'What's happened?'

'He's right here in the MIT room, cosying up to Jason Mulgrew.'

'Wondered why you were keeping your voice down. Have you tried telling him to piss off?'

'From the look on Mae McGovern's face, someone above her pay grade has okayed it.'

'Meaning Fox's bosses at Gartcosh. Funnily enough, I've just been there.'

'Oh?'

'Jasmine was modelling on a porn site.'

'That complicates matters. You took it to CEOP?'

'If by that you mean did I take it to a single solitary over-worked officer, the answer is yes.'

'Helpful?'

'Too early to tell.'

'Are you going to go public with it?'

'Not yet. Don't want those involved scurrying back under their various rocks.'

'What's the site called?'

'Young Fresh East Coast.'

'Hang on ...' Clarke listened as Esson tapped at her keyboard. 'Yeah, I'm looking at it.'

'Her photo's top row right.'

'None of the other models have come forward?'

'Would you?'

'If she was my friend, too right.' Esson paused. 'God's sake ...'

'What is it?'

'I think Fox and Jason are discussing "going for a jar". It's like I've tuned in to *The Likely Lads* or something.'

'I can't unsee that image.' Clarke began to laugh, sloughing off some of the tension.

'Or maybe *Steptoe and Son* would be more accurate,' Esson added.

'You're not old enough to have lived through either of those, Christine.'

'They've been huddled at Jason's computer for almost an hour. Fox probably knows more about the case right now than I do.'

'I very much doubt that. But I take it there've been no breakthroughs to report?'

'The square root of nada. I suppose I better go try to earn my keep. Another drink soon?'

'Going for a jar, you mean? Yes, let's do that. Bye, Christine.'
'Ciao.'

Clarke ended the call and put the music back on. The sat-nav told her she'd be at the Andrews house in under twenty minutes, but then the satnav didn't know Edinburgh and its roadworks like she did.

Both cars were still in the driveway. It was lunchtime, and James Andrews was chewing a mouthful of sandwich as he answered the door. He stared at her for a moment, then swallowed.

'They don't give up, do they? I'll get the apology done when my head's back in the game.'

'This isn't about Craig Fielding, Mr Andrews.'

Her tone alerted him that there was news, and not the good kind.

'I'll fetch Helena. She's in the kitchen ...'

Clarke was seated in the living room by the time husband and wife returned. Helena Andrews was brushing crumbs from her loose-knit jumper. Clarke gestured towards the sofa, and they complied, settling side by side.

'So?' James asked nervously.

'Nothing bad's happened,' Clarke reassured them, 'but there's something I need to share with you and I want you to be prepared.' She slid the computer from her shoulder bag and opened it. Without saying anything, she played the recording while keeping the screen hidden from view. Afterwards, husband and wife shared a look. Helena's mouth fell open and she placed her fingertips to her lips.

'I don't ...'

James Andrews had risen to his feet, heading towards Clarke with the intention of viewing the screen. She folded it shut.

'Is it Jasmine's voice?' she asked.

'I think so,' Helena blurted out. 'But those words ... I don't ...'

129

'AI,' her husband growled. 'You can fake anything these days. Someone's idea of a joke.'

'It's a website.' Clarke kept her voice level. 'People pay to watch teenagers perform.'

Helena Andrews' face folded in on itself. 'You're saying Jasmine was ...? That's ridiculous. Why would she do something like that?'

'Spite,' her husband answered. 'One way to get back at you.' He turned his attention to Clarke, looming over her. 'Is this why she's done a runner? Someone was about to shame her or blackmail her?'

'We don't know as yet.'

'It's a bloody good motive, though.' He gripped at his hair for a moment, as if about to yank some out. 'Who's behind it? Just give me a name.'

'James,' his wife cautioned, but Andrews waved this aside.

'Because if I catch them before you do ...' He stabbed a finger directly in Clarke's face.

'You're already on a warning, Mr Andrews.'

'Just because they used her voice,' Helena persisted, 'it doesn't mean it goes any further than that.'

'One of the site's users identified Jasmine,' Clarke explained.

'I hope you've got him in the cells,' James Andrews snarled.

'Look,' she ploughed on, 'this has come as a shock to you – of course it has – but I need you to think it over carefully. Maybe there were times Jasmine went out and wouldn't say where she was going, maybe messages she received or calls she took in her room, a name or address she let slip ...'

'That slippery little bastard across the fence,' Andrews said. 'Filming her in her bedroom, I'll bet. Tells her it's just between them, then goes and sticks it online!'

'It's not her bedroom,' Clarke corrected him.

'His, then!'

She shook her head slowly. 'We've spoken to Craig. He's currently not suspected of anything. And if you're thinking of confronting him, I'd strongly advise against it.'

'Of course it's not Craig,' Helena stated. 'He's a good kid.' She had risen to her feet and was walking to the window that faced the rear garden and the houses beyond.

'Someone obviously talked her into it, persuaded her – maybe for a dare or something.' James Andrews was staring at the back of his wife's head. 'What's that girl called? The cocky one?'

'Carla,' his wife responded.

'Yes, Carla. Right little madam, as we used to say.' He turned towards Clarke's computer. 'Is *she* on that thing?'

Clarke ignored the question. 'When we get pertinent information, we will of course share it with you.'

'Jas must have known she couldn't keep it secret for ever – porn's everywhere online and teenage boys probably hoover up more of it than most.'

'You seem well informed,' his wife muttered, half turning her head in his direction.

'Common knowledge, that's all.'

But Clarke noted the colour creeping up his face.

'What's the site called?' Helena was asking, turning away from the window, arms folded.

'That has to remain confidential for now,' Clarke told her.

'But it has photos ... videos of Jasmine?'

'We'll know more in due course. Right now, all anyone scrolling can see is a pixelated face.'

'But the voice is clear enough,' Helena said quietly, tears forming in her eyes.

'Whoever controls the site ...' her husband began, 'say she decided not to do any more ... say she told them she was going to the authorities ...'

'Christ, James.' Helena squeezed her eyes shut and pinched the bridge of her nose between finger and thumb.

'She's underage – they must have known that. How many more on that bloody contraption of yours? How many more kids like Jasmine?' His voice was shaking.

Clarke placed the computer back in her bag and stood up.

131

She made show of checking her phone, as though some urgent message had just appeared on its blank screen.

'If you can think of anything that might be of help ...' The sentence drifted off. She began to make for the front door and the safer world beyond.

'A fucking kid,' James Andrews was telling her. 'Taken advantage of. Abused. And your lot do fuck all about it. I swear I don't know how you can sleep at night.'

Clarke knew there were things she could say, things that would include CEOP and the National Crime Agency and the haunted face of Louise Hird. But she knew too that none of it would help in this moment, to this parent. But Andrews wasn't quite done with her. He stood in the doorway, one arm outstretched, finger pointed in her direction as she unlocked her car, pulled her seat belt around her and started the engine. When she risked a glance from the window, he was shaking his head slowly, judging her with absolute finality.

She switched the music back on and drove.

After a few hours at Gayfield Square, Fox felt he was beginning to be accepted. DC Paul Allbright had made him a mug of tea – terrible, weak tea, but Fox had sipped it as though he'd never tasted anything better – and DC Zara Shah had talked him through the search of the prison buildings and grounds. The night-shift officers were the focus of another investigative strand, but there were no signs as yet of sudden windfalls or big-ticket purchases. The interview transcripts and recordings told their own stories, each one leading to a brick wall. Fox had concentrated on officers Novak, Watts and Samms, but also on the chats with Darryl Christie and Everett Harrison. Those had been perfunctory at best, and he wished he could have been there to spice things up. He noted that Rebus had yet to be formally questioned and reckoned that was because he'd already said his piece to Christine Esson in private.

He had also found out a little more about Bobby Briggs.

Briggs had done a bit of work down the years for a Govan-based criminal called Mickey Mason – security, mostly. Time was, Mason had been a boxing promoter, Briggs paid to keep order at ringside or on the door. To Fox, the interesting thing was that Mickey Mason had recently been released from HMP Barlinnie after a short stretch for benefit fraud. According to intelligence, he was quickly settling back into his old ways, including ensuring a steady supply of drugs on the streets of suburban Glasgow. Fox didn't know what to do with this, but he could see possible links in a chain – a chain that might end with Shay Hanlon hanging from it like a precious stone.

When his phone rang, it was a colleague at OCCTU, a detective sergeant called Stevie Hodge. Fox leaned back in his borrowed chair.

'What can I do for you, Stevie?'

While he listened, he tried to keep his face neutral, aware that Shah and Allbright were nearby, Esson and Mulgrew having gone to their boss's office for a powwow – or, much more likely, to tell her everything Fox had been up to since arriving at MIT. Having ended the call, he rose to his feet and began to put his jacket on, without looking as though he was in any particular hurry.

'Tell the parents not to wait up,' he informed Shah and Allbright, gesturing in the vague direction of Mae McGovern's office. Once in the corridor, his pace increased. He exited to the car park, got into his car, stuck an address into the satnav and hit the accelerator. -

Stevie Hodge was waiting for him, parked kerbside on a quiet street of semi-detached Victorian houses in Mayfield. Fox climbed out of his own car and into Hodge's BMW. Hodge was in his early thirties, stocky and crop-haired, sporting a recent moustache, which he had taken to stroking as if it were a pet.

'Tell me again,' Fox commanded.

'Witness is out shopping. Supermarket car park. There's a car leaving, but a motorbike stops in front of it, blocking it. Rider gets off, pulls a pistol from his leathers and points it at the driver's-side window. Indicates for the driver to lower the window, which he does. Biker says something, then walks back to the bike and hoofs it. Our witness – a Mrs Clarkson, age fifty-three – didn't get much of a description of the bike or the rider, but when the car left its parking bay, she clocked the licence plate. Racing-green Jaguar F-Pace, registered to a certain Jake Morris at this address.' Hodge gestured through the windscreen. 'It's parked four cars further along.'

'And as we both know,' Fox drawled, 'Jake Morris is one of Darryl Christie's lads.'

'Very much a senior lieutenant,' Hodge confirmed.

'Are we getting CCTV from the car park?'

'For what it's worth – biker kept his helmet on throughout.'

'And Mrs Clarkson didn't hear what was said?'

'She did not.'

'Well, I suppose we better go and ask, then ...'

When they rang the bell, a chain slid across the door before it was opened from within, a woman's eyes visible through the gap. Fox showed her his ID.

'Could we have a word with Mr Morris, please?'

'He's not here.' The woman's eyes were heavily made-up, the hair jet-black and piled atop her head. She sounded English.

'When will he be back?'

'He's gone to visit family. In Yorkshire.'

'Sudden decision, was it? We notice his car's parked just along there.'

'Look, what do you want?'

'It'd be easier to speak inside.'

'I've only got your word for it that you're police.' She nodded towards Fox's ID. 'Anyone can fake a thing like that these days.'

Fox was digging into his wallet. He held a business card into the gap below the door chain. As she made to take it, he pulled it back. 'What are you scared of, Mrs Morris?'

'Who said I was scared?'

'Please tell Jake we want to help if we can.'

134

She took the card from him and studied it for a moment.

'At first I thought it was to do with Jasmine,' she said. 'When you said you were police.'

'Jasmine Andrews?'

He watched the woman nod. 'My daughter Carla's her best friend. She's worried sick.'

Fox tried for a sympathetic look. 'And now this ...'

Her face was giving nothing away. 'This what?'

'Jake having to scarper.'

'I told you, he's visiting family.'

'Maybe you could give me their address?'

But she was already closing the door on the two detectives.

'Remember, we want to help,' Fox said, raising his voice so she'd be sure to hear. He left the doorstep and took a couple of paces onto the lawn, but the living-room window had a net curtain across it, and there was no sign of movement within. So he headed to the pavement and approached the Jaguar. Its interior was giving nothing away.

'Taxed and insured,' Hodge commented.

'A nice law-abiding family,' Fox said quietly. He was thinking of the daughter, best friends with the missing girl. Could be something or nothing. He reckoned Siobhan Clarke might well find it of at least *some* interest.

But then again – why should he tell her?

Why indeed? he said to himself.

'So what do you reckon?' Hodge was asking.

'A falling-out among thieves?' Fox speculated. 'Or else a new player emerging.'

Which was why, though he wouldn't be sharing it with Siobhan Clarke any time soon, he would definitely be calling Thomas Glaze in London.

Glaze, he knew, would be interested. Interested *and* grateful ...

10

Rebus had been watching Blair Samms as best he could while the officer worked the day shift. This hadn't escaped Ratty's attention – very little did. He sidled over to Rebus and stood beside him as Rebus rested against the wall near his cell.

'Has he done something?' he asked in an undertone, scratching his nose to further muffle his words.

'What makes you think that?' Rebus kept his eyes on Samms as he spoke.

'You've got a sniper's look about you.'

'Is it that obvious?'

'You're actually doing a good job of acting casual. Proof of that is that Samms hasn't noticed you scoping him out.'

'What do you hear about him, Ratty?'

'Samms? No particular beef with anybody. Clocks on and clocks off. Bit of a closed book.'

'Doesn't do favours for anyone?'

'Bringing stuff in, you mean?' Ratty watched Rebus give an almost imperceptible nod. He rubbed at his nose again, thoughtfully this time. 'We all know it goes on.'

'But do we know who's doing it?'

'The good ones keep it well hidden.'

'I've heard the stories – get recruited, do the training, spend a while working for both sides, then skedaddle.'

'That's what you think Samms's game is?'

Rebus's mouth twitched. 'You heard anything new about Jackie?'

'Just that forensics found plenty fingerprints and DNA in his cell, belonging to cons and POs both. Stands to reason: Jackie was a popular guy, people liked to hang out with him.'

'And how do you come to know all this?'

'I keep in with the cleaning crew. They happened to be passing the governor's office ...'

Rebus nodded his understanding. 'A word with you in private,' he said, heading for his cell. He positioned himself by his desk, Ratty arriving a few moments later. 'Best leave the door open. Looks less suspicious that way.'

'You've got me worried.' Ratty gave a nervous grin.

'Any particular reason for that?'

'What's going on, John? Am I in trouble here?'

'You tell me.'

Ratty looked like he was thinking about it. Then he shook his head. 'Thought we were pals,' he commented.

'We are. But you work the kitchen and the serving-up.'

'You not getting enough? Want me to sneak you some rations? Watts and Samms keep tabs on everything, but I can see if—'

'And there's nothing you can tell me about either of them?'

'Not that I can think of.'

'How about the rest of the team – Devo and Malachi?'

'Fuck's going on here, John?'

'Mark Jamieson reckons he might've been slipped something the night he was KO'd. Either in his meal or his tea.'

Ratty gave a snort. 'He's covering his arse. Guy was self-medicated to the max and he knows how that's going to look in dispatches.' His eyes narrowed, making him appear more rat-like than ever. 'Maybe it was me, eh, John? That the way your thinking's headed? Why not just ask me flat out?'

'Because I've no real reason not to trust you. You've been decent to me. So I'm asking – Watts, Samms, Devo and Malachi. If one of them was spiking someone, who would your money be on?'

Ratty fell silent, moving to the chair and slumping down on it, elbows on knees, hands clasped. Samms passed outside, walking with the usual studied determination. He saw Ratty and his eyes moved to Rebus. Rebus pinched the fingers of one hand together and made an extravagant sign of the cross, as if he were taking Ratty's confession. Samms got the reference and grinned, moving on. Rebus hoped he'd continue to take it as a joke, or better still forget about it altogether.

Ratty looked up but saw only the empty doorway. 'Devo,' he said quietly. 'I'm not saying he did it, I can't for the life of me think he did. But if I had to choose.'

'And why him?'

'Partly because he was serving up that night. Serving the meat and gravy, I mean. Easier to plant something in that gloop without it being noticed by the person eating it. Potatoes and carrots – you'd notice, wouldn't you? Pudding was tinned fruit and ice cream – again, hard to spike without it being obvious.'

'How about the mugs of tea?'

'Well, you couldn't do the whole urn, could you?'

'Fair point,' Rebus conceded. 'The officers couldn't have intervened at any point?'

Ratty answered with a shrug.

'Tell me about Devo,' Rebus went on.

'What's to tell? Stole blind from everyone he ever met, including his gran and grandad. Been inside more than he's been out. Caught on CCTV lifting the charity tin from an Oxfam counter.'

'Who's he pals with?'

'Everybody and nobody.'

'Everett Harrison?'

'Most of us like to keep a respectful distance from Big H.' Ratty stared at Rebus. 'Why are you breaking your back on this?'

138

'It's what I do.'

'Trying to shift suspicion from Novak and his mates?'

'If that was the plan, you've just been a big help.'

'How?'

'By not fingering Watts or Samms.'

Ratty thought about this. 'Aye, right enough,' he conceded.

'Which is why I know I can trust you – you told the truth as you saw it, didn't try to frame a PO.'

'I'm a fool to myself,' Ratty said with a thin smile.

'Think you could maybe have a quiet word with Malachi, see if he saw anything during service that day? Without making it too obvious, I mean.'

'Might not be easy. Malachi's pretty bright. He'll soon suss the whys and the wherefores.'

Rebus had moved closer to the door, signalling that the meeting was over. 'I'd appreciate it,' he said. As Ratty made to pass him, he placed a hand against his shoulder. 'One last thing,' he said. 'If you *do* ever get hold of those extra rations ...'

'One Tunnock's equals two ciggies,' Ratty explained.

'I don't smoke, though.'

He swept the cell's interior with his eyes. 'Maybe a nebuliser, then. I can always find a use for a nebuliser ...'

After Ratty had gone, Rebus lay on his bed for a while with his forearm across his eyes. It was something you never thought about on the outside – the control you had over such simple everyday things as switching a light on or off. In here, someone else held sway. He reckoned that was one reason why ex-cons sometimes found life afterwards hard to adjust to. How the hell did you plan meals or do the shopping required – all those shelves, all those choices to be made?

Others, of course, took to prison life as if born to it, a simple extension of the schools or other institutions they'd known throughout the course of their lives. Rebus himself had gone straight from school to the army and from there to police training, but always with questions and never quite happy to blindly follow the rules and regs. He'd survived his share of

139

disciplinaries and reckoned he'd managed never to become just a cog, serving a function dictated from elsewhere in the machinery. If he'd wanted a quiet life he'd have refused the move to the general prison population, but the quiet life wasn't really his thing, never had been. All the same, he knew he wasn't the man he had been. More aches and pains, less likely to win any physical contest. Which was why, even with eyes closed, his ears remained alert to danger. Briggs would have been checking. Soon enough he'd be ready to call Rebus out on his spurious relationship with Shay Hanlon. That meant being watchful during free flow. But even here in Trinity Hall, there was Everett Harrison to consider. He was close to Briggs. So far he'd taken Rebus's side, but that might change at any moment – and he was only a cell away, a cell directly across from Jackie Simpson's. Jackie Simpson, whose misadventures had led to Harrison's sentencing.

Rebus could see it. An officer on the take; the unlocking of Harrison's cell; padding across the floor to where the same officer was opening Simpson's door; Mark Jamieson out for the count; a towel stuffed into Simpson's mouth and his throat cut.

How long would the whole thing have taken? Two or three minutes tops. Then the clean-up – bloodied clothing placed in a bag, to be carried out of the prison at shift's end, along with the murder weapon. Rebus knew that ceramic knives could be smuggled in, no metal detectors triggered. CCTV would have caught someone leaving Harrison's cell, but then CCTV could be wiped or altered, couldn't it?

Neat and tidy, and with the night-shift POs firmly in the frame ...

'A penny for them.'

He flinched at the voice, swinging his legs off the bed.

'Easy there,' Novak said from the doorway. 'Didn't mean to scare you.'

'Who said I was scared?'

'Just a convincing impression then.' He took a couple of steps into the cell, pulling the door until it was open only a few inches. He dropped his voice a level when he spoke. 'Blair Samms tells me you had Ratty in here earlier. Got him working for you?'

'I was just taking confession.'

'Aye, that tickled Samms.' Novak turned the chair towards him and settled on it.

'Say Samms *was* in somebody's pocket,' Rebus said, 'who would your bet be?'

'Darryl's the obvious answer. But then there's always Shay Hanlon's buddy.'

'Meaning Harrison?'

'Meaning Big H,' Novak confirmed. 'But there are probably others, too.'

'I've been hearing of threats against officers – not just here, but other jails. Your car went up in flames, but has there been anything else?'

Novak considered for a moment before replying. 'Drive-bys in the middle of the night, horns blaring. A dead cat lobbed over the garden fence. My wife even found a note in her trolley when she reached the supermarket till.'

'What did it say?'

'"Play nice."'

'Just that?'

'Just that.' Novak shifted on the chair. 'Could be something or nothing.'

'No notes since that one?' Rebus watched Novak shake his head. 'What do you think it meant?'

'Turn a blind eye; if you're asked to do something, do it.'

'You're sure it was meant for you?'

'Not really.'

'And *have* you been asked to turn a blind eye?'

'Not as yet.'

'Told Esson and her team any of this?'

'What's the point? If anything, it just makes me the more likely suspect.'

'How about your CID cousin?'

141

'Cammy? He's a bit busy working crimes he's got half a chance of solving.'

'If I was playing devil's advocate,' Rebus said after a moment, 'I'd now be saying that there's only your word for it about these threats. Whole thing could be made up to make you look either innocent or a scapegoat.'

'You're a hard man to please.'

'Mark Jamieson reckons his supper that night could've been spiked. Ratty, Devo and Malachi were on duty, supervised by Watts and Samms – the man you reckon might be on the take.'

'Is that what you were asking Ratty about?'

'He more or less vouched for Watts and Samms.'

'Leaving Malachi and Devo – if you're ruling out Ratty himself.'

'Either of them look likely to you?'

'It's easily done, a bit of powder or a pill. If asked by the right person, I'd say neither of them would say no.'

'Can't say I've noticed them looking any different since that night.'

'It's not like the person asking would suddenly be filling their cell with strippers and booze.'

'No, but they'd probably find themselves part of that person's charmed circle.'

'I've seen no sign of it, but I'll definitely be keeping watch.'

'For what it's worth, Ratty reckons Devo is the most obvious candidate.'

Both men became aware of voices rising down the hall, their heads turning towards the disturbance. Novak sprinted from Rebus's cell and turned sharp left. Rebus wasn't far behind. Prisoners had huddled around the figure of Darryl Christie, their shouts blurring with his. Officers were wading in. It looked to Rebus as though some prisoners were bent on protecting Christie while others were trying to get to him. There was a stick of some kind, jutting up above the various heads. Rebus recognised it as a pool cue.

As he got closer, he saw that one end of the cue had been

forced into Everett Harrison's mouth. Harrison was gagging on it, face almost purple. He'd been forced to his knees and was trying to dislodge the cue with one hand while beating against Christie's forearm with the other. Two of Christie's lieutenants were pressing down on Harrison's shoulders. When someone threw a punch at an officer, the alarm sounded, more bodies arriving. There was a look on Christie's face that Rebus had witnessed once before; an intense, vibrant madness. Aided by the fresh slew of white shirts, Harrison managed to free himself of the pool cue, retching and holding a hand to his throat as he stumbled to safety. Rebus had no idea what had lit the actual fuse, but he knew something like it had been in the offing – all that anger and resentment at Jackie Simpson's death, all the uncertainty and the feeling that to the outside world none of it – and none of *them* – mattered very much.

Order was being restored, Christie dragged away towards the gate and the corridor beyond. He locked eyes with Rebus and smiled with his teeth. Harrison sat, knees pulled up to his chin, back against the wall near the pool table. He was being checked over by Samms and Novak. The gathered prisoners now looked hesitant – whose side should they take? Some turned towards the gate through which Darryl Christie had been led. Christie was a local and Christie had power, but Harrison worked for Shay Hanlon, and Hanlon, being a lesser-known quantity, had a touch of the mythic about him. Everyone knew what Darryl Christie could do, but Hanlon's capabilities were all in the realm of the imagination. The uncertainty loomed large on several faces. Men who had been spoiling for a fight – any fight – now seemed bewildered and lost. They returned to their cells without fuss while Harrison was helped to his feet. He didn't argue when it was suggested he be taken to the nurses' station. He seemed unwilling or unable to speak, and kept one hand cupped around his throat.

'What was that all about then?' one officer asked, but Harrison just shook his head. Billy Groam, Rebus's neighbour, wondered aloud if the pool cues would now be put into cold storage.

'Happened with the dartboard after that one time,' he muttered, more to himself than anyone.

'Let's all go back in our cells,' Novak was advising. 'Leave things to settle down.' He had his arms outstretched, ushering his charges into their quarters. Rebus stayed put on the threshold, and when Novak approached, he told him he needed to speak to Christie.

'Way beyond my pay grade, John,' Novak informed him.

'That's why I need you to take it to the governor.'

Novak stared at him. 'Governor's probably got more pressing concerns.'

'Despite which, I need you to ask him.'

'Owe you a favour, does he?'

Rather than answer, Rebus retreated to his bed, lying down again, but this time without shading his eyes. He kept them open, unblinking, as he stared towards and beyond the ceiling.

It was a further hour before Graves arrived at his door and announced that the boss needed to see him. As they crossed the hall, Rebus noted that the pool cues and balls had indeed been removed. As they neared Howard Tennent's office, the man himself emerged, locking the door after him.

'I'll take it from here,' he said to Graves. Then, watching the officer retreat the way he'd just come: 'Is this absolutely necessary, John?'

'Afraid so.'

'Am I allowed to ask why?'

'Maybe later.'

They began to walk. 'Making any headway?' Tennent eventually asked.

'Of sorts – mostly ruling stuff out, but that can be useful in itself.'

'What just happened with Darryl and Everett?'

'Search me.'

'Are you about to ask?' Tennent watched Rebus angle his

head slightly. He looked around, but there was no one within earshot. 'The police inquiry has stalled – no one's saying as much, but it's obvious. Only DI Fox seems still to have some fire in his belly.'

'Probably a curry disagreeing with him.'

'You don't rate him?'

'One-star reviews across the board.'

'Well, I like what I've seen of the man.'

'Stick with it, he'll soon disappoint you.' Rebus paused. 'Can I ask you something?'

Tennent glanced at him. 'What?'

'Do you ever hear anything about my appeal?'

The governor shook his head.

'You'd tell me if you did?' Rebus pressed on.

'Look, John, I don't think you should be in here any more than you do. But no one's going to tell me before they tell you.'

Tennent focused on unlocking yet another solid metal door. They were headed to SRU, where Rebus had spent his first three months. Solitary was part of this complex – two cells, neither of them roomy, each with a sink and toilet with no privacy, every ablution visible from the spyhole. No phones or TVs here, no kettles or bookshelves. A solid concrete ledge for a bed, with only a thin mattress and blanket. Plus a sliver of window so high up the wall it was rendered all but meaningless.

The officer in charge of the unit was waiting for them. He nodded a curt greeting to Rebus as he unlocked the door and pulled it open. Darryl Christie sat on the ledge, head bowed.

'You need to wait out here,' Rebus told Tennent as he stepped inside, pulling the door closed after him.

'You sound like you own the place,' Christie commented without raising his head.

'That would mean filling your shoes, Darryl. I'm not sure they'd fit.'

'I own the square root of fuck all, that's the truth of it.' Christie couldn't contain the bitterness spilling out of him.

'What's happened?'

145

Rebus waited, but all he received was a slow shake of the head. After half a minute, Christie's head shot up, his eyes fixing on to Rebus's. 'You and Malcolm Fox go back a ways, aye?'

'We've had our moments.'

'He's Organised Crime – wankers crawled all over me back in the day, phone taps, the lot. Far as I know, their hard-on's not gone away just because I have.'

'What's Organised Crime got to do with this?'

There was that smile again, that dangerous smile. 'Everything,' Christie stated.

'How long do I have to wait for you to bring up his name?'

'Whose?'

'Shay Hanlon.'

'That bastard,' Christie snarled.

'Harrison works for Hanlon. The two of you have always seemed amicable, but something's changed. You can't get to Hanlon, but you can have a go at the next best thing – so you did.'

'Were you this smart in school? Arm always shooting up to answer the teacher's question?'

'Actually, I was pretty average. Bunked off a lot. I've tried making up for it since.'

Christie had made his mind up. He checked over Rebus's shoulder that the door was closed, but even so he rose to his feet, leaning his mouth in towards Rebus's left ear.

'A couple of my guys have been got at. Shooters pointed at them, told to leave the city or else. The attackers ride motorbikes and have Scouse accents.'

'Scouse means Hanlon,' Rebus agreed.

'The lads he's threatened are top of the class. When they walk, all that's left are the narrow passes and dunces.'

'Hanlon's making his play,' Rebus surmised.

'I need to know what Fox knows. Do you think he'd tell you?'

The only credible answer to this being 'not a chance in hell', Rebus kept his mouth shut. Not that Christie seemed to be paying attention, his head filled with fizzing energy.

'If Hanlon's back on UK soil, I can plan a hit. Even if he's not, I need to know who he's got in charge up here.'

'Pity you didn't ask Harrison.'

Christie considered for a moment. 'Aye, well ... that'd been on my mind, but then when I started walking towards him, he had a big smarmy grin on his coupon and I just wanted it gone – because that grin told me he knew that I knew. He reckons his boss can just waltz into my city, after all the sweat I've broken. I needed to show him, and there was Mark Jamieson lining up a shot, the cue almost winking at me as I made to pass him ...'

'I reckon that's a bridge burned then.'

'Which is why I need access to Fox and his shiny-suited brethren.'

Rebus pretended to be thinking. 'I'll need a phone.'

'Easiest thing in the world.'

'Not with you stuck in here for the foreseeable.'

Christie shook his head at Rebus's naivety. 'Third shower stall from the left. Reach down into the drain. It should have plenty of charge and credit. You can hang on to it after – call it your reward.' He stood back a little so Rebus could see the finger he was wagging at him. 'But I want that info, John. If I don't get it, I won't be a very happy monkey.'

'Lucky for me there are no pool cues left for you to use.'

'Don't you worry about that – I've been known to improvise. I'm sure I'll think of something to hurt you with.'

'Noted.' Rebus stepped past Christie and pushed open the door. Tennent was just the other side, his face giving nothing away. Either he'd heard or he hadn't. Rebus wasn't sure it mattered.

'We'll talk later, Darryl,' the governor said sternly.

'And to think they call it solitary,' Christie shot back. 'A man can't get five minutes' peace ...'

*

147

Rebus waited until late afternoon to roll up his towel and head for the showers. The younger guys, the ones who worked out, thought nothing of stripping off in their cell and walking there in flip-flops or trainers, a towel wrapped around their waist. But that wasn't Rebus's way. He undressed in the shower cubicle itself, stepping out to lay aside his clothes before going back in, hanging the towel over the chest-high door. The floor and walls were damp from the previous occupant. He turned on the water – it was never more than tepid at this time of day – and peered over the top of the door to check no one was in the vicinity. Then he crouched and worked his fingernails under the edge of the grating covering the run-off. Whatever screws it had once held had been removed, the fact disguised by thick dollops of soap pushed into each screw hole. The whole thing was prised off with ease.

Rebus stared into the drain, seeing nothing at first. But there was a thin wire hooked over the rim just below floor level, and when he pulled on it, he felt resistance. The clear polythene bag it was tied to eventually emerged. He could make out the small, dark lozenge inside. He unwound the wire and placed it back in the drain, then slid the grating into place. Turning off the water, he started drying himself. Had the police search neglected the showers? Or had it just not been thorough enough? He supposed the phone could have been placed in the drain after any search had taken place, but it must have been secreted *somewhere*. Furthermore, the drain could just as easily have concealed a weapon – maybe even a knife with a serrated edge.

The other stalls were empty, so he inspected them, but the drain covers were screwed down tight. His heart was beating a little faster than usual as he got dressed and, the phone wrapped in his towel, walked back to his cell, trying hard not to quicken his usual pace. The phone went into the little safe beneath his bed. For once, he locked it afterwards.

That evening, after bang-up, he clambered onto the toilet seat and fired up the phone, calling Christine Esson's number. She took her time answering.

'It's John,' Rebus whispered to the handset. There was no immediate reply as he listened to the background sounds. 'You're in a pub?' he guessed. He heard her hold the phone away from her as she explained to someone that she'd be back in two minutes.

'Which bar is it?' Rebus enquired.

'Jeremiah's Taproom,' Esson eventually said. 'It's near Gayfield Square.'

'Siobhan with you?'

'No.' She was out on the street now, low-level conversation replaced by traffic noise.

'Sounds like it's raining,' Rebus said.

'It has been. Stopped now. What is it you want, John?'

'What I *want* is to smell the grass on the Meadows after the rain's been. But what I *need* is to talk to Fox – have you got his number?'

'In more ways than one. What is it you plan to talk to him about?'

'Need-to-know basis, Christine. But nothing to do with your case, I promise.'

'Hang on a sec, then.' After a moment she began to recite a string of numbers, which Rebus copied with his pen on the back of his hand.

'Thanks,' he said. Then: 'How is the case progressing anyway?'

'Have you got something for me?'

'Mark Jamieson thinks his dinner could've been spiked. That's one thing. Chris Novak says he's one of the POs who's being targeted by people on the outside – not just his car getting torched but threatening notes and the like. So that's two things you probably didn't know. Oh, and Darryl Christie just rammed a pool cue down Everett Harrison's throat, apparently in retaliation for Harrison's boss targeting Christie's team on the outside. How about you – managed to dig up anything on Blair Samms?'

'Nothing of note. I listened again to the interviews we did

with him. Seems like a team player, parroting the same script the others on night duty gave us. And CCTV only shows him doing the one quick tour of Trinity Hall. In fact, he spends exactly seventy-three seconds there as opposed to two and a half hours on his backside drinking hot chocolate and reading a newspaper.'

'Okay, so you're being methodical.'

'Methodical *and* meticulous.'

'Without actually getting anywhere.'

'While you meantime have doubtless worked out who poisoned Simpson's cellmate?'

'I'm looking at likely candidates, though I'd much rather be looking at a fresh pint in this pub of yours.'

'They do a decent hamburger, too.'

'When I get out, first thing I'm doing is booking a table at Prestonfield House.'

'Am I invited?'

'As long as you're happy to go Dutch.'

'Is Christie the reason you want to speak to Fox?'

'If Darryl's gang are being targeted, he'd be the one who'd know.'

'He's attached himself to the inquiry, you know.'

'You have my sympathies.' Rebus paused. 'While I remember, do you know anyone in CID called Cammy?'

'Only Cammy Colson. He's currently partnering Siobhan. Why?'

'Nothing really. I'd better let you get back to the festivities.' Rebus's hips were aching from crouching on the toilet seat. 'If and when you have news, you know where to find me.'

He hung up and walked to his cell door, testing it. Of course it was locked, the sounds from outside muffled: coughs; someone still whistling 'Valerie'; a dull bass thump from one cell, which the POs would soon put a stop to. He could hear the gate to the hall being unlocked and then locked again – an officer coming or going. One of the things that drove Rebus near-demented was the constant unlocking and locking. A door or gate needed

150

to be unlocked, yet beyond it was only a corridor with nothing at the end but another locked door or gate. So why did the first need to be locked? It never seemed to bother the officers or his fellow inmates, but it bothered Rebus. He thought of Billy Groam – had he really heard a cell door opening? He gave his own a kick, hard enough to stub a toe.

'That'll teach you,' he muttered, retreating to his cot and thoughts of warm and inviting pubs and juicy steak dinners.

Esson stared at her phone's screen as Rebus ended the call. When it went blank, she pushed open the door and walked back to her table, shivering a little and brushing raindrops from her arms.

'Is that it starting again?' Malcolm Fox asked, blowing his nose. Across the table, Jason Mulgrew was rotating his pint glass, adding some foam to the surface. The initial arrangement had been between Fox and Mulgrew, but Esson wasn't going to let Fox get away with that, so had invited herself along.

'Sorry about that,' she said. 'Had to take it.'

'Work-related?' Fox asked.

'A source.' She paused, looking down at what remained of her vodka tonic with its three slices of lemon. 'They tell me members of Darryl Christie's network are running scared.' She looked up, meeting Fox's eyes.

'Is that right?' Fox reached for his water glass.

'You tell me.'

He offered a shrug. 'I didn't realise you had an interest.'

'You told me yourself Everett Harrison could well have had a grudge against the victim, and Harrison works for Shay Hanlon. Hanlon has his eyes on Edinburgh, but that can't happen until he deals with Darryl's team.' She rested her elbows against the table. 'Is Hanlon back in the country, Malcolm? Is that what's got London so rattled?'

'I've no idea if Hanlon is still in Brazil or not. But it's true that Christie's team is being picked off. Latest was a guy called

151

Jake Morris. A biker shoved a gun in his face and now Jake's in hiding.'

As Fox spoke, Esson noted that he had Jason's rapt attention – Fox sensed it, too, and was playing to his audience for all he was worth, gesticulating as he repeated the story, adding details that Esson soon realised were almost certainly fabricated. He spoke about his 'close relationship' with SO15 – 'You might have heard it called Special Branch, Jason, but it changed names a while back.' Then he moved on to Gartcosh and the various 'high-level' agencies based there. 'I'll show you round the place sometime if you like.'

Mulgrew bowed his head in a show of gratitude.

Eventually Fox ran out of steam and shifted his focus to Esson. 'I'm interested in this source of yours, Christine. They seem to know things that aren't exactly common knowledge.'

'I promised them anonymity. I can't go back on that.'

'I thought we were a team here.'

'Did you now, Malcolm?'

'I appreciate that you and I got off on the wrong foot ...' Esson knew he was talking about the meeting in his car. He was about to add something, but then noticed that his phone was buzzing. Esson guessed that his screen would be showing something like *No Caller ID*, Rebus on the other end of the line. Fox didn't bother answering, switching the phone off and pocketing it instead.

'My round, I think,' Mulgrew said, draining his glass.

'I think three's plenty,' Fox chided him. 'Nice clear heads tomorrow. But it's been useful, don't you think? A bit of bonding away from the office?'

'Absolutely. It was good of you to invite us, wasn't it, Christine?'

'Wouldn't have missed it for the world,' Esson replied, knowing her fake smile would fool only one of the men at the table.

'It's Rebus, isn't it?' Fox's smile was every bit the equal of hers. 'This source who knows what's happening around Darryl Christie. You need to be careful, Christine.'

'No lectures, please, Malcolm – not from you of all people.'

'But I'm right, aren't I? What else did he tell you?'

'Only that Chris Novak has been receiving threats and Mark Jamieson's meal could have been spiked the night of the murder.'

'Plenty Brownie points when you tell Mae McGovern all of that.'

'Yes, bloody well done, Christine,' Mulgrew added, sounding only slightly irritated.

'You'll get your moment in the sun, Jason, never fear,' Fox told him, reaching across to grip him by the arm.

'Calling it a night then?' Esson announced, keen for a break from the bromance.

'Until next time,' Fox said, his hand still on Mulgrew's arm, as if reluctant to let go.

'I've still got a couple of mouthfuls left, though,' Mulgrew complained, tapping his glass.

With a sigh, Esson got to her feet and left them to it.

Day Four

11

Jason Mulgrew was waiting for Esson on the busy pavement. She reckoned this part of the city would normally be sleepy and well ordered. A few school runs and early-morning grocery deliveries. Neighbours had emerged from their homes to watch the commotion. Two scene-of-crime vans were parked up, alongside four marked police cars.

'I was hoping you'd be the bearer of coffee,' Mulgrew said as he opened the door of Esson's car for her.

'Three pints a bit much for you, Jason?'

'It felt like the right thing to do. Malcolm seems a good guy, no bullshit about him.'

'You suffering from long COVID? Lost your sense of smell?'

His mouth twitched. 'At least I know now why you and John Rebus were having that little chat in Pastoral Care.'

'John wants a result, same as the rest of us.'

They had arrived at one of the vans, its rear doors open, an officer dispatching overalls, gloves and shoe coverings. Esson glanced in the direction of the two-storey house they were about to enter. 'Who was it told you?' she asked.

'The DCI got wind of it first thing, recognised the victim's name.'

The street was tree-lined and the branches above Esson were

dripping on her. She gave them a stern look as she tugged the hood over her head. Barnton to most Edinburgh residents was a neighbourhood they drove past on their way north and west. It tended to house professionals and those who'd done well for themselves. One middle-aged woman was complaining to the young constable who was setting up the cordon.

'Probably worried it'll affect the value of her house,' Esson commented. 'Who found the body?'

'Victim's mother. She hadn't heard from him for a few days – thought it unusual. Came for a look-see and let herself in. Soon after, she was phoning 999.'

'Where is she now?'

'They took her back home. Hoping to interview her properly as soon as she calms down.'

They had reached the front door, where they gave their details to an officer holding a clipboard. Then they were in. The living area was large, open-plan and lurid, the art on the walls apparently chosen for its screaming contrasts of colours. A TV projector was aimed at the one vacant wall. Two cream leather sofas were arranged in a V shape and shelving held an array of bottles, glasses, video games and football magazines. Zebra-patterned rugs partially covered the parquet floor.

'He was found in the kitchen,' Mulgrew stated, so that was where they headed next. The body was *in situ* but about to be removed. A camera technician was checking his footage, making sure he hadn't missed anything. The kitchen boasted a central island, topped with speckled white marble. Two of the forensics team were paying it particularly close attention. Even from a couple of metres away, Esson recognised the smear of liquid on one corner as blood. She hadn't known Zak Campbell in life – Siobhan Clarke was the football fan. But here he was, growing cold on his kitchen floor.

Haj Atwal, the scene-of-crime boss, recognised Esson and nodded a greeting. But then he saw Mulgrew and gave a growl.

'Hood, for pity's sake, man!'

Mulgrew, who had been giving his head a scratch, looked

158

mortified and quickly tugged the elasticated material over his head.

'I assume he didn't just slip and fall?' Esson asked from behind her face mask.

'Damage to his forehead was probably done by the worktop,' Atwal answered. 'As to why he toppled over ...' He nodded towards one of the evidence bags arranged on a nearby worktop. The detectives walked towards it. There was a six-inch kitchen knife inside, its blade smeared with blood, the handle showing traces of fingerprint powder. Esson looked to where, further along, a knife block exhibited one empty slot.

'Just the single puncture wound, delivered from behind,' Atwal went on. 'Knife was dropped on the floor afterwards.'

'Tell me we have prints,' Mulgrew said, staring at the body.

They watched Atwal shake his head.

Esson dragged her eyes away from the evidence bag. 'Who's running the show?' she asked.

'Gillian Reeves's team.'

'So where are they?'

'Upstairs maybe,' Atwal said. Esson turned and left the kitchen, heading for the hallway.

'What do you reckon?' Mulgrew asked as they climbed.

'All we know right now is Zak Campbell was good friends with Marcus Simpson and Marcus's father just happens to be our case.'

The walls of the upstairs corridor were covered in framed football jerseys and press cuttings from Zak Campbell's glory years. Every door stood open and voices were coming from the far end. Esson passed a bathroom, and what looked to be the main bedroom, plus a room turned into a home office. The final bedroom was where the gathering was taking place. Its curtains were closed, illumination provided by a pink light bulb in the ceiling. A digital camera stood atop a tripod, pointed towards the bed.

'Looks like he filmed his conquests,' one officer commented for the benefit of Esson and Mulgrew. Esson ignored him, her gaze fixed on the bed and the wall behind it. She had seen that pale striped wallpaper before.

'Oh crap,' she eventually said. Detective Inspector Gillian Reeves turned to look at her.

'What is it, Christine?'

'I know this room, Gillian.' Esson was trying to dig her phone out of her overalls, but it was proving impossible. 'And what Zak Campbell was doing here goes way beyond collecting notches on his bedpost ...'

The meeting took place in DCI Bryan Carmichael's office at St Leonard's, with its array of swimming medals and framed photos of his parents and long-term partner, Adam. By the time Esson, Mulgrew, Siobhan Clarke and Gillian Reeves had packed themselves in, there wasn't much space left and, it felt to Esson, almost as little oxygen. A line of sweat trickled down her back. She had explained the situation to Clarke in her phone call, and now both women had just finished telling their tale to Clarke's boss, while Esson's own boss had joined them via speakerphone. Clarke was holding her laptop open, the home page for Young Fresh East Coast visible, every model posed on the same bed against the same striped wallpaper. Reeves stood in stony silence to one side, hands clasped behind her back, eyes begging Carmichael not to take her case away from her.

'All right,' Carmichael said, focusing his attention on the phone in front of him. 'Seems to me, Mae, that there's a stronger connection to the misper case than the prison death, and seeing how Jason and Christine already have a murder to occupy them ...'

'I don't disagree,' the voice from the phone crackled. 'But I'd still like my team to have a foot in your camp. There's a tenuous connection to Jackie Simpson, but a connection nevertheless. I need to feel comfortable that it has no relevance.'

'That's fine by me. Christine and Siobhan have worked

together in the past, making Christine the obvious candidate.'

Jason Mulgrew bristled conspicuously.

'I sense a difference of opinion in the ranks,' Carmichael commented.

'With respect, ma'am,' Mulgrew began for the phone's benefit, 'shouldn't the more senior officer be given the responsibility?'

'I think it's already been decided, Jason,' McGovern stated icily from the speaker. 'And Christine, you'll be straddling two horses, but I don't want you to forget which mount is your favourite.'

'Understood.'

'We'll need you here at Gayfield Square as much as possible. And if it turns out that this incident has nothing to do with our own inquiry ...'

'Also understood.'

Carmichael leaned a little closer to the phone. 'We're a bit short of hands over here, Mae.'

McGovern's reply was preceded by a loud snort. 'Join the bloody club, Bryan.'

'So I'll be kept on?' Gillian Reeves interrupted.

'Of course,' Carmichael replied. 'And feel free to bring a friend or six ...' He paused. 'Is that everything, do we think?'

There were nods around the room, Mulgrew the only obvious dissenter. He was still scowling as the four of them filed out, leaving the two DCIs to talk tactics. In the corridor, he turned to face his three colleagues, eyes fixed on Christine Esson.

'I suppose that's me back to Siberia then,' he said. 'Will you be gracing us with your presence before the end of play?'

'Cheer up, Jason. Means you get to spend more time with your new pal Malcolm.'

He glowered at her before heading for the exit.

'I hope *you* don't think you're being shafted, Gillian,' Clarke said to Reeves.

'Not nearly as much as DI Mulgrew.'

'Boys and their feelings,' Clarke said.

'So what's the plan?' Reeves asked, folding her arms.

'I'm the only one who's not seen the locus,' Clarke answered after a moment's thought. 'Maybe Christine could show me once I've introduced you both to the team here. They need to be briefed so we can start the doorstepping and interviews. We'll rendezvous back here in a couple of hours and get that particular ball rolling.' She kept her eyes on Reeves, who nodded eventually.

'Then we're good to go,' Esson said, with what she hoped was a collegiate smile.

The forensics crew were still busy at Zak Campbell's house. The autopsy had been scheduled for the following morning. Campbell's mother – his father was long dead – had formally identified the body, going to pieces again afterwards. She was being comforted by a neighbour who was also her closest friend. The crime-scene tape stretched across one lane of the road outside Campbell's house. A queue of cars had built up to use the lane left available. Siobhan Clarke reckoned most would be the usual ghouls. Phones were being held out of driver's-side windows, filming and snapping, ready to feed the social media maw. She'd already had a text from Laura Smith. Just three words – *Quid pro quo* – but their meaning was clear: Clarke was in the journalist's debt and wouldn't be allowed to forget.

Meantime, the media had arrived, radio and TV vans parked up, narrowing the road still further. Questions were lobbed towards the two detectives as they passed through the cordon and got suited up. Someone had unlocked the door to the garage that sat attached to one side of the house. The car inside was a Maserati – bright red, naturally. Behind it could be glimpsed a motorbike of the same hue. Both were being checked for trace evidence. Inside, pretty much everything from Campbell's home office had been bagged and tagged and was in the process of being removed. Clarke stopped one of the officers and took a closer look at the evidence bag he was carrying. It contained an

A4-sized piece of white card with capitalised writing on it, done in black marker pen.

I'm horny as hell. Please choose me. I'll do anything your heart desires.

'I know,' Esson said, when Clarke looked at her.

'Computer's going to be crucial,' Clarke stated a minute later, moving towards the spare bedroom. Campbell's recording equipment was already gone. There was a metal-framed kitchen stool placed just behind where the tripod would have been. Clarke sat down on it, facing the bed. This, she knew, would have been Zak Campbell's perch.

'I need to talk to Louise Hird,' she said.

'Who's that?'

'The CEOP officer I told you about.'

'You reckon this is all Campbell's work?'

'Looks likely, wouldn't you say?'

'But could he have done it without help? Technical help, I mean?'

'I'm hoping we'll find out.'

'Police doctor reckoned he'd been lying on the floor for several days. Maybe from around the time Jasmine did her runner.'

'Yes.'

Esson was studying Clarke. 'It's a heck of a motive, Siobhan.'

'No question about that.'

'Do I sense a "but"?'

'Campbell could have made any number of enemies.'

'His minder might know.'

'Marcus Simpson,' Clarke agreed. 'That's another chat we need to have.' She walked to the side of the bed, whose sheets and pillowcases were on their way to the lab. The mattress looked new and pristine. She lifted it, but there was nothing beneath except the slatted wooden base. Dust balls were visible on the floor. Even if Campbell had employed a cleaner, he wouldn't have wanted them intruding. A glance towards the bedroom door showed that a lock had been fitted. She opened

163

the curtains and peered out. 'Comings and goings can't have escaped the neighbours' attention. I wonder what the hell they thought was happening.'

'They knew him as a footballer,' Esson speculated. 'Young and good-looking with money to burn. I think the phrase is "babe magnet".'

'There'd have been tuts of disapproval behind all those windows, though – this is Edinburgh, after all. We're going to be knocking on a lot of doors.'

'Let's hope our DCIs find us those extra bodies.'

'Let's hope,' Clarke echoed, moving towards the door.

The main bedroom didn't detain them long. Fitted wardrobes filled with designer clothes, a drawer containing women's underwear, almost certainly for use in the room next door. There was a TV on the wall opposite the bed. No reading matter of any kind.

'The team found a quantity of drugs – coke and grass and bags of pills.' Esson gestured towards the bedside table. 'Enough to give a group of people a good time. Traces in the living room, too.'

Downstairs in the kitchen they took out their phones and looked at the footage forwarded from the crime-scene photographer. Numbered Post-it notes had been placed in relevant spots.

'We can get prints from a granite surface, right?' Clarke checked with one of the team as they walked past.

'Shouldn't be a problem,' the officer said. 'Tell you what might be, though – the sheer quantity. Not on the murder weapon, but around the house; pretty much every room shows multiples.'

'Oh joy,' Esson muttered.

Five minutes later they were back at Clarke's car. Passing the media, Clarke spotted Laura Smith. They exchanged a look. When Clarke started driving, Esson probably wondered why she wasn't putting her foot down, until she saw that her attention was on the rear-view mirror. A few streets further on, Clarke pulled into a side road and waited.

'I think I know what's coming,' Esson said. Moments later, the rear door opened and Laura Smith climbed in, having parked her own car directly behind them. 'Bingo,' Esson said.

'You know Laura?' Clarke asked her.

'I know DS Esson,' Smith replied, reaching a hand into the gap between the front seats. Esson shook it. It was swiftly replaced by the journalist's flushed face. 'So what can you tell me?'

'As of now, not a whole lot.' Clarke was measuring each and every word. 'Zak Campbell seems to have been the brains behind Young Fresh East Coast.'

'And now he's dead and one of his girls has done a disappearing act.'

'Don't try to second-guess, Laura. We're not tying the cases together yet.'

'You are, though, otherwise you wouldn't be here. And how about you, DS Esson? I thought you were being kept busy with the Jackie Simpson murder? What's the connection?'

Esson said nothing.

'You wouldn't have got here without me,' Smith persisted, her attention shifting to Clarke. 'Surely I'm owed something for that.'

'I'll do what I can,' Clarke said. 'You know I will. But right now there's a lot that can't be made public. We have to think of the kids Campbell was exploiting. They have families. There are going to be awkward conversations. Best that those happen before the feeding frenzy.'

'You know this'll leak, right?' Smith pushed on. 'You lot are like a sieve. Only takes one set of loose lips to call it in to a news desk and I'll be left in the dust.'

'Laura ...' Clarke, hands clamped to the steering wheel, twisted her head as far as was possible, making eye contact with the journalist. 'I'll do everything I can. You'll be the first person I talk to. You've got my word.'

Smith turned this over in her mind, then leaned back against her seat. 'When's the press conference?'

'There's stuff to be done first.'

'Who's heading the MIT?'

'That would be me,' Clarke stated.

'Not Gillian Reeves? Her team was first on the scene – how does she feel about that?'

'We really need to be elsewhere, Laura.'

Smith took the hint, pausing for a moment before shoving open the door and making her exit. Clarke started the car and pressed down hard on the accelerator.

'Thanks for letting me do the running,' she said to Esson. 'Doesn't do to underestimate Laura. She's all on her own out there, no news organisation to back her up.'

'Meaning she needs views and clicks – and what better way to generate those than teen porn and a celebrity murder?'

'Something like that,' Clarke muttered. They were nearing a traffic light that was about to turn red. She sped up and flew across the intersection.

'All right, Lewis Hamilton,' Esson commented.

Clarke managed a brief laugh, releasing at least some of the tension. For the rest of the journey, she stayed just the right side of the speed limit.

12

Malcolm Fox was at the office in Gayfield Square. He'd asked where Esson and Mulgrew were, but no one seemed to know. He was studying the footage from the prison for the umpteenth time, but focusing on the cells of Harrison and Christie from before lock-up on the night of the killing. He was looking for interactions with officers or signs that either prisoner was more nervous or excited than usual. There was nothing obvious. Same went for the aftermath of the body's discovery. No officer looked unsurprised, while Harrison and Christie were their usual selves. Then again, whoever had been involved would have known they were being watched and recorded. They'd have been primed to act naturally. When he looked at the queue for supper the previous evening, he was pleased to see Rebus so low in the pecking order, over a dozen inmates ahead of him. Darryl Christie was, of course, first in line. The victim, Jackie Simpson, looked relaxed, three ahead of Rebus. When he was served, Fox could see nothing amiss, no tells from any officer or fellow con.

Fox stretched and cracked his vertebrae back into place. Next to his computer sat a printout detailing every recorded minute of the night shift, gaps marked where officers' whereabouts could not be verified. The toilet break taken by Novak and

Watts was the most conspicuous, since there was no evidence of either officer entering or leaving the lavatory. But as the interview transcripts showed, they were sticking to their story. Fox's eyes felt gritty from time spent peering at the camera footage, looking for any signs of shadow play, indicating activity just out of shot. He checked the printout again, its granular level of detail impressive without being in the least bit helpful.

When Jason Mulgrew walked in, hauling off his coat as if intending to do it actual physical harm, Fox got to his feet.

'What's happened?' he asked.

Mulgrew had come to a halt between the desks of Zara Shah and Paul Allbright.

'Our victim's son Marcus was pally with a local celeb called Zak Campbell. Campbell's just turned up dead and it seems he might be connected to that schoolgirl who disappeared. They've swiped Christine from us until further notice.' He looked at the two seated figures. 'They'll probably want to talk to you about your interview with Marcus Simpson. Make sure you're happy with whatever notes you took.'

He waited until Shah and Allbright had nodded their understanding, then went to the kettle and switched it on. Fox joined him.

'You're angry,' Fox stated.

'Should have been me, not Christine,' Mulgrew muttered, spooning coffee into a mug.

'I can see that – you're the senior officer. But you're in charge of *this* case, Jason, and I'm glad you are. You're a proper detective, and Christ knows this place could do with one of those. Judging by last night, Christine might've picked up too many bad habits from the likes of Siobhan Clarke.'

'Christine's a decent cop too, you know.'

'If you say so.'

Mulgrew seemed to be calming a little. He looked towards the desk Fox had been using. 'I don't suppose you've found anything?'

'Not much, no. I'm wondering about Valerie Watts, though.

On duty during the meal service, then locking Simpson's door at lights-out ...'

'Not forgetting that gap in the camera footage.'

'The famous loo break, yes.'

'You think we should talk to her again?'

'If we do, I wouldn't mind it happening away from her place of work. You can tell a lot from a person's home life and how they act there.'

'Out of uniform, as it were?'

Fox nodded slowly while Mulgrew added milk to his drink.

'Should have asked if you wanted one, Malcolm.'

'I'm fine,' Fox assured him. His eyes swept across the near-empty office. 'But with Christine out of the picture, I reckon I'm definitely needed here, wouldn't you say?'

'Absolutely,' Mulgrew confirmed. 'Wouldn't have it any other way ...'

The prison's visiting area was as light, airy and welcoming as it could be. There was even a corner with toys for inmates' children to play with while meetings took place. Right now, however, it was deserted, visiting time over for the day. Deserted apart from Siobhan Clarke, who was seated at one of the tables near the exit. Rebus was led in by an officer, who then stayed put by the far wall, giving them privacy. Rebus gave Clarke a questioning look as he drew near.

'I pulled a few strings,' she explained.

'A nice surprise, all the same.' Rebus pulled out the chair opposite and sat down.

'Who's she?' Clarke asked in a near-whisper, indicating the officer, who was looking interested.

'Her name's Valerie Watts.'

'She looks ... glamorous.'

'Just a bit of make-up and hair dye, Shiv. So why the burning need to see me?'

'You know Zak Campbell? The ex-footballer?'

169

'I know somebody topped him.' He saw the look she was giving. 'We're not completely cut off from the news agenda in here.'

'Marcus Simpson was one of his closest friends.'

'Son of Jackie?' He watched her give a slow nod. Glancing towards Watts, he saw that the PO was craning her head as far as possible while not quite edging her whole body forward from the wall.

'Join us if you like,' he called out to her. Her head snapped back to its original position.

'Word is,' Rebus continued in an undertone, 'she's Chris Novak's squeeze, him being the officer we're all supposed to think did for Jackie Simpson.'

'You're not buying it?'

'Never fall for the hype, Siobhan. Didn't I teach you that lesson?'

'Most of what you taught me I had to unlearn so they didn't kick me off the force.'

'Fair point. So who killed Zak Campbell?'

'He was running a porn website. Jasmine Andrews was one of the girls on it.'

'The runaway? You fancy her for his murder?'

'It's a scenario.'

'And yet?'

'You said it yourself, John – don't trust the hype. She did vanish around the same time, though.'

'A kindly knight came along and took revenge on her behalf?'

'And if she knew that was going to happen ...'

'Would that have caused her to run? And who would this knight be anyway?'

'It's early days.'

'A case like this, you do it by numbers – the interviews, the doorstepping, the lab and autopsy reports ...' Rebus broke off. 'Will the pathologist be Deborah Quant?'

'Want me to pass along your regards?'

'I doubt she'd accept them.'

'Maybe once that appeal of yours bears fruit. No word?'

'Christ knows what I'm paying them for. Luckily I have plenty to keep my mind occupied. Darryl Christie is fretting. He says Hanlon's lot are picking off his team. He had a go at Hanlon's right-hand man. I doubt that can end well.'

'Best keep your head down, then.'

'I'm famous for it. So if Zak Campbell connects to the murder here through Jackie's son ...'

Clarke gave a slow nod. 'Three inquiries become one.'

'Meaning you're teamed with Christine? Any noise from Malcolm Fox?'

Clarke's eyes narrowed. 'Should there be?'

'Not many pies go unfingered if Fox gets his way.'

'Charmingly put.'

'You need to keep your wits about you, Siobhan. With you having snubbed him, he might well see Christine as a ready replacement. At any rate, he's never going to have your best interests at heart.' He paused, weighing up his next words. 'I happened to be speaking to Christine last night. She was in a bar. She didn't *say* she was with Fox, but ...'

'Malcolm's interested in what happened here – stands to reason he might want a catch-up with Christine. And what were you phoning her for anyway? I assume it was on one of your illicit mobiles?'

'Maybe I just fancied a catch-up too. And unlike Fox, I can't offer drinks as a bribe.'

'Well, Christine's been seconded to my case now, leaving Fox twiddling his thumbs at Gayfield Square.'

'Then he'll just latch on to somebody else – most likely Jason Mulgrew.'

'You know Jason?'

'A brief encounter. But he struck me as hungry. Fox will sense that and try to use it.' Rebus sat back a little, resting his hands on his knees. 'Feel free to bounce ideas off me as often as necessary. But I doubt there's anything I can suggest that won't already be on your to-do list.'

'Are things going to be okay in here, John?' Rebus considered for a moment before shaking his head. 'And you won't be digging yourself a foxhole?'

'Smuggle me in a shovel and who knows?'

Clarke's mouth opened a fraction. 'Stupid of me – I didn't think to bring any wee treats.'

'The big kids would just take them off me anyway. You heading home or working a late shift?'

'The latter.' She'd been about to add something, but swallowed it back.

'What?' Rebus said.

'I was about to ask if you had plans.' She looked around at their surroundings. 'Sometimes I forget where we are.'

'Lucky you,' Rebus said, reaching out to pat the back of her hand. 'Oh, by the way, how's your own partner?' She looked puzzled. 'Cammy Colson, right?' he added.

'That's right.'

'Turns out he's cousins with Chris Novak, suspect number one.'

'And?'

'And nothing. I just wondered if he'd mentioned it.'

'He hasn't.'

Valerie Watts had taken a couple of loud steps forward, indicating that time was up. 'Back into battle,' Rebus announced, rising slowly to his feet.

'I'm hoping that's just a metaphor.'

'It hasn't kicked off in here yet, but it still might, and there's an ogre who wants a taste of my blood – I'm doing my best to keep out of his way.'

'Maybe I will smuggle in that shovel after all.'

'Make it a sharp one,' Rebus said.

He turned his head in Valerie Watts' direction as they strode back along the corridor.

'I know you're dying to ask,' he said.

172

She kept her eyes on the route in front. 'You'll tell me if you want to,' she said.

'It wasn't to do with in here, if that's what's bothering you.'

'Chris didn't do it,' she said firmly.

'Well, someone did, and there were only twelve of you on duty that whole night. CID are simple souls at heart. Give them an obvious conclusion and they'll leap to it. Chris Novak didn't much like Jackie Simpson. He'd already had a go at him once when they were alone in that cell.'

'Only according to your pal Jackie, who seldom told the truth when a lie would suffice. *He* was the one who'd been threatening to pay Chris and his family a visit once he got out.'

'And what would *you* do in that situation, Officer Watts? What might you be *driven* to do? Chris Novak had the means and opportunity to go with the motive.'

Watts stopped abruptly and turned towards Rebus, her eyes fiery. 'Those minutes that aren't accounted for,' she began. 'CID seem to think that's the "opportunity" you're talking about. But we weren't heading for anybody's cell.'

'Where, then?'

She paused, drawing in a deep breath. 'We were in the store cupboard along from the breakout room. That's all there is to it. There's a blind spot between the two doors – makes it easy. Some people go there for a smoke. Others ...' Her voice drifted off.

Rebus studied her face. 'Why are you telling me?'

'Because Chris seems to think you might be on his side.'

'So if not you and him – who?'

'He's already told you about Samms.'

'Samms didn't go off-piste for ten minutes that night, though.'

Watts took another deep breath and then exhaled. 'I'm going to defend him all the way, you know that? Even if it means his family finding out about us.'

'Because you're in love with him?'

'Because I know he's innocent,' she corrected him. She

173

started walking again, Rebus falling into step beside her. 'What was all that about earlier today with Darryl Christie?' she asked.

'He hates anyone who cheats at pool.'

This raised the vestige of a smile. 'Nobody seems ready to talk.'

'It's a territory thing.'

'Shay Hanlon, right?'

'Right.'

'Meaning we have to keep Christie and Everett Harrison a bargepole apart?' She watched him nod. 'Well, Darryl's going to be in solitary for a while anyway. Time enough for things to cool down.'

'I doubt he'll see it that way. The city's being prised away from him. He's only going to get keener to even the odds.'

'Fun times.' Watts unlocked the gate to Rebus's hall, ushering him through.

'Twelve of you on duty,' he reminded her. 'If not the two of you, that leaves ten.'

'Always supposing he wasn't already dead by lock-up.'

'You turned the key – I'm assuming you took a look inside at the same time?'

'I can't swear that I did.'

'Well, his cellmate says he was still breathing at lights-out.'

'This is Mark Jamieson we're talking about – guy's practically a zombie. Half his day's spent gouching – you reckon you can trust his memory?'

Rebus made show of considering the question. 'In here,' he told Watts, 'I'm not sure it's wise to trust anyone or anything.'

'Me included?'

'You've got more to lose than some,' he said, walking away from her towards his cell.

13

By the time Clarke got back to St Leonard's, Esson and Reeves had finished making their introductions. Space was tight and desks were being shared. Clarke couldn't help but think again of the few formative years she'd spent here alongside John Rebus, years when she'd seemed part of the fabric of the place.

These days she felt more like a visitor.

Esson was chatting with Cammy Colson, eyes already glazing over as he treated her to his full-bore drawl. Pete Swinton and Trisha Singh were keeping their distance, pretending to be busy with computer cables and extension leads.

Spotting Clarke, Esson excused herself from Colson, who carried on talking for a further few moments before realising he'd lost his audience.

'Is he always like that?' she said, leaning in towards Clarke.

'This is him on a good day. Everything all right otherwise?'

'Where did you disappear to?' Esson asked, ignoring the question.

'Visiting an old friend. How did you enjoy your drink with Malcolm Fox?'

Esson gave her a look. 'The drink was Malcolm and Jason; I just sort of invited myself along.'

'So Fox has dumped the pair of us for Jason Mulgrew?'

'I think you'll find *we* dumped Fox, remember?'

'Good point.' Clarke paused. 'Why did John phone you, though?'

'He didn't confide in you? Then maybe I shouldn't either.'

'You're not his lawyer, Christine – you're allowed to talk.'

'He had some info.'

'About the Simpson murder?'

'Yes.'

'Did he also mention Darryl Christie kicking off?'

'He did. He wanted me to talk to Malcolm about it, see if he knew what was happening with Christie's gang.'

'And since Malcolm was right there alongside—'

Clarke broke off as DCI Bryan Carmichael made his entrance, clapping his hands together to attract everyone's attention.

'As you can see,' he began, 'I've got my coat on. Alas, not on my way home to a log fire and a glass of malt, but a tedious bloody dinner I can't get out of. But I want to thank you all for staying late and putting in the hours. Someone needs to be chivvying forensics for their findings from the crime scene. Between us, DCI McGovern and I have managed to round up a football squad's worth of uniforms to start knocking on doors in the morning. Autopsy needs someone present who's not likely to faint, and the deceased's mother needs to be questioned again, plus any and all friends and associates.' He paused. 'And that's before we get to CCTV and doorbell footage. Plenty to keep you on the path of righteousness.' His eyes flitted between Clarke and Reeves – the two DIs in the room. 'Happy with everything so far?'

'Absolutely,' Reeves responded.

His attention shifted to Esson. 'I know you've got other plates to keep spinning, and if it starts getting too much, feel free to keep that to yourself and soldier on regardless – just don't tell Mae McGovern I said that.' He tightened the red cashmere scarf around his neck, trying to think if he'd forgotten anything. Then, with a final businesslike nod, he was gone. The room relaxed a little.

'Get a brew on then,' someone said.

Gillian Reeves manoeuvred between the desks, heading for Clarke and Esson.

'We've had a call from a woman the victim was seeing. I've invited her in for a chat.'

'A girlfriend, you mean?' Esson checked. Reeves gave a nod. 'When is she coming?'

Reeves made show of checking the time on her phone. 'In about twenty minutes. Oh, and we sent a couple of uniforms to Marcus Simpson's address, but there was no answer. They'll have another go in the morning.'

Cammy Colson joined the group. 'Any takers for the mortuary tomorrow?'

'Isn't that a man's job, Cammy?' Clarke said slyly.

'I'll do it if no one else will,' he eventually conceded.

'Knew we girls could rely on you.'

Colson rolled his eyes and readied to move away.

'By the way,' Clarke commented, 'you never mentioned you were Chris Novak's cousin.' She glanced at Esson, whose eyebrows had slid upwards a fraction.

'Is there a conflict of interest?' It was Colson's turn to look at Esson.

'I don't think so. Do you, Christine?'

Esson took a moment before shaking her head.

'Chris is a diamond,' Colson stated. 'I don't see him often, but he's solid – a family man, you know?'

'Has he spoken to you about what's happening at the prison?' Esson enquired.

'Like I said, we don't see much of each other.' He looked from Esson to Clarke. 'We done here? I've got stuff waiting for me on my desk.' Without waiting for a reply, he turned and began ambling across the room.

The team had settled to their tasks, having finally sourced enough chairs. The murder wall – a large whiteboard on wheels – had been set up and the pick of the crime-scene photos were being added to it along with a professionally posed shot of Zak

Campbell, lifted from his living room. Clarke stared at his face for a moment. Once it became public knowledge that he'd groomed and exploited a multitude of young teenagers, a lot of the sympathy for him would drain away, and with it the desire to aid the inquiry. They had to work quickly – and without any leaks. She remembered again that she needed to tell Louise Hird at CEOP, but it was too late in the day now. Trisha Singh was explaining to the room at large that there weren't enough mugs to go round, so they'd either need to bring their own or else rinse and return as soon as they'd finished their drink. Swinton added that there seemed to be only one working printer – and it was low on cyan.

'They always are,' Reeves answered. 'And do any of us even know what cyan is?'

There were a few chuckles as they got to work. Clarke gave a slow nod in Esson's direction: it wasn't a bad start. Then again, the room was high on adrenalin, as always happened at the start of a big case. The problem was maintaining momentum – which entailed making decent progress over the next day or two.

The desk sergeant appeared in the doorway, spotting Clarke and making for her.

'Young woman downstairs says it's about Zak Campbell.'

Clarke sought out Gillian Reeves, but she was busy with a phone call, so she looked at Christine Esson instead.

'Might as well,' Esson said, following her out of the room.

The new-build apartment block stood alongside the Union Canal, near Fountainbridge. There was a video entry system, so Fox pushed the buzzer and waited. He assumed he was on camera so held up his ID.

'Yes?' a female voice crackled.

'Ms Watts,' he said. 'My name's Fox. I'm here with DI Jason Mulgrew – I think the two of you met during your first inter-view. We just have a couple of follow-up questions.'

'So ask me at the prison.'

'We can certainly do that, but we felt maybe a bit more privacy ...' He tailed off, leaving her to read into his words what she would.

'The place is a tip.'

'I have a couple of pairs of blinkers in my pocket – we'd be happy to wear those.'

There was silence for a moment. Then: 'Give me two minutes.' The speaker went dead. Fox stepped away from the camera and studied his surroundings. A few canal boats had tied up and a pair of swans were gliding past.

'They've done a good job along here. Used to be a dump.'

'So is she busy getting her story straight or phoning Novak to ask him how to play it?' Mulgrew speculated.

'We just have to wait and see,' Fox said, rubbing his hands together and wishing he hadn't left his gloves in the car.

In the end, they waited more than two minutes, more even than five. Fox was readying to press the bell again when a buzzer indicated that the door had been unlocked. They took the lift to the second floor. Valerie Watts was standing in her doorway, barefoot and dressed as if for a gym session.

'You carry blinkers?' she asked Fox.

'Two pairs.' He patted one of his pockets.

She gestured for both men to follow her into a smallish open-plan living space. Nicely furnished, but with evidence of clutter having been shoved just out of sight. Watts pushed a hand through her hair. Fox had already settled himself on the narrow sofa, leaving just about enough room for Mulgrew. Watts hesitated, then perched on the arm of the only chair.

'So?' she said.

Fox gave her a reassuring smile and held up his phone. 'Mind if I record some audio – just in case I forget something?'

Watts fidgeted but didn't say no, so Fox hit record and placed the phone on his knee. 'Most of the weapons found in jails are actually made there, right?' he began.

'Sure,' she said. 'Soften the head of a toothbrush and jam a razor blade into it.'

'Creating a "shank", yes?' He watched her nod. 'But that isn't what we're dealing with here. The pathologist reckons a serrated blade, the sort of thing you'd only find in a kitchen ...'

'And all the staff and trusties who work on food prep have been asked about it.' She looked at Mulgrew. 'I explained it to you, didn't I? Knives are kept locked away—'

'Away from prisoners, yes,' Fox interrupted, 'but what about staff?'

'If they're taken out and used, they're counted at the end of the shift. Nothing is missing from the kitchen. We've checked and you've checked.' She looked at Mulgrew again. He nodded his confirmation.

'On the day of the killing,' Fox continued, 'the kitchen crew consisted of three trusties plus yourself and Officer Samms?'

'That's right.'

'What can you tell us about him?'

She blinked. 'Samms?'

'We know there's talk he might be for sale to the highest bidder – you'll have heard those stories?'

'I've heard them.'

'He worked the night shift too, alongside you and Chris Novak.'

'He did.'

'Was he there when you locked Jackie Simpson's cell that night?'

'He was in the vicinity.' Her voice had hardened, her spine stiffening.

'We can't actually see the cell, of course – that handily broken camera again.' Fox paused. 'And you really did lock it?'

'I think I've had just about enough of this.'

'Could another officer have unlocked it again?' Fox pressed on. 'An officer such as Blair Samms?'

She gave a slow shake of the head.

180

'Has Mark Jamieson's theory reached you yet?' Mulgrew broke in.

'What theory?'

'That his meal was spiked.'

'Give me a break.'

'That's what we're trying to do,' Fox stated softly. 'It's why this conversation is happening away from prying eyes and sharp ears.'

'I don't know anything about food being doped or a knife being lifted from the kitchen or Blair Samms being in anybody's pocket.'

'Contraband does get into the prison, though, doesn't it? To be sold on by Darryl Christie. That can't happen without someone from the outside world being involved, a PO or similar.' He paused. 'Anything you can tell us about Everett Harrison?'

'What's he got to do with it?'

'You know he works for a Liverpudlian called Shay Hanlon?'

'So?'

'Harrison might have had reason to want Jackie Simpson dead.' He watched her shrug. 'Well, if you can't help with that, maybe we should move on to the toilet break you and Chris Novak took.'

'Why?'

'Because it's ten minutes where neither of you seems to be anywhere. We know there are blind spots around the prison. We also know that staff would know them better than most. It might even be possible to get from the breakout room to Trinity Hall without appearing on a single camera.'

Watts was shaking her head again. 'I know you want Chris for this, but he was never out of my sight that whole shift.'

'Even when you went to the toilet?'

She considered for a moment, then indicated Fox's phone. 'Turn that thing off,' she said. He did as he was told, holding the screen up for her to check. She closed her eyes for a moment before opening them again and speaking.

'You're right about those blind spots. One of them is the

store cupboard next to the toilets. We went there for some private time.'

'Private time?' Fox echoed. 'Lasting how long?'

'Ten minutes or so.'

'You reckon your fellow officers remained clueless?'

She gave a twitch of her mouth. 'Nobody ever says anything out loud.'

'But it was a regular occurrence? It's why you work the same shifts so often?'

'It's also why I know Chris had nothing to do with Simpson's death.'

'He's being set up?'

'Looks like.'

'To protect who, though?'

'Isn't it your job to find out?'

'Hard to do when we're being fed a diet of half-truths and lies,' Mulgrew commented.

She ignored him, pulling her own phone from a pocket and checking the screen.

'Chris getting back to you?' Fox guessed. He saw the look on her face and gave a thin smile. 'He's married with kids, therefore stuck at home. You couldn't risk phoning to tell him we were here, so you texted instead.'

'He says I shouldn't even open the door to you.'

'Maybe you should message back that you've just helped save his neck.'

Watts tucked the phone away again and rose to her feet. Fox took the hint. He reckoned he had just about everything he wanted anyway.

'What do you think of the threats against Chris?' he asked, trying to make the question sound casual.

'Part and parcel of the job.'

'You haven't been on the receiving end of any?'

'I don't stick my head above the trench the way Chris does.'

'Meaning?'

'He wants more checks, better surveillance.'

'To stop the drugs getting in?'

'The drugs, the phones, the weapons ...' Her eyes locked on to Fox's. 'I'm telling you, Chris isn't the bad guy here. I wouldn't be with him if he was.'

Fox took a moment to consider this. 'Thanks for your time,' he told her. 'Enjoy what's left of the evening.'

'Just as soon as you two arseholes are gone,' Valerie Watts said, opening the door.

The two men sat in Fox's car for a moment, engine running, heating on. Fox had checked that the recording was audible.

'I'll send it over to you,' he told Mulgrew. 'Even though the best stuff came afterwards.' He angled his body towards the passenger seat. 'Did you notice how she closed her eyes, like she was about to repeat a piece she'd memorised? I reckon we're not the first people she's owned up to.'

'Who else?'

'I don't know. I told you, though, didn't I? It's always interesting to check out a suspect's home life. Little lesson for you there, Jason.'

'You know I'm the same rank as you, Malcolm? I'm not exactly fresh out of college.'

Fox knew he needed to backtrack. 'Same rank, but you're a lot younger. That speaks volumes. Sorry if I sounded patronising.'

'You called her a suspect – is that still your thinking?'

'Maybe not so much. So what now – fancy a quick one before home?'

'Not especially.' Mulgrew was scrolling down his phone's screen. 'I asked Christine for an update,' he explained. 'All she says is, Jackie Simpson's son is nowhere to be found.'

'Interesting. So that makes two people who've done a runner.'

'One single sodding sentence.' Mulgrew was still studying his phone.

'She's a busy woman,' Fox said, readying to set off. 'Are you sure I can't tempt you to that drink?'

'Ach, go on then,' Mulgrew said, putting his phone away.

Her name was Tamsin Oakley and she was busy on her mobile when Clarke and Esson entered the interview room, her elongated painted nails proving no hindrance as her fingers flitted across the screen.

Clarke saw that the spare chairs in the MIT office had been sourced from this room. Tamsin Oakley was seated, but nothing had been left for anyone else. There was also no video camera, but Esson had brought a couple of fresh tapes for the audio recording. Oakley broke off what she was doing and aimed her phone at the two detectives. Clarke placed her hand in front of it.

'Not allowed,' she said.

'It's just for the socials,' Oakley argued. Her accent was local. Her hair boasted highlights and extensions, her face was bronzed, eyelashes long and thick, lips painted dark red. Her outfit was loud but didn't look cheap. The Louis Vuitton bag on her lap might have been authentic or knock-off – Clarke had no way of knowing.

Esson had got the tape rolling, so the two detectives introduced themselves, adding place, date and time of recording.

'I'm Tamsin Oakley,' Oakley said, leaning towards the mic.

'We're sorry about Zak,' Clarke said, watching for a reaction. Oakley straightened up and her face dropped dutifully. She even produced a paper tissue from the depths of her bag.

'He was lovely. What happened exactly?'

'That's what we're trying to find out, and we're grateful you've come forward.'

'Theresa and Katie said I had to – they reckon I'm going to be famous.' She paused. 'They're my besties. I promised them pics of some detectives.' She studied the two women. 'Not sure you're what they had in mind, though.'

184

Clarke ignored this. 'How well would you say you knew Zak, Tamsin?'

'We were pretty steady.'

'"Pretty"?'

'I'm not saying he didn't see other people, but it was me he always came back to.'

'So you were close, then? Friends with benefits?'

'Maybe he saw it that way ...'

'You wanted more of a commitment?'

'Maybe.' Oakley produced some gum and held it up. Clarke nodded to let her know it was allowed, so she slid a piece into her mouth.

'What do you do for a living, Tamsin?'

'Hair stylist. Wilhelm's in Stockbridge.' Clarke and Esson felt her momentary appraisal of their own cuts.

'Is that how you met Zak?'

She shook her head. 'Bar on George Street. Theresa knew who he was – she had her eye on him, but it was me he bought a drink for. Back of the net.' She smiled at the punchline, one she'd obviously used before.

'How long ago was this?'

'Maybe three months.'

'And he treated you well?'

'I wouldn't have stuck around otherwise.'

'Ever visit his house?' Clarke watched Oakley nod. 'Often?'

'Stayed over a few nights. Zak wasn't always keen on that.'

'Why not?'

Oakley offered a shrug. 'Somebody killed him, yeah?' she enquired, eyes hungry.

'Looks like. Did he have any enemies?'

'Not one.'

'So why did he need a minder?'

She thought for a moment. 'You mean Marcus? He was just a pal from the old days who liked hanging around.'

'So you never saw any trouble when you were out with Zak?'

'Quite the opposite – VIP areas and cocktails on the house.'

'To get back to Zak's home life, were there others present when you visited his house?'

'Just me. He never really had parties – liked the place to himself.'

'You said he might've been seeing other people – any particular names?'

Oakley shook her head again, but then thought of something. 'He was in the kitchen once and a message popped up on his phone. It was lying there on the sofa so I took a look. It was a girl. Younger than me, judging by her photo – not that you can trust those.'

'How young, would you say?'

She looked at both detectives in turn. 'What's going on?' she asked.

'Ever take a look inside the spare bedroom upstairs, Tamsin?' This came from Esson, who was pretending to check that the tape was working. As if the question didn't really mean very much.

'No.'

'Because it was kept locked? Zak ever tell you why that was?'

'No.' Her voice had grown slightly fainter.

'To get back to his phone,' Clarke interrupted, 'you wouldn't happen to know the access code?'

'His birthday – he told me that once. He was useless with passwords.'

'You never thought to open it and check up on him?'

'Why the hell would I do that? We were too busy having a good time. Was he in trouble, is that it? Got that girl pregnant or something?'

Esson and Clarke shared a look, Clarke giving the slightest shake of her head – anything they revealed to Oakley would be internet currency within five minutes.

Oakley kept glancing down at her phone, its screen illuminating every few seconds.

'Theresa and Katie wanting to know how the meeting's going?' Clarke guessed.

'Just notifications.' Oakley turned the screen away from her so that it rested against her thigh.

'Is there anything else you want to tell us, Tamsin?' Esson asked.

'Just that you need to catch whoever did it. Zak was a bit special.'

'We'll catch them,' Esson said. 'And to that end, before you leave we'll need your address and contact number, just so we can keep in touch.'

'Plus a swab and fingerprints,' Esson added, 'for purposes of elimination. We're doing the same for everyone who visited Zak's house.'

Oakley seemed reassured, nodding her wary agreement. 'We were due to go to Prestonfield this weekend, staying overnight. He liked treating me to nice things.'

Finally the tears came. She dabbed at her eyes, trying not to interfere with her make-up.

They walked her as far as the front entrance. There were windows to the sides of the door, and they watched through the glass as she took a selfie in front of the Police Scotland sign, flicking her hair back and crossing one foot in front of the other.

'She's been told it makes you look thinner,' Esson commented.

'I might need just a bit more help than that,' Clarke replied. 'Didn't seem overly upset, did she?'

'Plenty more fish in Tamsin's particular sea,' Esson said. 'But if we check her socials later, I dare say we'll see waterworks.'

'Newspapers will tuck into her like she's sirloin.'

'Funny you should say that, Siobhan. John was telling me that when he gets out, his first appointment is going to be at Prestonfield – I think he has a notion for a steak.'

'It's a popular spot,' Clarke said, turning back towards

the MIT office. She started composing a text to the lab at Howdenhall, telling them to check the victim's date of birth against his phone.

'She's going to blab about the locked bedroom, isn't she?' Esson guessed. 'I maybe shouldn't have brought it up.'

'It's fine,' Clarke reassured her. 'Thing is, she hasn't a clue what he was up to. And she's proof of one thing ...'

'What?'

'His clientele might have wanted their meat on the raw side, but Zak liked his to be that bit more dry-aged.'

Day Five

14

As they queued for breakfast, a couple of prisoners asked Rebus
for news of Darryl Christie.

'Why not speak to one of his team?' Rebus asked back.

'They don't seem to have your privileges.'

'Privileges or not, I know hee-fucking-haw,' Rebus stated,
lifting his tray.

He settled on a seat across from Ratty. For once, Ratty had
his back to the servers. Rebus looked over Ratty's shoulder
towards them. 'The looks Devo's giving you are so filthy I could
probably sell them on Pornhub.'

'That's because I asked Malachi about him, and Malachi
grassed me up.'

Rebus understood now not only why Ratty had his back to
Devo but also why he was pushing the food around on his plate
rather than tucking in. 'You should eat it,' he nudged him. 'If
you start feeling funny, we'll know we've got our man.'

'It's not doping I'm worried about.'

Rebus shrugged and scooped a forkful of Ratty's eggs into
his mouth. Ratty watched his jaw moving.

'For what it's worth, Ratty, I don't think anyone slipped
Jamieson anything. Whatever he took, it was him doing the
taking.'

Rebus sought Mark Jamieson out with his eyes. He was seated with the Wizard. His fame had lasted almost as long as the compress that had been removed from his stapled forehead. Nobody was paying him the slightest heed. Rebus slid his tray towards Ratty. 'Have mine if you like,' he said. 'I don't seem to have much appetite.'

Ratty didn't need telling twice.

Rebus got up and walked over to Jamieson's table. 'All right?' he said by way of greeting, squeezing in next to Jamieson, who had to shuffle along to make room. 'Just need a word,' he told the Wizard. Jamieson had stopped chewing and was reaching for his tea instead.

'Let's say nobody spiked you that night,' Rebus began, his voice not much above a whisper – the other prisoners might have shown minimal interest in Jamieson, but the addition of Rebus to the equation was something else again. 'And you're sure that your cellmate was alive and well at lights-out ...' He waited until Jamieson nodded. 'But you were starting to feel out of it – more so than usual?' Jamieson continued to nod. 'So maybe whoever supplied you with your junk that day had added a little extra to the dosage. Is that a possible scenario?'

Jamieson stared at him, eventually giving a slow shake of the head.

'You hadn't been given a few more pills than usual?' Another shake. 'And you're sure they're the same pills you always got?'

This time Jamieson nodded.

'Had anyone palmed you anything that day, Mark. A little treat? Something new to try?'

'No.' Jamieson slurped at his tea.

'Then there's no reason why you were zonked the way you were.'

'Someone thumped me.'

'Yes, but you say you weren't conscious when that happened – you'd surely have heard them coming in if you had been. Which brings us back to the reason you were out of it. Something you'd been given, obviously.'

192

'Spiked,' Jamieson said, glancing in Devo's direction.

'I'm assuming you get your regular supply from Darryl Christie, yes? Him or one of his guys?'

'Darryl's not the only game in town,' the Wizard interjected. 'Plenty of stuff in here before he came on the scene.'

'But now he's here – you're telling me he'd allow competition?'

'Maybe he'd have no choice.' The Wizard held Rebus's gaze.

'Are you talking about Everett Harrison?'

He just shrugged and cleaned the last of his plate.

'Everything all right here?'

Rebus looked up towards the speaker. It was Blair Samms.

'Just dandy,' he told him.

'You're looking a bit pale, Mark,' Samms went on, ignoring Rebus. 'Need to see a nurse?'

'I'm okay,' Jamieson answered.

'I'll look after him,' the Wizard assured the officer. But Samms's eyes were on Rebus.

'See that you do,' he said, moving away.

Rebus watched him go, reminded that Samms had been on the meal shift that evening too. He turned his attention back to the Wizard.

'I suppose,' he began slowly, 'it's feasible the supplier wouldn't need to be a prisoner at all ...'

'We're banged up here, John. That goes for Darryl just as surely as it does you, me and Mark. But some people have the freedom to come and go. It would only take one.'

Rebus turned his attention back towards Jamieson. 'How about it, Mark? You ready to give me a name?'

'Why would he do that?' the Wizard demanded, voice stiffening. 'The boy's got enough shite to deal with without turning grass.'

'I'm trying to get justice for Jackie Simpson,' Rebus stated.

'A man you barely knew? All because the governor asked you to?' The Wizard gave a snort. 'Makes me wonder what's in it for you – other than your precious sense of "justice".' He waved his fork at Rebus. 'We all know who did it – the one

193

person Jackie said he'd be looking for when he got out. And nothing's going to happen to him. Your lot have already put the brakes on – any sign of them recently? Any POs suddenly scuttling off to be questioned?'

Rebus turned towards Jamieson again. 'It would help if somebody opened up.'

'And pointed the finger towards a fellow inmate, you mean?' The Wizard gave a cold chuckle. 'Just give it up, John. You're not going to—' He broke off as Blair Samms, having circled the hall, approached again.

'All getting a bit heated here, gents,' he commented. 'Maybe time for you to step away, John.'

But it was Mark Jamieson who bounded to his feet, grabbing his tray. 'I'm done anyway,' he muttered.

'Aye, me too,' the Wizard added, rising with his usual studied slowness. Rebus watched him dump his tray and follow Jamieson back to their shared cell.

'You seem to be good at getting up people's noses,' Samms said.

'Speaking of which – you wouldn't be bringing dope into the jail, would you, Officer Samms?'

Samms's eyes burned. 'Now why would you go making an accusation like that?'

Rebus considered his answer. 'Maybe because I'm at the end of my tether.'

'Then you need to step back a little, before that tether ends up choking you.'

Samms began to make another circuit. Rebus felt every eye on him as he sat alone at the table.

'Sod the lot of you,' he muttered to himself, squeezing his eyes shut and rubbing a hand across his brow.

Clarke sat at her desk, having finally managed to reach Louise Hird. She held a cup of takeaway coffee in her free hand, taking occasional sips.

'Just calling to give you an update,' she said.

'I was beginning to feel snubbed.'

'You've heard, then?'

'Have you got into his hard drive yet?'

'We're getting there. Both his phones are already unlocked, not that there's much on them. Almost as if he were trying to keep his two lives separate.'

'He wouldn't be the first. London will be interested in any data – and if your lab isn't up to the task of extracting it …'

'I didn't say that.'

'So are you any nearer to identifying the scumbag who killed the scumbag?'

'There's a mate of his who's gone walkies.'

'Not to mention a certain schoolgirl – can I come see what you've got?'

A buzzing told Clarke that someone else was calling. A mobile number, not one she recognised. 'I have to go,' she told Hird, picking up the incoming call.

'What the hell?' The man's voice was distorted with rage. In the background, a woman was adding to the complaint. It took Clarke a moment, but only a moment.

'Mr Andrews, is there a problem?'

'Yeah, you could call it a problem,' James Andrews growled. 'Since we've just found out our daughter was being used by that paedophile bastard. When were you going to tell us?'

Clarke put her coffee down and lowered her eyelids for a moment. 'You shouldn't have heard the news like this. I'm assuming the media called you?'

'Laura, her name was – wanted a comment. She said she thought we'd have been alerted by you lot. Why weren't we?' There was the sound of the phone being wrenched from Andrews' hand.

'I hope he rots in hell,' Helena told Clarke, voice trembling. 'And I'd give a bloody medal to whoever did for him.' She handed the phone back to her husband.

'What else did this journalist tell you?' Clarke asked. The

look on her face had made Christine Esson curious, and she was closing in on Clarke's desk.

'Wanted to know if we'd ever met this sleazebag,' James Andrews was saying.

'And had you?'

'No. Helena's sure Jas never mentioned him or brought him here.'

Clarke's eyes were on Esson as she spoke. 'Laura Smith was totally out of order contacting you. To answer your question, I intended breaking the news to you today in person.'

'Is Jasmine a suspect?'

Clarke tried to think of a diplomatic answer.

'You can't be fucking serious,' she heard Andrews snarl.

Esson had accessed Laura Smith's blog on Clarke's computer, but there was no update on the case.

'Other journalists will start pestering you,' Clarke was telling Andrews. 'It's up to you whether you talk to them or not, but it might not make our job any easier.'

'We just want her found. We need her back here with us.'

'I understand that. Would it help if we sat down and talked about it?'

'I doubt it. Just don't keep us in the dark.' Much of the anger had drained out of him.

'Again, I'm so sorry you had to find out like this ...' Clarke broke off when she realised Jasmine's father had ended the call.

'Unbelievable,' she muttered as she phoned Laura Smith's number. Esson stayed put, resting against the edge of the desk. Clarke kept her eyes on the homepage of Smith's blog. It changed just as she was being connected. She nodded towards the screen and Esson leaned in to look. There was a photo of Zak Campbell's house, taken from the police cordon. *Champagne Footballer's Secret House of Vice*, yelled the headline.

'I know it's not subtle,' Smith said when she answered. 'But then nuance doesn't pay the bills.'

'What the hell were you thinking?' Clarke was having trouble controlling her temper.

'You should have told them, Siobhan. I was genuinely gob-smacked you hadn't.'

'You know we wanted this kept under wraps.'

'But that was never going to last, was it? I had to get ahead of the pack. It's *my* story, remember – I'm the one who found you Pedro. You'd have been floundering otherwise.'

'In point of fact, *he* found *you*.'

'It's still my story.'

'For a few more minutes maybe – after which it's everyone's, so congratulations.'

'I've got London dailies bidding for me to write them the exclusive. Radio and TV interest, too. I can't give that up, Siobhan. This is what I have to do.'

'You've jeopardised our case.'

But Smith's mind was elsewhere. 'Jesus, do you see how many hits I'm getting? My phone's going nuts, too. I have to go, Siobhan. You'll still keep me in the loop, right? A promise is a—'

It was Clarke's turn to end a call while the speaker was still talking.

'What now?' Esson asked. Clarke gnawed away at her bottom lip for a moment, then rose to her feet, clapping her hands together much as DCI Carmichael had done the previous day.

'Heads up, people,' she said, voice raised above the hubbub. 'The story is out there – online for now, but everywhere else pretty bloody soon.' She saw officers look at each other. 'It wasn't a leak,' she assured them. 'Just one journalist who put two and two together and then jumped the gun. But it means we need to get a rush on, because everyone connected to Zak Campbell and his website will be deciding what stories to tell us and how much they can hold back.'

'I might be able to help there,' Gillian Reeves announced, holding up her phone and waggling it. 'Lab got into the deceased's computer using a password stored on one of his phones. Once inside, seems his security was woeful. They're sending us everything they've got. Should be on your screens any minute now.'

197

The whole room fell silent as they stared at their monitors, during which time Cammy Colson slouched into the office.

'Mortuary's livelier than this,' he commented.

'Anything to tell us?' Clarke asked with her eyes still on her screen.

'Single stab wound, punctured a lung. Probably rendered unconscious when his head connected with the kitchen island. Pathologist reckons he might've survived if he'd made it to A&E. But he lay there for three days, judging by rigor mortis and lividity. Fair bit of coke in his system and a last meal of Thai hot spice crisps – crinkle-cut, if you're interested.' He walked over to the kettle and started making himself a brew, looking in vain for an unused mug.

'No milk either,' someone piped up.

'Why does it always happen to me?'

No one answered, because the promised dump of data suddenly started to arrive.

'There's a ton of it,' Esson commented. She was peering over Clarke's shoulder towards her screen. Clarke got to her feet again, gesturing with a stretched arm.

'This side of the room, focus on the clients – their IDs and contact details. The other side, concentrate on the models – and feel free to call them victims if you prefer, because to my mind that's what they all are. Again, names and contact info. Then we start making phone calls. I want the punters brought here for questioning; the victims can be interviewed at home, parents present as necessary.'

'Some of the users are overseas,' Trisha Singh said, scouring the list.

'Those ones we email if we can't reach them by phone. This has to be done in a hurry. Mainstream media will soon be all over the story. I'm going to have Uber drop us off supplies of sugar and caffeine.'

'And milk,' Colson reminded her.

'All life's little luxuries, Cammy,' Clarke assured him. 'And we can add your report to the file once you've typed it up.'

'That might take a while,' Esson said in an undertone, watching Colson trudge towards his chair with all the easy grace of a Sasquatch. Her phone pinged with another text from Mulgrew. He had upped the ante to three question marks.

'Remind me,' Clarke said, looking from one side of the room to the other. 'Who's on clients and who's on kids?'

'I've already forgotten,' Esson admitted, shutting down her phone and returning to her desk.

Fox having been called in to a meeting of OCCTU, Mulgrew and Zara Shah had gone to HMP Edinburgh to question Chris Novak. Having driven post-meeting to Gayfield Square, Fox was given a copy of the recording, which he listened to on headphones. When asked, Novak denied any relationship, improper or otherwise, with Valerie Watts. There was no assignation in a store cupboard, and during those ten minutes, all he'd done was take a dump. Fox wasn't particularly surprised by the denials. Novak was married with kids.

'Whatever is said in here stays in here,' Mulgrew had stated.

'That why you're taping me?' Novak had responded.

'You're not really helping yourself, Chris,' Mulgrew had persisted. 'Think about it – if you were with Valerie, you've got an alibi.'

'I don't *need* an alibi.' Novak's words had been accompanied by a sound Fox guessed was the single definitive thump of a fist on a tabletop. The session had started going in circles not too long after. Novak was prepared to bad-mouth neither Valerie Watts nor Blair Samms. He didn't know anything about POs on the take, and why were they spending so much time harassing officers and so little quizzing the prisoners? If POs could be bought, why not detectives? And now could he please get back to the work the hard-pressed Scottish taxpayer was employing him to do?

Fox removed the headphones and took them back to Mulgrew's desk.

'Good job,' he said. 'If I'm allowed to say that without sounding condescending.'

Mulgrew had his phone in his hand. Fox had noticed him checking it every few minutes.

'Christine?' he guessed.

'Maintaining radio silence.' Mulgrew looked around the office. 'We could do with her back here. We're stretched and tired and getting nowhere.'

'We got somewhere last night with Valerie Watts,' Fox stated.

'Ruling stuff out isn't the same as ruling it in.'

He shook his head. 'I'm not ruling Watts out – or her lover, come to that. The more I think it over, the more a cell left unlocked at lights-out makes sense. Then all Novak has to do is head there instead of the storeroom.'

'Without any other officers seeing him?'

'Who says they didn't? Cover-up could be bigger than we think. Thing is, did he do it for his own reasons, or did someone else maybe grease his palm?'

'Bringing us back to Everett Harrison again ...' Mulgrew ran his fingernails along his chin. 'I don't know, Malcolm.'

'Just give it some thought, Jason.' Fox patted Mulgrew's shoulder and walked over to the murder wall. Zara Shah was standing in front of it, staring at the photos from the cell.

'What are you working on?' Fox asked.

'The blood,' she said. 'Specifically, what happened to it.'

'Vampire,' Paul Allbright piped up.

'There you go,' Fox told Shah. 'Every question has an answer.'

'In this case, a really stupid answer.' She gave Allbright a look.

'Bite me,' he said.

15

Everett Harrison was lying on his bed reading a legal textbook.

'Reckon you've got a chance?' Rebus asked from the doorway.

'Fuck do you want?' Harrison's voice was still croaky.

'Just wondering if you fancied shooting some pool.'

'It's not pool I fancy shooting, it's your bestie Darryl.'

'Everyone seems to assume we're friends.'

'He's been looking after you in here, hasn't he?'

'I didn't ask for it.'

Harrison placed the book aside and sat up, swivelling his feet onto the floor. He gave Rebus a good hard look. He had the usual sleeves of tattoos, most of them companion pieces to the Liverpool FC pictures covering his walls. Rebus had moved to within a few inches of the cell's only chair. He gave a questioning tilt of the head and Harrison eventually acquiesced. Rebus sat down, but not too comfortably.

'Is it true your boss is going after Christie's gang?'

'Christie seems to think he is.'

'Is he, though?'

Harrison gave a humourless grin. 'Got him rattled, eh?' He stroked his throat with a finger. 'That's what matters.'

'Are you saying Hanlon's not back in the UK?'

'Not back in the UK, not particularly interested in a minnow like Darryl Christie, and doesn't know you from Adam.' He pointed the same finger at Rebus. 'Despite what you told Bobby Briggs in the library. Bobby's not happy with you about that, and neither am I.'

Rebus was not to be deflected. 'So why are Christie's men running scared?'

'Running full stop from what I've heard.' Harrison paused to consider the question. 'Maybe they recognise a sinking ship when they see one.'

'Is trouble coming when Darryl gets out of solitary?'

'That'll be up to him. I can handle whatever he brings.'

'You seem fairly normal, though, if you don't mind me saying.'

'And he's not?'

'I once watched him shoot a man in the face. When that switch gets flipped, no telling what he'll do.'

'Maybe I should get my retaliation in first, then.'

'Or you could ask to be transferred to another hall.'

'For all the good that would do.'

'Funny, the two of you seemed pretty matey for a while.'

'He thought he could turn me. That's not the Scousers' code.' Harrison lay back down again and picked up his book. Rebus got up.

'I'm glad we could have this little chat, Everett. It's good to talk.'

'Off you fuck now,' Harrison growled. Regular service had been resumed.

Back in his own cell, Rebus decided to take a risk, pulling his door closed and climbing onto the lavatory with the burner phone. He'd jotted the number on his hand but then washed it off, confident that he had it memorised. He ended up speaking to a stressed-sounding woman, a toddler bawling in the close vicinity. So he thought for a moment and tried again, this time connecting to an MOT garage.

Third time's a charm, he told himself as he started over.

'Who's this?' Fox answered.

'Trading Standards, sir. We have reason to believe a Mr Malcolm Fox has been falsely presenting himself as a functioning detective.'

'Reduced to prank calls, John? Unless of course you've got something for me.'

'You're not very good at answering your phone, Malcolm.'

'Not when it's a number I don't recognise.'

'Do you really think Christie's men are being targeted?'

'Definitely. Latest was a gun shoved through a car window. Happened in broad daylight. A witness got the car's number plate. Belonged to one of Christie's gang, but the guy had skedaddled by the time we got to his house.'

'No luck ID'ing the attacker?'

'Crash helmet with the visor down.'

'What if I told you he had a Liverpool accent?'

'Did he?'

'Darryl Christie says so.'

'Meaning Shay Hanlon's gang.'

'Yet I've just been chatting to Everett Harrison and he says Hanlon's still overseas and not particularly interested in Darryl.'

'Well of course he'd say that! But Darryl seems to think otherwise, judging from the fact he tried screwing a snooker shot around Harrison's tonsils. Or am I being dim?'

'Of course you're being dim – dim is Malcolm Fox's whole brand.' Rebus listened to the growing silence on the other side of the line. 'I hope I've not hurt your feelings?'

'Esson's lot aren't making much progress, are they? But then she's got other fish to fry now.'

'Has she?'

'See, John, there's stuff I know that you don't.'

'You mean the Zak Campbell murder? Everyone and their dog knows about that. I'm serious, though, Malcolm. You need to think who else stands to benefit as Christie's empire crumbles.'

'I would have thought we all benefit.' Fox paused. Rebus

203

could almost hear the cogs turning. 'Hang on, you mean Mickey Mason?'

'Do I?'

'Recently released from the Bar-L and needing to get back into the game.'

'That's the fellow,' Rebus improvised.

'Has Bobby Briggs told you anything about him?'

'Keeping tight-lipped. The two of them were pretty close at one time.' Rebus tried to make it sound like statement rather than guess.

'And as you said yourself, Briggs and Harrison are chummy. Links in a chain, John, links in a chain.'

Rebus was looking in the direction of his cell door. He couldn't risk much longer. 'Maybe you're smarter than I give you credit for, Malcolm. Will you keep me posted? And in return, I'll keep my ears open here.'

'I'll think about it.'

'Oh, and Malcolm? Next time you don't recognise a number, answer the phone anyway.' Rebus ended the call and climbed down from the lavatory, smiling at the thought of all the sales cold-calls Fox might be opening himself up to.

After hiding the phone, he settled at his desk. He'd been there barely thirty seconds when Blair Samms yanked open his door.

'You all right in there?'

'Something I can do for you, Officer?'

'Just checking. With Darryl Christie elsewhere, could be that some of the prisoners will start getting ideas.'

'But I'm universally admired,' Rebus argued.

'You including Bobby Briggs in that list? Our lives would be a lot quieter if you went back to SRU. Boss says he's considering it.'

'Which boss?' Rebus tried to make it sound like an innocent question.

'Our boss – Mr Tennent. Who did you think I meant?'

204

'A man can sometimes have two masters. There was a stage play a few years back.'

'I've no idea what you're talking about.'

But Rebus could see in the young officer's eyes that he did. 'Why would you personally want me moved?' he asked.

'It's not personal.'

'Am I becoming a thorn in your side, Officer Samms? Asking too many awkward questions?'

Samms's face remained a mask. 'Governor's thinking over my suggestion,' he underscored, turning to leave. Rebus shifted in his chair so he was facing the wall, with its scratched graffiti and smudges and stains.

'If not Hanlon, then who?' he mused aloud in a quiet voice. Who stood to gain from the detonation of Darryl Christie's empire?

I would have thought we all benefit.

'You might have a point there, Malcolm,' he added. 'Though I doubt you're quite bright enough to see it ...'

He put in a request to speak to the governor, and was surprised when the man himself turned up at his cell door.

'I was looking forward to those biscuits,' Rebus said wistfully.

Howard Tennent was dressed in a winter coat that reached down past his knees. He was also carrying his briefcase. Rebus guessed that the combination lock would have been engaged before it left his office.

'I'm in a bit of a rush here, John,' Tennent said.

'Off somewhere nice?'

'I was presuming you've got something for me?'

Rebus was seated at his desk and saw no reason not to stay there. 'I don't want to be moved,' he stated.

'Who says you're being moved?'

'Blair Samms might have dropped a hint.'

'Blair Samms is not in charge of this prison.'

205

'His notion is, with Darryl elsewhere, knives might be out for me.'

'Well, he's got a point, hasn't he?'

'I'm not sure that's the reason he wants me moved. Could be he's more interested in the digging I've been doing.'

Tennent's eyes narrowed. 'And why would that interest him particularly?'

'You know there are rumours he's on the take?'

The governor bristled. 'Those have been looked into and dismissed.'

'Was he reckoned to be Darryl Christie's stooge or Everett Harrison's?'

'I've really not got time for this, John.'

'I want to visit Darryl again.'

'Why?'

'Couple of things I need to ask him.'

Tennent stared at him, wanting more, but all Rebus offered was his silence.

'To do with Jackie Simpson's death?'

'What else?'

'It seems to me you've not been great shakes in that department so far.'

'I don't see anyone doing better.'

'DI Fox provides me with regular updates – interviews are still being conducted, forensic evidence analysed ...'

'I'm ex-CID, Howard. All you're getting from Fox is the usual fluff. I'd be doing the exact same if I was making so little progress. You might think I'm being slow, but it's the way I work.' Rebus spun a finger around in the air. 'In circles, slowly inwards.'

'So there *is* news?'

'There might well be – once I've talked to Darryl.'

The governor gave a sigh. 'You're a pain in the hole, John – did anyone ever tell you that?'

'It gets a chapter in my autobiography.'

'You'll tell me the outcome tomorrow, okay?'

'Yes, sir.' Rebus held two fingers to one of his temples and gave a little flick, as if in salute.

Forty minutes later, he was on his way to SRU, accompanied by Eddie Graves.

'How are tricks with you?' Rebus asked.

'Back's playing up again. Sleep's not great either. Son dinged his car the other day. He's fine, but it's the third time. He's going to be uninsurable at this rate.'

'Could be worse, though, eh?'

Graves glanced at him. 'How?'

'Well, you might have to spend your days surrounded by the dregs of society.'

'Retirement can't come soon enough.'

'You'll miss us when you're gone.'

'I won't miss being called Michelle, though.'

'It's meant affectionately,' Rebus said. 'But to get back to my original question, I was actually meaning in here – with the murder and Darryl Christie kicking off and everyone's springs ready to snap ...'

Graves gave a shrug. 'It's like the old saying – what's for ye won't go by ye.'

'I always thought that was a bit bleak myself.'

'Your point being?'

Rebus found he had no answer to that, none that would offer consolation to Graves or change his worldview. So they walked the rest of the route in silence, all the way to Darryl Christie's cell.

The door was unlocked by one of the faces Rebus knew from his time in the unit. Both officers stood guard, door ajar, as Rebus entered the room's tight confines.

'I need to look up the word solitary in the dictionary,' Darryl Christie muttered.

He was lying on his bed, hands clasped together on his stomach. He half turned his head to make eye contact with his visitor.

'How's it going out there?' he asked.

'Everett Harrison's taken to sounding like a chain-smoking Fenella Fielding and Blair Samms wants me moved back here. The first of those was your doing, but what about the second?'

'He's got a point, though – up to now you've been tolerated, but you're still an ex-cop, and ex-cops tend not to thrive in the general prison population. Plus you're a marked man.'

'Meaning Bobby Briggs?'

'For one.'

'Who else?'

'How long have you got?' Christie drummed the fingers of one hand against the knuckles of the other. 'Anyway, what brings you to my throne room? Managed to speak to Malcolm Fox yet?'

'He knows I need a word,' Rebus improvised. Then: 'You're Mark Jamieson's supplier, right?'

'No comment.'

'See, he ended up KO'd. As a regular user, he'd know how much to take and the effect it would have. This went above and beyond.'

'You're saying the merch was tampered with?'

'Either that or switched.'

'By whoever it was who did for poor Jackie?' Christie nodded his understanding. 'They still had to unlock the cell, though, didn't they? And the one thing in here I have trouble laying my hands on is a magic key. I doubt any of us could get hold of one without taking an officer hostage – and that didn't happen, did it?'

'No hostage-taking required if the price was right. Who brings all the dope in? Blair Samms?'

'I could tell you, but then I'd have to kill you.' Christie offered a wink. It struck Rebus that he was a lot more relaxed than previously, a bit more pleased with himself.

'You sure it's Hanlon who's gunning for your boys? No other candidates you can think of?'

'I'm sure.'

'Why are you smiling?'

'I just got word we're fighting back. Scouse bastard stuck his gun through another car window, but this time my boy wrenched it out of his hand, near broke the shooter's wrist in the process. Roared off on his motorbike, tool and dignity left behind. That's the message my lot needed – these wankers can be beaten. Want to know the best bit?'

'What?'

'It was an air pistol. No threat whatsoever. You could maybe pass that on to Everett Harrison – no threat whatsoever.' Christie stared at the ceiling again, the smile spreading across his face.

'Unless Hanlon decides to escalate,' Rebus speculated.

'He'd better be quick then, now there's a bounty on his head.'

Rebus took a moment to digest this. 'How much?'

'Enough.'

'Plane fares included?'

'Hanlon reckons he's protected in Brazil – but that protection disappears in a puff of smoke if the offer's right.' Christie glanced in Rebus's direction. 'No plane fares needed.'

'I'm guessing this is something I shouldn't share with Harrison.'

'Maybe I'm testing your loyalty.'

'And maybe you're spinning me another of your lines. How many more days are you in here?'

'Out tomorrow, probably.'

'Back to Trinity Hall alongside Harrison?'

'That's up to the governor.' Christie paused and yawned, wetting his lips with his tongue. 'So is that the sum total of your progress on Jackie's murder? Mr Tennent must be disappointed.'

'A bit more cooperation would help.'

'You're telling me I should cooperate with an ex-cop who's been tasked with pushing the blame onto a con rather than a uniform? Jog the fuck on, John. Now if you don't mind, I could do with some shut-eye.' He yawned again. 'Waiting till after lights-out to start making business calls means I lose out on my eight hours.' He raised a hand and waved it towards Rebus, then turned on his side, face towards the wall. Rebus stood there for a moment before pushing open the cell door.

'You sent him to sleep,' Graves said, staring at the prone figure. He sounded almost envious.

16

Clarke and Esson were seated side by side in the office, going through a printout of names, email addresses and, in some cases, phone numbers.

It helped that Zak Campbell hadn't been versed in the ways of the dark web and had left behind plenty of instructions to himself on which passwords he needed to access the various domains. Subs and fees were paid by bitcoin to an offshore account, outwith the UK's jurisdiction. Still, by dint of having all the instructions they needed, they had accessed his balance and found that it was in the hundreds of thousands – at current rates of exchange.

He paid the models mostly by cash or with gifts of electronics and vouchers for online retailers. The twenty-three teenagers on his books were now real names and faces. Most of them had turned eighteen, but four could be classified as children. Jasmine was the only one from her school. Those awkward phone calls and visits to parents and family homes had already begun. So far, only Jasmine was AWOL. Swabs and fingerprints were being taken, so that they could be matched to the crime scene. Each step in the investigation had to be meticulous and defence-lawyer-proof. The Procurator Fiscal's office was in close touch with DCI Carmichael, and he in turn was checking regularly that things were being done in accordance with procedures and protocols.

The users they'd identified so far – there were almost a thousand regulars, with thousands more one-time payers – were men ranging from their twenties to their seventies, from all corners of the UK and beyond, stretching as far as Australia and Bermuda. So far only one woman, based in Hong Kong but Scots-born.

A few pseudonymous accounts were proving difficult to break down. Mae McGovern had been persuaded to accept CEOP's offer of help from the National Crime Agency, whose opinion was that these individuals were well used to covering their tracks and therefore probably breaking the law in other ways – either that or they were IT professionals. Clarke and Esson scoured the list again. One Glasgow councillor, a probation service officer in Derby, a company director in Aberdeen, a teacher in North Wales. Some had already been contacted. Peter 'Pedro' Cowan was there too, which made Clarke think of Laura Smith and the breaking of the story. The major incident team had been fielding requests ever since, the mainstream media hungry for a feed. Bryan Carmichael had hosted a hastily arranged press conference at which he shared the bare minimum of information, to the irritation of those gathered before him. The office had watched on their phones or computers, giving shrugs afterwards. The media would be far from satisfied and the usual keyboard warriors would be dusting off their pitchforks. Someone had already thrown paint at the downstairs window of Zak Campbell's home and sprayed the word *PAEDO* on his garage door.

'At least they can spell,' Esson had commented when shown a photo of the damage.

Someone had opened a window in the office to let out the smells of the various fast-food offerings delivered to the desks of officers who didn't have time or inclination to take a proper break. Clarke's last meal had been a sandwich, as had the meal before that. Not that she had much of an appetite. Coffee was keeping her going. Esson, as usual, drank only mugs of hot water – couldn't stand tea or coffee. As a result, she looked a lot less wired than Clarke felt.

'An awful lot of suspects,' Gillian Reeves commented, waving the same list of names in the air as she passed the shared desk. 'And still no sign of Marcus Simpson. One of our patrols checked again an hour ago.'

'What do his neighbours say?'

'Apparently it's not that unusual.'

'His car reg is out there, right?'

Reeves nodded. 'Everyone's on the alert.'

Clarke and Esson shared a look. Jasmine Andrews and Marcus Simpson: both known to the victim, both whereabouts currently unknown. The Jasmine inquiry was now a hunt for a murder suspect, DCI Carmichael convinced that the timing of her disappearance was no coincidence. But he had also stressed that no one outside of MIT – her parents included – were to be told this. Cammy Colson had been a bit more blunt in his summation: *She either did it or she got someone to do it for her ...*

'A lot of these we can probably put a line through, right?' Esson said, tapping the stapled sheets of paper. 'The overseas ones, I mean.'

'We can't rule anyone out, Christine – Fiscal wouldn't like that.'

'If we're ranking them, though ...'

Clarke nodded her agreement. 'Of course they're far less likely. We talk to locals first, but that probably includes Glasgow ... maybe even as far as our man in Aberdeen.'

'We've already got a few booked in for interview – with the promise of maximum discretion in return for their cooperation.'

'That room's going to be getting a lot of use. We'll have a video camera installed by tomorrow at the latest.'

Esson's phone buzzed. She checked caller ID and got up, stepping away from the desk. 'Hi there, Jason,' she said. 'Sorry I've not been picking up your calls.'

'I'm feeling decidedly neglected here, Christine.'

'Are you at the prison or Gayfield Square?'

'The latter.'

'Case hitting a wall?'

'Lucky for us the public's attention has moved elsewhere. Hasn't stopped Mae McGovern turning the screws, mind. How are things at St Leonard's?'

Esson turned from the window and studied her surroundings. 'Just ever so slightly manic. Campbell's computer has yielded most of his users.'

'Well, that's a huge step. Any interesting names?'

'Celebs, you mean? None to speak of. One ex-footballer, who'll have been shocked to know who was taking his money.'

'So the next stage is giving them all a grilling?'

'We're going to be kept busy.'

'Has Marcus Simpson turned up yet?'

'No. I don't suppose you can shed any light?'

'He still has family in town, that's about as much as I know. Except that he's got a burial to plan. Might be worth checking if he's still in touch with the funeral directors.'

'That's a good idea, thanks.'

'You'll come and lend a hand in return, yes?'

Esson couldn't help but smile at his persistence. 'Give me half an hour,' she said.

On her way back to the desk, she phoned the mortuary, where Jackie Simpson's body was being held. She asked about funeral arrangements and got a name and number. As she settled again next to Clarke, she made the call to a parlour in Greenhill. Clarke gave her a questioning look, but Esson was already speaking.

'Yes, hello there. This is Detective Sergeant Christine Esson. I'm attached to the inquiry regarding Jackie Simpson – he might be John Simpson in your records.' While she listened, she mouthed the words *funeral director* to Clarke, who nodded her understanding. 'Yes, that's right,' she continued. 'What I'm wondering is, are you in touch with his son, Marcus?' Esson watched Clarke give a silent round of applause. 'So when is he coming in for that meeting? Today?' She angled her phone

214

so that she could check the time on its screen. 'That's only an hour from now. He hasn't phoned to cancel or change the arrangement?' She listened for a moment, shaking her head for Clarke's benefit. 'Well, if he does get in touch, I'd be grateful if you didn't mention that I've spoken with you.' She listened again. 'Oh, I'm sure discretion goes with the territory. Many thanks again.'

She ended the call, grabbed a notepad and jotted down the details of the funeral parlour, handing them to Clarke.

'I need to be elsewhere,' she explained. 'It's Jason we have to thank for this, and he wants me to show my face at Gayfield Square.'

'Has there been a break in the case?' Clarke asked.

'Not even a minor fracture. Any chance you can keep Marcus waiting until I get back?'

'Depends how cooperative he's feeling – always supposing he turns up in the first place.'

'Oh ye of little faith,' Esson said, making for the door.

The first thing Marcus Simpson asked Clarke was whether he needed a solicitor. This was in her car. He had arrived at the funeral home in a minicab, Clarke and Colson intercepting him before he reached the front door. He'd looked resigned to his fate as they led him to the Astra, putting him in the back seat, where Colson joined him, having checked that the child locks were engaged – didn't want him making a dash for it at the first set of red lights.

'Do you think you need one?' Clarke had asked, making eye contact via the rear-view mirror.

'You tell me.'

'Well, it's up to you, Marcus. But all we really want right now is a chat.'

'So chat.'

'Once we get to St Leonard's.'

'St Leonard's?'

215

'This isn't about your dad – it's to do with your pal Zak.'

'What about him?' He had turned his head sharply, suddenly interested in the passing scenery.

'Never play poker, Marcus,' Clarke advised. 'Your body right now is one mahoosive tell ...'

At the station, he was invited to make himself comfortable in the interview room. Clarke provided a mug of tea and a KitKat.

'Preferential treatment,' she said. He had his phone in one hand, both knees bouncing. 'Who've you been calling?'

'Undertaker – had to apologise, didn't I?'

'That was decent of you. We won't be releasing the body for a while yet anyway.'

'Why wait? It's not like you lot are ever going to solve it.'

'What makes you so sure?'

'Stands to reason.' He lifted the mug to his lips.

'Where've you been hiding anyway?'

'I've not been hiding. Just staying at my cousin's. I do that sometimes. We play games – should see the set-up he's got: multiple screens, interactive chairs, VR headsets ...'

'You didn't think we might be wanting a word?'

'Couldn't care less one way or the other.' He took a loud slurp of tea. Clarke got the feeling he was trying to rattle her. She snatched the uneaten KitKat from the table, unwrapped it and took a bite.

'What happened to "preferential treatment"?' he asked with a scowl.

'That was before you started pissing me off.'

He jutted out his jaw and hoisted his phone. 'Maybe I should talk to your boss.'

'My boss?'

'DCI Fox.'

'How do you know Malcolm Fox?'

'My dad did him a few favours.'

'Did he now?' Clarke pushed the remains of the KitKat back across the table. Simpson just looked at it. 'What sort of favours?' She watched the young man shrug. 'Was he in touch after your dad died?'

'No. But I phoned him.'

'When?'

'I didn't want fingers pointed at me when Zak died. Fox said there was nothing he could do. Told me never to call him again.'

'That was the only time you've spoken with DCI Fox?' She watched him nod.

'Dad gave me his number a while back. He knew I might get in trouble one day and need a friend. Might've worked if Dad hadn't been killed. After that, Fox was done with us.' He picked up the KitKat, studied it for saliva and then took a bite. Clarke checked the time on her phone. She was hoping she wouldn't have to bring Colson in.

'We should probably save this for the interview,' she said.

'I thought this *was* the interview?'

The words were just out of his mouth when the door flew open and Christine Esson manoeuvred her way in, bringing a chair with her. 'Apologies if I've kept you waiting,' she said, sounding breathless. She started readying the recording equipment before she made herself comfortable, shrugging her way out of her coat and draping it over the back of her chair.

'Before you turn that on,' Clarke said, 'Marcus has just been telling me that his dad used to do favours for a DCI called Malcolm Fox.'

'Oh?' Esson stared at Simpson. 'What sort of favours?'

'Like an informant, I suppose. And see where it got him ...'

With the tape rolling, they identified themselves and told Simpson to do the same.

'I didn't do anything to Zak!' he burst out instead.

'Name, please,' Esson repeated. It was more order than question.

'Marcus Simpson,' he eventually relented.

'And what was your relationship to the deceased, Mr Simpson?'

'We were mates.'

'Yet you don't seem to be grieving.'

'You said the same when you were asking me about my dad. Maybe I just don't show my emotions.' He folded his arms, but then, perhaps mindful of Clarke's crack about poker tells, unfolded them again and stuffed his hands into his pockets instead. He was keeping the hood of his skiing jacket up, same as it had been when he'd stepped out of the cab at the funeral parlour. It didn't bother Clarke, but Esson asked him if he was feeling the cold.

'No,' he said.

'You were more than mates with Zak, weren't you?' Clarke enquired.

'No,' he repeated, bristling.

'I just mean you worked for him – sort of like a minder.'

'I looked out for him, same as any wingman would.'

'And he looked after you – financially, I mean?'

'He sometimes put his hand in his pocket.'

'But you've not seen so much of him lately?' Esson said. 'Is that because you found out about Young Fresh East Coast?'

Simpson shifted in his chair and hunched his shoulders, but kept his mouth closed.

'If anything,' Clarke added, 'it makes you more admirable, Marcus – not sticking by him once you knew. Of course, coming to us would have been even better. Could be Zak would still be alive, too—'

'Then again,' Esson interrupted, 'maybe what he did with those kids didn't bother you at all. Maybe you were even there, aiding and abetting. We're talking to every single individual he groomed and filmed, so we'll soon know either way.'

'I had nothing to do with it!' Simpson blurted out, face turning crimson. 'And you're right, it's why I walked away.' He puffed out his cheeks and exhaled. 'They were young at first, but not *that* young – eighteen plus. He'd chat them up in pubs and clubs. Seemed to have a sixth sense for the ones who might be willing. Christ knows where he got the idea from, but once it got going, it just snowballed.' He paused, checking to see

218

if there was anything left in his mug. 'But the punters kept nagging him, they wanted younger and younger, and they'd pay top whack. Zak started hanging around outside schools and youth clubs. He'd stand next to his Maserati and wait to see who took an interest. I was never there – ask anybody – but then he showed me one night ... showed me some of the footage, told me how young the girl was ...'

'Was this Jasmine?'

'Jas, aye.'

'You knew her?'

'Saw her at the house once, just to say hello to.'

'You didn't think to warn her off?'

'I know I should have.'

'When was the last time you saw her?'

'That one time in the house – maybe six weeks back.'

'Did Zak ever talk about his clients?'

'The punters, you mean?' Simpson shook his head.

'Would you be happy for us to take a swab and prints, Marcus?' Esson asked. He looked from her to Clarke and back again.

'I keep telling you I didn't kill him.'

'But you visited the house, and that means your DNA's almost certainly there.'

He removed his hood so he could run a hand over his head, growing edgier.

'We just want to get at the truth, Marcus,' Esson said quietly.

'Like with my dad, you mean?' He glared at her.

'I've actually just come from Gayfield Square,' she informed him. 'We're far from giving up on finding whoever killed your father.'

He lowered his head again.

'How did you *really* feel when you heard Zak was dead?' Clarke asked.

He took a moment to consider. 'I thought I must be hallucinating – first my dad, now this. My cousin says I'm like some kind of bad-luck charm.'

'But you were surprised?'

'Shocked, aye.'

'So he wasn't especially worried – in fear of being attacked, I mean? The fact he had you guarding him hints that he had enemies.'

'He just wanted to look big. Plus, aye, sometimes an arsehole in a pub or club would want a square go – but only because Zak was better off than them and didn't mind flaunting it. Swear to God, he could pick up any woman he saw – sweep her right out from under her boyfriend's nose and whisk her off in the Maz. He sometimes filmed them, too – had one of those wee cameras on a shelf by his bed.'

'We've seen some of the footage,' Clarke stated.

'Aye, me too. Zak wasn't the shy retiring sort.'

'But you've no idea who might have wanted him dead?'

'Not a scooby.' He slouched a little lower in his chair, knees still going up and down like caffeinated pistons.

'Something that's been bothering me,' Clarke said slowly. 'From what we've learned, Zak wasn't the savviest when it came to tech. So how come he was able to set up the website and everything around it?' She watched Simpson's face fall. 'He had to have access to someone with that kind of know-how – someone a bit like your game-playing cousin.' Simpson turned his head towards the far wall, as if there was something fascinating on display there other than scratched and peeling paintwork. Bingo, Clarke thought.

'Would the guy be in trouble?' he eventually mumbled.

'I can't think why.'

'Wish I'd never introduced the pair of them. Zak didn't even pay Tommy what he owed him.'

'We're going to need to talk to Tommy about the work he did for Zak,' Clarke stated with quiet authority. 'There might be bits and pieces he can help us navigate.'

'He'll know I've grassed him up.'

'He's family. He'll understand. And if it gets us Zak's killer, he'll be helping confirm your innocence. I'd call that a win for you and him both. Now we just need his address ...'

Simpson licked his lips while he made up his mind, then recited it into the microphone.

'Thank you, Marcus,' Clarke said. When she looked at Esson, Esson raised a single eyebrow. Clarke got the message and nodded her agreement.

'I think we're done here – for now.' She checked the time, adding it to the recording before Esson switched off the machine. The tapes went into evidence bags, Esson handing Simpson his copy.

He stared at the bag and its contents. 'You said he "groomed" them – it wasn't like that; nobody got hurt.'

'He did groom them, though,' Clarke countered. 'And you stood by and let him.'

Simpson's face darkened. 'I can go, aye?'

'Soon as we've swabbed you and got your dabs,' Esson said. 'So stay sitting where you are – might take us a few minutes to rustle up a kit.'

Simpson hoisted his emptied mug. 'Refill wouldn't go amiss.'

'You can stick your refill up your backside,' Clarke said, getting to her feet and making her exit.

17

A uniform was dispatched to the interview room to keep an eye on Simpson until a testing kit could be found. Clarke and Esson sat together in the office with fresh drinks.

'Malcolm Fox?' Esson said. 'Who didn't bother to tell me that my prison victim was his snitch?'

'We should probably have a word with him about that.'

'And this Tommy Simpson character – is he really not in any trouble?'

'I wouldn't go that far, Christine. For starters, Zak didn't pay him what he owed him. That gives us another possible motive.'

'So we bring him in?' Esson was studying an incoming text on her phone.

'We definitely bring him in,' Clarke confirmed. Esson was waggling her phone between thumb and forefinger.

'That was Jason,' she said. 'Fox has just landed at Gayfield Square – he was elsewhere when I dropped in. I won't say Jason was pining, but he couldn't shut up about him. And he's definitely still sore that he's not here instead of me.' She paused before holding up her car key in her other hand. 'Yours or mine?' she asked.

'Yours,' Clarke decided.

*

Gayfield Square police station was a utilitarian concrete eye-sore on an otherwise attractive New Town square. The staff car park was at ground level and open to the elements. Fox's car – his gloss-black pride and joy – was recognisable. With no other spaces free, Esson parked across its nose. She reached into the door pocket of her Skoda and offered Clarke some gum. The two women then sat chewing and thinking their thoughts.

'We could be here all day,' Clarke eventually said.

'It's nice to switch off, though, isn't it?'

'Yeah, like that's what we're doing.'

Esson took her phone out and started a text message. She showed Clarke the screen. 'What do you think?'

The text was addressed to Jason Mulgrew: *I'm coming back – got a bone to pick with Fox. Tell him to stay put!*

'Worth a try,' Clarke said, watching Esson press send. They only had to wait a further couple of minutes before Fox appeared, tugging his driving gloves over his fingers.

'The man never could stand a confrontation,' Clarke muttered.

Fox let out an audible complaint as he noticed someone had boxed him in, only recognising Clarke and Esson as he got closer. Clarke had slid her window down. His face appeared at it, saying nothing.

'Back seat,' she told him. He looked thunderous, but eventually climbed in.

'Very clever, Christine,' he said, teeth showing. The two women turned as best they could to face him.

'How are things with you, DCI Fox?' Clarke asked. 'Congratulations on the promotion, by the way.'

'I don't know what you're talking about.'

'Well, Plausible Deniability always has been your middle name.'

After a few seconds of silence, he caved. 'You've been talking to Marcus Simpson.'

'We have. He tells us his dad was working for you.'

'He was human intelligence, yes.'

'And that wasn't worth sharing with the murder team?' Esson bristled.

'I didn't think it germane.'

'That wasn't your decision to make!'

'I have operations I need to protect, Christine. Things well above your pay grade.'

'It wasn't accidental, was it?' Clarke added. 'Jackie Simpson breaking into that particular nail bar? He did it at your behest so you'd have a reason to walk in afterwards and take a look around. I can't believe him ending up in jail was part of the plan.'

'It wasn't. But he got sloppy.'

'Did you try to intervene in the case?' Clarke saw what the look on his face meant. 'No, of course not,' she went on. 'You said it yourself, you've got operations you need to protect. So you probably didn't go out of your way to help him in prison either?'

Fox twisted a little in his seat. 'I'm not sure this is getting us anywhere.'

'You told me about the break-in,' Esson interrupted. 'And about how Everett Harrison might go ballistic if he ever found out about the connection to Jackie Simpson.'

'You see? I was trying to help!'

'Help how?'

'By pointing you in the right direction.' Fox was starting to sound annoyed.

'After the fact,' Clarke said. Fox glared at her.

'What do you mean?'

'Your man was on the same wing as Harrison.'

'In a cell directly opposite,' Esson added. 'You could have had him moved.'

'But then he'd have been useless to you,' Clarke stated quietly. 'Placed where he was, he could be your eyes and ears. If Harrison or Christie let anything slip, Jackie Simpson might hear it. How did you communicate? Had to be by phone?' She watched Fox give a shrug. 'A very dangerous game, as it turned out.'

'As far as I know,' Fox said, his voice growing more confident, 'the inquiry still has no motive for the murder. In other words, you're getting nowhere, Christine. Possibly because you're spending so much time in Siobhan's pocket. It's Jason who's doing all the running – he's smart *and* he's a team player. An exemplary officer, in other words.' He made a show of angling his head towards the windows of the MIT office above the car park. 'Your colleagues aren't particularly happy about all the time you're spending elsewhere. Mae McGovern's strongly minded to reel you back in. A word from me and she'll do exactly that.'

'She might be a bit too busy pondering whether to have you charged with obstructing that same inquiry,' Esson responded. 'Goodbye to your dreams of promotion to DCI.'

Fox tried not to look flustered – tried but failed. 'The break-in was Jackie's idea, you know.'

'It's not us you need to convince,' Clarke suggested. 'It's McGovern, Jason and the rest of the team. You'll be saving us the bother of grassing you up.'

After a further moment's thought, he pushed open the door, but then paused. 'These are ugly people we're talking about – Harrison and Christie and Hanlon. Thugs who think they can operate with no fear of the likes of you and me. To take men like that down – to be in with even a *chance* of taking men like that down ... Sometimes there's no nice, clean way of going about it.' He got out and slammed the door shut. When he stopped by his own car, he seemed to be considering unlocking it and fleeing the scene, but instead he gave Clarke and Esson one final steely glare before heading back into the building.

'Those sounded like lines stolen from the John Rebus hand-book,' Esson said.

'Recited by an actor who's B-list at best.'

Esson turned towards Clarke. 'Enjoy that?' she asked.

'Almost as good as chocolate,' Clarke replied, returning Esson's smile.

Having said his piece, Fox stood ramrod-straight in front of Mae McGovern's desk, hands clasped behind his back, feet slightly parted. Jason Mulgrew stood to one side of him, arms folded and head slightly bowed as though deep in thought. McGovern had been glowering for the past several minutes, Fox failing to match her gaze for more than a few seconds at a time, try as he might.

The silence in the room stretched, though outside noises intruded, the normal sounds of a busy police station. Just for a moment, Fox was reminded of the one time in high school when he'd been summoned to the rector's office for skipping a class.

'I'm so very disappointed in you,' the rector had said solemnly. 'You of all people, Malcolm ...'

He heard DCI McGovern clear her throat. 'Well,' she said, 'this is all a bit of a sorry fucking mess, wouldn't you agree? You shoulder-charge your way into a murder inquiry without bothering to inform any of us that the victim was a close associate?'

'Not *that* close ...'

'Just close enough to jeopardise the prosecution case! Fiscal's office will be shitting brimstone when I tell them. You've compromised this inquiry, DI Fox.'

'I really don't think it's that serious.'

'Are you suddenly an expert on how the judicial system works in this country?'

'I'm not exactly unversed in the ways of the courts.'

McGovern cut him off with a glare. 'You need to be gone from here. I mean, right this minute. Back to Gartcosh while I decide what to do with you.' She leaned back in her chair. 'Meeting over. Dismissed.'

Fox stayed put, trying to think what else to say, but then felt Mulgrew's hand take him by the elbow.

'Come on, Malcolm,' he said, guiding him to the door and opening it.

'I should go say goodbye to the troops,' Fox muttered, once they were in the corridor.

'I'll explain things for you. The boss seemed pretty certain that she wanted you off the premises PDQ. I'm not sure it would do to cross her – any more than you already have, I mean.' Mulgrew gave a smile, shaking his head slowly. 'I've got to say, though – I do admire you. You've got hidden depths. Almost like a spy or something.'

Fox reached out and gripped Mulgrew's hand in his. 'Promise me you'll keep me in the loop, Jason. This case means a lot to me. And when all this is done, I'll give you the tour of Gartcosh that I promised you – access all areas. You'll meet a lot of useful people. Deal?'

Mulgrew checked that there was no one in the vicinity. 'Deal,' he said, returning Fox's handshake.

Gillian Reeves looked like she needed her batteries recharging as she rose from her desk, stretching her neck and spine before walking over towards Clarke. Clarke paused with her hands hovering above her keyboard – Reeves's face said it was not good news.

'Peter Cowan,' Reeves said. 'He was the first client you ID'd?'

'Aka Pedro,' Clarke confirmed.

'Well, he won't be available for future questioning – jumped from Salisbury Crags this morning. Body found by a jogger.'

'Poor sod,' Christine Esson said from the other side of the desk.

'I wonder if any others will do the same. Respectable married men with careers and kids ...' Reeves was already on her way back to her chair.

Clarke pictured Cowan. Living quietly with his family, a regular at the Mallaig Inn, world suddenly turned upside down, his secret self about to be made public. Her phone was telling her she had an incoming call: Laura Smith. She snatched the handset from her desk and answered.

'I just heard,' she said.

'And there I was hoping to give you the news as an olive branch,' Smith said.

'Do you know if he left a note?'

'I've not been to his house yet.'

'But you will?'

'I'm driving there right now.'

'I'm sure the family will be thrilled.'

'Can't say I'm enthusiastic myself, Siobhan, but it has to be done.'

'Why?'

'So the story I write is as truthful as it can be. I'm not going to apologise for that. You just beat me to the funeral home, you know – I hope Marcus Simpson was talkative.'

'Goodbye, Laura.' Clarke listened as Smith attempted a long, weary sigh.

'Fine then,' the reporter said, ending the call.

Clarke walked to the kettle, checked the water level and switched it on. While she waited, she approached Cammy Colson's desk. He was digging into Zak Campbell's personal life, mostly by dint of studying his social media postings.

'If it wasn't for the fact he's lying in a chiller cabinet at the mortuary, I might be envious,' Colson said. 'Booze and glamorous women, nightclubs and fast cars ...'

'The women were all consenting adults, yes?' Clarke peered over his shoulder at his screen.

'Seem to be. But in his private messages, the ones between him and his mates, there's plenty of what you might term misogyny.'

'Meaning you wouldn't call it that?'

Colson turned his face towards her. 'Don't go pointing that gun at me, Siobhan. When have I ever—'

'I'm sorry, Cammy.' She held up her hands in surrender.

'I know you're one of the good guys, just like your cousin the prison officer. So many good guys in the world – maybe one of them is sheltering Jasmine.'

'On that subject ...'

'Yes?'

'I've been thinking about the murder weapon. No prints – so was she wearing gloves, or did she wrap it in a towel or something?'

'Maybe she wiped it clean.'

'But it all points to a degree of planning, doesn't it? Rather than spur of the moment? She's fourteen, never been in trouble, seems keener on K-pop than *Line of Duty* ...' He broke off. 'She didn't do it, did she? But does that mean she persuaded Marcus?'

'He says he barely knew her.'

'So she's not hiding out at his cousin's place?'

'We'll ask him when we see him ...'

Half an hour later, there was scattered applause as a couple of boxes were brought into the office. Clarke could make out the clinking of glass from one of them. Trisha Singh had grabbed the accompanying note.

'Beers in one, softies in the other,' she announced. 'Compliments of DCI Carmichael.'

'Reckon that makes it knocking-off time,' Esson said, watching her fellow detectives choosing their favoured drinks. Clarke's look indicated that she didn't necessarily agree . 'We've done loads,' Esson assured her. 'Don't want people burning out too soon.'

It was true – energy levels had been dropping for the past hour or so, but now spirits were lifting again. Carmichael knew what he was doing.

'Race you,' Clarke told her, rising to her feet.

Rebus had noticed at dinner – the prison officers seeming more frazzled than usual. He focused on his fellow inmates but saw no reason for the examples of short-temperedness and lack of humour coming from the POs. He wondered if something had happened – another targeted threat or attack on an officer's car. None of the faces he saw seemed in the mood to be asked, so he ate his food and kept his counsel. Ratty had noticed too, of course, his eyes darting around the room. As Rebus met the Wizard's gaze, the old man gave a slow blink and a nod – he too could sense it. Then Billy Groam tried a bit of gentle teasing with Kyle Jacobs, and whatever Jacobs said back to him had Groam leaping to his feet, instantly combative. Two more officers intervened, while a third rested his hand close by the alarm panel. Everett Harrison just laughed, like this was entertainment he was paying for.

'We've missed the church bells again,' the Wizard commented.

Mark Jamieson looked to Rebus. 'Every single day,' he said.

'I think only the Wizard really hears them,' Rebus obliged.

Slowly things settled. Curfew was nearing and prisoners began to focus on last-minute arrangements – books and DVDs to be borrowed or swapped; maybe a cigarette or two handed over, tomorrow's leisure activities diarised. Sometimes Rebus wondered if a shared cell would be preferable, someone to swap a bit of chat with. Yes, but then they'd be sharing toileting and nightly farts, too.

'No thanks,' he said to himself as he stood just inside his open door, waiting for an officer to lock him in. If things were going to come to a head, this was when it would happen. Inmates could get edgy and even slightly psychotic at the thought of that lock turning, the long hours ahead until morning's release.

'Who you talking to?'

Rebus realised he had been heard by Billy Groam in the adjoining cell. He peered out into the hall and saw Groam's head looking back from his own doorway.

'Just myself,' he responded. 'What was that all about earlier?'

'Kylie can usually take a joke,' Groam said. 'But they've been stretched thin today – thinner even than usual. It's definitely got to them. Even Novak's pulled a sickie. Not like him to miss a shift.'

'What's wrong with him?'

Eddie Graves was arriving to shut them up for the night, so Groam decided to risk asking him. 'Hope Chris Novak hasn't caught the 'rona,' he said.

'DIY accident,' Graves answered, sounding less happy even than usual. 'Fell off a ladder and did for his wrist.'

'No self-abuse for him for a while then, eh? Tell him I'm taking up the slack.'

'Very decent of you, Billy. Now step back from the door.'

Rebus listened as Groam's door was closed and locked. Then it was his turn. *Fell off a ladder and did for his wrist ...* By the time Graves checked through the spyhole, Rebus was on his bed, eyes facing the ceiling. Not that he was ready for sleep. His mind was too busy, and would be for a while yet.

Malcolm Fox stayed late at Gartcosh, long after all the offices around him had emptied. The chief super hadn't asked to see him yet, which was something. Then again, maybe Mae McGovern only wanted to prolong the torture. He had sent a text to Jason Mulgrew – *Don't forget your friends!* – but had yet to receive a reply. It was true what he'd said – the break-in *had* been Jackie Simpson's idea. And Fox had debated long and hard with himself before agreeing to it. Not that he'd shared any of that with Thomas Glaze and SO15. Would Glaze get to hear about his humiliation? What would London think, now that he was no longer attached to the murder inquiry, meaning even less access to Christie and Harrison?

There was an email on his computer from a CID detective in Glasgow detailing the past exploits of Mickey Mason. The man had been about to flood the city with fentanyl prior to his arrest. Fox found that interesting – the drug was being found more and more in other Scottish cities and towns, including Edinburgh. If Mason was back to his old ways – and why wouldn't he be? – then he would either become a fresh adversary for Shay Hanlon or a useful ally. Hanlon did need someone on the ground. Everett Harrison was incarcerated, but friendly with Bobby Briggs. Briggs gave him a connection to Mason. Working together would make shorter work of the competition, meaning Darryl Christie. Why send muscle all the way from Merseyside to put the frighteners on Christie's gang when willing bampots were available just forty-five minutes to the west? The more Fox thought about it, the more sense it made. It was too late in the day to phone Glaze, but he would make contact in the morning. Maybe SO15 could persuade Fox's boss to free up some manpower for surveillance of Christie's remaining troops. Hanlon would be sure to strike again. All it needed was for one attacker to be caught and identified.

You need this, Malcolm, Fox told himself. But more than that, you deserve it ...

Day Six

18

It was when Rebus looked like missing breakfast that his neighbours became curious. Groam and Harrison found him on his bed and having trouble catching a breath. They alerted an officer, who got the duty nurse to come and look. Rebus's nebuliser wasn't helping. His heart rate was high, as was his blood pressure. His breathing remained laboured and speaking was a problem.

'Hospital job,' the nurse told Blair Samms. 'And I know from experience that an ambulance will take a while.'

'Do we have a spare van?' Samms asked Valerie Watts, who had joined the group in Rebus's cell. Rebus could see fellow inmates crowding around the doorway. Ratty gave him a little wave, but Rebus's focus was on the discussion Samms and Watts were having. Watts took a step towards him.

'There's a fold-up wheelchair in the nurses' station. We'll use that to get you to my car. Staffing means it'll just be me – are you okay with that?'

Rebus squeezed his eyes shut and managed to nod.

The governor arrived and listened to the nurse's report, his eyes fixed on Rebus, lips clamped. He was still studying the patient as he checked with Watts that her projected course of action was proper and necessary. After which he gave the briefest of nods and turned away.

'Nice bedside manner,' Rebus managed to comment, after which the staff got to work hauling him into a pair of joggers and his green sweatshirt.

Ill or not, there were protocols to be followed, bits of paper to be signed at the reception desk next to the first-night centre. Rebus hadn't been there since he'd arrived and undergone induction. The same lugubrious face was behind the desk. He didn't so much look *at* Rebus as *through* him. And he did enjoy his admin. But eventually they were outside, Samms waiting in the yard with Rebus while Watts fetched her vehicle.

'You're white as a ghost,' Samms said after studying the patient.

'Thanks for the vote of confidence.' The words spluttered from Rebus's mouth. He was clutching his nebuliser in one hand like some version of rosary beads. There hadn't been time to think of what else he might need to bring. The nurse was going to phone ahead with his details. She had warned Watts that the wait in A&E could stretch for hours.

'The snack machine will be your friend,' she'd added.

Watts's car was a nippy-looking Alfa Romeo. Rebus decided its colour would be called something like 'midnight blue' in the sales brochure. Samms tried not to look impressed as he helped Watts guide Rebus into the passenger seat and do up his seat belt.

'When did you get the wheels?' he asked her.

'Last weekend.'

'You sure we're on the same pay grade?'

'I cut a deal.'

Rebus watched as Samms closed the passenger door and started pushing the chair back into the main building.

'Hope we can snaffle another of those from A&E,' Watts said, doing up her own seat belt. 'I don't fancy carrying you.' Then, turning towards her passenger before setting off: 'You're not going to give me any grief, John, right? Not in my spanking new car?'

'No grief,' Rebus assured her.

The Alfa was given a final check at the gatehouse, boot opened, underside examined, then the gates trundled open in front of them and suddenly they were outside the high prison walls. Rebus couldn't help staring. Such an expanse of sky, so many puffy clouds. Then traffic, and people, and houses and shops and ... everything.

'Comes as a shock,' Watts commented, reading his mind.

'It's been a while,' he agreed.

She drove with one hand mostly, the other resting on the central console. At the first pedestrian crossing she glanced towards him.

'Bit more colour to you. Breathing seems steadier, too.'

Rebus turned from his window and stared at her. She wasn't stupid, far from it. He could see her working it out, trying not to let anything show on her face, eyes on the road ahead.

'I need to stop somewhere on the way,' he eventually stated.

'Jesus, John.' She gave a sort of embarrassed grin, head angled downwards momentarily. 'What the hell is this?'

'I have to see Chris Novak.'

'No way.'

'You know I'm on his side – his side *and* yours. But to help him I really need to see him.'

'Not going to happen.'

'A phone call won't do it – has to be face-to-face.'

'Why?'

'Because he's in trouble. Not too much trouble as yet, but it's only going to get worse – and it could get a *lot* worse.'

'You're a piece of work, John. This whole thing was a con?'

'Took a bit more effort than I thought. At one point I reckoned I actually was about to keel over.'

'And what if you hadn't had me as your escort? What if we'd found an ambulance?'

'Plan A was to scarper from the hospital.'

'And?'

'Go find Chris's house.'

'How would you have done that?'

'Maybe I'd have phoned you and asked. Then later on I'd hand myself back in, no harm done.'

'Except that your escort would be getting a rocket for letting you loose in the first place!'

Rebus was still staring at her. 'It'll take five or ten minutes max. We both know he's stuck in the house.'

'Under the watchful eye of his wife.'

'I'm just a friend from work who's come to commiserate.'

'In a prisoner-issue top?' Watts was shaking her head slowly, eyes not moving from the road. She was gripping the steering wheel with both hands now, practically throttling it. Rebus was relieved she was taking it out on an inanimate object rather than his own neck.

'Jesus, John,' she repeated, with a little less force than before. Then she looked at him. 'He's really in trouble?'

'Yes.'

'What sort?'

'Better if he tells you.'

She was still shaking her head as, teeth bared, she executed a sudden U-turn, horns blaring around her. She pushed down on the accelerator and did a quick calculation.

'Might take us fifteen or twenty minutes. I don't know if A&E will phone the prison when you don't show.'

'Why not call them yourself and tell them I'm a lot better – too well to bother burdening them?'

'And what do I say when we get back to Saughton?'

'That we visited A&E and they checked me out and everything's fine.' Rebus offered a shrug. 'I'm improvising here.'

'It's only my head on the block,' Watts muttered, but she ended up making the call anyway. Then they drove on in silence until she turned left into a modern housing estate.

When they passed Novak's house, she pointed it out to Rebus.

But she turned into another street before stopping. 'Can't let her see me,' she said.

'You've been here before?' Seeing the look on her face, Rebus held up a hand in apology. 'None of my business,' he agreed, undoing his seat belt. As he was opening the door, she gripped his forearm.

'Do not mess me about, because if you do, I will fuck you up – understood?'

He nodded slowly, unable to think how else to respond.

Then he was out of the car, striding along an actual pavement, past pebble-dashed two-storey houses with trimmed lawns and flagged driveways. A Waitrose van was making a delivery. The driver gave a nod and a smile. Rebus nodded back. His skin was tingling and he drew in lungfuls of air. He could hear a plane overhead – and was that a train in the distance? Maybe a school playground, too, ball games and squeals. A red-liveried Royal Mail van crawled past, part and parcel of the rhythm of the day.

All too soon he was outside Novak's house, but before approaching the door he studied the adjoining garage. It's up-and-over doors weren't quite closed, giving him a glimpse of a sleek white BMW and, poking out from behind it, an equally sleek motorbike.

He rang the doorbell and waited. He'd been expecting the wife, but it was Novak himself who answered. The wrist of his right hand was strapped up, but he still raised it as if expecting a blow of some kind.

'What the fuck?' he blurted out.

'I was just passing,' Rebus said. Novak was looking to right and left along the street.

'How did you get here?'

'Not going to invite me in?'

Novak all but hauled him inside with his uninjured hand, slamming the door shut afterwards.

'Nice place,' Rebus commented, studying his surroundings.

'Not too flash – your wife's taste or yours? Where is she, by the way?'

'Never mind her.' They were in the living room, facing one another. Rebus doubted there would be any offer of a seat or a drink, which suited him fine. 'To repeat the question, John – what the fuck?'

'I think I've worked it out,' Rebus said casually. 'But I need you to confirm it.'

'Confirm what? Christ's sake, did you just break out? Are you on the news yet?' Novak dug out his phone, but with only one working hand, a search proved difficult.

'Hospital appointment,' Rebus explained. 'Just stopped off here en route.'

'Where's the van ... your escort?' Novak peered out of the window.

'Not important. But here's what is – you need to stop, you need to stop right now.'

'Stop what?' Novak tried for a puzzled look.

'Christie told me one of his men wrestled a gunman's weapon away from him, nearly broke his wrist in the process. The guy was on a motorbike – that'll be the one in your garage. Leathers, gloves and a crash helmet with the visor down – probably a set of fake plates, too? I can see all of that, and I don't suppose a Scouse accent is hard to pull off if you've practised and you're not trying it with actual Liverpudlians.'

The air was leaking out of Chris Novak in real time. He kept his eyes averted from Rebus, looking at his phone's screen saver instead. It showed a boy and a girl not yet in their teens. 'I'd be worrying about them if I were you, Chris,' Rebus said softly. 'Because if this game of yours spirals out of control ...'

'It's no game, John. They've been at me and at me and at me. Torching my car, sending threats – not just me, either. Lots of other officers who refuse to turn a blind eye or do as they're told. Christie reckons he *owns* that prison. Well not on my watch he doesn't.'

'You learned about Hanlon, heard the rumours he was

240

interested in Christie's patch. You decided to make it seem like it was really happening – I'm guessing your CID cousin tipped you off regarding movements and addresses. All you then had to do was put the fear of God into Christie's team, weakening him while making him furious in the process.'

'Furious *and* impotent, John.' Some pride had entered Novak's voice. 'Because there are things he can't do from inside, plenty of things he can't control, and it's all starting to dawn on him.'

'But now he knows you were only using an airgun. Next time you try something, his team won't be scared. They'll be ready – maybe tooled up themselves – and they'll want their pound of flesh.' Rebus studied Novak's right hand. 'How bad is it?'

Novak flexed his fingers. 'Day or two off's all I need. I'll be fine.' His eyes met Rebus's. 'So what's your next move?'

'Apart from returning to jail?' Rebus shrugged. 'I don't have a next move – and you shouldn't have one either. No room for masked vigilantes in *this* Gotham.'

'I'm not going to roll over for him, John.'

'You said it yourself – you've already weakened him. Somebody'll walk into town eventually and take over. And you *have* given him a fright – I'm not sure he'll ever get over it. Right now he still thinks his bogeyman is out here.' Rebus nodded towards the window. 'And that's going to keep gnawing away at him. Job done, Chris. Time to call it a day while you still can.'

'How about *your* job, John? Have you done anything about Blair Samms?'

'What do you suggest? I can hardly shine a bulb in his face and sweat him like in the old days. Until someone breaks ranks ...'

'I doubt that's going to happen.'

'Then the killer gets away with it.' Rebus gave another shrug. 'Until someone breaks ranks,' he echoed. He drank in his surroundings, the quality furniture, family photos, TV with sound system. 'You're a lucky man, Chris. Try to keep it that way.'

Novak offered his left hand, and Rebus clasped it. At the front door, he asked Rebus how he'd managed to track him down.

'I've not lost the old touch,' Rebus answered. 'I'll see you back at the ranch in a couple of days, aye?'

'Listen ... I appreciate you doing this. You took a hell of a risk.'

'And now I just have to tunnel back into Colditz – wish me luck.'

Novak gave him a little salute and made to close the door. Rebus pushed a hand against it so it stayed open.

'You did put a choke on Jackie, didn't you? In his cell that time? He wasn't lying about that?'

'Fucker threatened to come after my family, John.'

'After *you'd* bad-mouthed his son,' Rebus stated. 'If someone's framing you, you did a pretty good job of climbing into the picture all by yourself.'

'Tell me this then. Say you'd become a prison officer rather than a cop – how well would you have coped, day in, day out?'

'Oh, I'd have killed someone long before now,' Rebus said, turning away.

When he got back to the car, Watts still had a tight grip of the steering wheel. 'True to my word,' he told her as he climbed in.

'I've been calculating,' she said as she started the engine. 'If we head back now, they'll never believe we got seen so quickly.' She glanced at him. 'There's a drive-through Burger King not too far away – what do you reckon?'

'If that's the only offer on the table.'

'Pub's out of the question, if that's what you're thinking.'

'I'd settle for coffee and a bacon roll.' He saw the look she was giving him. 'But Burger King's fine too.'

Their route took them past Novak's house. He was watching from the living-room window. Watts met his gaze. A minute or so later, music filled the car, Bluetooth telling her she had a call. She let it ring out.

'Need to think about what I'm going to say to him,' she explained to Rebus. Then: 'Is he still in trouble, John?'

'Not if he heeds my advice.'

'Did the advice include steering clear of me?'

'Not in the least.'

She turned her attention back to the road. 'Thanks.'

'But if it turns out you're both killers,' Rebus added, 'I want you to know I'll be very disappointed.'

When she saw the glint in his eye, she gave a little laugh, Rebus joining in.

'Burgers are my treat,' she said.

'They'll have to be.' He patted his empty pockets.

'So you'd have high-tailed it from the hospital with no idea where Chris lived and no money or phone? *That* was the extent of your plan?'

'And yet somehow it all worked out. It doesn't always ...' Rebus rested his head against the back of the seat and watched the big, beautiful world roll by.

19

Louise Hird had made the trip from Gartcosh to see how things were progressing. The DCI had decided that she merited a meeting in his office. He was seated behind his desk, facing Hird and Siobhan Clarke.

'We've interviewed most of Campbell's victims,' Clarke said. 'One of them, she's nineteen now, had told her parents what was going on. Pitched it to them as a modelling job, not much different from a lingerie shoot. One thing she didn't say was that Campbell wanted her to dress and act younger than her years.'

'And the parents were generally okay with it?' DCI Carmichael asked.

'Campbell never laid a hand on her. Quite the gentleman, according to their daughter.'

'Were they ever introduced to him?' Hird asked, tapping notes into her phone. Clarke shook her head.

'Nobody ever met Campbell apart from his models.'

'What angle are you taking as regards his murder?'

Carmichael decided to answer that before Clarke could. 'We're keeping a very open mind, Louise.'

'No sign of forced entry,' Clarke added. 'Plenty of security.'

'Cameras?' Hird interrupted.

'Aimed at the doorstep and the garage – but he hadn't bothered switching them on.'

'And inside the house?'

Clarke shook her head again. 'Whoever it was, looks like they were invited in.'

'Campbell takes them through to the kitchen,' Carmichael continued, 'probably to fix a drink or something, turns his back on them and ...'

'They slid a knife from the block,' Clarke added.

Hird saw what she was getting at. 'They didn't arrive tooled up. If this was a falling-out among thieves, they'd have been more professional in their approach. You're not ruling out one of the victims then – and I'm guessing that puts Jasmine Andrews at the top of the leader board?'

'We've scoured town and country for her,' Carmichael said. 'She still hasn't used her debit card or phone.'

'So which is she – a very smart and ruthless cookie or locked up in a killer's cellar?' Hird held up a hand. 'Sorry to be frank.'

'A further complication,' Carmichael continued, 'is that there are no prints on the weapon, meaning it was either meticulously wiped afterwards or ...'

'The killer wore gloves,' Clarke said.

'Taking us back to malice aforethought,' Hird commented. 'DNA?'

'Not telling us much as yet.'

The three of them sat in silence for a moment. Carmichael lifted his mug without drinking from it. He'd rustled up a plate of digestive biscuits, but they sat untouched on his desk.

'Well,' Hird eventually said, 'London have taken a look at everything they were sent. It doesn't seem the deceased was part of a wider network. In other words, no one was buying his wares for use in overseas markets. Doesn't mean there won't have been piggybacking, of course.'

Carmichael leaned forward. 'Piggybacking?'

'A punter records what they're watching so they can sell or share it elsewhere. You need to make the victims aware that

245

their presence could linger online for some time to come.' She shifted a little in her chair. 'From the messages between the clients and Campbell, some definitely wanted the models to go further – and they got angry when Campbell said no, giving another possible motive.'

'Do we have grounds for a prosecution of any of these men?' Carmichael enquired.

'A question for the Procurator Fiscal. I'd say it's a grey area, but you should definitely be handing out warnings, even if only to give them a fright.'

'One has already committed suicide,' Clarke said quietly.

'Not your fault, Siobhan.' Hird turned her attention back to Carmichael. 'Do you have enough family liaison officers for the workload?'

'We've managed to get hold of precisely two,' Carmichael told her. 'With a third on the way from Dundee.'

'Going to be busy then. I've found them invaluable in the past – they get the confidence of the family, and that's when the unsaid starts to be spoken out loud. How about the men who stumped up for the abuse, the ones still breathing? Any likely murderers among them?'

'Not so far.' Clarke lifted her own mug, cupping her hands around it. 'There's one client we're having real trouble with,' she confessed. 'Calls himself Valerio.' She spelled the word out. 'Just that and a string of numbers after. The numbers don't seem to mean anything, but we googled Valerio and got a couple of shops – we've visited both and ruled out any connection. It's a masculine name, Italian or Spanish, means strong or healthy.'

'One thing you can be sure of, it won't be their real name. Local, you think?'

'We've no idea – they seem savvy about security and the dark web. No way for us to get beyond that username.'

'I can nudge London, see if they can help.' Hird met Carmichael's eyes. 'From my perspective, this could have been much worse. But I acknowledge that from yours, you've a lot of work still to do. Did Campbell's mother have any inkling what her son was up to?'

'None whatsoever,' Clarke answered.

'She's been told now, though?'

'And Zak is still her blue-eyed boy. Always will be.'

'I don't suppose he vented to her about any enemies or threats?'

'No, but the list keeps growing. He would hit on women in bars and clubs – their boyfriends didn't always like that. Had an old school pal acting as his shield. He tells us they parted company because of Zak's online activities.'

'Nothing useful so far from forensics?'

'Twenty-three young people were regular visitors to the house,' Clarke said. 'Makes for a lot of matching and checking.'

'Not that we'll dismiss a single strand of hair,' Carmichael said defensively. 'Everyone's working flat out.'

'Never in doubt,' Hird said. 'But I wouldn't mind a tour of your operation anyway, if Siobhan's willing.'

'Happy to oblige.'

'Anything you're particularly interested in, Louise?' Carmichael asked.

'I'm just jealous of all the manpower,' she answered with the thinnest possible smile.

As Hird was readying to leave, tour complete, a man was being led along the corridor by Gillian Reeves, accompanied by DC Pete Swinton. The man was in his early twenties, overweight and with bad skin and hair. He wore the branded T-shirt of a metal band under a grubby Harrington-style jacket, baggy jeans brushing the floor.

'Thomas Simpson,' Reeves said as they passed, as though there were any doubt. Marcus's cousin was ushered into the interview room.

'I can see myself out,' Hird assured Clarke. 'But keep me posted.'

The chair Esson had deposited in the interview room was still there, though Esson herself had been summoned to Gayfield Square for a meeting with Mae McGovern. Simpson and Reeves were already seated, Swinton fussing with the newly installed video camera. He gestured to let Clarke know she could have his perch, but she shook her head and rested her back against the wall, peripheral to the cousin. It was a lesson learned from Rebus many years back. You remained a presence – and an ominous one at that. The interviewee couldn't guess what you might be about to do. She crossed one foot over the other as the interview started.

Preliminaries over, Reeves referred to the inch-thick contents of the file in front of her, waiting a few beats before starting.

'Did Marcus ever tell you why he felt the need to hide from us?'

Tommy Simpson swallowed hard and spoke as though he'd been in the desert for a week. 'He often kips at mine.'

'He means his mum's,' Reeves said for Clarke's benefit. 'He was fast asleep in bed when she let us in. In the end, we all traipsed upstairs to rouse him. Sleeping bag on the floor, presumably for visitors.'

'And the rest of the bedroom like the bridge of the *Enterprise*,' Swinton added. 'Never seen so many screens and cables.'

'I'm a games designer,' Tommy said.

'Any we'd have heard of?'

'Not got that far yet,' he mumbled.

'But you set up websites on the side, eh? Like you did for Zak Campbell?'

'If you say so.'

'It's your cousin Marcus who says so,' Clarke chipped in. 'How much did Zak owe you?'

'A couple of grand.'

'That must have rankled.'

Tommy Simpson's whole face seemed to be in movement as he sat there, a mass of tics and blinks, like organisms were

248

writing just beneath his flesh. 'Marcus should have kept his mouth shut.'

'Are you Valerio, Tommy?'

He half turned to meet Clarke's eyes. 'Who?'

'A username on Zak's site.'

'I've never visited it.'

'Never?'

'Not since I finished building it.'

'Not even slightly curious?'

'I don't get off on that kind of thing.'

'Did Marcus?'

'Not while he was with me. Too busy with MMORPGs.'

'That's games a whole bunch of you play online?' Reeves enquired. Tommy answered with a thumbs-up. 'You knew that wasn't what Zak wanted, though, right? He wanted to stream porn to paying customers.'

'Easiest thing in the world.'

'Despite all the encryption needed?'

Another thumbs-up.

'Ever visited his house since the site's been up and running?'

'Never invited.'

'He owed you a chunk of cash, though – not tempted to go knock on his door?'

'I got Marcus to ask a few times, but then him and Zak fell out.'

'And what did Marcus tell you about that?' Clarke asked.

'Just that he didn't like the way things were going.' Tommy paused and swallowed again. 'Age-wise, I mean.'

'Can't have been comfortable for you, Tommy,' Reeves said, trying to add a note of concern to her voice. 'You must have known then that what he was doing had crossed a line – when we came gunning for him, you'd be in our cross hairs too.'

'It's not like I left footprints. You've been into the site – I bet you've not found any trace of me.'

'Unless you're Valerio,' Clarke said.

He turned his head towards her again. 'Why's this Valerio so important?'

'Because *he's* good at not leaving footprints too.' She paused for effect. 'Like a pro.'

Tommy was shaking his head. 'I've told you, I've no interest in any of that.'

'It's your baby, though, you created it – means you might be able to help us dig a little deeper?'

'Give me a keyboard and some decent bandwidth.'

'It'd have to be at our lab with one of our tech officers,' Clarke said. 'But it would definitely be points in your favour.' She paused once more to let this sink in. 'So you've not been to Campbell's house in some time?'

'Months and months.'

'Any objection to us taking your prints and a swab? For purposes of elimination.'

'Do you keep stuff?'

'Not for any length of time.'

'Erased from the system?'

'We're not Big Brother, Tommy – not yet, at least.'

'I did ask him why he was bothering with real flesh-and-blood humans when avatars are cheap, almost as lifelike and unlikely to say no.'

'Did any of Zak's models say no or start getting reluctant?'

'How would I know?'

'Your cousin might have said.'

'He didn't, though.' Tommy started gnawing at the skin next to his right thumbnail.

'Did Marcus ever mention a girl called Jasmine?' Clarke asked.

'No.'

'You know who I'm talking about, though?'

'Aye.'

'And Marcus hasn't got her hidden away at your place?'

'Ask them, they've been there.' He gestured towards Reeves and Swinton. The silence stretched as the three detectives realised they had run out of questions. Clarke gestured towards Swinton. 'Stay with him, Pete. Call the lab and see who's available to sit at a computer with him.'

Swinton nodded, readying to end the recording while Clarke and Reeves left the room and headed to MIT.

'Still living at home with his mum,' Reeves reiterated.

'And him such a catch.'

'If he did it, I'm guessing video games will get the blame.'

'Do you think he did?'

'I'm past the point of guessing. Far too many suspects; it'd be nice to narrow the field.'

They heard the hubbub before they walked in, the team huddled around Bryan Carmichael and looking agitated. He motioned for Clarke and Reeves to join the fray. It was Trisha Singh who had news to share.

'A handful of clients paying a lot more than anyone else,' she said, sounding out of breath. 'We thought maybe some VIP level of access – even actual physical hook-ups. But the people we've interviewed so far ruled that out. Now one of them's phoned us. He knew we'd be paying him a visit so he decided to take the initiative. Retired businessman, lives in Gullane.'

'Spit it out, Trisha,' Clarke said.

But Cammy Colson got there before Singh could.

'Sextortion,' he said. Maybe he liked the feel of the word in his mouth, because he repeated it. Clarke looked to DCI Carmichael, who said it too. She asked Singh for the man's name.

'Alexander Urquhart.'

'Time to bring him in for a chat, then.'

'He's housebound, apparently,' Carmichael said. 'Basically lives in a wheelchair.'

'So give me his address.'

Carmichael couldn't help but notice Singh going up and down on her toes, desperate not to be overlooked. He nodded towards her. 'The two of you go,' he said.

251

Clarke turned towards Reeves. 'Make sure to pair Tommy Simpson with one of the lab's finest nerds.'

'Will do,' Reeves said. Then: 'Go get him, girls.'

20

Clarke let Trisha Singh do the driving, leaning back against the headrest and even closing her eyes for a bit. Was the investigation spiralling outwards or inwards? She was too dizzied by it to be able to tell.

'How did he sound when you spoke to him?' she eventually asked.

'Calm. Not embarrassed or anything. Posh.' Singh wasn't a talkative driver, preferring to focus on the traffic. They'd hit rush hour, though these days much of the city seemed to suffer nothing but. Singh's car didn't have a blue light, so there wasn't much they could do – and it wasn't as if Urquhart was about to abscond. Once they were out of the city, the vehicles in front sped up, their owners keen to get home to comfortable, middle-class East Lothian. They passed farmland and occasional dwellings, the Firth of Forth to their left. Gullane itself wasn't much more than a main street with its share of shops and restaurants. The big draw was its golf courses, including Muirfield. Singh's doctor husband had played many a round there.

'Are women allowed these days?' Clarke asked.

'Yes, but my handicap's too high.'

'Maybe don't use that word in front of our wheelchair user,' Clarke advised. Singh's mouth formed a little O. 'Only teasing, Trisha,' Clarke said.

'I'd never thought of it, though.' Singh checked her dashboard satnav. 'Nearly there,' she said.

Urquhart lived in an Edwardian-era house built in the baronial style, with a turret and crow-stepped gables. The gates opened onto an expansive gravelled driveway. As they approached the varnished oak front door, it was opened by an imposing-looking woman dressed in tweeds, thick woollen socks and brown brogues, her hair tied back into a tight silver bun.

'Mrs Urquhart?' Clarke guessed.

'*Miss* Urquhart,' the woman corrected her. She had the demeanour of a schoolmistress from decades past, her face gaunt but largely unlined, her eyes hawk-like. 'You'll be the police. Alexander said to expect you.'

They were in the large wood-panelled hall by this point. Urquhart's sister closed the door and examined her guests. 'He was pretty tight-lipped as to why you're here.'

'Care to hazard a guess?'

'It's not my place.'

'Are you his carer, Miss Urquhart?' Singh asked.

'Since Julia died,' the woman confirmed.

'Julia being his wife?'

'Who else?' She paused and lowered her voice a fraction. 'You know he's a JP? *Was* a JP, I should say. I just felt it's something you should be aware of.' Neither detective said anything, which seemed to disappoint Miss Urquhart. She led them to a door, knocked and pushed it open. 'Your guests, Alexander,' she said, ushering them in. 'Does anyone require tea?' Clarke and Singh assured her they were fine, so she closed the door slowly, staying outside.

Alexander Urquhart's wheelchair was set behind an ornate antique desk, in front of an entire wall of glass-fronted bookcases. The man himself was in his seventies, silver hair sprouting around the base of his bald dome. He wore half-moon glasses and was in the middle of writing in an oversized notebook.

'Not my confession, you understand,' he told them, slapping his hand against the open page.

'Mr Urquhart, I'm DC Singh. We spoke on the phone.'

'Indeed we did.' Urquhart bowed his head slightly in greeting. 'Which region of India do you call home?'

'Blackhall.' While Urquhart's brow furrowed, Singh turned towards Clarke. 'And this is Detective Inspector Clarke.'

'Two charming young women – such a pleasure.'

'From the New Town,' Clarke pretended to elucidate. Then: 'Is it really a pleasure, sir? Most people in your position wouldn't be quite so relaxed.'

'Am I relaxed?' He considered the question. 'I suppose I am.'

'Is that because you're no longer in the clutches of the man who was blackmailing you?'

'They call it sextortion, don't they? I think he decided I was worth the candle when he looked me up online and found I was a justice of the peace – I bet Marjory told you I was a JP too, didn't she?' He gave a smile, no answer required. 'She thinks you might go easier on me, whatever it is I've done.'

'Will you actually tell her?'

Urquhart stretched out his arms. 'Well, what *have* I done?'

'Watched underage girls stripping off online for starters,' Singh commented.

'But I'd no idea they were underage until he tried to wring money from me.'

'Tried and succeeded,' Clarke felt it necessary to add.

'Once or twice, yes. But then I thought: why the hell should I? So I stopped and told him to go hang himself. He could out me to the world if he liked but I wasn't giving him a sou more, and if he didn't stop harassing me, I'd go to the police myself.'

'You didn't do that, though, sir,' Singh said, her tone cool.

Urquhart was busy manoeuvring his way from behind the desk. He headed to a space near a sofa and gestured for his visitors to

255

be seated. Singh and Clarke followed him but remained standing.

'Throughout all this,' Clarke said, 'did he ever identify himself?'

'He used an alias. Actually, more than one – he seemed to message me from a different email address every single time.'

'How was the money transferred?'

'A digital wallet. He had to take me through it step by step. I still use a chequebook, for God's sake.' Urquhart drummed his fingers against the wheelchair's armrests. 'I got the inkling he was probably local,' he eventually conceded. 'Mainly because the models on the screen were – you could tell from their accents.'

'They spoke to you and you spoke to them?'

'The conversation, such as it was, was strictly one-way. I typed in a message and sometimes they typed something back, but they might also say something.' He paused and rattled the chair's metal arms. 'Even if I *had* discovered his identity, doing away with him wouldn't have been straightforward in this contraption.'

'Maybe so, but a man of your means could have paid for the privilege.'

Urquhart fixed Clarke with a look. 'But that didn't happen, Inspector.'

'I'm assuming you must have encountered one or two unsavoury characters during your time as a JP.'

'It's not like we kept in touch afterwards.' The thin smile had returned.

'The site's other users, you never knew any of them in real life?' Clarke watched him shake his head. 'And you didn't invite any like-minded friends to join the club?'

'I did not.'

'Is there anything else you want to tell us, Mr Urquhart?' Singh asked.

'Just that I bitterly regret getting mixed up in the whole sorry business.'

'Can I ask how you found the site in the first place? Were you just browsing, or did someone recommend it?'

'The internet is an extraordinary sphere,' Urquhart said. 'The most innocent soul is never more than a few clicks away from everything they could ever imagine and much more besides.'

'Your way of telling us that this was your first foray into online abuse?'

He winced slightly. 'You're correct, of course. It can almost certainly be termed abuse, with the benefit of hindsight.' He looked from one detective to the other, seeking something he wasn't going to find. 'So what now?' he asked.

'A formal interview,' Clarke stated. 'It can be recorded here. Plus we'll be passing your details to our colleagues at Child Exploitation and the National Crime Agency, obviously.'

Some of the light left Urquhart's eyes. 'Of course,' he mumbled, chin resting on his chest.

Without saying anything else, Clarke headed to the door, Singh following.

'Enjoy the rest of your day, officers,' Urquhart said, automatically. Good breeding and all that.

His sister heard the door and emerged from the kitchen, a tea towel in her hands, apron tied around her waist.

'Everything all right?' she asked.

'Someone will be coming back to take a statement.' Clarke met her gaze. 'Your brother has a penchant for underage pornography, Miss Urquhart. I hope you find that as troubling as we do.'

The woman gave a sniff. 'I don't find it the least bit troubling. Alexander has done a power of good in this world, but no one is without flaws – probably not even you.' She pulled open the door. 'My brother is not a criminal, and you'll have the devil of a job convincing me otherwise. I'll be contacting his solicitor as soon as I'm done with you.'

No more words were exchanged as Clarke and Singh walked across the gravel to Singh's car.

'What a piece of work,' Singh commented as she unlocked the doors. 'She knew all along, didn't she?'

'I'd say so.'

'And was fine with it?'

'Looks that way.'

'Weird old buggers, the pair of them. And that house gives me the creeps.' She turned towards Clarke as she started the engine. 'So what do you want to do now?'

'Stop in Port Seton for chips,' Clarke said decisively.

'You're the boss, Siobhan. And that's definitely a strategy I can get on board with.'

Jason Mulgrew was providing an update to the governor in his office at HMP Edinburgh when the door opened and Malcolm Fox walked in.

'Mind if I join you?' Fox asked. 'Howard and I are old friends – I hope I can say that, Howard?'

The governor hesitated for only a moment before nodding.

'So what have you been chatting about?' Fox asked Mulgrew, gaze fixed on him.

'We were just getting started,' Mulgrew replied.

Fox nodded: nothing had been said as yet about his dismissal. He smoothed his tie and crossed one leg over the other.

'I was just telling Jason,' Tennent said, 'that there's still some tension on the halls, not exactly helped by Darryl Christie having a go at Everett Harrison.'

'Christie's in solitary?' Fox checked.

'But due back in Trinity Hall today. I sat him down in here with Harrison.'

'What was their beef exactly?'

'These things can come out of nowhere, Malcolm.'

'Maybe so, but this one came from the fact that Christie's business is under threat from Harrison's boss. His men are being targeted. I'm not convinced sitting them down will provide much more than a sticking plaster.'

'What would really help,' Tennent said, 'is a break in the case.' He turned his eyes towards Mulgrew.

'I'm sorry to say progress has been limited – not helped by one of my officers being temporarily poached by a rival inquiry. Nevertheless, we aren't stinting, I can assure you of that. Our current thinking is that, despite the cellmate's evidence, Jackie Simpson was attacked prior to lock-up.'

'Meaning it could have been another prisoner?' Tennent had the look and sound of a man grabbing at a straw.

'Putting Everett Harrison back at the top of the list,' Fox said.

'Only if he knew Simpson was responsible for him being in here in the first place,' Mulgrew cautioned, 'and I doubt that's the sort of thing he'd be likely to admit to us.'

'Not "us", no,' Fox said, 'but he might well have told *someone* ...' He turned his attention back to the governor. 'You've an inmate called Bobby Briggs in one of the other halls. He's pretty close to Harrison, I hear.'

'And equally unlikely to share with us anything Harrison has said.'

Fox pretended to consider for a moment. 'Does Briggs ever get visitors?'

'I would assume so,' Tennent said.

'Would there be a list of names? One in particular I'm interested in – Mickey Mason.'

'I know that name,' the governor said, eyes narrowing slightly. 'Comes with a reputation attached.'

Mulgrew was looking at Fox. 'What's your thinking, Malcolm?'

'Just joining the dots, Jason, from inside to outside and back again.'

'Even supposing Harrison did commit the murder, he still had a knife to get rid of.'

Fox shrugged. 'Someone smuggled it out for him.' Tennent looked ready to object, but Fox held up a pacifying hand. 'Not necessarily a prison officer.'

'So how do we get to Harrison?' Mulgrew eventually asked.

'I'm not sure we can,' Fox admitted. 'Anyone who clypes would have a target on their back.' He turned his attention to the governor. 'Any chance of a bit of bribery, Howard? Special privileges in exchange for information?'

'From what you've been saying, those privileges would have to include round-the-clock protection from Harrison himself.'

'You could always request that he be moved to another jail. That might help loosen tongues.'

'It's a thought,' Tennent conceded, folding his arms.

'The falling-out with Christie gives you the perfect excuse,' Mulgrew added.

Tennent began to nod his head slowly. 'Leave it with me,' he said.

A few minutes later, they wound up the meeting. Fox and Mulgrew walked together towards the exit, led by Tennent's secretary.

'Thanks for not saying anything,' Fox said in an undertone. 'About me being shipped back to Gartcosh, I mean.'

'No problem.'

'And of course there's no reason for anyone to know I was here.'

'Did you know about the meeting?'

'Complete coincidence.'

'And you were coming to ask about this guy Briggs?'

'Briggs and Mason, yes.'

'Not connected to Jackie Simpson's demise?'

Fox gave another shrug. 'Is Christine not back in the body of the kirk yet?'

'It's imminent.'

'Any more news from St Leonard's?'

'If there is, she's not been sharing it with me.'

They entered the reception area, the secretary waving them off. Both men retrieved their phones from the lockers.

'Drink later?' Fox asked.

'Aye, maybe,' Mulgrew said.

They shook hands on it.

As Fox neared his car, he got an incoming text from Stevie Hodge at OCCTU.

Jake Morris is back on our radar. Worth catching up with him?

Leave it with me, Stevie, Fox messaged back.

You sure?

Dead sure. Talk soon.

'No rest for the wicked,' he said quietly to himself as he opened the driver's-side door. Jake Morris: a gun waved in his face, going into hiding, now back in circulation. *Worth catching up with him?* Most definitely – and without anyone like Stevie Hodge hogging the stage.

21

Having given a promise of best behaviour, Darryl Christie was back on Trinity Hall.

Rebus knew the governor was making a mistake, but two inmates on another hall had had a go at one another with home-made shanks. As a result, Christie's isolation cell was required. He gave an open-armed grin in Rebus's direction as he marched into the hall, bouncing on the balls of his feet. There were some whistles and handclaps, none of them appreciated by the scowling Harrison, who had emerged from his cell to watch.

'Game of pool later, Darryl?' someone called out.

'Only if they've disinfected that cue,' Christie shot back. His eyes met Harrison's and he raised one hand, forming it into a pistol, which he pretended to aim and fire. Harrison stood his ground for a moment before retreating into his cave.

It was a further half hour or so before Christie arrived in Rebus's doorway. 'What are you reading?' he asked.

'A biography of John Martyn.'

'He a footballer?'

'Guitarist.' Rebus put the book to one side. 'Bit of a loose cannon in his time, pissed off friends and foes alike. Can't think who he reminds me of ...'

'Reckon I could pick up some tips?' Christie's face grew more serious. 'How's the phone? Still plenty of charge?'

'It's fine.'

'That tells me something.'

'Oh aye?'

'I might occasionally piss off some of my friends, but at least they're there to *get* pissed off. You on the other hand don't have anyone who'd want to hear from you.'

'You think you've won this round with Hanlon, but there's a long way to go. If you start getting cocky or complacent—'

'My guard's always up,' Christie interrupted. 'Same as yours should be. Seen anything of Bobby Briggs lately? He's always on the lookout for you during free flow.'

Rebus ignored this. 'It won't be an airgun next time, Darryl. Hanlon will know he has to ramp things up, especially if you've really put a price on his head.'

'Are you my fucking mum or something?' Christie was scowling, his good humour all gone.

'I'm just saying riling Harrison gets you nowhere.'

'I don't know about that. Could be I've a guardian angel or two looking out for me.'

'Officers taking your bungs, you mean?'

'Besides, there's a recruitment drive under way – out there and in here. If you weren't such a crock, I might even have asked you.'

'Gee, thanks.'

Christie gave a twist of his mouth. 'Better be off – business won't look after itself.'

'Who did you put in charge while you were in solitary?'

Rebus's question was answered when Billy Groam arrived at Christie's side, Christie resting a hand on his shoulder before leading him away.

Rebus went back to reading his book, but his head wouldn't let him. It was important to keep up the pretence that the attacks were Shay Hanlon's work – both to protect Chris Novak and because it kept Christie rattled. But Everett Harrison wouldn't take much more teasing. He too would be talking to his troops, shoring up their morale and preparing them for a potential war. There were some on the hall who could safely stand on the sidelines, but Rebus knew he wasn't one of them.

'Stuck in the middle, John,' he muttered to himself, 'just like Gerry Rafferty always said ...'

Siobhan Clarke was on the phone to Howdenhall to see how they were getting on with Tommy Simpson, only to be told that Tommy was no longer there.

'He basically took one look at our set-up and laughed,' the technician explained.

'So where is he?'

'Back at his. Jeff went with him.'

'Jeff being your computer guy?'

'Soon as Simpson started detailing his rig, Jeff's eyes lit up.'

Clarke was resting one elbow on the desk, fingers massaging her forehead. She noticed that Singh and Swinton had their coats on, Swinton carrying a box that she knew would contain recording equipment. Alexander Urquhart was about to be paid a second visit.

'Have you got a mobile number for Jeff?'

The technician recited it while Clarke copied it onto her writing pad. She ended the call and rang Jeff. When he answered, she could hear explosions in the background.

'Yes?' he asked.

'Jeff, it's DI Clarke from the Zak Campbell inquiry. Sorry to interrupt your game ...' She listened as Jeff tried to muffle his phone while hissing at Tommy Simpson to turn the volume down. Then he placed the phone back to his ear.

'Just showing me his system's capabilities,' he improvised.

'I believe there's a sleeping bag in the vicinity if you're thinking of pulling a late one.'

'Sorry,' he eventually said, sounding sheepish.

'Pass me over to Tommy, will you?'

Jeff explained who was on the phone and handed it to Tommy, who immediately explained that they'd been working.

'That's good,' Clarke drawled. 'So what have you got for me?'

'There's not a lot you've not already accessed.'

'Well, for a start, there's Valerio's real identity.'

'Whoever they are, they're pro level. I'd have more luck cracking open MI6. They're certainly a lot more security-conscious than Zak – he left holes everywhere, despite the lectures I gave him.'

'So someone could have worked out who he was?'

'Easy – he had avatars and any number of false names and email accounts, but they all lead back to Zak Campbell.'

'So our anonymous friend Valerio would have been able to ID him?'

'Given a few hours' screen time, yes, definitely.'

'Anything else before I let you get back to your shoot-'em-up?'

'I really was just showing Jeff the graphics. He's putting his jacket on, ready for the off. I'll pass you back to him.'

But Clarke had already ended the call. She crossed to Esson's desk. Esson held up a forefinger as she finished typing a message into her phone. Having hit send, she gave Clarke her full attention.

'I was just going to offer to make you a mug of hot water,' Clarke said.

'No spare mugs last time I looked.'

'Swear to God I'm going to keep a couple locked in my desk drawer.'

Esson's phone pinged and she checked the screen. 'Jason Mulgrew again,' she informed Clarke.

'Wanting to know when he'll be seeing you?'

'He's after another progress report. You'd think he was in charge of *this* case rather than his own.'

'Well, ours has got media traction – gilded footballer, teenage girls ...'

'HMP Edinburgh certainly can't compete with that. Then

again, with Fox out of the game, we really are short of hands. I doubt I'll be here much longer.' Esson leaned back in her chair. 'Are we in danger of getting diverted, do you think?'

'How do you mean?'

'Tracking down all these clients, checking them out ... Jasmine Andrews is still our prime suspect, right? Otherwise why did she run?'

'We don't know that she ran,' Clarke felt it necessary to qualify.

'What then? She was in the house and the killer took her with him? In which case, we don't find her until we catch him.' Esson turned this over in her head, tapping her pen against the edge of her desk.

'That could get quite annoying after a while,' Clarke pointed out. Esson clamped the pen in her fist.

'I wasn't here at the beginning, back when she was just a misper. You talked to her parents and schoolfriends?'

'Including her ex, who lives over the back fence.'

'I can't believe nobody knew what she'd got herself into.'

'Someone did mention Jasmine suddenly being flush.' Clarke paused. 'Was it Carla?'

'Carla?'

'Her bestie.' But Clarke was shaking her head. 'No, I think it was the ex. His name's Craig.'

Esson had transferred the pen to the corner of her mouth. 'What about this Craig?'

'An amicable split, instigated by Jasmine.'

'No resentment?'

'I think he's past it.'

'So she's not locked away in a cupboard?'

'Without his parents noticing?'

'Jasmine's suddenly got money – we know the source now – and she doesn't tell anyone, not even her best friend, where it's coming from?'

Clarke considered this. 'If she did, Carla wasn't about to tell

266

us. I did think at the time maybe there was something she was holding back.'

'You've not questioned any of them since the website came to light?'

'No,' Clarke admitted. 'But then nobody else from her school was on Campbell's books.' She met Esson's eyes and narrowed her own. 'What's your thinking?'

Esson made show of checking the time on her phone. 'Schools will be out soon.'

'Probably best talked to at home, no?'

'Oh, absolutely. Teenage girls always open up more when their 'rents are in the vicinity.'

'Sarcasm *and* pen-tapping? What a catch you are, Christine.'

Esson was smirking as she started shrugging her way into her jacket. Clarke had gone back to her desk to retrieve her bag, phone and keys.

'You're never here,' Cammy Colson complained as she passed him. The rest of the team weren't about to comment, but they were giving her looks – even Gillian Reeves. Clarke knew what those looks meant: we're stuck here doing the heavy lifting. She gave the room at large a regal-style wave as she made her exit. Esson went one better, adding a curtsy in the doorway.

22

Rebus was re-shelving books when Megan Keighley appeared at his shoulder and asked a favour.

'I hope it's not insensitive,' she began, 'but Jackie Simpson had a DVD out on loan. It's one of those *Fast & Furious* things with Jason Statham, and there's a growing waiting list. Mr Statham is very popular.'

'Can't say I've seen him in anything.'

'Me neither, yet he seems to earn a crust.'

'You want me to fetch it?'

'If it's still in his cell.'

Rebus thought for a moment. 'Chances are it'll have been taken by the scene-of-crime posse, but no reason for them to hang on to it. I'll see what I can do.'

'That's kind of you, John. I did ask Mark Jamieson if he had it, but apparently not.' A new group of prisoners was arriving, and she went off to serve them. Valerie Watts was the officer in charge. She rewarded Rebus with a slight incline of her chin, after which Rebus's view of her was blocked by Billy Groam. He was interested in the shelf next to Rebus.

'Psychology, Billy?' Rebus commented.

'Is that what the sign says?' Groam peered at it. 'Thought you might have wanted a word with me.'

'I'll admit I was surprised. You're a bit of a dark horse.'

'I arrived here same time one of his lads was getting out – I suppose that left a vacancy.'

'So you didn't know him on the outside?'

Groam shook his head. 'Though one of his crew drank in one of the places I worked.' His brow furrowed. 'I feel a bit bad, actually. There was a guy called Jake Morris used to drink there too. New in town and needed a bit of work, so I introduced him to Darryl's man. Next thing, he's doing well for himself – right up until someone stuck a gun in his face. Jake did a runner.'

'So what's your deal with Darryl?'

'While I'm in here, my family's provided for.'

'Wife and one kid, right?'

Groam nodded. 'For the record, I was against you being sprung from SRU. To me, you spelled trouble. But Cafferty was always a thorn in Darryl's side and you plucked that thorn out. Fair play to you. Just a shame Darryl was locked up in here when it happened – made it harder to capitalise on the fact.'

'He seems to run his operation pretty well, all things considered.'

'Until Hanlon came along. City doesn't have oxygen enough for both of them, John, and Darryl's team on the outside are short of talent where it counts. Darryl's itching to have that threat extinguished ...' Groam waited until a prisoner nearby had moved on. 'Even if it means cooperating with your lot,' he eventually concluded.

'Then he should be speaking to Malcolm Fox.'

'Darryl's not a grass, though.'

'Need to hurry it up,' Valerie Watts called out. 'Another hall's on its way.'

'We've hardly been here any time!' someone complained.

'Schedule must have got snafu'd.' It was as much of an apology as Watts was about to issue. Megan Keighley was processing the borrowings as quickly as she could.

'I need to go help,' Rebus told Groam.

'You'll speak to Fox?' Groam demanded. 'You've got a phone, so there's no excuse.'

Rebus moved towards the desk. He was halfway there when the next tranche of prisoners arrived. A figure towards the rear was jostling them, barging them aside. Bobby Briggs's eyes were wide and staring, flecks of saliva at the corners of his mouth, teeth bared. Rebus looked to left and right, but there was nowhere to go. He had his mouth open, but before he could do any more than that, Briggs was on him. Rebus tried to wrench himself free, but Briggs's grip was fierce. One of his paws grabbed the back of Rebus's head, propelling his face into the nearest shelf of books. Tears streamed from Rebus's eyes and blood from his nose. Briggs's hand went from Rebus's head to his throat and started squeezing, while he placed his garlicky mouth next to Rebus's left ear.

'Where's Everett Harrison when you need him, eh?' he hissed.

Rebus could feel his eyes bulging from their sockets, his heartbeat pounding in his ears. A punch caught him in the kidneys. He clawed at Briggs's wrist, to no effect whatsoever. Briggs had taken something, and it had given him strength to accompany his rage. Rebus had a sudden flashback to fights he'd had when younger. Christ, he'd even wrestled Big Ger Cafferty when the man had been a mountain. He'd always been a scrapper, but scrapping wasn't what was required here. This was altogether different. There were voices all around, some egging Briggs on, others warning him to stop. But Briggs was beyond reasoning. The only thing that mattered to him in this moment was Rebus's ultimate demise. The room started to shimmer at its edges, the figures becoming ghostly.

Groam's fist caught Briggs squarely on the side of the head. Rebus could almost hear the man's jaw crack. It took a second identical punch before Briggs relaxed his grip on Rebus and squared up to his new foe.

'Come on then,' Groam said, bending slightly at the knees, a boxer's pose. Watts meantime had sounded the alarm and backup was starting to arrive.

270

'Way I hear it, your boy Christie is yesterday's man!' Briggs roared at Groam.

'Enough!' Watts barked. 'Unless you like the thought of solitary.'

Briggs stared at her and gave a humourless grin. 'Those cells are jam-packed, if you didn't know.' He was turning back towards Rebus, fists bunching, when Groam dropped him with an uppercut. Briggs buckled and keeled over, his lights extinguished. Rebus watched it all from behind his hands, which were cupped to his nose and filling with bright red blood. His eyesight was still blurry, but he knew a trained fighter when he saw one, and he recalled seeing Groam heading to the showers after gym sessions, T-shirt soaked with sweat, hair dripping. He remembered now: he'd been a doorman rather than bar staff – an enthusiastic doorman at that.

Briggs's breathing was being checked by a white-shirted officer. Rebus risked a glance in Megan Keighley's direction, hoping she hadn't been traumatised, but she looked more excited than anything, one hand at her crucifix, her cheeks flushed as she took shallow gulps of air. She was staring at Billy Groam as if seeing him for the first time. Watts meantime had reached Rebus and was pinching the bridge of his nose between her thumb and forefinger. Someone else produced a clump of paper tissues.

'We've got a gusher,' a voice called out, as the two groups of prisoners were separated and led out into the hallway. By the time a nurse arrived, Briggs was coming round. Watts had already told Groam to be on his way but prepare for repercussions. He stepped past without Briggs noticing. The nurse was asking Briggs if he was on anything.

'Adrenalin and stupidity,' Watts murmured to Rebus by way of answer.

Rebus met her eyes. 'You talked to Chris yet?'

She just nodded, saying nothing.

'Everything okay between you?'

A shrug.

271

A second nurse had arrived. She homed in on Rebus. 'Let's have a look at you,' she said, taking him by his arm. With a prison guard accompanying them, they walked the short distance to the nursing station. Rebus sat on a chair in one of the cubicles while the nurse got gloved up.

'My prostate's fine,' he told her.

'At your age, I very much doubt that.' She prodded at his nose and got him to open his mouth wide to check for loose teeth. 'There'll be bruising,' she warned him. 'Your eyes will probably puff up.'

'I believe the prescription for that is a juicy steak.'

'Not so much in here. Your nose isn't broken and your mouth seems fine.' She stood back and looked at him. 'You're having a day of it – how did it go at the hospital?'

'Fine, aye.'

'Funny that, they told me you never arrived. Felt better en route and didn't want to waste their time – very public-spirited of you.'

'What can I say?' Rebus managed a shrug.

'Don't worry, your secret's safe with me.'

'What secret?'

'But you better pray that Chris Novak doesn't catch on.'

Finally Rebus understood. 'It wasn't ...' he started to say, but then realised that a lie might suffice where the truth wouldn't. 'That's very much appreciated,' he said instead.

'Valerie's a good lass. Just maybe that bit too free-and-easy at times.'

'Could be, aye,' Rebus said. He got to his feet, somewhat shakily, as the nurse began to peel off the rubber gloves. But then she paused.

'Maybe you want me to check your ...' She waggled a finger.

'That's a smashing offer, but I think I'll pass.'

'Would you turn Valerie down as readily, though?'

Rebus felt himself blushing – actually blushing – as he opened the door and made his escape.

23

They waited at the school gates and heard the bell ringing, signalling the end of lessons. A couple of parents waited in their cars for their sons or daughters to emerge.

'A Volvo and a Range Rover,' Esson commented. 'We could do them for sitting on double yellow lines.'

'These are the people who pay our salaries,' Clarke reminded her.

The first children to emerge were a boy and a girl, each toting a violin case as well as a backpack. Probably first years, Clarke thought, spindly and awkward and with some way to go before adulthood. When the older ones appeared, they had more surface swagger, the boys keen to be noticed, aiming swipes at each other, chasing and being chased. Several already had their phones out, checking them with urgency. A few of the boys sported the beginnings of facial hair. The girls of similar age huddled and gossiped but looked altogether more grown-up.

'Can you remember that far back?' Esson asked, a touch of nostalgia in her voice.

'I was a swot,' Clarke answered. 'Had a few friends but we were all like-minded. Homework before boys. Homework before *everything*.'

'My school was party central. Well, the park behind the school was. Even had a bit of woodland you could disappear

273

into with a bottle or a bloke. Had to watch out for the creeps, though – pervs who seemed to be always hanging about. Glad to put it all behind me.'

'Happiest days of your life, Christine.'

'I know. It's such a depressing thought. But at least we didn't have the internet to deal with – the way it is now, I mean, filled with men like Zak Campbell.'

Clarke watched through the windscreen. 'Here she comes,' she announced. Carla was alongside the same friend who'd been seated next to her in the classroom during Clarke's visit – Stephanie, was it? There was a boy with them, too – Craig Fielding. 'That's Jasmine's ex,' Clarke told Esson. 'Lives in a house just behind hers.'

'Who's he interested in – Carla or her pal?'

'The pal, I'd say.'

'She's not as bonny, but then he's hardly catch of the day himself.'

'Jasmine saw something in him, though her dad's not a fan.'

'Fathers and daughters,' Esson commented. 'Shall we?'

They unclipped their seat belts in unison, got out of the car and crossed the road. Craig Fielding saw them first and muttered something to the girls. Some kids started making nee-naw noises, mimicking a police siren – they'd obviously been in class that day and remembered Clarke.

'Lock them up!' someone yelled from a safe distance, to peals of laughter.

'Anyone want some weed?' another joker called out.

Clarke took up position in front of Carla, who averted her eyes. 'You're Stephanie, right?' she asked Carla's companion. The girl looked to Carla for advice, but none was forthcoming.

'You don't have to tell them anything,' Craig Fielding said in a show of bravado.

'At least they're not panicking, Craig,' Clarke shot back. 'Did he tell you he tried to outrun a police car? Just a silly wee boy.' Craig immediately backed down and started shuffling his feet, eyes cast downwards.

'Yes, I'm Stephanie,' Carla's friend admitted.

'Nice to meet you. Would you mind if we had a word in private with Carla? I'm sure she'll fill you in later.'

'What about me?' Craig asked. Clarke turned towards him.

'You still here?' She managed to sound incredulous. Craig took the hint and started walking. Other boys were waiting for him, wanting to know the score. He pulled back his shoulders, ready to put on an act.

'I'll message you,' Carla told Stephanie, who nodded and moved away, albeit with some reluctance.

'Let's go sit in the car for a minute, Carla,' Clarke said. They flanked her as they crossed the street. The nee-naws were rising into the air again. Phones were out, recording the moment for posterity. Clarke opened the rear door and waited till Carla was in before heading around the car and climbing in next to her. Esson got the hint and settled in the driver's seat, knowing full well that she was really a passenger in this scene.

'You know what's interesting, Carla?' Clarke asked. The girl's lips were pressed together. She held her backpack on her lap, gripping its handle. 'What's interesting – to me at least,' Clarke continued, 'is that you never asked us if there's news or what we're doing here. That's what a friend would do, a friend who didn't know anything.'

'Is there news?' Carla blurted out. Clarke eventually smiled.

'Bit late for that,' she said.

'Stephanie and Craig didn't ask either.'

'But it's *you* we're talking about here, Carla, Jasmine's closest friend and confidante, even if she maybe wasn't yours. We haven't spoken since news broke of that website. Must have come as a surprise – or maybe not?'

'Of course it was.'

'She never said a word, dropped any hints? It's a hellish big secret to keep.'

Esson had started the car and was moving off. Clarke realised it was because some of Carla's schoolmates were still filming on their phones.

'Are we going to the police station?' Carla asked.

'We're just driving,' Esson informed her. 'We can drop you home if you like?'

'We can just drive,' Carla said.

'So when you found out what Jasmine was doing online,' Clarke continued, 'you must have thought the same as us ...'

'What?'

'That she killed him and that's why she ran.'

'She's not ...' Carla broke off and bit her bottom lip. Clarke leaned in towards her.

'You know where she is, don't you, Carla?'

The girl gave a vigorous shake of the head.

'She's a murder suspect, and she'll remain one until we find her and she talks to us. We *will* find her, by the way – no one stays hidden for ever. But the sooner we hear her side of the story, the better.'

'She didn't do anything.' The words were spoken so softly, Clarke almost didn't catch them.

'You know that for a fact? Because she told you? Meaning you're in touch with her.'

Now that they were a few streets clear of the school, Esson had pulled over to the side of the road again, watching proceedings on the back seat from the rear-view mirror.

'Carla,' Clarke went on, trying to soften her voice, even though a current was coursing through her, 'the only way we can know for sure that she's innocent is if she tells us herself.'

'She could write it all down, no?'

'Tells us herself,' Clarke repeated. 'She's not been using her debit card for food. We know she had a bit of cash, but that would mean going to a shop or paying a delivery driver. Her photo's been everywhere for days now – someone would have come forward if they'd seen her. That tells me she's lying low, protected by a friend or friends.' She paused. 'Does Craig know?'

Carla snorted. 'All Craig knows is that he fancies Steph.'

'How does Jasmine feel about that?'

'She's not bothered. Craig and her were never really ...' She broke off, realising she'd already said too much. 'I think I'm going to be sick.'

Esson got out of the car and opened the rear door for her. Clarke emerged too, watching as Carla bent forward, hands on her black-stockinged knees, taking gulps of air, producing nothing but some dry heaves. After a few moments she reached into the car and pulled a water bottle from the side pocket of her backpack, taking sips from it.

'Better?' Clarke asked. The girl nodded, but there was a sheen of sweat on her forehead.

'I could tell her to get in touch with you,' she offered, eyes focused on Clarke.

'That all takes time, though, and she might say no. You're her friend, Carla, and she trusts you, but *we're* having to depend on you now, too. The running-away has to stop. We have to hear the story from her own mouth. After that, everything will be a lot easier for everybody. So what do you say? I think you know in your heart that it's time – and it really *is* time.' Clarke pressed her palm gently against the shoulder of Carla's blazer. Carla looked back at her unblinkingly.

'You offered me a lift home ...'

Clarke nodded. 'And then we'll go and see Jasmine, yes?' Carla was still staring at her. Clarke sucked in some breath as the truth struck. 'She's at yours? Has been all this time?' She watched the girl give a slow nod. 'How did you keep it from your parents, Carla?'

'You'll see,' Carla said, climbing back into the car.

They drove to a semi-detached house in Mayfield. As Esson pulled to the kerb, Clarke was staring at a car already parked there.

'What the hell?' she muttered. She started pulling herself out of the back seat, gesturing for Esson to stay with Carla. Fox was out of his car by now, gloved hands clasped in front of him like an undertaker.

277

'What the hell's going on, Malcolm?'

Fox ignored her, looking towards her car. 'Is that Carla? I wouldn't mind a word with her.' He made to move forward, but Clarke pressed her hand solidly against his chest.

'I asked you what the hell you're doing here!'

'Her father works for Christie – didn't I tell you?'

'You know damned well you didn't.'

'Well he does, and he's been lying low but now he's back. Maybe Carla knows where I can find him.'

'You knew all this and you kept it to yourself, same as you held back from Christine that you knew Jackie Simpson? That's two big lines you've crossed, mister.'

Fox leaned in towards her, holding up one gloved hand, thumb and forefinger almost touching. 'I'm *this* close, Siobhan. *This* close.'

'And what are we, Malcolm? Your colleagues, I mean – what are we in this great scenario of yours?'

There was no emotion in his eyes as he met hers. 'Don't get in my way, Siobhan.'

'DI Fox,' she said quietly, 'if you don't return to your vehicle and drive away right now, I'm going to have you arrested.'

He gave a snort. 'For what?'

'I'll think of something – obstruction maybe.'

'You wouldn't dare.' But the sneer on his face didn't stay there long. It was obvious from her eyes that she'd seldom been more serious. To reinforce the point, she was already digging her phone out of her jacket.

'Right now,' she repeated, holding it up in front of her.

Fox managed a look of disgust as he backed away, getting into his car and starting the ignition. As his car roared off, Esson and Carla emerged. Clarke looked at Carla.

'How's your dad doing?' she asked.

'He's okay.'

'He's been away, aye?'

'For a bit. He's back now.'

'Not at home right now, though?'

Carla just shrugged, so Clarke gestured towards the house. Carla led the way, unlocking the door and calling out. There was no answer. The interior was tidy and homely, IKEA furnishings everywhere and a blown-up photograph of the family on one wall.

'Dad's idea,' she explained. 'Mum and me hate it.' She sloughed off her blazer and dropped her bag on the floor. Clarke and Esson followed her through the living room and dining area into the kitchen. She seemed distracted, maybe having second thoughts.

'We're here now,' Clarke said quietly. Esson was gazing through the window, her attention on a shed behind the garage. But after a few more seconds, Carla led them back into the front hall and began climbing the stairs to the upper floor. She stopped on the landing and pressed what looked like a light switch. A section of the ceiling began to open with a motorised hum, a ladder descending.

'Dad cleared it out years ago so I could have it as a play-room,' she explained. Then she started to climb, Clarke and Esson following.

The attic space had been floored, and large Velux windows installed. There was heating and a thick carpet, plus a sofa, computer desk, games console and TV. The posters on the walls showed Asian pop stars, just as in Jasmine's bedroom. Clarke noted the duvet draped along the sofa. A waste-paper bin was stuffed with used fast-food cartons, drinks cans and crisp bags. Carla looked around, saying nothing. She turned to Clarke for help, so Clarke cleared her throat.

'Jasmine,' she said, 'my name's Siobhan. I'm from the police and I really want to help you if you'll let me.' They waited, holding their breath, until they heard a noise from behind the sofa. Jasmine Andrews had wedged herself there and was now rising tentatively to her feet.

'Hi there, Jasmine,' Clarke said. The smile that accompanied her words was wide and genuine. But Jasmine was looking at her friend. And when tears started falling from her eyes, Carla began bawling too.

279

24

The child protection officer was called Terence Hayes. He sat alongside Jasmine in the interview room while her parents waited outside. Their reunion had been emotional, though some anger seemed to be simmering just below the surface of both wife and husband. The mood in the MIT office had been buzzy when Clarke and Esson arrived with Jasmine.

'Long way still to go,' Clarke warned Gillian Reeves. 'Make sure everyone gets the message.'

Hayes had asked for a couple of minutes alone with Jasmine. The DCI had offered the parents his office, telling them it was 'just a bit more comfortable'. Clarke caught his eye and nodded, knowing Helena and James Andrews were being kept out of the way.

When Hayes announced that they were ready, Esson and Clarke entered the interview room and started the recording. Once preliminaries had been dispensed with, Clarke took a moment to clear her head. She hadn't brought any of the paperwork with her. Esson had a small blank notepad in front of her and was holding a ballpoint pen. Probably nothing was going to put Jasmine at ease, but they were trying their best. Her blonde hair had been washed recently and her clothes were clean, though she looked awkward in them. Clarke guessed they belonged to Carla.

'You did well to hide for as long as you did,' Clarke began. 'Can't have been easy.'

'Carla looked after me.'

'How did you manage to use the bathroom?'

'Waited till her parents were out.'

'What made you do it in the first place, Jasmine?'

'Hide, you mean? Or the other thing?'

Clarke found herself swallowing, her throat dry. 'What other thing?'

'Letting Zak film me.'

She gave a slow exhalation. 'How did you get to know him?'

'Online. He liked the TikToks that Carla and me did. We started messaging on Snapchat.'

'Did you know how old he was back then?' Clarke watched Jasmine nod.

'First time I went to his house, he took some photos in the living room. On his phone, I mean, some of the two of us and some just of me. He said I was like a model.' She raised her chin, but then dropped it again. 'Second time I went, he was busy in his studio.'

'Meaning the spare bedroom?'

'When the girl left, he told me all about it. Then he showed me the pictures on his site. Good money, he said. We had a drink and a smoke, but nothing else happened. Third time I went ...' Her voice trailed off and she reached for the glass in front of her. Having swallowed some water, she spoke again. 'I didn't want to let him down.' She used the sleeve of her jumper to wipe a tear from her cheek. Hayes produced an unopened packet of tissues, which she took from him. The room remained silent until she was ready. 'Then that one time I turned up at the house ... He knew I was coming, but he didn't answer the door. And when I went to see if the back door was maybe unlocked, I saw him through the window ... lying there in the kitchen in all that blood. I just freaked.'

'And ran to Carla's?' Clarke asked. 'Why not go home?'

'To my mum? Fat chance. Tell her what I'd been doing at Zak's? Besides, we'd had a falling-out.'

'Oh?'

'Over her and Craig.'

'Craig Fielding?'

'She couldn't bear the thought of him fancying me. She was always hovering, getting his attention – at her age. "Mrs Robinson", Dad calls her – that's from some old film. Drives *him* mad as well. And Craig fucking fell for it.'

It suddenly made sense to Clarke – Fielding asking after Jasmine's mum. She remembered him saying something like *Helena must be worried sick*. Not just the genuine concern, but the casual use of her first name. She should have seen it at the time. And then Craig visiting the house after Jasmine's disappearance ... She knew now why James Andrews had attacked the boy.

'Zak would have sent Mum tonto,' Jasmine went on. 'And if not her, then Dad.' She broke off and looked at both detectives in turn. 'And I couldn't go to the police, could I? Not without you asking what I was doing there in the first place. Besides, somebody'd killed Zak – maybe I was on their list too. Carla eventually told me I was being stupid, but by then I'd made my little nest at hers. I was happy enough there.' She had finished her water and shook her head when Hayes suggested a refill.

'Who do you think killed Zak, Jasmine?' Clarke asked.

'No idea.'

'Did you know any of the people who used his website?'

'God, no.'

'So the name Valerio doesn't mean anything to you? He's one of Zak's customers.'

'I know the name. He ... watched me a few times.'

'No actual interaction, though?' Clarke watched the girl shake her head. 'What can you tell us about him?'

'He always wanted ... more. Zak sat at the camera and computer. He'd monitor what was being asked. I'd see him shake

282

his head if he didn't like it. Valerio was willing to pay, but Zak said no.' She paused. 'This Valerio – he'll be in the black book, won't he?'

Clarke's eyes narrowed. 'What black book?'

'Zak kept it in his pocket – used to take it out and wave it about, saying my head would melt if I knew who was in it. He kept teasing, but I don't think he ever showed it to anyone.'

Clarke made eye contact with Esson: no book, black or otherwise, had been found on Zak Campbell's body, or anywhere else for that matter.

'You met some of the other models, didn't you?' Esson asked Jasmine.

'Zak threw a few parties. I know some of them did twosomes for him, but I didn't want that and he never pushed it. That was the thing, he wasn't pushy. You felt like you were the one in charge.' She paused. 'But he was a prick, wasn't he? A complete fucking scumbag.'

'Maybe one of the other models came to that realisation a while back,' Esson commented.

'And killed him? I can't think of any of them who'd have done that.'

'You did confide in Carla, though,' Clarke said. 'You know who her dad is?'

'He's hardly ever around. I know he has shouting matches with Carla's mum after a drink – no surprises there.' Her eyes met Clarke's. 'He's some sort of gangster, isn't he?'

'Do you think Carla could have told him about Zak?'

'She promised not to tell a soul.'

'How about Marcus Simpson? He had a falling-out with Zak, didn't he?'

Jasmine shrugged. 'Zak never said anything about that. I only met Marcus one time, I think ...' She paused again. 'My mum and dad are raging, aren't they?'

'I'll explain things to them if you like?'

Clarke watched the girl nod. Esson seemed to have nothing to add. Hayes looked from one detective to the other.

'We're done here?' he guessed.

'For now, though we'll need prints and a swab.'

A look of alarm flitted across Jasmine's face. 'Nothing to worry about,' Hayes tried to assure her. Jasmine was wiping away more tears as they got to their feet. Clarke reckoned she knew what the girl was seeing and would continue to see for months, maybe even years to come.

A kitchen floor.

A body lying there.

And blood, copious amounts of blood ...

Journalists had gathered outside the station, so Jasmine and her parents were taken home in an unmarked van that had benches in the rear but no windows. Esson started whistling 'Mrs Robinson' as she watched.

'Subtle,' Clarke said as she started checking her phone. She had a dozen missed calls and as many messages from Laura Smith. She walked over to where Esson had just started filling in Reeves and Colson.

'We need to ask Carla if she told her dad,' she said to the group.

'I can do that,' Esson replied.

'What about this black book?' Reeves asked. 'If the killer took it ...'

'It was to stop anyone else having it,' Clarke said, nodding. 'It also means whoever has it has access to the sextortion list. We need to check if anyone's contacted the likes of Urquhart, trying to restart the scheme.'

'You think that's why it was taken?'

'It's one scenario.'

'But not the most obvious.'

'No,' Clarke conceded. She stepped away from the huddle and called Marcus Simpson.

'I need to ask you something,' she said when he answered. 'Did you ever see Zak with a little black book?'

'That thing? Sort of like a diary? Aye, he always had it on him.'

'Did he say what it was?'

'Names and numbers, that's what he told me – not that I ever saw him open it up. Could've been blank pages for all I know.'

'Thanks,' Clarke said, ending the call. She watched DCI Carmichael walk in her direction.

'Well, that's at least one happy ending,' he said.

'Maybe.' Thinking back to what Jasmine had gone through and the home awaiting her, she wasn't so sure.

'But I'm here to give you a strong reprimand – you and Christine both.' He folded his arms. 'The Fiscal's not happy at you grabbing a schoolgirl off the street and grilling her in your car.'

'We just had a couple of casual questions – didn't feel the need to make it formal.' Clarke had already rehearsed with Esson what to say when they were asked. 'Once she was relaxed, she opened up to us, no grilling required. In fact, in an interview room, surrounded by adults, I'm not sure she'd have told us much of anything.' She paused. 'Besides, it got us Jasmine, safe and sound, didn't it?'

'No denying that.'

'So the Fiscal might not be happy, but how about you, Bryan?'

Carmichael leaned in towards her and lowered his voice. 'I'm over the bloody moon, Siobhan – and I couldn't be prouder of you.'

'In which case,' Clarke said, looking past his shoulder, 'you can do me a favour.'

'Name it.'

She took a step back and nodded towards the figure who had appeared in the doorway. 'Get rid of that ghoul.'

Fox had spotted Clarke and was zeroing in on her. 'I need access to Jasmine,' he stated. 'To both girls, actually.'

Clarke held a hand out towards her boss. 'DCI Carmichael, I think you know DI Malcolm Fox?'

Fox took his eyes off her long enough to grace Carmichael with the curtest of nods.

'OCCTU have been investigating Darryl Christie's various dealings for many months – a lot of money and man-hours expended. Carla's father is part of Christie's gang and was targeted recently by persons unknown. We need information on who might be behind that attack.' His words were aimed at Carmichael, but his focus remained fixed on Clarke.

'So talk to the father,' Carmichael said.

But Fox was shaking his head. 'He's a criminal – he's hardly likely to tell us anything. When he was safe and secure inside his own home, *that's* when he'd have opened up – and those girls could well have heard something. Either the adults talking, or a telephone conversation, maybe another gang member visiting ...'

'This can be dealt with in due course,' Carmichael stated coldly. 'But right now we have a murder inquiry on our hands, and Carla and Jasmine are crucial to it. Once things are on an even keel ...'

Fox glowered at him. 'Listen to yourself, man! An even keel? Scotland's been holed beneath the waterline. Whole communities are in danger of drowning. I tend to think that takes priority over someone whacking a cut-price pimp!'

Carmichael stared at Fox, the silence between the two men lengthening. 'Your boss at Gartcosh is Phil Pratchett, yes?'

'Detective Chief Superintendent Pratchett,' Fox said.

'Phil and I go back a ways – I assume you have his blessing for this ram raid of yours?'

'Hardly a ram raid.' Fox shuffled his feet, eyes on the floor.

'Does he know or doesn't he?'

'In an operation like this, parameters have a way of widening suddenly.'

'I'm not sure even *you* know what you mean by that – it just sounds good to your ears.' Colour was creeping up Fox's neck. 'I think the best thing you can do right now, DI Fox, is go back to OCCTU and let us get on with our job without interference.

Find another way of tackling Christie and his kind – maybe even try the gloves-off approach.'

Fox was still wearing his leather driving gloves. He flexed a hand, eyes on Clarke.

'I thought that's what I *was* doing,' he said. 'With precious little help from my supposed colleagues in this city.'

'I look forward to reading your complaint,' Carmichael said. 'Don't let me detain you from writing and submitting it. Meantime I'll be talking to your chief super. Goodbye now.'

He made a sweeping motion with one hand. Realising that the whole office was now watching, Fox sniffed, turned and made his exit.

'Was that good enough for you, Siobhan?' Carmichael asked as soon as he was out of sight.

'Just about perfect, I'd say.'

'So now we can get back to the main business of solving our case?'

'Absolutely, sir,' Clarke said. 'With pleasure.'

After bang-up that evening, Rebus called Christine Esson. It wasn't easy seeing the numbers through eyes reduced to slits by the violence earlier. He felt light-headed, and his heart rate was failing to come down. Without Billy Groam, his knight in shining tracksuit, he reckoned he'd have been a goner. He knew too that Bobby Briggs would never be appeased, meaning Rebus would have to be even warier than usual, his guard up until one of them was no longer inside.

'News travels fast,' Esson told him when she answered the call.

'What news?'

'Jasmine Andrews. She's back with her family.'

'I hadn't heard.'

'So why are you phoning?'

'I need Fox's number.'

'I already gave it to you.'

'And I thought I had it memorised – stuff happens.'

'We found out that Jackie Simpson was Fox's guy.'

'How do you mean?'

'Before he got himself arrested, he was Fox's snitch. Malcolm Fox is the reason he broke into that nail bar in the first place, so Fox had an excuse to go in there looking for anything incriminating to do with Hanlon.'

'He hit the jackpot.'

'But Fox couldn't stop Simpson going to jail.'

'Where he ended up dangerously close to Everett Harrison.' Rebus thought for a moment. 'That reminds me,' he said eventually, 'if the lab's done with the *Fast & Furious* DVD, any chance of it coming back? I told the librarian I'd ask.'

'Don't see why not, but it might be a lowish priority.'

'How come you're not out celebrating the misper turning up?' he asked.

'Because Zak Campbell's killer still needs to be caught.'

'And Jackie Simpson's too,' Rebus reminded her.

'That goes without saying.'

'Doesn't sound like you're getting very far with it.'

'We do seem to have hit a wall,' she confessed. 'I'm hoping our man on the inside might have better luck.'

'Your man on the inside's hit a wall too, Christine.' He probed at his aching nose. 'So the missing girl didn't kill the pornographer?'

'We don't think so.'

'That narrows your list of suspects then.'

'Small mercies, John,' Esson said, reciting Fox's number and bringing the call to an end.

He had the same difficulty with Fox's number. Plus the phone only had about fifteen per cent charge left.

'What do you want?' Fox barked.

'I'm phoning on behalf of the Jackie Simpson Memorial Fund. Thought you might be minded to make a substantial contribution.'

'You're a prick, John.'

'And you sound like you're still at your desk. Got other lives to ruin, I suppose?'

'I did what I could for Jackie.'

'Did you, aye? Because my guess is you were pleased as punch when he ended up in the same hall as Darryl Christie and Everett Harrison. How did he get his reports to you?'

'Those little booths they have for video calls.'

He was so quick to reveal this, Rebus knew it was because he reckoned it ingenious and therefore worth sharing.

'Any of the staff here know what was going on?'

'Far as anyone knew, I was Jackie's solicitor. Well, obviously the governor had to be in the loop, but no one else. And you're right – I am still at work, more determined than ever to get some justice for Jackie.'

'Well, I might have some news for you. Darryl Christie isn't quite ready to step into the dead man's shoes, but he says he'll cooperate with you if it will bring Hanlon crashing down.'

'I'm not convinced Hanlon has anything to do with it, John – not directly.'

'Oh?' Rebus was trying to work out how Fox could have identified Chris Novak.

'I'm coming around to the idea of Mickey Mason. He got out of the Bar-L a few weeks back – the timing clicks almost exactly.'

'Mason's muscling in on Edinburgh?' Rebus hoped the relief didn't show in his voice.

'In cahoots with Hanlon. Think about it: Hanlon needs someone on the ground. Mason is pals with Bobby Briggs. Briggs has regular chinwags with Harrison – that's how the two bosses communicate. In Glasgow Mason pushed more ketamine than a vets' school – and right now Edinburgh's awash with it.'

'You've got it all figured out, Malcolm,' Rebus said, trying to sound impressed. He was about to muse on why Mason might be using a motorcyclist with a Liverpool accent, but he didn't want Fox jumping to anything but wrong conclusions. 'So you've got eyes and ears on Mason?'

'Not yet. I'm trying to convince my boss.'

'If anyone can do it, you can.'

'So maybe I won't have much need of your chum Darryl.'

'He seems blissfully unaware of Mason's involvement.'

'Let's keep it that way – I'd like to get Mason before Christie does something stupid.'

'I won't say a word.' Rebus pressed an exploratory finger against one of his puffed-up eyelids.

'But I do appreciate you taking the trouble to call me.'

'I'll let you get back to the grindstone, Malcolm.'

'One last thing, John.'

'Yes?'

'I said that I've got Mason in my sights, but I'm ruling nothing out. If not Mason, then Hanlon direct, and if not Hanlon ...'

'Who?' Rebus felt his chest tightening a little.

'Think about all the enemies Christie's made. Someone might have thought it was time for a bit of vigilante justice.'

'I'm not sure I understand,' Rebus said, understanding only too well.

'A lone wolf, someone with a grudge.'

'Unlikely, I'd have thought.'

'They'd need help, of course – to track Christie's men. But a few quid slipped to the right people ...'

'I don't know, Malcolm, the way Everett Harrison acts ...'

'And how exactly is that?'

'Like he knows precisely what's going on.'

There was silence on the line. 'You're keeping something from me, John – what is it?'

'I'm telling you everything I know.'

'And why would that be, when you've always hated my guts?'

'I just think you're in danger of taking a wrong turning.'

'Or maybe a right one, eh? Is that what's worrying you?'

Rebus was still trying to think of some convincing line to spin when he realised Fox had hung up on him. He cursed under his breath as he clambered from the toilet pan. So the governor knew that Jackie Simpson had been reporting to Fox.

Rebus speculated about that for a minute or two as he lay on his narrow bed, hands clasped behind his head. And Fox wasn't ruling out the lone wolf theory – a theory that, taken to its conclusion, would bring Darryl Christie down on Chris Novak's head. Along the hall, someone was singing behind their cell door. It sounded like 'Hurt'. Rebus knew Johnny Cash didn't write it, but it was Cash's version he liked. He recited the words silently until a mix of pleading and angry voices stilled the singer.

Folsom Prison to San Quentin to Saughton.

Quite the journey.

'Are you driving?' Fox asked Jason Mulgrew when his call was connected.

'I promised Christine a gin and tonic. Everything okay with you, Malcolm?'

'I don't suppose there's any news from the prison?'

'What do you think?' Fox heard Mulgrew give a heavy sigh.

'Can I let you in on a secret?' he asked.

'Of course.'

'I visited Carla's home – Jasmine's best friend. Took an OCCTU colleague with me. We were looking to speak to Carla's dad. He works for Christie, but someone stuck a gun in his face and he went into hiding. But here's the thing – while Carla's mum was lying through her teeth about the father's whereabouts, Jasmine was already ensconced in the attic. How crazy is that?'

'There was no way you could have known – I assume the mum had no idea?'

'How am I supposed to answer that when they won't let me talk to Carla?'

'Siobhan Clarke's warned you off?'

'She got her boss to do her dirty work for her.'

'What's your thinking?'

'Carla's parents might have let anything slip during their

291

various chats. Anyone in the house could have heard. Could be stuff about Christie, the gunman, Harrison or Hanlon ...'

'Or even Simpson's murder, if there's a Christie connection.'

'See, that's what I'm thinking, Jason. If the request to interview the girls came from the Simpson inquiry ...'

'You think I'm likely to have any more luck than you?'

'You could hardly do worse. Maybe pitch it to your DCI, see what she thinks.'

'You're tenacious, Malcolm, I'll give you that. Shall I pass on your best to Christine?'

'Might be better not to mention me at all.'

'Understood.'

'And Jason? Only soft drinks if you're driving afterwards. Wouldn't want you failing a breath test ...'

Christine Esson had a G and T in front of her when Mulgrew walked into the bar. It was actually her second, but he wasn't to know that. A pint, with plenty of life still in it, sat on a coaster waiting for him.

'Thought we agreed this was my shout,' he said, settling next to her.

'Second round's yours.' She leaned back and exhaled.

'You've had a pretty good day,' he said, hoisting his glass in a toast.

'Only because Carla was bursting to tell someone.'

'Incredible they could keep Jasmine hidden.'

'It maybe helped that the father was elsewhere.'

'He works for Darryl Christie, yes?'

Esson nodded and lifted her glass.

'See, that's interesting from a Jackie Simpson perspective.'

Esson stared at him. 'Are you sure you don't mean a Darryl Christie perspective? This you doing Fox's work for him, Jason?'

'Simpson is *our* case, Christine – maybe you've been forgetting that?'

She decided to allow him this. He lifted his own drink and took a sip. She didn't think he was planning on finishing it. Safety first; clear head – Fox again.

'So Jasmine is back with her family,' he commented, 'but nothing to suggest she's the killer?'

'There's a client called Valerio. We could do with pinning him down.'

'Like valerian, the plant? Or Valerie Watts?'

'Or a hundred other permutations. See, Zak Campbell's blackmail scheme could have backfired on him. There's a missing book, a sort of diary with names and details.' Esson paused. 'Actually, we don't know what's in it, if anything.' She began to deflate a little, compensating with one more mouthful of gin.

'You want to stick with this to the bitter end, don't you?' he asked quietly.

'If Mae McGovern will let me.'

'I really doubt she will. You don't know the pressure she's under.'

'Her and every other cop in this city.'

Mulgrew was looking at her. 'You need an early night, Christine.'

'Some women would read that as a chat-up.' She saw his face change. 'Don't worry – I know Zara Shah's more your type.' He seemed ready to protest, but Esson lifted a hand, palm towards him. 'You're right,' she said. 'When I came in here, I intended having three or four, but I think I'm done. I was about to apologise, but you're not really in the mood either, are you?'

They both studied his barely touched pint.

'Another time, DS Esson?' he said.

'Another time, DI Mulgrew,' she replied.

Day Seven

25

After breakfast, Rebus visited Everett Harrison in his cell.

'What the hell do you want, Rocky?' Harrison growled.

'Just a bit of clarity. Did you know who Jackie Simpson was? Why he was inside, I mean?'

'Breaking and entering, as per.'

'It was your nail bar he went into, though, the one with the stash in the back room.'

'You're shitting me.'

Rebus shook his head. 'You didn't know until now?'

'No.'

'And if you had known?'

'I'd have ripped his throat out.'

'Exactly.'

'But I didn't.' Harrison scratched a hand across his jawline. 'So was it a coincidence or what?'

'No coincidence. Police knew your boss had trafficked stuff to that location. They wanted to search it for proof.'

'Simpson was working for your lot? That's what you're saying? Well they're not getting me for stiffing him – go tell them that.'

'So if not you and not Novak ...'

'Who says it wasn't Novak?'

'I do.'

'You sure about that?'

Rebus gave a nod. 'One more thing,' he said. 'Does your boss know Darryl's put a hit out on him, money no object?'

'Yeah, right,' Harrison sneered. 'You think Christie's reach stretches more than half a mile beyond the city bypass, never mind halfway round the world?'

'Hanlon really isn't interested in Edinburgh, despite the dope haul that put you in here?'

'*Because* of the dope haul that put me in here,' Harrison corrected him. 'Shay wants cities with a big enough market to make the occasional bust worthwhile – turns out Edinburgh's not worth the hassle.'

'Even so, doesn't do any harm to make Christie think he has competition.'

'He obviously *has* got competition – pistol-packing biker's proof of that. Local scrotes, though, if you ask me. That's just about the level of threat Darryl Christie merits.' Harrison broke off as Kyle Jacobs appeared in the doorway.

'Change your top, John, you've got a visitor.'

'He's a popular fellow, is our Rocky,' Harrison commented as Rebus was led away.

Siobhan Clarke was waiting at one of the tables when he arrived. There were other prisoners present, catching up with family. A couple of kids played in the corner set aside for them. Rebus checked out each prisoner's face. He didn't know any of them.

'What happened to you?' Clarke said, eyes widening.

'I tripped on the stairs. Remember the good old days when a lot of suspects did that on their way from the interview room to the cells?'

'Before my time, thankfully.'

'Anyway, what brings you here?'

She had turned her head towards the visitors' door. 'I had a surprise, but now ...' She got to her feet and headed to the exit, opening the door and stepping through. A couple of minutes later she reappeared, bringing Samantha with her. The two women sat down opposite him.

'What's going on?' he demanded.

'We brought Carrie,' Samatha explained, studying the damage to his face. 'Siobhan's right, though – can't let her see you in this state. What the hell happened, Dad?'

'I got in a fight – and yes, you should see the other guy.' Rebus was peering as best he could in the direction of the door. 'Where is she?'

'An officer is keeping an eye on her.'

'Maybe I should go sit with her?' Clarke gestured towards the door and Samantha gave a grateful nod. Father and daughter watched her leave.

'You look as gorgeous as ever,' he eventually said. He could see that she'd made an effort, while recognising that a prison wasn't a catwalk. Muted shades but her clothes looked new-bought. 'How's Carrie doing?'

'She misses you.'

'And Brillo?'

'Ditto, though he's fallen big-time for your granddaughter.'

'You know I don't want her seeing me in here. Because then she could never *unsee* it – if that makes sense.'

'You're still her grandad. None of this changes that.' She handed him a folded sheet of paper. Carrie had drawn Brillo and her.

'She's got talent,' Rebus said.

'She really has. Loves going to galleries, too.'

He nodded towards the door Clarke had exited through. 'Was this her idea or yours?'

'Mutually agreed.' Samantha reached across the table and gave his hand a squeeze. 'She really does want to see you, and none of this would faze her.' She swept the room with one hand. 'Maybe once your face heals, eh?'

'Maybe,' Rebus conceded.

'Fancy a drink or something?' She nodded towards the row of vending machines.

'Maybe a Highland Park with a splash.' He shook his head. 'No, I'm fine.'

'Any news from the lawyers?'

Another shake of the head. 'Bastards are avoiding me. So do me a favour and take my mind off it – tell me about you and Carrie ...'

As she spoke, Rebus felt as though a weight was being lifted from him. But with five or so minutes left, Clarke came back and asked if she could have a quick chat with 'the old man'. With a final hug and kiss, Samantha headed for the door. Clarke sat down and met his eyes.

'I screwed up, John, and I'm sorry. But I did it with the best of intentions.'

'What did you tell Carrie?'

'That you're not feeling a hundred per cent but you'll be better soon and she can come see you then. Okay?'

'Aye, maybe.'

'Anyway, I forgot to say – Christine told me to tell you that the lab are done with the DVD box, so it's on its way back.'

'Box? No actual disc?'

'Just the box.'

'Someone nicked a Jason Statham film?'

'Well, he's very popular.'

'So everybody keeps telling me.' He met her eyes. 'Good work getting Jasmine back.'

'I'm not sure it takes us any closer to Zak's killer. There's one name we're having trouble identifying – Valerio.'

'Like the song?'

She spelled it for him.

Rebus nodded. '"The Great Valerio" – I think he's a tight-rope-walker. It's Richard and Linda Thompson. Are you telling me you don't know the *Bright Lights* album?'

'It's also a hairdresser's and a chip shop – none of which have been much help.'

'I could sing it to you if you like?'

'What a pity visiting time is up,' she said with a smile.

He gave her a brief hug as they stood. She leaned back to study his face.

'Not angry?' she asked.

'I'm always angry, Siobhan – it keeps the fire lit.'

'You're too old to be fighting, John.'

'This was more by way of a surprise attack. I'll be ready for him next time.'

'That shovel's looking more and more essential.'

'Maybe change the order to a sledgehammer.'

'Carried under my coat?'

'Why not?'

'Then it's a done deal.' She gave him another hug and was gone.

On the way back to the hall, Jacobs seemed to want to talk, but Rebus stayed quiet until the message got through. When he reached his cell, he decided to risk a daytime phone call, hoping the battery would last. It was to a number he knew by heart, but the secretary told him that his solicitor wasn't available and would have to get back to him later in the day.

'Is there a message I can pass on?' she asked.

'There certainly is,' Rebus told her. 'I want out of here as soon as humanly possible, though quicker than that would be preferable. So if your lazy-arsed boss could take my case off the back burner and get some proper heat under it, I'd be grateful. That's what I thought I was paying you for, after all.' He paused. 'Need me to repeat any of that for you?'

'I think I caught the gist.'

'I reckoned you might.'

He ended the call. The battery level had dropped yet again. Well, he was damned if he was going to ask Christie for a top-up. He knew there'd be a price to pay, and that price, whatever it was, would be far too steep.

*

Clarke was seated at her desk with the lyrics of the song displayed on her computer screen when her phone buzzed: Jason Mulgrew.

'What can I do for you, Jason?' she asked, pinching the bridge of her nose.

'I just thought I'd reach out, Siobhan. Christine's about to be summoned back to base, but I'm hoping you'll still feel able to keep us in the loop.'

'Even though there's no connection between my case and yours?'

'I think we can agree there's *some* connective tissue.'

'Well, I'll keep that in mind. How's Fox, by the way? I take it he stays in touch from Gartcosh?'

'He's a pro, Siobhan. I appreciate that you and Christine might have a different take on him, but we're all trying to get to the same place.'

'A word of caution, Jason. Malcolm Fox is your ally only for as long as you have something he needs. He kept crucial intelligence back from your inquiry because he hates to share. Everything he does, he does for himself and himself alone. In my books, that's the opposite of a pro.'

'You're not exactly objective, though, are you?'

'Because I refused the role of his protégée, you mean? Do I really come across to you as being so small-minded?'

'I'm not saying that.'

'Look, I've said my piece. You're a big boy, and if you want to dance with him, feel free. But it'll be his steps, his tune and him who decides when the music stops.'

'I'm not much of a dancer, though.' Mulgrew paused. 'You'll keep us posted on any progress? If not for my sake, then for Christine?'

'Goodbye, Jason,' Clarke said. Having ended the call, she got the song up on her phone and found her earbuds in a drawer of the desk. Then she hit play and listened.

*

302

When Esson walked up behind Clarke, she saw that she had her earbuds in and was staring at what looked like a poem on her computer. Realising she had company, Clarke yanked one of the buds out.

'It's a song by Richard and Linda Thompson,' she started to explain. 'Valerio is a high-wire act in a circus.' She offered Esson the free bud and put the song on again, the pair of them studying the lyrics.

'Mr Thompson,' Clarke said, 'was in a band called Fairport Convention. He still plays, as does Linda. They split as a couple a while back.'

'I'm sure Jason's mentioned them. He likes all that folkie stuff. I told him once he and Rebus were made for each other.'

'It was John who put me on to the song.'

Esson was still reading the lyrics. 'So he has a safety net, but it's not really needed because he's so good, and everyone down below is craning their necks in awe of him. Does that get us anywhere?'

'I'm not sure. Jason was just on the phone, actually – I should have mentioned the song to him.'

'What did he want?'

'Kept in the loop, especially once you're back at Gayfield Square.'

'Jesus, he never gives up.'

'He wouldn't happen to be a whizz with computers too, by any chance?'

Esson thought for a second. 'He is actually.'

Clarke looked at her. 'I was joking.'

'Naturally.' Esson got up after a moment and paced back to her own desk as though walking a tightrope. She sat there for a while, oblivious to the bustle around her, thinking of the plaintive song and the music Mulgrew always seemed to have on in his car; the way he had reached around her at her desk and with a few keystrokes got her computer working. He'd done the same for Zara Shah, too, impressing her with his command of IT jargon.

Valerio: the high-wire act ...

Then there was the way he'd acted at the murder scene, forgetting to put his hood up before they entered the kitchen, adding potential contamination to the locus. Jason: so meticulous and careful, always prepared, getting everything right – except that one time, Haj Atwal chiding him for his mistake.

Valerio: so different from the crowd far below ...

She remembered his annoyance at missing out on attachment to the Campbell murder, the way he kept pestering her for updates and news.

And when she'd mentioned the name Valerio to him, he'd blanked it. A name he should have recognised, just as John Rebus had ...

No. Nope. Nah. She shook her head as if to wipe the marker board clean.

She tried working for a while but just couldn't focus. So she switched gears and pulled up the CCTV footage from the major routes around Zak Campbell's neighbourhood. One of the team had been through it all and added a list of vehicle makes and any legible registration numbers.

It only took her ten minutes to find Jason's silver Audi, caught on camera half a mile from Campbell's house on the same evening as the murder. She tapped her pen against the edge of her desk until the looks from her colleagues made her stop. She had pulled up 'The Great Valerio' lyrics so she could read them again for herself. Then she googled the musicians. Wikipedia led her into a sixties and seventies music scene filled with artists Mulgrew had mentioned or whose songs he played in the office and car. When her phone trilled, Jason's name came up. She almost didn't answer, but eventually relented.

You're being stupid, she told herself. Working too hard, seeing things that aren't there ...

'Hey, Jason,' she said, realising at once how fake her tone sounded – too bright and breezy by far.

'Been taking the sunshine pills, Christine?' he enquired.

'Trying for a positive outlook. Are you at Gayfield?'

'Just arrived at the prison,' he informed her. 'I've got Zara with me.'

'More interviews?'

'We have to keep trying.'

'So who's in the frame today?'

'Everett Harrison.'

'I'm surprised Fox hasn't abducted Zara and taken her place.'

'Harsh.'

'But fair, I think you'll find. Are you expecting Harrison to give you anything?'

'Not really,' he conceded.

'Well, I assume you're dying to know, but there's really not much going on here either.'

'Actually, the reason I'm phoning is to tell you that our boss wants you back here pronto. Skeleton crew's been noticed by the brass and they're not best pleased.' She waited for him to say that he'd just been speaking to Siobhan, but he didn't. 'It was only a matter of time,' he said instead.

'True,' she agreed.

'So I can let Mae know you're packing up your stuff?'

'Absolutely. Thanks, Jason.'

'See you soon, Christine.'

Esson stared at her phone. A look from Pete Swinton told her she was tapping her pen again. She smiled an apology and rose from her chair, shrugging herself back into her jacket. Jason was at the prison. Jason would be there for a while. As she headed to the door, Clarke asked where she was going.

'Just something I need to check,' Esson told her. 'Won't be long.'

It was a short drive to Gayfield Square, though the usual roadworks in town didn't help. Esson parked in the car park and strode into the building, making for the CID suite. Paul

Allbright was there, which made a change, and Jack Tilley seemed to have survived his latest bout of COVID.

'Hello, stranger,' Tilley said in greeting.

'I could say the same, Jack.'

'Thanks for the get-well-soon card.'

'The one I didn't send?'

'I'm sure the thought was there.'

She turned her attention to Allbright. 'Teeth okay, Paul?'

'Fine, aye, though the dentist says my gums might have to go.'

'That line's older than you are.'

'Jason's got more interviews at the jail,' Tilley told her. 'Took Zara with him – reckon those two have something going?'

'I wouldn't put anything past DI Mulgrew.'

The two men were staring at her. 'You okay, Christine?' Allbright asked.

'I'm fine. It's just, workplace romance never ends well, does it?' She sat down at her desk, slipping out of her jacket and placing her bag on the floor next to her. After a few moments, she pretended to be sifting paperwork in search of something. Not finding it, she crossed to Mulgrew's desk and began looking there. The drawers were unlocked and messy, but contained nothing of interest. Tilley asked her what she'd lost.

'Nothing important,' she replied. But she checked again before returning to her own chair, where she sat, head in hands, staring at everything and nothing.

'I've got ibuprofen,' Allbright offered. Esson shook her head slowly.

'Any news I should know about?' she eventually enquired, trying to sound interested.

'Clutching at straws really,' Allbright stated. 'Talking to people who've already been talked to. Going back over the lab reports, autopsy result, CCTV. Unless someone blabs, I think we're stuffed.'

'What was with that DVD?' Tilley asked.

'Librarian wanted it back,' Esson explained.

306

'Because nothing ever goes missing from a prison, eh?'

'Nothing except the odd Jason Statham film,' Esson responded with a weak smile. She stayed for as long as it took them to share a hot drink. Tilley wanted to know about the Campbell case and Jasmine Andrews' sudden reappearance.

'No real connection with Marcus Simpson then?' Mae McGovern said, entering the room with arms folded. Esson gave a shake of the head. 'Well, it's good to have you back with us in a full-time capacity, Christine.'

'Though I still need to clear my desk at St Leonard's,' Esson countered.

'The work of five minutes, I'm guessing.'

'Sooner it's done, sooner I can refocus my energies.'

'A bit of energy would certainly make a change.' McGovern's attention was directed at Allbright and Tilley, who were pretending to be interested in their computer screens. She gave a theatrical sigh and checked the time on her wristwatch. 'Off you go then, Christine. I'll expect you back here within the hour – and for keeps this time.'

'Understood,' Esson said, reaching for her things.

She had just reached her car when a horn sounded. A moment later, Siobhan Clarke emerged from her own car and walked towards her across the car park.

'How did you know I'd be here?' Esson asked.

'Because we're sisters from a different mother. Besides, I was watching you before you left, your mind turning and turning. So talk me through it.'

They returned to Clarke's car. She had two bottles of water in the front, one of which she handed to Esson while she uncapped the other. Esson took her time as she spoke. She didn't want to sound like a lunatic.

The musical interest.

The IT skills.

Ensuring there was an excuse for his DNA being at the locus.

The traffic-cam footage.

His annoyance at not getting himself attached to the case –

where he could be more confident of causing roadblocks along the way.

'And on top of all that,' she concluded, 'just a weird feeling that it all makes sense.' She took a slug of water and screwed the top back on.

'Okay,' Clarke said into the silence, drawing the word out. 'But you can't just ... I mean, it's one hell of an accusation.'

'He phoned me just before I came here,' Esson ploughed on. 'And he didn't even mention that he'd called you half an hour before. This is a man who keeps things locked away, Siobhan – keeps bits of *himself* locked away. No wonder Fox was so smitten.'

'And this has nothing to do with that?'

'With what?'

'Fox stealing your partner from you, filling his head with empty promises?'

'Absolutely not.'

Clarke studied her, then turned her attention towards the windows of the MIT office. 'You were looking for evidence of his involvement.' It was statement rather than question.

'Jason's busy at Saughton, so I took my chance.'

'But didn't find anything? Does he know about the diary?'

'I *might* have mentioned it last night,' Esson confessed.

'Last night?'

'He wanted to meet for a drink.'

Clarke was still staring at the windows. 'Well, if he's Valerio, it'll have been destroyed – so tell me how we're going to find any solid connection?'

Esson could only shrug. 'What about Marcus's cousin? No progress in ID'ing Valerio?'

'He seems better at designing safes than unlocking them.'

They sat in silence, concentrating on their bottles of water, trying to find options. 'Gut instinct isn't really enough these days,' Clarke eventually said. 'In the past, we could've fitted him up for some other crime and got him sent down that way.'

Esson managed a smile. 'Pious perjury, right? It's what John

Rebus would have done.' She turned towards Clarke. 'So why can't we revive a venerable CID tradition?'

Clarke was forming an answer when a silver Audi glided into the car park, finding the final unused bay and slotting into it. Zara Shah was in the passenger seat, looking pleased with herself, as if she had won something – the something being Jason Mulgrew.

Esson had climbed out from Clarke's car, Clarke herself only a couple of steps behind. Emerging from the Audi, Shah saw her and gave a broad smile.

'Hey, you,' she said. 'Welcome back.' She made to close the passenger door, but Esson held it open.

'Would you mind waiting a minute, Zara? I need a quick word with Jason.'

Shah looked quizzical, but gave a nod, Esson climbing in and closing the door after her. Clarke had taken up a position alongside Shah, both women visible from the driver's seat. Mulgrew, halfway out of his own door, eased himself back in and closed it.

'What's with the welcoming committee, Christine?' he asked. 'It's not like Harrison helped us break the case.' As he locked eyes with the silent Esson, his relaxed demeanour began to change.

'Tell me you're not Valerio,' she said with quiet firmness.

'What?'

'I mentioned that name to you and you stonewalled me, yet it's a song by one of your favourites – why wasn't that the first thing that sprang to mind?'

'Valerio?'

'Richard and Linda Thompson. Is that how you see yourself, Jason – walking your tightrope far above the world? If so, did I just take the net away?'

He gave a bark of laughter, but his eyes had clouded over as he tried to work out which mask to choose. Shah had approached the passenger-side window and was asking what was going on. With Mulgrew distracted, Esson yanked open the

309

glovebox. It was empty. Mulgrew's left hand was pressing down on the armrest of the car's central console. She tried prising it off but couldn't, so she bent down and sank her teeth into his wrist.

'Fuck!' he roared, lifting his hand away. She flipped open the console and scrabbled for the small black book wedged there. He grabbed at her wrist with his uninjured hand, squeezing hard.

'Give that back, you bitch!' he snarled. Esson got the door open wide enough to toss the book from the car. Mulgrew's hand went for her throat but eased off as he watched Clarke pick up the diary and open it. He released his grip completely and started the ignition, preparing to drive off with Esson on board.

'It's me or the book, Jason,' she told him, breathing heavily. 'You can't have both.' He changed his mind and cut the engine. But by the time he was out of the car and striding towards Clarke and Shah, Esson was right alongside her colleagues. Mulgrew stopped in front of the three women, hand outstretched. Then he looked over Esson's shoulder to where Mae McGovern was emerging from the building, knowing something was going on but unsure what. One floor above, Allbright and Tilley had their faces pressed to the glass.

'You've got your audience now, Valerio,' Esson said. Mulgrew looked ready to explode. His eyes sought out the book, but it had vanished from view, Clarke having tucked it into her clothing.

'Jason?' Mae McGovern enquired. But he ignored her, letting out a howl aimed at the world at large as he stalked back to his car and got in, slamming the door shut and roaring out of the car park with a squeal of tyre rubber.

'We need to put out a call,' Esson told her boss, trying to control her shaking voice. 'All vehicles to be alerted to a silver Audi. Suspect in the Zak Campbell murder at the wheel. Unarmed but possibly dangerous.' She saw the look of disbelief on McGovern's face. 'Trust me, ma'am,' she said. Hearing

310

Esson's tone, then looking at Siobhan Clarke, McGovern absolutely did.

Zara Shah was staring towards the car park exit, mouth open. Esson gave her shoulder a squeeze – *never ends well* – and started to lead the way back into the station, ready to explain her thinking to DCI McGovern. Clarke meantime was on the phone to her own boss, but she managed a moment's eye contact with Esson and gave a slow nod: job well done.

Job bloody well done ...

26

Rebus was surprised to see Megan Keighley standing in his cell doorway. He had heard a few whistles but reckoned they were aimed at the TV or some new female officer. Jacobs, who had escorted the librarian to Rebus's cell, was scowling in the direction of the whistlers. The inmates, undeterred, were already starting to parade past the door, checking Keighley out from behind her back.

'Megan,' Rebus said, rising from his bed. She was casting an eye over the interior.

'You keep it neat,' she said.

'Spartans had the right idea,' he answered. She rewarded him with a smile.

'I wanted to see how you were doing after yesterday.'

'Surviving,' he offered.

'Looks sore.' She was studying his face.

'I've had worse.' He paused. 'By the way, it's bad news about your film – police lab only has the case it came in.'

'Oh.' She looked over her shoulder towards Jackie Simpson's cell. It had been unlocked after repainting. Rebus had been told that a couple of cops had visited it earlier while he'd been with his visitors. They'd given the nod for it to get back to being used. 'It couldn't still be in the machine, could it?' she asked.

'We don't have DVD players as such.' Rebus gestured towards his own wall-mounted TV. 'There's a slot in the back for DVDs. SOCOs aren't that sloppy.'

'SOCOs?'

'Scene-of-crime,' Rebus explained. She nodded her understanding as more prisoners sauntered past, Jacobs having given up trying to warn them off.

'Tidy,' one of them called out once he was safely past the doorway. 'I definitely would ...'

'You're excused library duties,' Keighley was telling Rebus. 'If you're not up to it, I mean.'

'I'm fine, Megan. The man who went for me is the one you won't be seeing for a while.'

'That's good.' She noticed the photo lying on his bed, the one he'd been holding when she arrived. 'Your family?'

'Daughter and granddaughter.'

She angled her head. 'A good-looking pair. Did you pass the reading habit on to them?'

'I'm not sure about that, but my granddaughter's turned into a bit of an artist.' He unfolded Carrie's drawing.

'Impressive. Will you stick it on the wall?'

'And spoil the aesthetic?' He made show of looking around the bare cell.

'You don't like to give much of yourself away, John, do you?'

He answered with a shrug.

'How long till the puffiness goes down?'

'You don't think I look good as Jabba the Hutt?'

'I wouldn't have taken you for a *Star Wars* fan.'

'I saw the DVD case in the library.'

She smiled, but then thought better of it. 'That man was going to kill you, wasn't he?'

'I reckon so.'

'Until Billy Groam stepped in.' She was running a finger up and down her crucifix. 'He's in the next cell along, isn't he? Billy, I mean?'

'But at the gym right now, as far as I know.'

Her face fell a little. 'Well, I'll see you back in the library soon.'

'I really appreciate you dropping by, Megan.'

Jacobs ushered her away, a line of prisoners following in close procession. Rebus lay back down again. He didn't think he would put Carrie's drawing on display. It would stay hidden, alongside the photograph. He turned his head towards the doorway. With the entertainment over, the noise level was settling down. A couple of younger prisoners strode past in their underwear, flip-flops clacking, headed for the showers. Rebus thought about the phone hidden in the drain there. Hiding places: prisons were full of them. Hiding places and secrets. He remembered the arrival of Haj Atwal's SOCOs. They would have stepped into many a crime scene, but none quite as intimidating or as strange and disorientating as a jail. Shouts from the locked cells all around them; doors and gates that had to be opened and closed as they made their way inwards from the reception desk. ID checks and scanners. Uniforms and creeping claustrophobia, the smells and sights, a secret world to which they resolutely did not belong.

No wonder one or two of them had looked unnerved, minds not wholly committed to the job at hand. Wanting out asap.

SOCOs aren't that sloppy ...

But what if ...

What if, this one time, they *were*?

There was a new arrival standing just outside his cell: his neighbour, Billy Groam, fresh from his workout, sweat glistening on his skin.

'I think your librarian's taken a shine to me,' he said. 'Bit of colour in her cheeks as she passed me just now. Reckon I could be in there?'

'I'd see you swing first.'

'They don't do hangings in here any more, John.'

'Has peace broken out between your boss and Harrison?'

'I wouldn't go that far.'

'No more of Darryl's boys have been targeted on the outside, though?'

Groam shook his head. 'And Jake Morris is back in town. Whether he'll live down the embarrassment of doing a runner is another thing.' He paused. 'You know his girl is friends with the one who went missing? Seems she was keeping her hidden in Jake's house without him knowing.'

'He doesn't exactly sound like the brightest and best.'

'Jake's all right. Just not sure he's cut out for the life.'

'The life *you* introduced him to,' Rebus reminded him. Groam's face hardened.

'I'll see you in the library, John. I think I'm going to become a regular. Just don't rely on me always being there at the same time as that maniac.'

After Groam had left, Rebus waited a couple of minutes before rising from his bed and leaving the cell. He was crossing the hall when Valerie Watts intercepted him.

'Off somewhere nice, John?' she asked.

'Library is missing one of its DVDs. Jackie Simpson had it last. Just wondered if it might still be inside.'

'Jackie's cell's been stripped, though.'

'Inside the TV,' he explained. 'The slot at the back.' Watts considered for a moment before nodding.

'Let's take a look then.'

She accompanied him into the cell. They stood for a moment smelling the fresh paint, both of them staring towards where Jackie Simpson had spent his last night on earth. Then Rebus walked over to the TV, switched it on and pressed eject. There was a brief whirring noise but nothing else.

'Slot's empty,' Watts said.

But Rebus was peering into it as best he could. 'No, it's definitely in there,' he said. 'But it looks ...' He tried focusing his swollen eyes.

'Looks what, John?' she asked as he straightened up.

'Looks as though someone from Haj Atwal's team will be getting a rocket,' Rebus eventually answered. He fixed her

315

with a look. 'We need to step back outside. And you need to call the MIT.'

She frowned and brushed past him, staring into the slot for herself.

Without waiting, Rebus was on his way back to his cell. He pulled out his chair and sat down, elbows on the desk. For five or so minutes he didn't move. When he did exit into the hall, he saw that Simpson's cell was being locked again, Watts standing some distance away, walkie-talkie pressed to her mouth so she could keep her voice low.

He settled himself at a table, watching a game of pool, and then another, the players pleased to have their cues returned. Watts was a pro, her demeanour giving nothing away. None of the prisoners had taken much notice of the door being locked or the conversation Watts was presumably having with the governor. Someone tried handing Rebus a cue, but he shook his head. The Wizard was seated a few feet away, studying him as though seeing him through fresh eyes. Another prisoner, high on something, was marching up and down, counting as he went. Rebus joined him, remaining a few steps behind. At a certain point, he stopped, rooted to the spot, the other prisoner having eventually to manoeuvre past him. He ran the palm of his hand across his jaw.

'Yes,' he said to himself, starting to walk again, this time in the direction of the Wizard's cell.

Mark Jamieson was seated at the desk, playing patience with a greasy set of cards.

'No king or queen of diamonds,' he told Rebus. 'Probably used for roaches.'

'Can I show you something, Mark?'

Jamieson looked up from his game. 'What?'

Rather than say anything, Rebus gestured for the young man to follow him into the hall. 'I'm going to get the quote wrong,' he began, 'but it's from a Sherlock Holmes story, I think. Did you know Conan Doyle was born here in Edinburgh? Got out as soon as he could, mind.'

'What are you on about?'

'The quote's something to do with ruling out the probable and improbable. Once you've done that, even if the solution seems impossible, that's what it has to be.'

'You taken some gear, John?' Jamieson enquired. But Rebus just shook his head and nodded towards Jackie Simpson's cell, which was being unlocked again while the governor stood by, accompanied by two detectives Rebus didn't recognise. He watched for a reaction from Jamieson and was about to get one when a hand landed heavily on his shoulder. Darryl Christie had arrived behind both men.

'A word, please, John,' he said, plenty of steel beneath the calm.

'What happens now, Darryl?' Jamieson stammered, the blood draining from his face.

'You keep your trap shut, Mark, that's what happens. I've got the best defence lawyer in the country on speed dial. It's all going to be okay and your mum's being taken care of – remember that.' Christie steered Rebus away.

'His mum?' Rebus asked.

'MS – needs a ton of help, and none of it comes cheap.'

'That was the deal? Easy enough to convince him, I suppose, since you also control the tap that drips out his various fixes. Free highs for life, was it?' Rebus paused. They had reached a neutral stretch of wall between cells and rec area. 'Why Simpson, though?'

Christie looked around for potential eavesdroppers. 'Can't you guess?'

'Because Novak would be the obvious suspect, and it was him you were really after. Meaning you'd no actual beef with Jackie?'

'They call it collateral damage.' Christie stared at Rebus, his eyes gleaming. There was that madness again, never far from the surface, same as when he'd shot a man, same as when he'd so nearly turned the gun on Rebus. 'Novak's a pain in the hole,' he went on. 'I've enjoyed watching him sweat.'

317

Rebus swallowed back the temptation to say that Novak had been a bigger pain than Christie knew. 'Why not get Samms to do it?'

Christie screwed up his face. 'Samms isn't my guy. I don't need any of that these days. A drone can deliver to the exact open window you tell it to. But Novak wants cameras on the outside walls, pointed at the skies rather than the ground.' He gave a shake of the head. 'Very bad for business.'

'And Billy Groam didn't really hear a cell door being unlocked? That was just another piece of misdirection?'

Christie gave a slow wink.

Rebus turned towards the murder cell. 'It's about to come spilling out, Darryl.'

'Not if Mark does what he's told. All they know now is the *how*.'

'They'll put together a case whether he talks or not. You robbed a man of his life – that can't go unpunished.'

'Listen to yourself! Look at where you are! How exactly are they going to punish me?' Christie burst out laughing, the laughter so sudden and loud that the governor emerged from Simpson's cell. Christie lifted his hand in apology.

'You know I'm going to tell them,' Rebus stated.

'You do that. I can help you get onto the roof if you like – you can shout it from there, for all the good it'll do. Welcome to the real world – and you didn't even have to choose a pill.' He paused, leaning in a little closer. 'Remember when you first arrived here? I told you I could get you anything. I was so hoping you'd say yes. Know why? *Control*. The idea I could control you was catnip to me. Something *I* could use to make the walls melt away.'

'Sorry if I disappointed you.'

'You seldom disappoint me, John.' Christie stared in the direction of Jackie Simpson's cell. 'Though you *can* be full of surprises.' He paused. 'Not all of them pleasant, and some loaded with repercussions.'

'How do you mean?'

But Christie had already turned and walked away, accepting a proffered pool cue and lining up his shot.

Fox was at home in Oxgangs, evening meal finished, feet up on the sofa, when he got the call from London. He had been both expecting it and dreading it. He steeled himself as he answered.

'SO15 never sleeps,' he said.

'So after everything,' Thomas Glaze drawled, 'looks like a simple spat between cellmates. You got us all worked up over nothing, Malcolm. I think it's safe to say we're feeling a bit let down by our colleagues north of the border.'

'I'm holding a violin the size of a thimble here, Tommy.'

'I'm not sure I like your tone, Malcolm.'

'I've busted a gut for you over this. I've kept fellow officers in the dark and told them lies, all to protect our operation. I got a man sent to jail and he ended up dead, for Christ's sake.'

'A good detective is one who gets results – wasted effort is often wasted because it was misjudged in the first place.'

'That's easy for you to say, sitting in your cushy office in London while others put themselves on the line. It's *me* who has to start picking up the pieces.'

'I believe the offices at Gartcosh are fairly cushy too, DI Fox. You shouldn't stray too far from that desk of yours – you're not very good at the other stuff, the *real* stuff of policing.'

'Listen to me, you little—'

But Glaze had already ended the call.

Fox stomped into the kitchen, pacing it from one end to the other, having forgotten why he'd gone there in the first place. He filled the kettle and waited, his anger ceasing to abate. Then he realised he hadn't flicked the switch on the kettle, so he grabbed a can of Appletiser from the fridge and opened that instead.

'These bloody shitty people,' he muttered to himself as he returned to the living room, where his discarded phone was ringing again. Not Glaze this time, but Fox's boss.

Again, not wholly unexpected, though he'd been hoping to defer the conversation until morning.

'Good evening, sir,' he said, resting on the very edge of the sofa.

'Jason Mulgrew, Malcolm?' Pratchett began without preliminaries. 'The officer you reckoned was just about ready for a promotion to Internal Affairs or Organised Crime?'

'I think it's come as a shock to all of us, sir.'

Pratchett ignored this. 'That's twice you've fallen short, which is twice more than I like. And to think some of us reckoned *you* might be ready for a step up ...'

Fox closed his eyelids. 'I'm assuming that thinking has been somewhat adjusted?'

'Insofar as you can kiss it goodbye, yes.'

'And my suggested surveillance of Mickey Mason?'

'All predicated on those famously reliable instincts of yours? Not a cat in hell's chance. You've two strikes against you, Malcolm. Might not take a third to send you on your way.'

Fox allowed himself a grim smile. Where had he heard that before? Answer: Siobhan Clarke. Strike one: keeping secret from her his connection to Jackie Simpson. Strike two: not mentioning his interest in Carla's dad or who Jake Morris worked for.

'I wonder if we could take this up again in the morning, sir, before I say something I'll probably regret?'

The line was silent for a moment.

'If you've something to say, say it,' Pratchett eventually said.

Fox stared at the blank television screen in front of him, seeing himself reflected there. 'I just think I've had enough – enough of the thankless job and the budget cuts, enough of the smugness from those at the top who'd struggle to find the cheeks of their arse with both hands, and enough of all the utter fucking fannies I'm surrounded by, fannies up to and including your good, useless self.' He paused. 'With respect, sir.'

This time the line was silent for longer. Fox even checked to be certain that the call was ongoing.

'Nobody at Gartcosh will stand in the way of your resignation, DI Fox, I promise you that.' A slight but evident tremor had entered Pratchett's voice. Well, well, Fox thought, I got through to you at last. 'Many will be glad to see the back of you,' Pratchett continued, 'along with your failed instincts and your ludicrous schemes. I'm bound to say I count myself chief among them. Goodbye, Malcolm – and good luck.'

Fox switched off his phone and tossed it across the room.

'Goodnight, Vienna,' he said quietly, giving his reflected self a rueful smile.

Rebus went through everything he knew as he lay in bed that evening, staring towards the ceiling. Mark Jamieson had been questioned under oath with a solicitor present. The interview had taken place in the governor's office, after which the young man was taken to the SRU. Rebus had tried calling Esson to tell her to transfer Jamieson to a cell at Gayfield Square, or St Leonard's – or *anywhere* – but his call had gone straight to messaging. He'd asked to speak to the governor, only to be advised that Tennent was up to his eyeballs. Jamieson would be shivering in his cell, more from shock than cold. Did he have anything secreted about his person? Very probably. It would dull the pain, but only so much and for so long.

A DVD, snapped in half to create the necessary jagged edge. Jackie Simpson asleep, vulnerable, unwary. Mark would have stripped naked so there was no blood on his clothing when he carried out the attack. He would wash himself after, towelling himself dry. Blood on the towel now, but he'd been told what to do – stuff it into the dead man's mouth, giving a plausible reason for it being in the state it was. Rinse off the DVD too, before cajoling it back into the TV slot. Then all he had to do was get dressed again and climb into his bunk, downing a bigger than usual dose of drugs – gratefully received. Finally he would have smashed his head against the wall a number of times – the pain dulled, the damage necessary – before waiting for the blackout to come. The story about his evening meal having been tampered with was yet more misdirection. Everything had to point away from cell and cellmate. And towards the POs, especially Chris Novak.

None of it for Mark himself, of course, not really even for his ailing mother. But all to satisfy the cravings of Darryl Christie, who would remain untouched even if Jamieson sang like a bird.

Besides, that wasn't going to be allowed to happen. Rebus knew it in his churning gut.

He awoke next morning and was told at breakfast. Mark Jamieson had OD'd in the night. Billy Groam leaned down towards where Rebus sat with his breakfast tray, none of it eaten.

'He wasn't supposed to survive the first time,' he whispered. 'The boy was tougher than he looked.'

Rebus sprang to his feet, eyes on the figure of Darryl Christie, seated two tables away with a spoon paused halfway to his mouth, watching Rebus.

'You won't get within five feet, John,' Groam warned him. 'So sit yourself back down and behave.'

Rebus knew he was right. He sat down again, picking up his spoon, holding it tight.

Afterwards

27

Jason Mulgrew's legal team reckoned the case might not even reach court. They had statements from DCs Allbright and Tilley to the effect that DS Christine Esson had made a search of her colleague's desk without a warrant. Same went for his car. His mobile phone and computer showed evidence of deletion, but MIT had yet to find a bank account with evidence of money paid to Zak Campbell. At each recorded interview, Mulgrew said the same two words – 'No comment.' His lawyers agreed that samples of his hair might well have been found in Campbell's kitchen, but their client had explained the momentary lapse in concentration that had led him to give his head a good scratch while the hood of his overalls hung loosely down around his neck.

At the end of one of the interviews, after the equipment had been switched off, Siobhan Clarke had placed a hand on Mulgrew's arm as he went to join his lawyer in the corridor.

'Why hang on to the book, Jason? Just tell me that?'

He leaned in so his lips were almost touching her ear. 'All those names, Siobhan. I just got greedy ...' His lawyer cleared his throat in warning and Clarke released her hold.

There was tidying-up to be done elsewhere. Jasmine's parents had started the process of filing for divorce and Jasmine wasn't sure if she would stay with her mother or travel south with her father. The media clamour had died down and would only be rekindled if and when the Zak Campbell murder trial started. The names in Campbell's little black book would become public property then. Proceedings were actually being considered against at least three of his clients who had pestered him for younger and younger models. Siobhan Clarke wondered if Peter 'Pedro' Cowan would be the only one to take his own life.

She went to see Rebus, knowing that Samantha had set up her own schedule of visits with Carrie. There was still some bruising on his face, but his eyes were back to normal, more or less.

'Good result,' she told him, having fetched cold drinks and chocolate from the vending machines.

'Except that with Mark Jamieson dead, you lot will draw a line under it.'

'"You lot"?'

'I'd probably have done the same back in the day. Mystery solved, end of. But it was Darryl Christie who plotted it and Darryl Christie who made it happen.'

'The only thing missing is concrete evidence.'

'*I'm* the evidence, Siobhan.'

'Which is why you need to play nice, John – you've seen what can happen when Christie feels cornered. Gartcosh reckon you should leave it to them.'

Rebus snorted. 'I wouldn't trust Fox to take down a shower curtain, never mind organised crime.'

'You've not heard?'

Rebus took a bite of chocolate. 'What?'

'Fox has tendered his resignation. He was grooming Jason Mulgrew for greatness. That didn't go down too well. Added to everything else, there's a good chance he was due to be bounced down the ladder anyway.'

'Just like him to take the coward's way out.'

Clarke gave him a look. 'I'm not sure that's *strictly* fair.'

'Do I have time to phone him for a gloat?'

'Stop it.' She sipped from her can, stifling a burp. 'It's good that you've agreed to let Carrie come visit.' Rebus just shrugged. 'Are things settling down now? In here, I mean?'

'Harrison's being moved to Perth. Darryl Christie seems to have grown a couple of inches. Everyone knows what he did to Mark Jamieson. No way I'm ever forgiving him for that.'

'Remember what I said about playing nice?'

'I'm not sure I can, though.' He was wrapping up what was left of the chocolate, ready to tuck it into his pocket for later consumption or bartering. 'Every day I'm in here, the feeling gets stronger – somebody needs to do *something* to take the bastard down.'

'Doesn't have to be a retired cop who's pushing seventy, though, does it?'

'You think I've not got it in me?' Rebus made show of puffing out his chest. Clarke gave a little laugh and shook her head.

They chatted more generally until time was up. Chris Novak was standing ready to escort Rebus back to Trinity Hall.

'Everything all right with you?' Rebus asked him.

'We seem to have got away with you paying me a visit,' Novak answered under his breath.

'What about Valerie?'

'We've decided to break things off.'

'Her heart was in the right place, you know – telling the investigation about your relationship, bringing me to see you ...'

'I know that, John. But I can't live two lives.'

'It was three, actually, with your vigilante act.'

'Aye, well that's gone, too.'

'And yet Christie's operation needs bringing down more than ever.'

Novak nodded solemnly. 'I got a message from DI Fox, you know.'

'Oh aye?'

'He said he knew who it was under that bike helmet. He'd looked at which POs had family or friends in CID. He also said *you'd* done your best to throw him off the scent. But one other

327

thing he'd heard was that some gangster in Glasgow had come to realise how fragile Christie's hold on Edinburgh was ...'

'Mickey Mason,' Rebus stated, his eyes on Novak. 'And you think the city would be better off in Glasgow's hands than Darryl Christie's?'

'I think a lot of threatened prison officers might be.'

'Speaking of threats, the governor still owes me a favour.'

'I know you want Bobby Briggs sent elsewhere. Governor's doing his level best ...'

Rebus had stopped walking and was holding up a finger, face angled upwards. 'Do you hear that, Chris?'

'What?'

'I thought I heard bells.'

'No churches near here, John.' Novak listened and then shook his head.

Rebus was readying to move off towards Trinity Hall, but Novak tapped him on the arm.

'We're taking a detour,' he said, leading him towards the row of clear-walled cubicles set aside for private visits. 'You've got someone waiting.' He indicated the booth at the far end. Then he held out his hand and shook Rebus's. 'I'll be here when you're done, John. Fingers crossed ...'

As Rebus walked towards the booth, he saw his solicitor already seated, sorting through some paperwork in front of him. He hesitated a moment before opening the door and stepping through.

'John.' The lawyer reached across the gap to grasp his hand. 'Take a seat, please.'

Rebus did so, his fingers seeking a grip around the smooth lip of the table. The solicitor read on for a few further seconds, then looked up at him. The man's mouth broke into a widening smile.

'Finally there's news, John,' he began. 'There's very good news indeed ...'

Acknowledgements

There is a real HMP Edinburgh, situated in the same area of the city as the prison in this novel, but of course this is a work of fiction and the two should not be confused. I am grateful to staff and inmates (present and past) who spoke to me and allowed me to tour the facilities. I have taken a few necessary liberties, but I hope I have also managed to show that prisons are places where compassion and hope can be manifested on all sides, church bells or no church bells.

I.R.

JOHN REBUS RETURNS TO TV

Stream REBUS on BBC iPlayer now – starring Richard Rankin as a young Rebus and set in contemporary Edinburgh, the series follows Rebus as he is drawn into a violent criminal underworld by none other than his brother Michael.

VIEWERS ARE GOING WILD FOR REBUS...

'Love the new Rebus... It's time for this reboot'

'I want more, please!'

'Can't wait for season two'

'Love it!... BBC drama at it's best'

© HAMISH BROWN

KEEP UP TO DATE WITH THE WORLD OF

IAN RANKIN

Follow Ian ✗ @Beathhigh

Find him on Facebook **f** @IanRankinBooks

Keep up-to-date with Ian's latest news
and subscribe to his newsletter:
www.ianrankin.net

THE JOHN REBUS SERIES

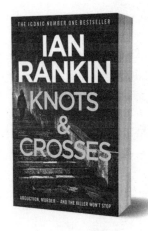

#1 KNOTS AND CROSSES

The modern classic which introduced the world to Detective John Rebus. In Edinburgh, young girls are being abducted. Soon, messages begin to arrive – knotted string and crossed matchsticks – taunting Rebus with a puzzle only he can solve.

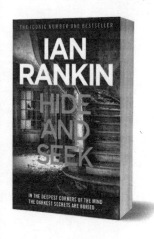

#2 HIDE AND SEEK

It starts with a dead junkie in a forgotten corner of Edinburgh. Nobody cares, but when Rebus starts to dig, he finds more than murder – and uncovers the dark heart of the city.

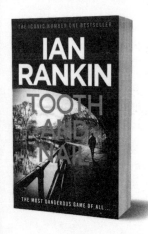

#3 TOOTH AND NAIL

A murderer targets London's East End. Rebus is called upon, due to his expertise in serial killers. But navigating the politics and prejudices of a new city is dangerous work – both for his career and his life . . .

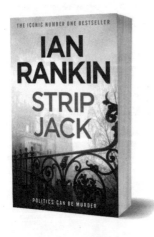

#4 STRIP JACK

A police raid on a notorious brothel ends the career of a promising local politician. But when the man's wife disappears, Rebus suspects the young MP is more than just unlucky. Someone is out to destroy him . . .

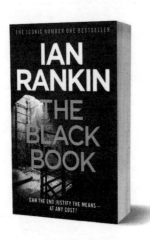

#5 THE BLACK BOOK

After a fellow officer is brutally attacked, Rebus is drawn into a case involving a hotel fire, an unidentified body, and a puzzle that not everyone wants solved – perhaps not even Rebus himself . . .

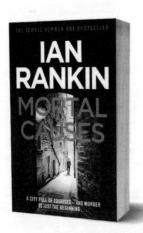

#6 MORTAL CAUSES

August in Edinburgh, and a brutally tortured body is discovered as the Festival is in full swing. When the victim turns out to be a notorious gangster's son, Rebus knows all hell is about to break loose . . .

'One of the great creations of modern mystery fiction'
Observer

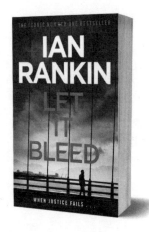

#7 LET IT BLEED

Far more used to investigating Edinburgh's underworld, when Rebus is invited to the home of the Scottish Office's Permanent Secretary he discovers a world in which crime really does pay – and people who are beyond justice.

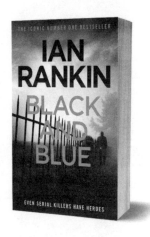

#8 BLACK AND BLUE

The award-winning masterpiece in which Rebus juggles four cases trying to nail one murderer – a copycat who may lead to the infamous serial killer Bible John. If that wasn't enough, he has to do it while being accused of a miscarriage of justice in the eyes of millions . . .

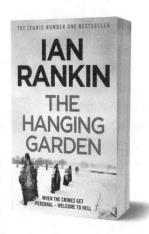

#9 THE HANGING GARDEN

Rebus is buried under paperwork, investigating the history of a war criminal now living in Edinburgh. As a turf war between two gangsters boils over – and targets his daughter – Rebus is dragged back to the present . . . ready to do a deal with the devil.

> '**In the Rebus books Rankin has created an Edinburgh that is textured, vivid, plausible, perhaps even real**'
> *Express*

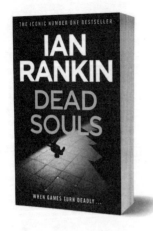

#10 DEAD SOULS

Should the past remain in the past? Rebus faces the question on all fronts: whether to out a supposedly reformed paedophile; or look into the disappearance of the son of an old friend; and whether to believe a notorious convicted killer has served their time and now walks free . . .

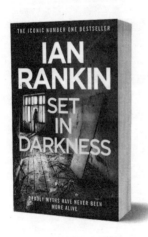

#11 SET IN DARKNESS

The new Scottish parliament opens slap bang in the middle of Rebus's patch. But when a body is discovered, a seemingly easy assignment might just turn out to be the hardest yet — and bring him face to face with Edinburgh's most notorious criminal.

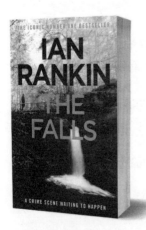

#12 THE FALLS

When a student goes missing, Rebus has a gut feeling there is bad news waiting. A carved wooden doll in a toy coffin in her home village, and clues on an internet role-playing game bring the ancient and the modern to-gether in a cocktail of secrets, lies and murder.

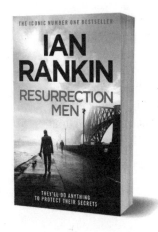

#13 RESURRECTION MEN

Following an outburst, Rebus is sent for 'retraining', where he is assigned an unsolved case alongside the other officers at the last chance saloon. While the newly promoted DS Siobhan Clarke, trying to solve the murder of an art dealer, is drawn dangerously towards 'Big Ger' Cafferty . . .

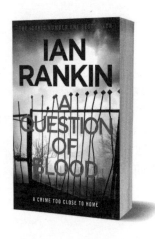

#14 A QUESTION OF BLOOD

Two students are killed by an ex-army loner who then turned the gun on himself. The mystery takes Rebus into the heart of a shattered community. Ex-army himself, Rebus becomes fascinated by the killer – who had friends in high places and enemies to spare . . .

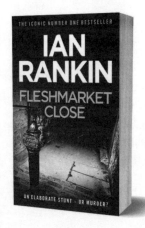

#15 FLESHMARKET CLOSE

Two skeletons discovered beneath a cellar floor in Fleshmarket Close are considered an elaborate stunt – but whose? Investigating the murder of an illegal immigrant Rebus starts to wonder if the case is linked, and just who might be hiding bodies around his town . . .

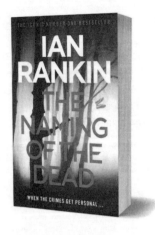

#16 THE NAMING OF THE DEAD

As the G8 summit gathers in Scotland, the apparent suicide of an MP connects to clues that a serial killer is at work. Warned off the case as protests turn to riots, Rebus was never one to follow orders – even if it sets him on a collision course with both sides of the conflict.

#17 EXIT MUSIC

As Rebus ties up loose ends before retirement, one last case arrives. A Russian dissident is found dead while a delegation of Russian businessmen are in town. Then, a brutal assault on Cafferty suddenly means Rebus might not survive long enough to retire . . .

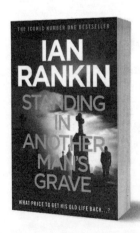

#18 STANDING IN ANOTHER MAN'S GRAVE

Rebus has been working as a civilian in a cold-case unit. When a string of disappearances stretching back decades becomes apparent, can Rebus be the man he once was and still stay on the right side of the law?

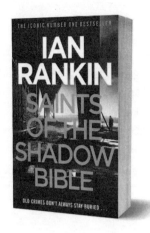

#19 SAINTS OF THE SHADOW BIBLE

Rebus is back on the force, with a chip on his shoulder and a marked card, as a case he worked thirty years ago is re-opened. Who are the saints and who are the sinners? And can one ever become the other?

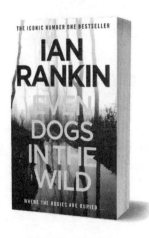

#20 EVEN DOGS IN THE WILD

Retirement doesn't suit Rebus. DI Siobhan Clarke knows what the answer will be when she asks for his help with a case. A lawyer has been murdered, a note found on the body. Across town, 'Big Ger' Cafferty gets an identical note and a bullet through his window. In the city, as in the wild, it's dog eat dog.

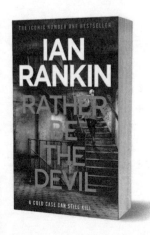

#21 RATHER BE THE DEVIL

Some cases never leave you. For Rebus, the unsolved murder of a socialite in a luxury hotel still haunts him. Meanwhile, as a dangerous young upstart muscles in on Cafferty's turf, Rebus refuses to believe his old adversary is as retired as he claims . . .

'Rebus is one of British crime writing's greatest characters: alongside Holmes, Poirot and Morse'
Daily Mail

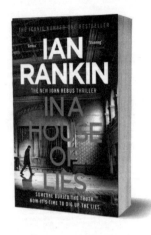

#22 IN A HOUSE OF LIES

When the body of a missing private investigator is found – in an area that police had already searched – Detective Inspector Siobhan Clarke discovers that everyone involved with the case is hiding something. None more so than her own mentor: Rebus.

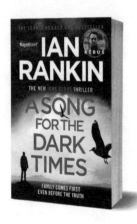

#23 A SONG FOR THE DARK TIMES

When his daughter Samantha calls in the dead of night to say her husband is missing, Rebus fears the worst and knows she'll be the prime suspect. He rushes to her aid – but is he going as a father or a detective?

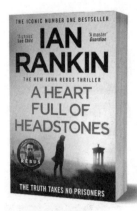

#24 A HEART FULL OF HEADSTONES

John Rebus is on trial facing the rest of his life behind bars. DI Siobhan Clarke tackles Edinburgh's most explosive case, as a corrupt cop harbouring huge secrets goes missing. When it comes time to choose sides, it becomes clear: after a lifetime of lies, the truth will break your heart...

OTHER NOVELS

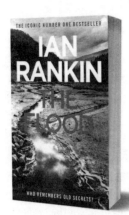

THE FLOOD

Mary has always been an outcast. Now she is a single mother, caught up in a faltering affair. Her son, Sandy, has fallen for a strange homeless girl. Their search for happiness isn't easy, as they both must face a dark secret from their past.

WATCHMAN

Bombs are exploding in the streets of London, but life has laid more subtle traps for Miles Flint – a spy who is desperate not to botch his latest case. But a trip to Belfast quickly becomes a flight of terror, murder and shocking discoveries.

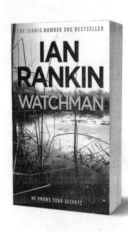

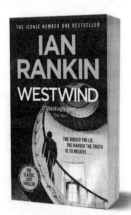

WESTWIND

After his friend suspects foul play at the satellite facility where they both work – and then disappears – Martin Hepton is determined to uncover the secret everyone is trying to keep hidden. But he isn't prepared for what he finds . . .

DOORS OPEN

Mike Mackenzie is a self-made man with too much time on his hands. When he and his friends make a plan to rip-off the National Gallery of Scotland, the real trick is make it look like there was no crime at all . . .

DETECTIVE MALCOLM FOX NOVELS

#1 THE COMPLAINTS

Nobody likes The Complaints — cops who investigate other cops — but that's what Malcolm Fox does. When he reluctantly takes on a new case, he soon discovers there's more to it than anyone thinks…

#2 THE IMPOSSIBLE DEAD

Malcolm Fox is investigating a simple case of misconduct — but it is soon complicated by a brutal murder and a weapon that should not even exist. When the body count rises, Fox finds himself in mortal danger.

PLAYS

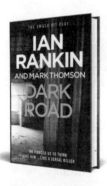

DARK ROAD

It's been 25 years since Alfred Chalmers was convicted of the gruesome murder of four young women, and Isobel McArthur, Scotland's first Chief Constable, has been haunted by the case ever since. Now, with her retirement approaching, McArthur decides the time has come for answers. But her decision rips opens old wounds and McArthur is soon caught up a web of corruption, psychological mind-games and deceit . . .

LONG SHADOWS

After the daughter of a murder victim turns up outside his flat, Rebus is determined to solve this cold case once and for all and enlists the help of his old friend DI Siobhan Clarke. But Clarke has problems of her own, problems that will put her at odds with her long-time mentor and push him into seeking help from his age-old adversary: 'Big Ger' Cafferty.

A GAME CALLED MALICE

A splendid dinner party in an Edinburgh stately home concludes with a murder mystery game created by the hostess. A murder needs to be solved. But the guests have secrets of their own, threatened by the very game they are playing. And among them is Inspector John Rebus. True crime is his calling. Is he playing an alternative game, one to which only he knows the rules?